Books By Rick Bentsen

The Blademaster Chronicles
The Blademaster

The Chronicles of Xarin
The Crucible

Dawn of a New Age

The Blademaster

By Rick Bentsen

Steel Drake Press
Taunton

The Blademaster
Book 1: The Blademaster Chronicles

All Rights Reserved © 2014 Rick Bentsen

First Print Edition

For information, contact the author at
rickbentsen@rickbentsen.com

www.rickbentsen.com
www.facebook.com/RickBentsenAuthor

ISBN: 0615981879
ISBN-13: 978-0615981871

Praise for The Blademaster

"Up until I'd read "The Blademaster" by Rick Bentsen, the closest thing I'd come to reading or seeing a story in this genre was "The Lord Of The Rings" that I saw at the theater several years ago because my husband wanted to see it.

I wanted to read "The Blademaster" because Rick and I have been cyber friends since around 2000 and I wanted to support him and his new book.

So, kind of to my own surprise, when I started reading the saga of Alana Steeldrake (First Blademaster to be named in over 300 years) and Colwyn Starseeker (Protector to Alana Steeldrake and heir to the title of First Lord of the Valendale Territory) I found myself really enjoying it!

The story flows with just enough descriptions that keep the story moving and on course.

All the characters, even the secondary ones, are really well developed. I felt like I knew all the characters in the book, even the bad guys, by the time I'd finished it.

I'm impressed with Rick's writing ability. I'm amazed at his imagination. I'm intrigued with the names of places, characters, and phrases he came up with and how they perfectly fit the tone of the story. And I appreciated the underlying moral code of love and honor that he threaded throughout the story.

And I can totally see this story becoming a movie!"

--Pat Ballard, author (Abigail's Revenge, Wamted One Groom, and others... The Queenor Rubenesque Romances...)

The Blademaster

Foreward

February 21, 2014

The book that you are holding in your hand has been a labor of love for me. When I started writing this novel in 2005, I had a half baked idea and had no idea just how far that half baked idea would take me.

Almost ten years after I started working on this book, I am working on getting the manuscript ready for publication. Odds are good that this book goes off to the printer by the end of this weekend.

I find myself to be both excited and nervous about this.

As I said, *The Blademaster* has been a labor of love, an ironic choice of words considering that the focus of this story was to discover the power of love on a person's life.

As I said, it was a half baked idea when I came up with it. "Let's write a story about the power of love on a person's life." Half baked and very vague. And yet, that is exactly what this story is.

A love story.

Don't get me wrong. You haven't bought a romance by accident. This is definitely the start of an epic fantasy series. But at its core, this story is a story about the love two people, in this case Alana Steeldrake and Colwyn Starseeker, share with each other.

Alana and Colwyn have become two of my favorite characters to write. I think that, when an author starts working with a new set of characters, those characters tend to consume the author's every thought for a long time. That was certainly the case with Alana and Colwyn in my case. I would have dreams about their adventures. Some of those dreams made it into this book. Some are stories for future books. And some are stories just for me.

But, as I said, this is a story about love. Love is a very powerful thing. It has certainly guided my steps a lot in my life. I have been called a hopeless romantic. I think, perhaps, that may have rubbed off on some of my characters.

The Blademaster

I enjoyed writing this book. It was a lot of fun to write. I hope that my readers enjoy reading it and appreciate the work that went into creating this world for all of you.

There are many many more stories to tell on the world of Calthea. I hope that you will continue along the journey with me. It's going to be a wild ride!

For now, though, I leave you with this thought. Love whoever you can, whenever you can, in all the ways that you can for the rest of your lives. Follow the First Law of the Blades* and your life will be enriched.

Dia duit!
Rick Bentsen

* So you don't have to go look it up, here's the First Law of the Blades: *You are commanded to love. Love your friends. Love your enemies. Love without reservation. Love without hesitation. Love without condition. Love without expectation of return. If you must fight, then fight with love in your heart. If you must kill, then kill with love in your heart. Never kill or fight with hate or anger in your heart. Hate leads to impotence, but love brings power. This is the law a Blademaster must live by more than any other or else she will be powerless to serve as she should. It is the First Law of the Blades because it is the most important. Live by it, or you will die.*

Acknowledgements

When I started down the road as a writer, I thought that writing was a solo adventure. I did not ever expect how wrong I would be. While the actual writing of the story is a solitary venture, any successful author has a team behind them. I am certainly no exception. And I have got an amazing team that backs every book I put out.

I always tell my readers that they can skip this and just go to the meat of the story. I will repeat that here. Feel free to consider this a free pass to skip this part. You won't offend me if you do. But these people deserve to see their names in print. This book would never have happened without any of them.

First of all, as always, I have to thank the Lord above for the gifts of my overactive imagination and my ability to put words on paper. Without those two gifts, I'd never have been able to do this.

To my parents for their unconditional support over the years. They helped pick me up when I had fallen to my lowest point.

To my brother, who taught me more about how to build a good story and how to create engaging characters in one day than any teachers have ever been able to in entire courses.

To my continuity expert, Joanna, for everything she does to make this series so rich. She knows these characters possibly even better than I do and she has always believed in this series from day one.

To my friends Tony and Andre from High School. They helped me create the characters for my first novel, Dawn of a New Age. Without that start, I don't think there would be any other books.

To my frind Paul Carhart, a fellow author, who helped ot edit this book. Thank you for helping ot make it the best it can be.

To my readers, because without you, there would be no point to doing this. I love each and every one of you.

To Alana and Colwyn. You two are very special to me. Thank you for letting me tell your story to the world.

The Blademaster

.

The text of 1 Corinthians 13 as it appears in this book is taken from the New International Version of the Bible. The following copyright information must appear as a result of this.

Rick Bentsen

*For the woman who has brought out
the hopeless romantic in me.*

The Blademaster

Rick Bentsen

The Blademaster

The first book in
The Bladmeaster Chronicles

The Blademaster

Chapters

The Prophecy of the Coming of the Age of Darkness
As prophecied by Bahalla Maranal, the Dream Weaver
31 Years after the Great Purge

In the waning days of the Age of Light, one who wears the white shall fall to the rites of the Dark One. Only the true power of the Child of Light can save her soul.

When the One born of the Light goes to the twice dead city, she shall fall to the darkness, as one of her own shall betray her. Only the slim blade of the Second Law of the Blades can save her.

When the twice dead city falls empty a third time, the storm clouds will gather, and sabres will rattle in their scabbards. The blight of war shall be upon the land, and only the One born of the Light can lead the charge against the darkness.

On the wings of war comes the Age of Darkness.

Prologue
Midnight Sacrifice

The high priest of Thraal slowly made his way up the steps of the ziggurat. His face was obscured by the hood of the black outfit of his office. The rest of the assembled priests of Thraal were happy for that, as many had seen his face on occasion and it was a face that could only be described as maniacal, dangerous, and skeletal.

He fingered the ceremonial dagger on his belt and grinned evilly. *Yes, it should be a good sacrifice tonight,* he thought with glee. Aloud, he said, "Is the girl ready for the sacrifice, Adouon?"

"Yes, my Lord," the priest beside him nodded. "I believe you will, without a doubt, find her quite suitable. And to heighten your pleasure, we found you a screamer."

"Very good," the High Priest nodded. "She has not been touched, I presume?"

"No, my Lord. She has not," Adouon confirmed with a sinister smile. "Not one of our men would dare touch her after I told them what the consequences would be."

"I need not know the details, but I presume the consequences were sufficiently nasty that I would have approved of it had I been consulted?" The High Priest looked at his assistant with a wicked smile on his face.

"Of course, my Lord," Adouon nodded his head. "Very nasty and very painful."

"Adouon, you are well on your way to becoming High Priest when I pass," the High Priest cackled. "Thraal himself will be pleased with you, I believe."

"All I am, I give to my Lord Thraal," Adouon said softly, bowing at the waist.

"Very good," the High Priest smirked. "Now go and make sure all our men are ready for the sacrifice. Tonight, Thraal will definitely have a message for us."

Adouon ran the rest of the way up the ziggurat, leaving the High Priest below to contemplate the upcoming sacrifice.

It was well known that the High Priest of Thraal loved the sacrifices to the Dark God. Indeed, there were many in the priesthood who said he took too much pleasure in them. None would say such aloud, of course, because they knew that, in the end, Thraal preferred his High Priest to enjoy the sacrifices as much as possible. In fact, the more the High Priest enjoyed it, the better the sacrifice was received.

But for this High Priest, at least, the pleasure came not from the sexual component as many of the young priests believed. Oh, he enjoyed that aspect to be sure. Indeed, he loved the feel of the sacrifice writhing beneath him in her death throes as he took her virginity. But it was the sacrifice's screams that thrilled him the most.

He gained the utmost gratification hearing the primal screams of fear that escaped the beautiful young women his priests found for the sacrifices. The euphoria caused by the screams sated him for days or weeks at a time.

The last two sacrifices, unfortunately, had been disappointing. Both of the young women had refused him the satisfaction of hearing them scream. But this new sacrifice was going to be a different matter altogether. Already he could hear the woman screaming in terror. *Oh yes,* he thought, *this will be a truly gratifying sacrifice indeed. Lord Thraal will surely be pleased by it.*

The High Priest pulled the dagger from his belt as he stopped on the top of the ziggurat. The priests in their black robes were all dancing about and chanting dark prayers to Thraal, dark prayers that most definitely pleased the Dark God. The sacrifice was tied onto the altar above the Great Fire that would receive her body when the ritual was complete.

He slowly made his way over to the altar and looked over the young girl tied spread eagle on the stone platform. *Yes,* he thought as he ran his fingers along her breasts. *This one will do very nicely indeed.* The young woman had temporarily stopped screaming when he approached her, looking at him with morbid curiosity. Her wide eyes darted back and forth, looking for a way out. But when he reached down and felt the folds of her sex to make sure she was still pure, her screaming and thrashing resumed, much to his immense delight.

"It is time," he rasped. "Thraal will be well pleased with this sacrifice."

The priests began chanting faster. The High Priest placed the dagger between the woman's breasts with the blade pointing up to her head.

The woman had gone quiet again, but the High Priest knew that the silence wouldn't last long. He began to disrobe. The sacrifice watched him with wide terrified eyes. When he stood naked before her, basking in the warmth of the Great Fire, she screamed in earnest again. She squirmed harder and harder against the ropes that held her. Even some of his priests shuddered when they saw him.

It was no wonder that his appearance evoked terror in the woman. He was hairless from head to toe, and his grey mottled skin was stretched tight over his bones. Where his eyes would have been, blue flames smoldered instead. He no longer appeared to be human. Indeed, he no longer even appeared to be alive.

He was, in fact, a lich.

The flames of his eyes took in the naked sacrifice before him. His dry, lizard-like tongue rasped over his thin lips. He bent over and flicked his tongue over her right nipple. She gasped in shock. Then he closed his teeth around the nipple and bit deep into her flesh, causing her to wail in pain.

"Please let me go," the woman wept. It was the first time he had heard her speak. He found her voice pleasant, if not pitiful.

"Even if I wanted to, I could not let you go," the lich rasped. "You are to be my mate this evening. After we mate, your soul will be released so my Lord Thraal can speak to us."

"Taelin's light protect me," she uttered in prayer "Keep the soul of me, your servant."

"It is a little late for prayers of protection, my mate," the lich cackled. He climbed up on the altar and knelt between her legs, his phallus just barely entering the folds of her sex. She quivered and writhed trying to dislodge him. "The so called Bringer of Light will not be able to help you here."

"He may not be able to protect me from you, but he can still keep my soul safe with him!" the woman declared. Her faith brought her a bravado that had been previously lacking. "I am a priestess of Taelin. He will take care of me for my service to Him."

"A priestess of Taelin!" the High Priest cackled with glee. "Yes, my priests have chosen very well. This will, indeed, be a sacrifice pleasing to Lord Thraal." He picked up the dagger and held it against the skin between her breasts. "Lord Thraal, the Dark One. The Darkbringer and the Great Destroyer. Accept this sacrifice so that we may gain your wisdom and hear your words!"

He plunged the dagger deep within her heart at the same time he thrust his phallus into her. She rolled her eyes back into her head and would have died, one last prayer to Taelin on her lips, had the dagger not been imbued with the power to keep her alive until the lich was done with her.

It did not take long for the lich to finish mating with her. When he had fully expended himself, he withdrew from her and stood up from the altar. He pulled the dagger from her heart and her soul was released. Her soul floated up from her body, a silvery apparition of the beautiful woman she had been. It floated off towards the limbo that all souls released by the dagger went to, denying her the right to be with her beloved god, Taelin.

At once, all the candles atop the ziggurat were extinguished, leaving only the light from the Great Fire atop the ziggurat. The priests all looked at each other. This was something out of the ordinary, something that had never happened before. They could only wonder at what it meant.

That's when the body of the dead priestess snapped the bonds that were holding her down and stood up. Several priests bolted down the stairs of the ziggurat in panic. None of them had ever seen anything like this during a sacrifice before.

The woman's eyes opened to show two flaming red coals. She opened her mouth and spoke, but the voice was not the same as before. This voice was much deeper and masculine. So deep, in fact, that it vibrated the very bones of the priests standing atop the ziggurat.

"Those who do not wish to burn in the Great Fire must leave now," the voice said. "Only High Priest Drakkhous may remain."

The priests took no time at all to follow the voice's command. They all went flying down the steps of the ziggurat, leaving only the lich to stand atop the ziggurat.

Drakkhous fell to his knees in obedience and respect. "My Lord Thraal. I am your humble servant. What may I do for you, Your Greatness?" the lich rasped.

"Arise, my friend," the Dark God said softly. "You have, as usual, done well."

"Thank you, my Lord," the lich said as he stood. "Now, what is your command?"

"The accursed Taelin has found a way to bring the Blademasters back," Thraal explained. "Even now, one walks the world. I do not yet know her identity, but you are to find her and sacrifice her to me. Only then may I walk the world again."

"It shall be done as you say, Lord Thraal," the lich bowed.

"Good," Thraal smiled. "I leave you to your work. Do not fail me, lich. You know the consequences for failure."

The red glow faded from the woman's eyes and she fell into the Great Fire. But Drakkhous did not notice. He was caught up in his own thoughts. *A Blademaster walks the world again?* he thought to himself. Amusement tugged at his thin lips. *That will certainly make life more interesting.*

The lich dressed and crept back down the ziggurat, smiling evilly all the way.

Several hundred miles south, in a room at the Temple of the White in the city of Ravendale, a young man awoke with a start. His name was Balaam Otakis and he was a young priest dedicated to the service of Taelin, with the rank of the Master of Acolytes for the priesthood of Taelin. He did not know what it was that had torn him from his deep sleep. But he now felt that something of importance had just happened.

Balaam got out of his bed and padded over to the table by the window. He poured himself a glass of water and peered out the window at the stars. It was a clear night, and he could make out the constellations that represented each of the gods in the pantheon. He frowned when he encountered the constellation for Thraal. The stars that comprised the constellation were shining brighter than he had ever seen them before. He did not know what it meant, but he suspected that it had to do with the uneasy feeling that had replaced a night of deep sleep.

As he watched, the stars resumed their usual brightness. Balaam finished his water and went back to bed, noting that he would have to tell the High Priest of Taelin of his experience the next day.

Part 1
Destiny

Chapter 1
Awakenings

The sound of an arrow hitting the wall outside the room she was in was enough to wake her from a sound sleep. She did not think that she was somewhere where an arrow would be fired at her room, but she did not remember where she was, so she could not be sure. As such, she felt that the sound merited some investigation. She quickly propped herself up on her elbows and immediately crashed back down onto the bed. A wave of dizziness and nausea flowed over her, making her retch.

Well, she thought bitterly. *That was a mistake. Must have been some strong drink last night.*

She propped herself back up, much slower this time, and was rewarded by only a mild headache from the movement. She looked around the room and noted to herself that it appeared to be just like any other inn room she'd ever encountered in the Southern Dales. At least, she was assuming that she was still in the Southern Dales. While she couldn't remember much of the past few days, she couldn't imagine traveling that far in that time without remembering it.

Or being saddle sore.

It was a pretty standard inn room. The walls were painted a muted green, and the furniture was all simple oak workmanship. With the exception of the golden knobs and hinges, the dresser and washbasin were unadorned. The chamber pot in the corner was closed, but stank a bit of vomit. A hearty fire was blazing in the corner fireplace, although the fire wasn't doing much to warm up the room. When she looked towards the window, she saw why. The window to the outside was open and a chill autumn wind was blowing in, cutting her to the bone. She wrapped the blankets closer around her and stood up carefully. The act of standing caused another wave of vertigo to pass over her, but she steadied herself against the dresser. She slowly padded her way over to the open window and gathered up the handles to close it. But she paused for just a moment, frowning. Then she ducked her head to the side.

An arrow whizzed by right where her head had been mere moments before, barely disturbing her deep auburn hair.

Cursing aloud, she slammed the window shut and drew the curtains.

"What kind of insane moron would shoot an arrow though an open window?" she fumed.

Now with the window closed and the curtains drawn, she felt no need to keep the blanket wrapped around her, so she let it fall to the floor where it gathered around her feet. The warmth from the fire flowed deep into her bones. Then she turned her attention to the arrow.

Most rangers marked their arrows. So she figured a quick glance would help her figure out where the arrow came from. It had hunter green fletching and two blue bands around the shaft near the feathers. An ornate C in a circle, all in the same shade of blue as the bands, was present between the two bands. She was certain she knew the mark, but for some reason she could not place whose it was.

Must have been a good deal of very strong drink then, she thought dourly to herself.

It was then that she noticed the message tied to it.

Who in their right mind would send a message this way? she grumbled to herself.

She pulled the message from the arrow.

"My dearest Alana," she read. "I have been looking for you for two days. The High Priest of Taelin has requested your presence. I think he is finally ready to answer some of your questions. Meet me at the Lucky Minotaur tonight. I have to go find the halfling. Col."

"Col?" she asked herself. The name sounded familiar.

Then it hit her like a ton of bricks. Not just who Col was. But also what had happened over the past three days. Now she remembered how, three days ago, Colwyn Starseeker, the love of her life, had proposed to her. And how, instead of saying yes, like she had wanted to, she had run and hidden herself away, drinking. For three days? Her eyes opened wide with the shock of what she remembered. She sank down on the bed, still holding the arrow and the note.

She shook her head.

"Oh, Col," she cried. "How could I do that to you? How could I just run off on you like that? Especially when I had been wanting you to ask me to marry you for so long. I finally get what I want and I run? How could I be so cruel?"

It took everything she had to keep the tears from her eyes and she wiped her eyes with the backs of her hands anyway. She knew that she would have to make this up to Colwyn somehow. She would meet him at the Lucky Minotaur, all right. And she would tell him what she should have told him when he asked her in the first place. She would tell him that she would be only too happy to be his wife.

"But if I'm going to present my best face to him and agree to marry him, I have to be dressed appropriately," she said resolutely as she went over to her pack.

Out came her favorite hunter green traveling dress. It was made of the finest elven feithidí silk, a very expensive fabric. She had spared no expense for the dress. feithidí silk was resistant to stains and difficult to cut. It was finely woven and very soft to the touch. This dress was her favorite dress, and she wore it as often as she could. She had designed the dress herself, and she was very proud of it. The dress was long and flowing and featured folds that reached from the waist to the hem of the dress, which barely dusted the ground. Hidden in the folds were slits that coincided with the daggers she usually wore on a garter underneath. The front of the dress was low cut showing off her ample bosom, but it came around straight at the neck in back. She had another small dagger that she carried in a specially designed sheath that rested between her breasts. The dress was just the right shade of green to accent her eyes. When she wore the dress, she wore it with a pair of feithidí silk slippers that caressed her feet just right.

Once she was dressed, she slipped the daggers into their sheaths and checked herself in the mirror. Satisfied, she snatched up the message and let herself out of her room.

Lucky Minotaur, here I come!

It had actually taken three arrows to wake Alana up. Colwyn Starseeker was a ranger that was good with his bow. The three arrows quivered right next to each other, lined up in a row right outside Alana's window. He would have to go into the inn at some point and retrieve the three arrows later on. It would be a pity to waste them.

Colwyn sighed as he watched Alana slam the windows shut. He was a little annoyed at how close he had come to hitting her with the arrow. Rangers are typically good archers but even he had cut that one a little too close. While he knew he could count on her reflexes, she had been a little slower than he had expected. He decided that she must have been drinking heavily the past three days. He'd breathed a huge sigh of relief when she had ducked out of the way and it had taken a certain degree of self control not to laugh out loud when she had cursed and slammed the windows closed. But it would not do to laugh at her.

Especially now.

Colwyn did not know what he had done to cause her to run. He could not fathom what could possibly keep her from agreeing to marry him. He knew that she wanted to say yes. Indeed, he had expected her to say yes, as had all of their friends. No one had expected that she would run and hide for three days.

He had not wanted to chase after her at first. But after his recent conversation with a certain young priestess, he knew he had no choice but to go and find her.

Priestess Naomi Mastairs had come to find Alana the day after she had run off. When he had told Naomi that he had not seen Alana since the night before, the priestess had demanded that he find her and bring her to the Temple of the White. He had agreed to bring her as soon as he found her. Without a second look, the priestess had turned on her heel and left him with more than a slight feeling that she did not like him. But then again, he didn't really care.

Colwyn went back to his horse and stroked its head gently. The horse huffed and nuzzled his hand. He'd always had a way with animals. They seemed to trust him, and that was one of the reasons he had become a ranger. Befriending and tending to animals were a large part of his job. He smiled at the horse then moved back to the saddle where he lashed his bow. Then he hopped up on the saddle in one fluid motion.

"Come on, boy," Colwyn urged softly. "We've got a date at Lucky Minotaur."

The horse started off at a slow trot, heading down the main street of Ravendale. Colwyn nodded at people he knew as they went by. He was in no real hurry to get to the Lucky Minotaur, so he let the horse go at his own pace. It took several long minutes, but the Lucky Minotaur came into sight. He sighed. He could no longer put off this task.

Colwyn dismounted and strung his bow across his broad chest. He lifted his sword from its scabbard just a few inches and then let if fall back, assuring the sword was clear for drawing. He had a bad feeling that finding the halfling would be fraught with a great deal of trouble. The halfling and trouble went hand in hand after all.

Ash, the young stable boy for the Lucky Minotaur smiled as he came up to Colwyn. "Stable your horse for you?" he asked. The young boy was related to Gwen, the waitress that he and Alana liked at the Lucky Minotaur and Ash had always been eager to please them.

"Thank you, Ash," Colwyn smiled. He pressed a gold coin into the boy's hand. "Tell Gwen that Alana will be in shortly. We'll need a table for two. She knows which table to give us. You'll see to it for us?" Colwyn held another gold coin up for the boy to see, making it dance across his knuckles.

The excited young man grinned from ear to ear. "I'll see to it right away!" Colwyn tossed him the second coin and the young man snatched it out of the air.

Colwyn watched and smiled to himself as Ash took the reins to his horse and led it off to the stables. Now that the arrangements for the horse and the table were set, Colwyn could get down to the business at hand. He needed to find the halfling.

If Colwyn were to be honest with himself, he would just come out and admit that he disliked Meryn, the halfling. He did not understand how Alana could stand to be around the halfling. Meryn was loud, obnoxious and she got the two of them into no end of trouble. And, to be brutally honest, it was very rare that Meryn did anything worthwhile for the party. She was simply a burden.

Still, Alana liked the halfling for some reason.

And so, when he had not seen her all day, Colwyn knew he was going to have to go find her. He would eventually have to go look for the mage too. He was not nearly as worried about William though, for he knew the mage could more than take care of himself. And it was not unreasonable for William to go missing for several days before a journey. There were times that William would take days just to find all of his spell components. So for William to be gone for three days was really no cause for concern.

On the other hand, the halfling being out of sight for any measurable amount of time was cause for absolute panic.

Colwyn pulled a small emerald stone from a belt pouch. He could feel its warmth in the palm of his hand. He closed his eyes and concentrated on the stone.

"Find Meryn Swiftfoot," he commanded under his breath.

The stone floated into the air up to eye level and slowly circled his head about a foot out from him. After a moment, it glowed a bright green whenever it was pointing in a specific direction in relation to Colwyn. That was the direction he would have to go in order to find Meryn.

The finder's stone was a peculiar bit of elven magic. Most non-elves didn't even know they existed. Designed to point the way to whatever the owner wanted to find, it was a small emerald imbued with elven magic. Unfortunately, it didn't always point out the easiest path, but it would locate the object of the owner's desire. It was a rare item to be found outside the elven nations, but it wasn't uncommon for elven rangers to carry one. This particular finder's stone had been given to Colwyn by an elf maiden he had once loved. Three years ago, she had told him to use it to find his way back to her when the Council of Elders had forbidden him from marrying her.

But when Colwyn had asked the finder's stone to find his true love, it had led him to Ravendale where he had met Alana.

Since then, they had been inseparable.

He turned his attention back to where the finder's stone was guiding him. A groan escaped his lips.

She is not stupid enough to go into the forest alone, is she? he pondered. *She couldn't be that stupid. I've warned her myself about the forest, and I know Alana has as well.*

But the finder's stone had never been wrong for Colwyn. And now it was telling him that Meryn had gone into the forest. Which meant that he was going to have to go into the forest after her.

Sighing deeply, he trudged off towards the forest, wondering if there was any place he'd rather go less than where he was headed.

He couldn't think of any.

"Into the forest it is, then," he sighed as he started off.

It was true. Meryn had wandered off the path. She knew it was not the smartest thing to do, but staying on the path had not helped her find William. She had been annoyed that no one had gone looking for the mage. Colwyn had been more concerned with finding Alana, and Alana, naturally, had been missing for three days. While she could understand why Colwyn would find it more important to find Alana, it still annoyed her that he didn't think William was important enough to find. Regardless of what the ranger felt about William, the truth was that Meryn loved the mage. She wouldn't ever tell him that, but she did love him.

She was just afraid to tell him.

It was that love and concern for him that had driven her to go into the forest after him. Someone had to, after all. And no one else was lining up to do it.

But now she was off the path and wandering around looking for William. And the trick of it was to make sure she didn't get lost while trying to find him.

And she was growing tired. After leaving the path, she had to fight her way through underbrush and it had worn at her. She didn't have the woods-sense of Colwyn or the strength of any of her larger companions. Now she was trying to stay awake by sheer force of will. And it wasn't working! She stumbled into a clearing. She just needed to rest. That's all. She slumped down to the ground and drifted off with a sigh.

She slipped into a deep sleep. As the fog of slumber descended over her, she could swear she could see things moving in the trees, but she dismissed it as her head lolled to the side. She dreamed of William and a life with him. It was a pleasant enough thing to contemplate. She wanted to stay in the dream and follow her life with William to its conclusion, but a loud voice roared through the dream, waking her.

It was a war cry! And she would know the source anywhere. Colwyn!

She sat up in fear, her eyes wide in terror as Colwyn notched and fired two arrows in quick succession. The arrows arced towards her. She dropped to the ground to avoid them. She heard them thunk into something very solid behind her.

She heard the death rattle of whatever creature the arrows had hit. With a wince, the halfling peered around just in time to see a forest orc with two arrows embedded in his chest, flop face first to the ground.

Colwyn leapt into the clearing, dropping his bow and drawing his sword all in one motion. There were six more forest orcs encircling the horrified halfling. And while they had not been expecting an attack, they reacted very quickly to the new threat. Quicker, in fact, than Colwyn would have thought possible.

But not quickly enough. Colwyn charged, sword brandished. With his first swing, he lopped off the closest orc's head. Before they could regroup and mount any kind of attack, two more orcs had been cut down, one with a thrust through the heart and the other with a mighty swing that cleaved the creature in two from shoulder to waist. Three forest orcs remained, gazing at their fallen comrades in disbelief.

However, their doubts faded quickly, and the forest orcs charged at the young ranger. There was no skill or coordination to the charge, although one of the orcs, ostensibly their leader, hung back and waited to see what the ranger would do to his fellow orcs. With one great swing of his sword, Colwyn took the heads off the two charging orcs. Then he dropped into a crouch and waited for the leader to make his move.

When the orc leader finally came, it was not without some trepidation. The orc pulled a spiked club from off of his back. He swung it twice experimentally and then paced back and forth just out of the ranger's reach. A moment later, the orc launched its attack, swinging the club for

Colwyn's head. The ranger brought his sword up and parried. He swept the sword around, disarming the orc and then slashed across the orc's body. But the orc fell back. Colwyn moved in, thrusting. He caught the orc just above its sternum. The tip of his sword sank deep into the orc's chest. He kicked the orc in the belly and it slid off with a wet sound. Colwyn sneered at the orc blood on his sword in distaste. With a sigh, he wiped the blood off on the orc's shirt and slid the sword back into its sheath.

Meryn was trembling when Colwyn knelt down next to her. He lifted her head up by the chin and inspected the unbridled fear in her eyes.

"You shouldn't be walking around in these woods all by yourself, Little Bit," he breathed. "You might end up as dinner for forest orcs."

"I-I'm sorry, Colwyn," the halfling sniffled as she stood. "I didn't mean to cause any trouble. It's just that William has been missing for three days and no one seems to be concerned enough to go out looking for him. I know that finding Lady Alana was important too, but I figured that, while you were looking for her, perhaps I should take the time to look for William. Someone had to. I know that we probably are going to get a new mission soon, and I know we'll need his magic when we do. I just got so tired that I couldn't keep my eyes open. I didn't mean to drift off like that, though. I guess I'm just lucky that you came around to look for me. I would have been dinner for those orcs if you hadn't. Did I thank you for saving me yet?"

"No," Colwyn sighed. To himself, he added, *I should have let the orcs have you. Maybe then I'd have some peace and quiet.* But he couldn't say such thoughts aloud. If it got back to Alana that he was saying such things to the halfling, Alana would never let him live it down.

"Well, in that case, thank you," the halfling beamed. She stretched before following Colwyn out of the clearing. "It was very brave and noble of you to risk your life to save me like that. Even if it really didn't look like it was really all that much of a risk. You made pretty short work of those orcs. They never really had a chance. You made it look too easy. But we still need to find William. I can't just leave him alone in these woods. I mean the forest orcs almost ate me. I'd hate for him to have to face down forest orcs as ferocious as those were."

"William can more than take care of himself, Little Bit," Colwyn reminded her. It took every ounce of self control that he had not to roll his eyes at her. "He has proven that on more than one occasion."

"I know, Colwyn," the halfling nodded. They started down the path leading from the clearing back to Ravendale. "But I still worry about him. Because I love him just like you love Alana." Colwyn's eyes opened wide at this admission. It was not something he had been expecting to hear. "But don't tell him, okay? I really think I need to be the one to tell him. I just haven't figured out the best way to tell him yet. If you have any ideas on how to tell him, please help me. Because Lord Taelin knows I need all the help that I can get..."

This time, he could not control himself, and he rolled his eyes as she continued in this vein and the two of them trudged further down the path.

From his seat in a tree overlooking the clearing, William Stonehands, Mage of the White, watched Colwyn and Meryn go. He had been perched in the tree through the whole battle. Indeed, he had watched the forest orcs approach the sleeping halfling and was getting ready to intervene on her behalf when Colwyn had shown up. He once again was amazed at the lengths that Colwyn would go to keep Alana happy, even to the extent of rescuing the halfling, even though he knew full well that Colwyn did not like the halfling in the least.

However, the revelation of the halfling's feelings for him had taken him by surprise.

The truth was, William loved the halfling as well, but he had been afraid to tell her how he felt for fear of rejection. But now that he knew that she felt the same way, there was no fear of rejection. Indeed, he planned on telling her how he felt as soon as an opportunity presented itself.

He checked the pouch where he had stored the tail feathers of a thrynda bird. It was one of the more esoteric spell components that William used, and it was also one of the hardest for him to gather. The tail feathers had to be plucked from a live bird, and the thrynda bird was notoriously hard to catch. But he had finally caught one in the tree he was sitting in.

Once he was sure that the feathers were secure, he dropped to the ground. He collected the arrows that Colwyn had used, cleaning and repairing them with a silent command.

"Off to the Lucky Minotaur, I think," he muttered to himself before taking the same path Colwyn and Meryn had taken towards Ravendale. "I should get there not long after Colwyn and Meryn do. I think that, once more, I will be fashionably late."

He whistled softly to himself as he started down the forest path leading towards Ravendale.

Chapter II
The Lucky Minotaur

he tap room of the Lucky Minotaur was very busy that night. And crowded. Gwendolyn was busy rushing from here to there, but still managed to stop by her friend Alana's table. After all, she hadn't seen Alana in three days and was concerned about her friend's well being. It was common knowledge that Colwyn had proposed to Alana, but Gwen also knew that Alana had never given Colwyn a response. Instead, she'd run. And Gwen hadn't seen her since.

"So, Alana, have you seen Colwyn since...?" Gwen asked softly as she slid into a chair next to the young warrior woman. A slice of chocolate pie materialized in front of Alana as if out of nowhere.

"Yes and no," Alana snorted. "The boy shot an arrow through my window to get my attention, but I didn't actually see him." She took a bite of the chocolate pie and smiled. "Still the best chocolate pie in all of the Southern Dales."

"Albert has always said you have excellent taste," Gwen laughed. She looked over at a table that had several large and tough looking mercenaries sitting at it and grimaced as they waved her over. She sighed and rolled her eyes as she turned to face her friend. "I know I have no right to ask you this. Promise me that you won't get into a fight tonight, Alana."

"You know I never *intend* to get into a fight, Gwen," Alana reassured her. "Trouble just seems to have a way of finding me."

"Well, Albert is a bit upset over trouble always seeming to find you here in the Lucky Minotaur," Gwen shook her head. She stood up and picked her tray back up. "He wouldn't bar you from coming here because he likes your money too much, but he doesn't want any more damages."

"I'll do my best, Gwen," Alana smiled. She took another bite of the pie. "Could I get another kava juice please?"

"Of course," Gwen smiled. "I'll bring it to you as soon as I tend to those thugs over there."

Alana flashed her a smile and took another bite of her chocolate pie. It was, as she had said to Gwen, the best chocolate pie in the Southern Dales. She would never allow herself to have too many of the pies, but every once in a while she craved one. They were her reward for doing things well. And since she had decided to accept Colwyn's proposal, she felt she had earned one.

Her thoughts returned to Colwyn. They had been so happy for so long, and now it came to this. She wondered how mad he was at her for running like she had. She hoped that he would forgive her. Especially since she had come to the decision that she loved no one but him and would very much like to be his wife. She wanted nothing more than to have a simple life with him. Unfortunately, she had a very strong feeling that "simple" might not be easy to come by.

It never had been.

She watched Gwen scurry over to the table where the mercenaries continued to call to her and gather their orders. One of the more brutish men at the table put his hand on Gwen's behind and squeezed. Alana grimaced. If they kept that up, it was very likely that she was going to have to break her promise to Gwen. Trouble was calling. And if it called her, she would answer.

But the situation with Colwyn was forefront on her mind. She felt guilty for having run off like she did, but she had panicked. Her reaction surprised even her because it was what she wanted.

But just because it was what she was hoping for, didn't mean she was expecting it, or even that she was ready for it. It wasn't logical. It actually made no sense whatsoever. But it was what she had done.

She took a sip of her kava juice and sighed. She knew she had hurt Colwyn by running. She only hoped that he could forgive her. If he didn't forgive her, she would have lost the best thing in her life.

She took another bite of chocolate pie and pondered about what she would say to him when he arrived.

"So, what are you going to say to him when he gets here?" Gwen asked as she plopped in the chair opposite Alana.

"I'm going to apologize to him for running and tell him I'll be happy to marry him," Alana smiled.

There. That sounded simple, she thought to herself. *I just hope it ends up being that simple.*

From where Alana was sitting, the door was in plain view. That was not an accident. Alana noticed Colwyn enter the tap room. He scanned the room briefly and started towards her table. With her back to the door, Gwen couldn't see Colwyn enter. Alana, however, had to fight to keep a straight face as she watched the big ranger sneak up on Gwen. When he got right behind her, Colwyn reached down and tickled her on both sides at the same time.

Gwen jumped about five feet in the air.

Gwen shrieked. "Colwyn Starseeker, you are a very mean man!" she chastised as she whirled around. She swung her tray at him and it bounced off his head.

Colwyn just laughed as he took the blow. The bar maid huffed and flounced off towards the bar. He chuckled as he sat down and smiled at Alana.

"Hi," he said simply, his smile growing wider.

"Hi." She smiled back. Then she wrinkled her nose in disgust at the odor coming from Colwyn. "Is that orc?"

"I know," Colwyn grunted. "You just can't get the smell out. I've already bathed twice. I'm going to have to burn one of my favorite outfits. All because the farking halfling got it into her head to go off into the forest to chase after the mage."

"Meryn went into the forest by herself?" Alana raised an eyebrow. "Is she crazy?"

"Either that or stupid. She decided that she would go find out what happened to William since no one else was doing it. And then she went and fell asleep in a clearing," Colwyn sighed. "If I hadn't come along when I did, she would very likely have been eaten by five hungry forest orcs. Maybe I should have let them have her. At least then I wouldn't have their stench all over me."

"Don't say that!" Alana laughed. "I don't think I'll ever understand what you have against Meryn."

"And I don't think I'll ever understand what you see in the farking halfling," Colwyn shrugged. He looked around for Gwen before turning back to Alana. "Listen, I'm sorry about the arrow thing. I had such a hard time finding you. When I found out where you were staying, I had to make sure it was you in the room before I could leave the message. I didn't mean to almost hit you in the head."

Alana nodded. "I understand, and I'm not mad at you," She reached across the table and took a hold of his hand. She gazed into his eyes as she continued. "I am sorry for worrying you though. I just shouldn't have run off like I did. But when you asked me to marry you, I panicked. It doesn't make any sense. I had wanted you to ask me for so long." She took a sip of her kava juice and glanced coyly at him over the edge of the glass. "In case you were wondering, the answer is yes, I'll marry you."

"I'm afraid that it's not that simple," Colwyn sighed, turning away to break their eye contact. He was shielding her from what? Pain? He patted her hand affectionately when he continued. "There's nothing that I want more than to be your husband. But I fear that, whatever it is that Lord

Caiaphas wants to talk to you about will prevent that from happening. I don't want to get my hopes up just to have you yanked away from me. I thought I had lost you once when you ran off like that. I can't go through that again."

Alana reached over and turned his head so he was looking her in the eyes. "Now you listen to me, Colwyn Starseeker. You are not going to get out of marrying me quite so easily. I've given this a great deal of thought. Don't you think I haven't already considered that? The worst Caiaphas can tell us is that I'm a princess and that I need to marry someone from a noble home. Remember that I don't know anything about my parents. But even if that is the case, you were born to a noble house, so that wouldn't even be a problem for us. See? I've worked it all out."

"I suppose you're right." A weak smile worked its way across Colwyn's handsome face.

"Still, it does kind of bother me with the timing of the summons," Alana frowned.

"I suppose," Colwyn said as he raised his mug of ale to his lips and took a deep drink from it.

She took another sip of her juice. "I mean, it can hardly be coincidence. It's been over a month since we returned to Ravendale after our last mission for the White Temple and we've heard nothing until now. And then, right after you propose to me, all of a sudden, the High Priest decides to summon me."

"Probably not a coincidence, no," Colwyn admitted what he'd already been thinking. "Which is why I fear what he has to say. A priestess named Naomi came to see me two days ago. She told me that we had been summoned to see the High Priest."

"Really?" Alana put her glass down. "*We* were?"

"Or, should I say, you were summoned. She didn't seem to care if I came along or not. Actually, maybe I'm not summoned after all but I won't let that stop me. I rather got the impression that she didn't like me all that much."

"Who doesn't like you, Colwyn?" Gwen giggled as she appeared back at the table. "Other than the occasional tickle attack, I think you're a pretty alright guy."

"Thanks for your vote of confidence, Gwen," Colwyn snickered.

"Any time, Colwyn," Gwen laughed as she placed a fresh mug in front of him. But her demeanor turned more serious when she placed a fresh glass of kava juice in front of Alana. "Alana, you know Albert and I love you like family. Right?"

"Yeah."

"I wouldn't even ask this, but I don't want anyone getting hurt. You promised me that you would at the very least try to avoid trouble."

"Okay." Alana caught Colwyn's frown. She shrugged as if to say she had to make the attempt.

"So, those men over there. I think they're looking for trouble tonight after all," Gwen sighed softly as she placed a mug of ale next to the glass of kava juice she had just put on the table for Alana. "They sent this ale over to you. Would it be too much to ask for you and Colwyn to call it a night?"

Alana glanced over at the rowdy men she had noticed earlier. One of them raised his glass to her when he saw her looking his way. It was the one who had put his hand under Gwen's skirt. She looked back at Gwen with a grimace on her face. "Tell you what. Since you asked so nicely, I think I will call it an early night. I'm not sure I like the company here at the moment anyway. Colwyn, would you take me home, please? It's been a very long three days, and I would very much like to sleep in my own bed tonight. Especially if I'm going to have to deal with Lord Caiaphas in the morning. I think I'm going to need to be well rested for that."

Colwyn nodded. "As you wish, Alana," he said with a broad smile. He drained the contents of his mug, because he hated to waste good ale or the coin that purchased it. Then he stood up and offered his hand to Alana.

The warrior woman smiled and took the offered hand. She stood and the couple started toward the tap room door. But they hadn't made it more than a few steps before trouble again found Alana. As it always did.

"Hey, Girlie," one of the brutes hollered. "You forgot yer drink."

"Girlie?" Alana whispered, tensing up at the insult. Her hands flexed near the slits at the sides of her dress as if she were itching to draw the daggers held within.

"Just ignore him, Alana," Colwyn urged under his breath as he ushered her towards the door.

The brute called out again. "Hey, Girlie!" That ale cost Hubie a whole gold coin. The least you could do is drink it."

Alana set her jaw and clenched her hands into fists. But she and Colwyn did not stop in their slow journey to the door.

"Well, Girlie," another of the mercenaries, presumably Hubie himself, drawled. "If you're not gonna drink it, maybe you should just wear it."

What happened next seemed to happen in slow motion. There was dead silence in the tap room. It was probably the first time Alana had ever heard it completely without sound. Even the bard had stopped singing. The ale splashed all over the back of Alana's feithidí silk dress. It was a line that should not have been crossed, and everyone in the tap room, except for maybe Hubie and his friends, knew it. Chairs scraped against the floor as the other patrons of the tap room scrambled out of harm's way.

Albert groaned behind the bar. "Here we go again..." he muttered. He loved Alana like a daughter, but it annoyed him to no end that there were more bar fights on the nights that Alana was there then at any other time. Even though Alana never started the fights, she did seem to always be in the center of them. And she had a way of finishing them. The damage usually wrought to Albert's tap room tended to be excessive, though. And while William was often on-hand to repair the damage with magic, it was still annoying to have so much damage on the nights that there were such fights.

And he knew there would be plenty of damages.

Alana turned slowly around, with her false smile plastered across her face. Anyone who knew her well was aware that this particular smile didn't bode well for those men. The mercenaries, on the other hand, were oblivious to the danger they were in. All they saw was a beautiful woman that they wanted to have their way with finally paying them some attention.

"I hope you have your daggers stashed under that beautiful dress of yours," Colwyn muttered.

Alana winked at Colwyn but otherwise gave him no indication that she had heard him. She rounded on the mercenaries, focusing the majority of her attention on Hubie.

"Hey, Hubie," one of the other brutes grinned broadly. "Looks like she likes you after all! I guess you're going to get it tonight!"

"Oh, yes, Hubie," Alana said breathlessly. "You're going to get just what you deserve."

She came forward, backing Hubie up to the wall. Hubie, for his part, was transfixed. His oafish features were screwed into a tangle of confusion, unsure of what to make of this sudden change in Alana's personality.

He never saw the strike coming.

In one fluid motion, almost too quickly to be seen, Alana drew a dagger from under her dress, flipped it so she was holding it by the point and let fly with it. The dagger spiraled swiftly towards Hubie and skewered him to the wall by his genitals.

Naturally, Hubie screamed in pain and perhaps a touch of fury.

"You can't do that to Hubie!" one of the other mercenaries yelled. "All he did was buy you a drink. You should have kissed him, not hurt him."

"Did you, by chance, notice that I was already with someone?" Alana raised an eyebrow. "And maybe that someone would turn out to be far better for me?"

"So?" the brute scoffed. "Everyone knows that no one denies Hubie what he wants."

"I rather think I just did," Alana grinned.

"Kill her!" Hubie screamed as he tugged at the dagger, still obviously in great pain. "Kill her for this outrage!"

The men drew their knives and advanced on Alana. Colwyn drew up next to her and drew his own sword. The other two daggers Alana had secreted on her person appeared in her hands.

One of the men lunged for Alana, thrusting his dagger at her chest. It was a clumsy strike, one made even clumsier by drink, and she easily dodged it. She thunked him solidly on the head with the hilt of her dagger, eliciting a painful grunt.

Another of the men came for Colwyn, but the ranger swatted the man's wrist aside with the flat of his blade. Alana and Colwyn had made an unspoken agreement not to kill the brutes, opting instead to subdue them. It was a conscious decision that most fighters wouldn't have chosen, but Colwyn and Alana were not most fighters.

The mercenaries were about to launch another attack when the entire room was plunged into an unnatural and almost palpable darkness. Colwyn and Alana knew immediately what had happened, but the brutish men were not so lucky. The darkness caught them completely off guard.

"Now, now boys," William's magically amplified voice mocked. "That's no way to treat a lady. I think you should put those knives away now."

"Yes, sir," the brutes gulped in unison.

William chuckled. "I can't leave you alone for a couple days without you getting into trouble, can I, Alana?" William asked, his voice now unenhanced. "What would you do without me?"

Alana growled. She'd been spoiling for a fight and was a touch annoyed over William having spoiled her fun. "You know, William, I could have handled those men without your help. Colwyn and I had things well under control."

"Oh, I don't doubt it," William laughed. "But there are no bodies to bury and no more damage for me to repair for Albert when things are done my way. And then everyone's so much happier. Aren't they?"

"They threw ale on my dress," Alana whimpered. "They deserved the ass kicking they were getting."

"All this over a little spilled ale?" William laughed harder, rolling his eyes slightly. "Tsk tsk tsk. I'm a bit disappointed in you. I thought you had more self control than that. Put your daggers away, Alana. This fight is over."

Alana liked to keep the hiding places for her daggers secret, and so she used the cover of William's darkness to sheath her daggers. There the mage stood, looking upon Alana with an amusement staining his face.

Upon seeing that there was not going to be any more fighting, the patrons of the tap room moved their chairs back to their tables and resumed their meals and conversations. Albert breathed a huge sigh of relief and nodded his thanks to the mage. William nodded to Albert in return with a smile.

Alana glared at the men, who were all cowering in fear not far from where Hubie was still pinned to the wall by Alana's dagger.

"By his genitals, Alana?" William asked, his eyes wide. "That's a little harsh, even for you, don't you think?"

"He had his hand up Gwen's skirt earlier in the evening, William," she said softly.

"Perhaps not harsh enough then," William nodded.

Alana shrugged and walked over to where Hubie was pinned to the wall. She smiled sadistically as she grabbed a hold of the hilt of the dagger. He winced in pain. Sweat began to pour down his face in rivulets as she slowly twisted the dagger. A small whimper escaped his lips.

"You were a very bad boy tonight, weren't you, Hubie?" she asked.

"Yes, ma'am," he whimpered.

"You shouldn't have put your hand under Gwen's skirt without her permission should you have, Hubie?" Alana sneered.

"No, ma'am!" Hubie squealed.

"And you shouldn't have bought me a drink when I was clearly with someone already. And definitely, you shouldn't have thrown the drink on me." Alana continued to twist the dagger. "Should you have, Hubie?"

"No!" Hubie gasped.

"And you're never going to do any of that again, are you, Hubie?" she asked, giving the dagger a particularly sharp jerk.

"I swear it. Just stop twisting the dagger," Hubie screamed. "Please!"

"If I ever hear about you putting your hand under Gwen's skirt again, I will find you and make *this* a pleasant memory," Alana grinned with an evil glint in her eye.

She yanked down with the dagger, tearing through flesh and leather alike. Hubie collapsed on the floor. His friends picked him up and hurried him out the door. After the group of mercenaries left, the rest of the patrons stood and applauded.

"I guess Hubie and his boys are not all that popular," William smirked.

"I guess not," Alana smiled. Gwen came running over to them. "I don't think Hubie will be bothering you any time soon, Gwen."

"I should say not after what you did to him!" Gwen giggled with glee. "Albert's so happy that those boys finally got their come-uppance that he's giving you all your food and drink tonight for free. And he's not even mad about the hole in the wall."

"Well, then," Alana's smile widened. "Since Albert's paying, I want a WHOLE chocolate pie! And I'm not sharing either!"

They all laughed because they knew she wasn't joking.

The three friends sat back down at the table. Alana's hand found Colwyn's. William noticed and could not suppress his grin.

"Said yes, finally, did you?" he asked Alana.

"So it would seem, yes," she replied.

"William, we need a favor," Colwyn said softly, his mood turning serious.

"Name it."

"We need you to watch over Meryn tomorrow," Colwyn continued. "We've been summoned to see Lord Caiaphas in the morning, and I'm rather averse to the idea of taking her with us. Quite frankly, I'm still annoyed with her."

"Yes, I saw your handiwork earlier," William chuckled. "Very noble. But I have to ask. If you don't like the halfling so much, why save her?"

"Because I wouldn't like to have Alana mad at me for letting the halfling die," Colwyn shrugged. "Although, if truth be told, I'd rather Alana's wrath than the stench. I hate forest orcs."

"Well, I'll be happy to keep an eye on Meryn for you tomorrow," William nodded. He took a sip of his wine and stretched. "Lord Caiaphas has finally decided to tell you what your destiny is, huh?"

"So it appears," Alana shrugged as Gwen put the chocolate pie in front of her. "Although, to be honest, all I expect is more riddles. I don't think it likely that, after all this time, he's suddenly going to give me a straight answer. Especially not in light of how fond he is of jerking us around."

"You'll have to let me know what he says," the mage nodded. "I'm ready for a new journey, so I'm rather hoping he sends us on a mission."

"Well, the halfling is at the Golden Dagger Inn," Colwyn said softly. "She's in the Green Room. They claim the room is halfling proof. As if such a thing were possible."

"Well then, I'll leave you two love birds to enjoy the rest of your evening," William stood. He leaned his staff in the crook of his right arm and grasped his wrists with the opposite hands, letting the arms of his robes fully cover his arms and hands. "I am going to go check on dear Meryn. She's had quite the ordeal today."

Colwyn stared after William, a look of shock on his face.

"I don't believe it," he said. "Who would have ever thought?"

"What is it?" Alana asked.

"The mage is in love with the farking halfling."

Alana laughed. "You've just now realized this, Col?"

"You knew?" Colwyn gasped at her.

"Of course I knew," Alana laughed even harder. "He looks at her the same way that you look at me. I'm surprised that you never noticed. You're usually far more observant than that!"

Colwyn said nothing, but rather put his head on the table and began to weep the tears of the insane.

Chapter III
The High Priest of Taelin

Caiaphas was dying.

He had known it for some time, of course, but the fact was, he was dying. And soon, he would be walking with his god, Taelin. He looked forward to the walk, but at the same time, he regretted leaving Calthea before fully completing the work that had been set aside for him to do. It was important work that would determine the fate of the world. But now it would be left for his successor to complete. And so, he had to hold on long enough to pass along instructions to he who would succeed him.

He waited in his chambers for Balaam, the priest he had decided would be his successor as the High Priest of Taelin. He hoped that the young priest would be able to do what needed to be done. He believed the young priest would live up to his expectations. Taelin would not have guided him to choose the young priest as his successor otherwise.

The young man came into the small quarters that Caiaphas was staying in. He was carrying a tray containing a bowl of stew, some bread and a cup of wine.

"You wanted to see me, Lord Caiaphas?" he asked tentatively as he set the tray down on the table next to the old priest's bed.

"Yes, Balaam, I did," the old man sighed, trying to sit up. Balaam helped him to a sitting position then offered the bowl of stew to him. Caiaphas waved the stew away. "I will eat when I am ready. I called you here for a reason, Balaam. That reason is not so you can feed me."

Balaam bowed. "No disrespect was meant, Lord Caiaphas."

"And none was taken, Balaam." Caiaphas smiled. "I will very soon go to walk with Taelin, my child."

"No." Balaam shook his head. "It cannot be so."

"Wishing for something to be different than it is will not make it so," Caiaphas rasped. "That is a lesson you still must learn, Balaam, if you wish to become High Priest."

"Of course," Balaam lowered his head and nodded. "I thank you for your wisdom, my lord. But I doubt I will ever be High Priest. I am nowhere near the Priest of Taelin that you are. Nor is it a position that I would even aspire to."

"And did you think I was always this way, Balaam?" Caiaphas laughed, wheezing. "I was just as you are now when I was named High Priest. It will not be an easy road for you, but you will be the High Priest when I pass."

"I am honored, Lord Caiaphas, that you would think I am worthy of being named High Priest," Balaam said softly. "But I am not worthy."

"The very fact that you would think yourself unworthy is proof enough, Balaam. Power goes to those that do not seek it," Caiaphas rasped. "You will be High Priest. I have so ordered it. Lord Taelin has approved it. There is to be no more discussion on it. There is much I have to teach you before I pass. That is why I have summoned you."

Balaam nodded and leaned closer to the old man. "What do I need to learn?"

"Some things that I must tell you will cause you pain, Balaam." Caiaphas whispered. "Are you sure you are ready to hear them?"

"Whatever you have to tell me, I can handle," Balaam said.

"Do not be so sure," Caiaphas said. He reached over and took the bowl of stew. After sipping several spoonfuls, he put the bowl down and sighed, a deep rattle in his chest. "I am afraid that Merinda Delwyn has been killed."

Balaam did not hear all of what Caiaphas told him about Merinda Delwyn. As soon as he heard her name, all he could do was to think about her.

He had not seen her in seven months.

The memory of the last day they were together came back in a rush...

Balaam was tired. His job at the Temple of the White in Ravendale for the past two years had been to train the new acolytes. He had been happy to be the one to guide the new acolytes onto the path of enlightenment. It fulfilled him in ways that he had never expected. But he had never given any thought to anything other than training the young priests to be.

Until Merinda Delwyn had come to the Temple of the White.

When Merinda Delwyn had first arrived at the Temple of the White to be an acolyte in the priesthood of Taelin, he was intrigued by the young woman. He had easily five years on her, but he could not help but feel the attraction to her. And she had felt the same way from the very first. He had had to consult with the old texts to make sure that there was nothing that would be against the two of them being together. When he found that there was no rule against it, he was pleased beyond words. They had gone to Caiaphas together and had received his blessing to court.

The relationship had grown quickly, and the two were rarely seen apart. Caiaphas had been impressed that they had managed to not let their relationship interfere with her training or his duties for that had been his one true fear for the two of them.

The morning had come for the graduation from acolyte to priesthood for the small group of acolytes that Balaam had been training. He had been proud to watch all of the acolytes take their rightful place in the priesthood of Taelin.

But he was most proud to watch Merinda Delwyn become a priestess of Taelin.

He waited for all of the festivities to be over so that he could be alone with Merinda. He had invited her for a walk through the city in the afternoon. She had readily agreed to go with him. They had gone to the Lucky Minotaur for a late lunch and then had gone for a walk through the merchant district.

They walked for a time in silence. Merinda had put her hand in his, and they walked along happily. But Balaam had a dark feeling that something was soon going to cut into his tranquil bliss. And he suspected that he would discover what it was before they returned to the Temple of the White. He dreaded the end of his happiness. So he did nothing to unearth the source of his suspicions.

"I love you, Balaam," Merinda said softly. She stopped to look at the merchandise on a roadside table. She ran her fingers along a medallion. "I hope you never doubt that."

"I never would," Balaam smiled at her. He pulled out his coin purse in case she decided that she wanted the medallion. "I'm curious. Why would you think that I would?"

"I have been given my assignment, Balaam," she said quietly. She picked the medallion up and Balaam counted out the coins to pay for the medallion. "I will be leaving Ravendale tonight."

Balaam wanted to object. Instead, maintained serenity. "For how long?" he asked softly.

She shrugged. "I don't know. I'm being sent to Tornith in Dracomyr to teach some of the acolytes there. It will not be forever, my love."

"Why Tornith?" Balaam asked as they moved off down the road. "Did anyone say?"

"Because I am needed there, Balaam," Merinda shrugged. "Why else?"

"You're needed here too, Merinda," he breathed.

"I know I am, Balaam," Merinda smiled up at him. "I know you need me. But I am needed there as well, and as much as I love you, I have to follow the calling of our Lord Taelin to Tornith. You know this. You were the one to it teach to me."

"I'm glad you learned your lessons so well, Merinda," Balaam said. His voice betrayed nothing of his inner thoughts. He wanted to scream out against the woman he loved being sent to the largest city dedicated to the Dark God where the largest ziggurat dedicated to Thraal was located and the priests of Taelin were hunted for sport. But what could he say to her? If her calling was to Tornith, there was nothing that he could do or say to stop her from going. Finally he said what he was expected to say. "I wish you weren't going to Tornith. But I understand why you are going."

"As I said, Balaam, it will not be forever." She smiled broadly at him. "When I return, I still intend to marry you."

Balaam smiled back. "Then I look forward to that day. For now, why don't we just enjoy the rest of our last day together before you have to be on your way."

"That's a splendid idea." Merinda grinned. She looped the medallion over her neck and let it fall between her breasts.

As they had gone through the rest of the day, Balaam had mixed emotions about what she had said. He was proud of her for following the calling of Lord Taelin, but he was torn, because he had a feeling that he would never see her again. Was that feeling unfounded? He did not know.

It was seven months later that he'd had that odd night when he had awoke with a start and had noticed that something was not quite right with the stars.

The following morning, he had gone to tell Caiaphas what he had observed. But he had been turned away without seeing the High Priest. He suspected then that there was more going on than he had first thought.

"Balaam," Caiaphas rasped, pulling Balaam from his memories. "Come back to the present. You must deal with this now."

"I am sorry, my lord," Balaam said quietly. "I did not hear everything you said."

"I said that Merinda Delwyn has been killed," Caiaphas repeated quietly.

"No!" Balaam thundered. "Not Merinda!"

"Silence!" Caiaphas ordered. "You must hear this out. There is a time for grief but this is not it."

"Yes, Lord Caiaphas." Balaam nodded, chastened.

"Merinda Delwyn was killed by a lich named Drakkhous in the service of Thraal," Caiaphas continued. "It seems she was sacrificed to Thraal."

"When did this happen?" Balaam frowned, the memory of the night he woke feeling strange still fresh on his mind. He had a feeling he knew the answer, but he had to ask the question anyway.

"Five days ago," the High Priest rasped. "At the time that the moon was full."

"For what purpose was she sacrificed?" Balaam whimpered. "Why would she be sacrificed? What could Thraal gain from such a sacrifice?"

"I believe that Thraal has found a way to escape his prison in limbo," Caiaphas coughed. "If I am right, he used the sacrifice of Merinda Delwyn to relay that information to his High Priest."

Balaam slumped back into the chair that he was sitting in and closed his eyes. The spoon fell from his hand and splashed into the bowl.

"Do you know what Thraal's plan is?" Balaam asked weakly.

"I know only that it involves Alana Steeldrake," the old man wheezed.

Balaam frowned. "Why her?"

"Because she is chosen by Taelin," Caiaphas smiled. The old man's voice was growing weaker as they continued talking. "I only wish I were the one who could tell her what she must do. This is the most important thing I will tell you, Balaam. You must help Alana."

"What must I do?" Balaam nodded.

"You must accompany her where she goes. She is to investigate the death of Merinda Delwyn and stop Thraal from succeeding in breaking free from his prison," Caiaphas instructed. "But there is a journey she must take first. It is time that she finally learn what she is."

"What she is? Don't you mean who she is?"

"I did not misspeak."

"What then is she?" the younger priest asked, his curiosity piqued.

"Alana must journey to Valendale to seek the sage Isaiah. It is he who will direct Alana to her final destination, the Temple of the Blades."

Caiaphas smiled, knowing that Balaam would get the reference.

"Is it true? Is she really...?" Balaam trailed off, not wanting to say the word for fear of it not being true.

"It is true. Lord Taelin and Lady Laeyra have done what only they could do to stop the coming darkness," Caiaphas fell to a fit of coughing. When his coughing eased, he continued. "My time grows short. You have been named, Balaam, and you know what you must do. Leave me now. I wish to die alone and in peace."

"As you wish, Lord Caiaphas," Balaam nodded. He stood and bowed to his mentor. "It has been a great honor to serve as your assistant. I promise to make you proud of me as your successor."

"You already have made me proud of you, Balaam," Caiaphas said weakly. The old man closed his eyes and quickly fell into a deep sleep.

Balaam bowed again and left the room, wiping tears from his eyes as he went.

When Alana and Colwyn arrived, the Temple of the White was in an uproar. Indeed, neither of them had never seen the temple in such a state. Priests were running everywhere on the grounds. Alana wasn't sure what was going on, but she was determined to get this over with. After all, she had been summoned.

She led the way up the marble steps to the great oak doors and pushed her way through them. She did not look happy, and the priests in the great hall noticed and got out of her way. One priestess was not so lucky, and Alana seized the unfortunate woman by the sleeve of her robes.

"I am in a foul mood, and do not entertain the notion of games today," Alana said through clenched teeth. "I have been summoned and I intend to speak to Lord Caiaphas immediately."

"I-I'll get the High Priest immediately," the priestess stammered.

Alana nodded as she watched the priestess go. Colwyn started to say something, but saw the glint in her eyes and thought better of it.

The warrior woman paced around the great hall, inspecting artifacts as she went. The longer she waited, the more she fumed. She was not, by nature, a patient person to begin with. But the games that had been played by the High Priest of Taelin were greatly upsetting to her. She felt as if she was being used as a pawn in some grand scheme, but she didn't know what the game was, who the players were, or what the rules were. She was hoping to get some clarification with this meeting with the High Priest, but the longer she waited, the less she expected that she would.

Alana had just picked up a particularly priceless and ornate statue when the priestess returned with Balaam in tow.

"Alana Steeldrake," Balaam smiled warmly. "It is good of you to come. I wish the Temple were in a little less of an uproar, but we can only do what we can do."

"I asked to speak with the High Priest, Lord Balaam," Alana said impatiently. "Where is Lord Caiaphas?"

Balaam cast his head down. "I am afraid that Caiaphas has passed, Lady Alana. That is why there is such chaos today. I have been named High Priest in his stead."

"I am sorry," Alana said with a frown, her head bowed in reverence. "Lord Caiaphas and I did not always get along, but he was a good man. His leadership will surely be missed in the Temple of the White."

"Yes, he was," Balaam nodded. "Come. He left me some instructions for you. We'll go talk in the peace of my inner sanctuary."

Alana nodded. She and Colwyn followed the new High Priest into the High Priest's sanctuary, all the while taking in the bustle of activity in the temple. As they neared the inner sanctuary, they encountered fewer priests. By the time they reached the door to the inner sanctuary, it was just the three of them. Balaam opened the door and ushered them inside.

The sanctuary was a small room, about ten feet wide to a side. A small altar was along the wall to the back. A cabinet was on the wall to the left and three small chairs were in the room. Despite so much stuff occupying the small room, it still did not feel cluttered.

Alana took a seat uninvited, but Colwyn waited for Balaam to sit down first. The High Priest pulled a scroll from the cabinet and sat facing at Alana.

"I am not allowed to tell you your destiny, Alana," he began quietly. "I have been forbidden to tell you by Lord Taelin himself as was Lord Caiaphas before me. However, I have been instructed as to what I can tell you."

"If you can't tell me what I'm supposed to be, then we're wasting our time," Alana said quietly.

"No we are not," Balaam responded. "Please listen carefully. You are to go to the city of Valendale to meet the sage Isaiah. He can direct you as to the next phase of your journey. This must be done before you can go on your next mission for the Temple of the White."

"Ah, see, now we get down to it," Alana nodded. She stood up and started towards the door of the sanctuary. "There's something you want me to do for you. What is it this time? Vampires? Goblins? Perhaps slay a dragon?"

"I understand your bitterness and I sympathize," the young man said quietly. And she realized that he was, indeed, a young man, not more than two or three years older than she was. "But this is important, and you will listen to what task I have for you to do."

"Very well," Alana sighed, returning to her chair and sitting back down. She crossed her arms a bit defensively. "What can we do for the Temple of the White today?'

"One of our priestesses was killed in Tornith," Balaam explained. "You are to investigate the priestess's death and bring whoever was responsible to justice."

"And our pay?" Colwyn asked. It was the first time he'd said anything since they'd entered the temple.

"You and your companions will be compensated at your usual rate, of course," Balaam chuckled. "But before you can go on that mission, you must go to Valendale and meet with Isaiah. Once you do what Isaiah instructs you to do, you can go to Tornith and take care of your mission."

"Very well." Alana stood. "We'll leave in the morning. Thank you for your time, Lord Balaam."

"There is one more thing, Lady Alana," Balaam said quietly. "I will be going with you."

"That's not necessary," Colwyn said.

"I assure you that it is."

"We'll be riding fast and hard," Colwyn continued. "You won't be able to keep up with us."

"I'm going. I was forced to promise Lord Caiaphas that I would go," Balaam stated flatly. "There is no choice in the matter, Colwyn Starseeker."

Colwyn snarled and stormed out of the sanctuary.

"We'll be at the Lucky Minotaur in the morning, Lord Balaam," Alana said. "If you are not there when we are ready to leave, we will leave without you."

"I will be there."

Alana turned and left the sanctuary. When she caught up with Colwyn, she put her hand on his shoulder.

"I don't like it," he growled.

"I don't like it either." She nestled in his arms and smiled up at him, content to be in his embrace. "But there's really nothing we can do about it. Go gather the supplies. We'll meet at the Lucky Minotaur in the morning for one of Albert's wonderful breakfasts." She touched his cheek gently. "At least we are going to go through this together, even if we have an extra mouth to feed on this journey."

"At least there's that," Colwyn simpered.

Chapter IV
The Trek South

At that hour of the morning, the tap room of the Lucky Minotaur was quiet. In fact, Alana was, at that point, one of only two people present. That suited her just fine. She wanted to have time to herself before the rest of her companions arrived for breakfast. It gave her the time to think about things. And she had a great deal to think about. Her trip to the Temple of the White had created more questions than it had answered, as was often the case.

Not the least of which were questions revolving around the journey she was about to take to Valendale. What could the sage tell her that the High Priest of Taelin couldn't tell her? It was certainly something curious to her that the sage in Valendale would know more than the High Priest of Taelin did about a destiny that was supposedly set by Lord Taelin. She suspected that the High Priest of Taelin knew more than he was telling her. Of course, she couldn't prove that until she found out what it was she was supposed to be. And she apparently wouldn't find that out until she spoke to the sage.

She could only wonder about what awaited her in Valendale. Although Alana had been to Valendale in the past with her companions, she had never had the opportunity to talk to the sage. But she was annoyed, as she knew that Colwyn was, that the High Priest of Taelin could not be bothered to tell of her destiny. The choice to send her to Valendale to talk to the sage instead was an irksome one to her at best. At worst, it was just plain infuriating. But there was not a whole lot that she could do about it. The way was the way, as the old saying went. And all that she could do at this point was to go to Valendale and consult the sage. She truly hoped that the sage would be more helpful to her than the past two High Priests of Taelin had been. Indeed, she doubted that he could be of any less help to her.

Alana scrutinized the table which had been set for five. She knew that Colwyn was not happy about the High Priest of Taelin joining them on this journey. In truth, she was not happy about it either. But there was nothing she could do to keep the priest from tagging along. She did think that it might be nice to have a healer present in some circumstances. But she had a feeling that there was more to the priest's wanting to go with them than he was telling them. She didn't have a clue as to what it could be though. It did not much matter what the reasons for his joining the party were. Truth be told, the decision as to whether or not he would be joining them had been made without her consultation. And the more she pondered it, the more it seemed that the decision had been made not by Balaam, but by Lord Taelin himself. And that unnerved her to no end. Why would the God of Wisdom take such an active interest in her? Surely this destiny that no one seemed to be able to tell her about was wrapped up in it somehow. But what were the particulars?

She gazed around the tap room which was as near to empty as she had ever seen it. The only other person present was a merchant that had just arrived in town the day before. The merchant was trying to catch a quick bite to eat before he started work on preparing his small market. Alana had every intention of looking over the man's merchandise before they left on their journey for the odds were good that he would be long gone by the time they got back. Small merchants like this one tended to travel around rather than stay in one city. One thing was for sure though. She hated to miss an opportunity to check out new goods when they were in Ravendale.

Alana had made certain she arrived at the Lucky Minotaur early. Even though she knew that they would not leave until much later, especially since Albert would insist on providing a hearty breakfast before they left, she'd had a hard time sleeping. It was a fairly normal occurrence for her to have trouble sleeping on the night before a journey. The adrenaline and excitement associated with a new journey always filled her the night before it began. She had tossed and turned for a good portion of the night before finally just giving up and prepping her gear, which now sat on the floor by her feet. Naturally, she was garbed in her full leather armor, her weapons polished, sharpened and at the ready. Alana in her weaponry and armor was an impressive sight. Some would even say she was intimidating.

When Alana had first arrived, roughly an hour ago, Gwen had brought her a kava juice and then disappeared back into the kitchen. Alana figured that Gwen had gone back to help Albert prepare the breakfast. Albert did not like to get up early, but he would have also been greatly offended if she and her companions had gone off to Valendale without having had their usual hearty breakfast at the Lucky Minotaur. And, to be perfectly honest, it would never have occurred to Alana to skip breakfast at the Lucky Minotaur before leaving anyway. It had become something of a long standing tradition for the companions to have their farewell breakfast there, and she knew that Albert loved to be the one to feed them and see them off.

Alana wondered what Albert had in mind for breakfast. The food at the Lucky Minotaur was renowned throughout the Southern Dales. Albert saw to that. And the chocolate pies that Albert made were regarded far and wide as the best chocolate pies in all of the Southern Dales. But the breakfasts that Albert prepared for Alana and her companions when they went off on a journey were truly something special.

Gwen emerged from the kitchen with a yawn and a shrug. She didn't much like getting up early either. But just the same, she would not miss an opportunity to send her friends off on a journey. And this time was even more important because she knew that this journey would mean a major change in her friends' lives. And as a result, it would signify a major change in her and Albert's lives as well, although she did not yet know how. But with this huge potential change in all of their lives, Gwen wanted to be there for her friends at the start of the journey.

Gwen walked over to the table and slumped into a chair. It was clear to Alana that the young woman had been working hard over the past couple hours. What she had been doing in the kitchen, Alana could not even begin to guess. She had been carrying two sacks, and Alana could tell that each sack was not very light. The young woman plopped the sacks on the floor under the table and smiled at Alana.

"These are the provisions that Colwyn ordered," she said to the warrior woman. "Well, there are three more sacks in the kitchen actually. We made one sack for each person in your party. There's enough for a two-week journey. I hope that will be enough."

"Enough for a trip to Valendale and back," Alana nodded. "If we need more than that, we can forage for it as we go."

"Good. I'm glad we were able to get you the supplies you needed," Gwen smiled tiredly. "Just wait until you see what Albert has prepared for you guys for breakfast. He's pretty well outdone himself again. You guys will definitely be ready for your journey with this breakfast."

Alana smiled back as she took a sip of her kava juice. The cold juice soothed as it flowed down her throat. She was ready for the journey, but at the same time, she was a bundle of nerves. She knew that her life would never be the same after this trip to Valendale. This was the most anxious that she had ever been at the start of a journey. She did not like the anxious feeling that was filling her so completely. It was something that she would have to control once they were on the road. Anxiety like this could cause her to be careless and get herself or one of her companions killed.

The door opened and Colwyn walked into the tap room. From where she was sitting, Gwen couldn't see the door open, nor could she see Colwyn sneaking across the room towards the table they were sitting at. Alana could, though, and she had a hard time keeping a straight face as she watched Colwyn slip up behind the young barmaid. Difficult as it was, she maintained a straight face.

When Colwyn got right behind Gwen, he reached down and tickled her. The young woman squealed and jumped up in the air. She whirled around and slapped him hard on the arm.

"You are a very mean man, Colwyn Starseeker!" she squealed. Then, fixing him with a withering glare, she slugged him a second time.

"So you keep telling me, Gwen," Colwyn chuckled as he dropped into the chair next to Alana. He leaned over and gave her a kiss. "But you still like having me around. Admit it. I make you smile."

"Sometimes you do," Gwen considered. "And sometimes you just infuriate me. I think that you do it on purpose."

"Sometimes," Colwyn laughed. He gave Alana's hand a little squeeze, then he smiled at her. "We have five horses ready and waiting in the stables. They're good, fast horses. I got the best that we could afford. We could probably shave a day or two off our journey with them if we ride hard. Ash is, at the moment, grooming and saddling them for us. They'll be ready when we are. "

"Good," Alana put down her glass. "We'll leave after breakfast. I want to stop and check out the merchant's wares on our way out of town."

"Merchant?" Colwyn frowned as he took a sip from the mug of ale that Gwen had left for him. He was instantly on his guard. It was not in his nature to trust new people, especially where Alana was concerned. "What merchant are you talking about, my dear?"

"That one," Alana said pointing to the merchant who had just gotten up from his table. The man gathered up his belongings and made his way out of the tap room. Colwyn followed the man with his eyes, taking the measure of him. He decided that he did not like what he saw.

Just after the man left, the door to the tap room opened again, revealing William and Meryn. They were both dressed for a journey, although for William, that did not exactly involve any kind of wardrobe change. He always wore the same robes no matter what the occasion was. Wizards never wore anything other than their robes. The right to wear a wizard's robes was earned through trial and pain, and no wizard would dishonor that hard work by wearing anything else.

The halfling, on the other hand, had made some major changes to her outfit. She usually wore a fine silk shirt and breeches when in town. But when she was adventuring, Meryn preferred more practical leather armor. The problem had always been that it was always hard to find leather armor in her size. But Colwyn had made sure that her armor had been made in the right size. It had been difficult finding an armorer that made armor in Meryn's size, and it had not been cheap to make. Alana had been kind enough not to point out that, if he didn't like the halfling, he would not have had armor made for her. Or paid for it for that matter. Of course, she knew that, had she pointed these things out, he likely would have stopped talking to her for days.

The halfling and the mage sauntered over to the table. Meryn tucked a napkin into the collar of her tunic, for she did not want to make a mess of herself when she bit into the food that Albert had prepared. She was a notoriously messy eater most of the time, something that often annoyed her companions. Of course, there was very little they could do about it. Meryn would always be Meryn, after all.

The door opened once more, and Balaam stepped inside. Colwyn glowered at him, eliciting a soft sigh from Alana. Alana wondered if these two would ever get along. If this journey were to be at all successful, they would have to find a way to coexist. From what Balaam had said in the Temple of the White, a great deal depended on this mission being successful. So it was in all of their best-interests to get along.

After Balaam took a seat at the table, Albert brought out a huge platter full of plates and passed the food out to the companions. Albert had, as he always did with these breakfasts, outdone himself with regards to the food. There were three kinds of eggs, scrambled, fried and hard boiled, all seasoned with various herbs and spices. A heaping plate of his spiced potatoes was also presented. Shredded cheese was on another plate; it was there to spread on top of the eggs or potatoes should any of the companions desired such. He had also made four kinds of sausages, a plate of bacon and several loaves of freshly baked honey wheat bread. It was an impressive feast by any standard. Alana could not remember a more extravagant breakfast that Albert had ever prepared for them. Alana suspected that Albert had known that this would be a special journey without anyone having told him.

The five of them ate in silence for a few minutes, save for the occasional appreciative noises.

"Alana, my dear, could you pass those sausages that are by you?" Colwyn asked as he gently took hold of her hand.

"I hardly think that that was appropriate, Sir Colwyn,' the priest said softly. He set his mug down. "You have no right to speak to Lady Alana in that fashion."

William and Meryn backed their chairs away from the table. Albert, who was still standing not too far from the party, grimaced, clearly fearing for the damages these two men might cause to his establishment.

Colwyn stared in disbelief. "I'm sorry?" Alana shot him a glare. She knew how dangerous the ranger was when the timbre of his voice dipped in such a way. Colwyn continued, "I'm afraid I didn't quite catch that, Lord Balaam. Are you telling me that I'm not allowed to talk to my fiancée in an informal, loving way?"

"I am saying that you may not be able to marry her at all," the priest shrugged. "It is, in fact, not a decision that is up to you."

"Nothing will stop me from marrying Alana," Colwyn growled. "And if you aren't going to be any more forthcoming about this so called destiny, then you have no right to interfere in our lives, Lord Balaam." Colwyn threw his napkin down and stood up. He drained the rest of his ale and turned to Alana. "I'll be outside when you're ready, my love. I've lost my appetite. I find I don't much care for the company."

With that, the ranger glared at Balaam once more then stormed out of the tap room.

Alana sighed and took her last bite of egg before she too left the tap room. When she caught up with Colwyn, she gently put her hand on his shoulder. He looked back at her and smiled. But the smile had a touch of sadness to it. She could feel his worry about what the priest had said. It was a worry she shared.

"Don't worry, Colwyn," Alana reassured him, sending him a genuine smile to take the touch of sadness away from him. "I won't let anything keep us from being married."

Colwyn nodded and shrugged. "I just can't stand the way he doesn't give us the information we need."

"I know," Alana nodded. "It bugs me too. Now, let's gather William and go see this merchant. I want to be on our way within the hour."

"As you wish," Colwyn smiled again. This time there was less sadness and worry than there had been before.

The merchant's shop was small and not entirely tidy. Crates lay everywhere, some open and some still sealed. The merchant himself was, at that very moment, laying out a series of black and red leather bound books on the shelves behind the counter. The shop, about half the size of the Lucky Minotaur's tap room, featured long shelves along each wall. A counter stood along the back wall, behind which the merchant would stand, waiting for customers. Not all of the shelves yet had items on them.

The merchant looked up as Alana, Colwyn and William entered the shop. They had decided that Meryn would not be going into the shop with them, and Balaam had volunteered to stay outside with the halfling. Apparently, shopping wasn't all that big a deal for the priest. The merchant came around the counter to meet the companions.

"We're not really open for business, my lady," the merchant said quietly. "Probably won't be for another day or two, in fact."

"I'll likely be out of town when you are ready to open," Alana shrugged. "I'm about to take an extended journey and I thought I might browse your wares before we left just in case there was something that we might find useful. I understand that you don't have everything out and ready to sell, but would you be willing to allow us to browse what you do have out? You might make some money today."

The merchant nodded. "Of course, my lady. And if there's anything specific that you would like more information about, please feel free to ask."

"Actually, I am quite interested in those books that you are putting up on the shelves," the mage said. "What are they?"

"Old books of spells and prophecies," the merchant shrugged. "I have no way of knowing exactly what is in any of the books because they are books of magic and that sort of stuff is beyond my expertise. They are nothing that I can read, but perhaps you can. And so, I would be willing to sell the entire set to you for forty gold pieces. If you are interested, Mage of the White."

"Sold." William pulled a pouch off his belt and counted forty gold coins out of it, nearly emptying the pouch. "I am sure that there will be something useful in those books."

"I will have the crate held for you until you return, Master Mage," the merchant bowed after taking the coins. "Unless you have other arrangements you would like me to make instead?"

"I will look through some of them briefly while my companions continue to browse," William said softly as he ran his fingers over the bindings of the books still in the crate. "Whichever books I don't take with me should be delivered to Albert at the Lucky Minotaur."

"It shall be done as you say." The merchant smiled and proceeded to put the books back in the crate. After he placed the re-sealed crate on the counter for William, he turned his attention back to Alana and Colwyn. "Is there anything that I can help you two with?"

"How much for these arrows?" Colwyn asked as he ran his fingers along one of the arrows' shaft. Whoever had made the arrows had been an expert fletcher. Quality like this only came from one source in Colwyn's experience. "Elven. If I'm not mistaken?"

"You have a good eye, my lord. They are indeed elven made," the merchant rubbed his hands together. "I cannot tell you which clan made them because I was not there when they were made, but they are fine arrows indeed. I will give you all twenty for ten gold coins."

"Agreed."

Colwyn counted out the gold and the merchant pocketed it. He turned to Alana, raising an eyebrow, silently asking if there was anything she needed.

Alana smiled, but she shook her head at the man. She watched William flipping through his new books for a few moments before turning her attention back to the young ranger. "I'm ready when you are, Col."

Colwyn nodded and put the new arrows in his magic quiver. Two years prior, he had come up with the idea of a quiver that would allow him to put any number of arrows inside and it would store them and then dispense them as needed. All he had to do was think about the arrow he wanted and it would appear in the quiver for him to draw. It had cost him a great deal to get a mage to cast the enchantments that made the quiver work. As each arrow was placed inside, it disappeared into the massive storage capacity of the quiver where they would remain until he called for them. When all twenty arrows had been put into the quiver, he looked over to where William had put the last of the books that he was taking into his pack. The rest of the books had been put back into the crate. With a word of magic from the mage, the crate sealed itself back up so that it only William could open it when he was ready to read one of the remaining books.

"Looks like we're ready," Colwyn announced.

"Good." Alana said. She turned to the merchant. "Thank you for letting us browse your wares, Master Merchant."

"Thank you for your business, my lady," the merchant bowed. "You and your companions are welcome back at any time. Master Mage, this crate will be at the Lucky Minotaur before you and your companions are even out of town."

"That will be fine," William bowed. "I did not expect to find such an eclectic collection of material as this. A great deal of it is, unfortunately, beyond my current expertise as well. In time though, I will make full use of these books."

"Then I am glad these books have found their way into your hands," the merchant bowed to William again.

The companions made their way out of the shop and met back up with Meryn and Balaam. The five of them then went across the road to where their horses were stabled. Shortly thereafter, they came galloping out of the stables and were soon beyond the borders of the town.

The merchant shuffled back to the counter and pulled out a sheet of parchment and a quill. He wrote out a message on the parchment and then looked it over for accuracy, reading it several times to make sure there were no mistakes. When he was satisfied, he folded the parchment up and melted a bit of sealing wax on the fold. He pressed his ring into the sealing wax and smiled to himself.

With a whistle, he summoned his pet falcon. The falcon landed on the counter and he tied the message to the falcon's leg. He stroked the falcon's crest, ruffling the feathers affectionately.

"Take this message to my master, Caltharis," the merchant said softly. "Take it to him quickly."

The falcon pecked at the counter once and then launched into the air. The merchant chuckled as the bird flew off into the early morning Ravendale sun.

"Yes, my lord," he muttered. "I am sure that you will find the information in that message to be very helpful indeed. I truly hope that you will know what to do with it. And I hope that you will remember me when the time is right. For I am now and always will be your faithful servant."

Still smiling to himself, the merchant went back to stocking the shelves in his store.

After they left Ravendale, Alana and her companions rode hard for the rest of the day. It was normally a nine day ride from Ravendale to Valendale, but Colwyn's observation about the horses was accurate. They were both strong and fast. Alana had no doubt at all in her mind that if she and the others rode hard, they would be able to make Valendale in seven days. They ate their lunches in their saddles, passing food back and forth as they rode. They rode for roughly twelve hours each day, resting for the other twelve hours. It was a hard ride, but the companions, especially Alana, were determined to get to Valendale as quickly as possible.

And so it was that as dusk fell on the seventh day of their journey, the companions crested the hill overlooking the city of Valendale.

"We'll camp here overnight and go into Valendale the first thing in the morning," Alana said softly.

The others agreed and began to set up camp.

Chapter V
Isaiah Talon

In the heart of the Ziggurat of Thraal in Tornith, Drakkhous paced back and forth in front of the altar to Thrall. He reread the message that Adouon had just brought him. The lich glanced at his assistant with a sadistic smile, licking his lips.

"You are sure of the validity of this message, Adouon?" Drakkhous rasped.

"The bird that brought me this message came from one of my most trusted informants, my lord." Adouon shrugged. "He has never proven to be wrong so far. If he says that it is the way of things, then I have no reason to doubt his word. And neither should you."

"Very good, Adouon. You have done well."

"Thank you, my lord." Adouon bowed. "It is a pleasure to serve our Lord Thraal."

"And you serve him well." The lich nodded. "Of course, she must be brought to me alive. She is no good to our Lord

Thraal either dead or defiled. Select three teams of our best priests and warriors to capture her. I do not care if they bring me her companions. But I want her brought directly to me. Assemble the teams before me and I will send them through the portals to where they are to search."

"Very well, my lord. And may I ask where will you be sending them?"

"Two teams will be sent to Valendale and the other team will be sent to the Elven Woods," Drakkhous replied. "I am serious about this, Adouon. I want her."

"It will be done, my lord." Adouon bowed again before leaving the High Priest of Thraal.

The lich never saw his assistant leave, for he was too intent on reading the message again. A slow and malicious smile stretched across his skinless lips.

"Much news, my lord Adouon, and your master will be pleased by it," the lich read aloud. He chortled at the messenger's confidence that he would be pleased by the news. He was, of course, but he was still amused by the confidence exhibited by the messenger. He continued to read aloud, "Caiaphas, the High Priest of Taelin has died. His successor is young, impulsive and inexperienced. I believe that this can be used to your great advantage, as can the information that this new High Priest was betrothed to a priestess of Taelin that your master recently sacrificed. We all know that a desire for revenge can make people do stupid things. Perhaps this new High Priest can be goaded into acting rashly. If so, perhaps he can be turned against the one he protects in the end.

"And there is one other thing that your master will find most important and be the most pleased with, I am sure. I have found the Blademaster for him. She does not yet know what is in store for her, but she is the one. She travels in the company of a mage, a ranger, this new High Priest of Taelin, and a halfling. I believe that your master will find that her companions may be her undoing. I am sure your master can see the truth of what I am saying. The one you seek is heading to Valendale. No doubt she will be directed to the Elven Woods and what lies within for her, at that point. I suggest that Valendale might be a good location for an attempt to capture her and her companions."

The lich held the message in his hand and let a small thread of his power leak into it, causing the paper to ignite. The flames consumed the paper instantly.

Another thought occurred to the lich. "Adouon," he called. "Come back here. I have some additional instructions."

"Yes, my lord?" Adouon popped immediately back into the altar room.

"I want her companions brought to me alive as well." The lich sneered. "Ensure that the teams are large enough for the task."

"It will be done, my lord." The human priest bowed.

"Good," the lich nodded. He never even noticed Adouon leave to carry out his instructions because he was reveling too much in his imminent plans

"Soon, Blademaster," he hissed, "soon you will be mine."

The five companions entered the city of Valendale from the north road. The long trek south from Ravendale had worn them out and they all wanted a warm bed to relax in. However, the urgency of their mission pushed them on. It was not easy for Alana to keep the party focused on the mission when she herself wanted to take a nap. But more than she wanted a nap, she wanted to find the sage and to discover what he had to tell her. She desperately wanted answers. She just hoped that whatever the sage knew was worth the exhaustion that just getting to him was bringing on. The constant hard riding on the road between Ravendale and Valendale had taken a lot out of her. She could tell it had taken a lot out of the others, too, although they never complained. None of them would have. Every one of her companions knew how important it was for Alana to finally learn the truth.

As they entered Valendale, Alana could sense that something was not quite right. The uneasy look on Colwyn's face told her that he sensed it too. No one seemed to be present in town. Alana and Colwyn were both disturbed, surprised and confused by this fact. Where was everyone? They had both been in Valendale many times before and they knew many of the people in the city. The companions called many of the residents of Valendale friends. Alana hoped that everyone was all right.

But there was something else that bothered Alana about the situation.

After a few moments of thought, Alana whispered, "It's a trap."

"Just because no one's here doesn't necessarily mean that it's a trap, my love," Colwyn said, playing devil's advocate for a moment. "It's possible that there is some other logical explanation."

Alana rolled her eyes at Colwyn, not feeling that his comment was worthy of a reply. She had a strong sense of these things, and she knew without a doubt that it was a trap. Which meant time was of the essence. Even though she knew that, deep down, he knew there was something seriously wrong with the situation, Alana didn't have time to convince Colwyn of the trap using a logical argument. But she knew what her instincts were telling her, and her instincts had yet to let her down. She lived by her instincts, and now was not the time to stop trusting them.

"Go find us a room, Colwyn," she urged. She turned to him with a reassuring smile. "I guarantee that I'll want to rest after I talk to the sage. In the meantime, I am going to go find him and finally get the answers to my questions."

Colwyn nodded. The companions started down the road towards the White Horse Inn, where Colwyn and Alana often stayed when the companions had reason to visit Valendale. But they had only gone two steps before two arrows came out of nowhere, barely missing Alana. She glanced quickly at the arrows where they were stuck in the wall behind her and quickly gauged the direction they had come from. She caught a glimpse of two black robed figures dashing down a side street before they skidded around a corner. Her anger flared and her desire to act kicked in.

"I told you it was a trap," Alana grunted. "Get the room. Watch for other attackers. Those two are mine."

Colwyn did not have time to respond for Alana had already charged down the side street she had seen the black robed figures run down. The distinctive ring of steel announced her twin long swords were now breathing the cool air. Alana would kill her ambushers, but not before they told her everything she wanted to know.

"I would not like to be those two when she catches up to them," William chuckled. "I do not envy them the pain that she is going to deliver when she catches up to them."

Colwyn glanced at the mage and shook his head in amusement. Then he looked around for more of the black robed figures. He didn't spot any others so he shrugged and led the others towards the White Horse Inn. "Let's get that room Alana asked for."

The lack of people in and around Valendale greatly disturbed Colwyn despite what he said to Alana. He remembered Valendale as a bustling city. Seeing it devoid of life and lacking the people he and Alana knew and cared about distressed the ranger. He hoped that the people of Valendale were all right. When this was over, he would make it a priority to find out what happened to the people of Valendale.

So Colwyn was fully on guard. Something was seriously wrong. And he knew without a doubt that Alana had been right.

Valendale was indeed a trap.

When they got to the White Horse Inn, they tied up their horses and Colwyn led the way inside. He strode over to the bar and was less than surprised to find it unmanned. He spied the open guest book and flipped through it, looking for the last registered guests.

Colwyn frowned. "That's odd."

"What?" William asked, as he stepped over to look over the ranger's shoulder.

"They haven't registered a guest in over a month." The ranger's frown deepened. "What is going on here? Where could everyone have gone?"

"Very good questions, Colwyn," William nodded. "But now is not the time to ask them. Someone is coming. We should hide."

"Not the innkeeper?" Colwyn raised an eyebrow.

William tensed for a moment, focusing on what he was sensing, before shaking his head. "Definitely not the innkeeper."

Colwyn motioned for the others to hide. He took a moment to make sure they were out of sight. Balaam dove into a booth. William hid behind an overturned table. The halfling took advantage of her small stature and wedged herself between the bard's pit and the bar. Satisfied, he leapt behind the bar.

He was just in time, too, for just as he ducked his head behind the counter, heavy footfalls lumbered down the stairs and into the tap room. Whoever it was, Colwyn had the distinct impression that they were people that were going to cause a great deal of trouble for the companions. His fears and impressions were confirmed when their leader spoke.

"Spread out and find them," the man growled. "They must be in here somewhere. They tripped the alarms coming in. They haven't left. And be careful. They are most certainly armed, and are definitely dangerous."

Colwyn listened to the people moving about the tap room. Keeping them from being discovered was his first priority. But how to keep that from happening?

He pulled an arrow from his quiver as the shadow of the leader moved across the bottles above the bar. Slowly, he rose up, keeping his bow flat. When he was high enough that he could see the room reflected in the mirror behind the bar, he stopped and took in the scene, finally getting his first look at their pursuers.

And it only took one look to tell him exactly what they were dealing with.

Scattered around the room were thirteen black robed followers of Thraal. And they were getting closer and closer to the companions' hiding places. Even if he were to start firing, he would never be able to get all of them before they could retaliate. But perhaps he could buy time for the others to get into the fight. They would have to jump into the fray quickly, and he trusted his companions to do exactly that.

Quietly, he drew the arrow all the way back. As he tracked one of the black robed figures, a male, came very close to where Meryn was hiding. Just as the man was about to come upon the halfling's hiding place, Colwyn let the arrow fly.

It zipped along and thunked between two of the man's ribs. The man spun around in surprise as a second arrow that Colwyn quickly readied, aimed and fired sank deep into the man's heart. The man fell down onto the ground with a thud, blood seeping from the wound.

The attack had not gone unnoticed, however.

Their leader whirled to face Colwyn and immediately brought his sword down to cleave the ranger in two.

He never made it.

A dagger flew through the air and pinned the leader's wrist to the wall. The sword fell to the floor. The leader screamed in pain as he reached for the dagger to try to free his himself. But a second dagger sang out and connected with the man's other hand, also pinning it to the wall. His screams of agony turned into screams of rage as the leader ordered the other followers of Thraal to attack.

The four companions all leapt from their hiding spaces. But the Thraalish warriors were not caught off guard as Colwyn had hoped. They responded quickly, drawing weapons and grouping up on the companions. Two set themselves against the halfling, and three squared off against each of the three remaining companions. Nevertheless, Colwyn regarded this as a relatively fair fight.

Colwyn brought his sword up to parry a thrust to his head. In his periphery, the mage pulled, in his own good time, a thrynda bird tail feather from one of the pouches on his belt. Colwyn had seen William do this once before and knew what was coming. He turned away from the bright flash of light that he knew would be coming and parried the next attack just in time to see the tail feather land gently on the shoulder of one of the nearby Thraalish followers. The feather flew away again and Colwyn knew that it was off to mark another target for William. He wondered for a moment how many of the attackers William's spell would take out, but he didn't have much time to contemplate. Another

Thraalish follower took a slash at him. This time, rather than parry, Colwyn ducked under a table and covered his eyes.

Just in time, too.

"*Ashrak menzinthos,*" William intoned, bringing his hands up.

The feather zipped back to float in front of the mage. An electrostatic charge bubbled around William's hands. An electric hum started to build up, filling the air of the tap room, as the electrostatic charge surged around William's hands. Finally and without much in the way of warning, a bolt of electricity burst forth and hit the thrynda bird feather. When it hit the feather, it split into seven sub-bolts, each finding a victim previously marked with the thrynda bird feather. Seven Thraalish followers hit the ground twitching as the electricity fired off neurons and nerves in the body. The smell of charred flesh and ozone filled the air of the tap room.

Four followers of Thraal remained, not counting the leader who was still pinned against the wall. Two of them were in mid-lunge for Balaam and the other two stopped attacking Colwyn to gaze down at their fallen comrades in shock.

The rest of the battle was quick. Balaam cast a spell that held the remaining free-standing followers of Thraal in place. He then went around and methodically knocked them all out with one quick blow to the base of each of their skulls with his club. While many priests of Taelin used flanged or spiked maces, Balaam had never felt the need to carry a weapon that could cause so much harm. Although Colwyn did not like the priest, he still respected the young man's choice to respect life. It was a choice he made himself whenever he could.

The leader of the followers of Thraal shrunk back in terror as Colwyn approached. The ranger grasped the hilt of the dagger that was pinning his adversary's right wrist to the wall and gave it a quick twist. The man grimaced in pain but did not cry out.

"I am going to ask you some questions, and you are going to give me the answers that I am looking for," the ranger snarled.

"Or else what?" the leader scoffed. "You'll kill me? I really don't think you have it in you, ranger."

"Why are you after us?" Colwyn asked with a twist to the dagger to emphasize the importance of the question. "What does the Dark God want with us?"

The man gasped in pain before replying. "We don't know why we were sent to capture you."

"Wrong answer," Colwyn grunted as he twisted the dagger a third time. "Again. Why are you after us?"

"I swear I don't know," the man said. He was now heavily perspiring. "All we were told was that we were to subdue the five of you and bring you all to the High Priest of Thraal. We decided that the best way to do that would be to separate you four from the woman. A whole team of fifteen men are waiting for her. She will be captured and taken to Tornith."

"Over my dead body," Colwyn scowled.

The ranger punched the man across the jaw, rendering him unconscious.

He turned to the others. "We go after her," he declared. "Alana was right about this being a trap. But she has no idea what she's in for."

"The holding spell won't keep them for too long once they awake," Balaam added. "I suggest tying them up before we leave."

"Leave that to me," William announced. He pulled a small ball of feithidí silk from a pouch and whispered, "*Mishtha entrosh.*"

The feithidí silk left his hand and wrapped itself around the followers of Thraal that were still alive. With them all bound up, including the leader, the mage removed the daggers from the leader's hands and returned them to the halfling. Meryn snickered as she wiped them clean and replaced them on her belt.

"Fine," Colwyn agreed. "Now. Let's go find Alana and make sure that the followers of Thraal don't get their hands on   her."

Alana did not look back at her companions as she charged after the two figures she had seen. She knew that her companions would not have followed her, especially since she had told them not to. She felt more than ready to take on two followers of Thraal on her own. A little exercise would help with the tension and frustration she had been feeling over the past week. Even if it was a trap, she was always more than ready for whatever came to pass.

The two figures were leading her on a merry chase through the city. Although the companions had visited Valendale several times over the year, she was not nearly as familiar with the city of Valendale as she was Ravendale. She kept mental notes of the route they took so she could find her way back to the White Horse Inn when she was done. As they passed a long sloping path, she noted a sign at the end of the path read "The Sage Isaiah." She made note of the path's location and vowed to return there have a chat with Isaiah even before she returned to the others.

After what seemed like hours of running, even though it was only maybe fifteen minutes, the ground under her feet started to feel different. The ground was more sandy and less solid here. She was heading onto the beach on the outskirts of Valendale. She was aware that sand would make for some tricky footing for fighting, but she'd fought in worse. She would just have to be careful.

She could do careful.

She burst out of the alley and onto the beach proper. The two black robed figures were on the far end of the beach, still running the other way. Alana pulled two knives from her belt and threw them both in one motion. The knives whistled through the air, each taking down one of the running figures. Alana was quick to join them to retrieve her knives.

"What have we got here boys?" a gruff voice called from off to the side. Alana glanced up. Fifteen black robed figures were slowly advancing towards her. "Looks like we got ourselves a troublesome little minx."

"I think it might be best if you just leave now," Alana said evenly, still kneeling by the two fallen men. She pulled the knives free and wiped them clean. Then she put them back on her belt and drew her swords again. "You've been warned. This is your one chance to go. Otherwise, I doubt if you'll get to leave at all."

"Big words for such a pretty little girl," the leader of the fifteen men snorted "But it won't be that easy for you. You're outnumbered fifteen to one. No one can survive such odds."

"I'm not no one," Alana derided. She twirled each of her swords once and set herself into a ready position. "Bring it."

"You asked for it," the leader chortled.

The fifteen black robed followers of Thraal circled Alana, drawing highly polished swords as they went. None of them used a shield, Alana noted, which was all right by her because it meant one less thing to worry about and fifteen swords was enough of a concern. Fifteen to one odds were not something that Alana would normally consider to be too much to handle. But while she had definitely faced worse odds in the past, she did not relish the idea of trying to keep fifteen swords from slicing her while fighting on shifting sand.

The battle was not pretty. The men were not exactly skilled fighters, but their sheer numbers still weighed in their favor. Alana gave herself over to the rhythm of the battle, parrying a thrust here and launching a quiet counter attack there. She did not try to overpower her opponents. She did not even try to out finesse her opponents. To conserve energy, she used as little motion as she could. She forced herself to go battle-blind, her vision limited to the fifteen men and her immediate surroundings. When she took down an adversary, she did not take the time to gloat; she simply brought her sword around to block the next attack.

As the battle wore on, Alana suffered several scratches, but nothing very serious. She delivered far more than she received. And she did not worry herself with the minor injuries that she received during the fight. She worked methodically and carefully. When she had the opportunity to launch an attack with the same movement from a block, she took it. After a few minutes of fighting, three of the men charged at her.

With a vicious slice, Alana cut the head off one of the charging men. The head rolled off into the surf. His body fell to the ground, spilling blood and viscera onto the wet sand.

The remaining seven black robed figures froze, their eyes glazing over as they toppled to the ground, their swords falling from their grasp. She dropped her own swords and dropped to a crouch, hands on knees and gasped loudly for air.

The slow methodical sound of clapping came from behind her. She whirled around, her swords back up in a ready position, to find an older man standing behind her, applauding.

He folded his hands across his chest, fingers grasping opposite wrists inside the sleeves of his robe. His staff was resting in the crook of his left elbow where it was within easy reach. The pose was reminiscent of one that William often used. The man had short-cropped grey hair and piercing blue eyes. The eyes reflected a deep and abiding wisdom. Alana had never seen him before, but she knew without a doubt who was standing in front of her.

It was the sage, Isaiah Talon.

"Very well done, my dear Alana," he praised. His voice had a strong tonal quality despite being soft and low. It was also kind, which was not what she expected. Then again, she wasn't really sure what she expected.

"I could have handled them without the help," she shrugged as she wiped the swords clean and returned them to their scabbards.

"Probably. But that was not the point of the exercise, and letting them hurt you more would accomplish nothing," Isaiah shrugged. "I saw what I needed to see. I am sure that you are the one."

"The one for what?" Alana furrowed her brow.

"The one that was foretold. You are, my dear, a child of prophecy," Isaiah smiled. "The High Priest of Taelin sent you to me, did he not?"

"Yes," Alana nodded. "In fact, he made the journey with me."

"Not surprising," the sage nodded as he stepped toward her. "You have passed the final test. I can't tell you what your destiny is, but I can feel confident in pointing you to where you need to go."

"You don't know what my destiny is either?" Alana sighed. "I made this journey for nothing?"

"I didn't say I didn't know what your destiny is, Alana Steeldrake," Isaiah smiled. "I simply said that I could not tell you what it is. I have been forbidden from doing so. That is the cost I had to accept to gain the knowledge needed to help you." His smile faded and his eyes flashed with pain. "Part of the cost at any rate. The remainder of the cost was far more. Almost too much for one man to bear."

Alana closed her eyes and sighed. "Where must I go?"

"I believe that your companion, Colwyn, will be able to guide you where you need to go," the sage sat on a rock. "You will travel to the Elven Woods. To enter the woods, you will need the help of the Forestwalker elves. In the middle of the woods, there is a temple. It is at this temple that you will finally learn the destiny that Lord Taelin has for you."

"There will be no more legs to this wild goose chase?" Alana opened an eye and fixed him with her gaze. "There will be no more waiting and wondering?"

"I promise that when you get to the temple, all of your questions will be answered." The sage smiled broadly but his smile faded quickly though. "It will not be an easy journey, especially for Colwyn. For in as much as this journey is to learn your destiny, it is also a journey to learn his destiny as well."

"Colwyn's destiny?" Alana raised her eyebrows. "I must admit, I have never given much thought as to what his part in this is other than the fact that I want him to be by my side."

"If he is to be by your side, then it will be a hard journey for him indeed," Isaiah remarked. He reached over and touched her cheek. "I am sorry, Alana. Whether he is to be your husband or not , he will have a hard time of it. I wish it were different. But try as I might, I cannot see which way it will go. I only hope that it ends up in the best way possible for the both of you."

"The best way would be for him to end up as my husband," she breathed. "Anything else would not be fair."

"If it helps any, I don't think Lord Taelin would have put him in your life were the outcome to be different than that. But as I said, I cannot see what will happen in this case. It's hard to say that as a sage. I wish I had the answers for you." He looked up at the sound of running feet. "Ah but look, your friends come for you. I daresay they had a bit of an adventure themselves and hope to make sure you're all right."

"Thank you, sage," Alana stood. "The Elven Woods, you say?"

"There is a temple deep within the Elven Woods, yes," Isaiah affirmed. "That is where your answers are to be found, my dear. Good luck to you. And good luck to us all."

With that last cryptic statement, Isaiah disappeared in a column of billowing smoke.

Alana shook her head in amazement and turned to where her companions were running across the beach towards her. As they slowed, they looked around in amazement at all of the black robed figures lying prone on the ground.

"What happened here?" Colwyn asked as he stepped up to Alana.

"They had a little accident," Alana shrugged. "I had a little help though."

"You usually don't need help," Colwyn snickered. "Listen, we were ambushed."

"I know," Alana nodded. "We need to leave Valendale right away."

"Not until we get what we came for," Colwyn crossed his arms. "I'm tired of getting the runaround from everyone."

"We have what we came for," Alana declared. "We are headed to the Elven Woods. Apparently there's a temple in the middle of the forest that we have to go to. Isaiah says that all my answers are there."

"I've been in the forest a number of times and I've never seen any temple there," Colwyn frowned, rubbing his chin. "I guess we could ask the Forestwalkers for help," he muttered. "I'm not crazy about that idea, but... the way is the way."

Alana smiled at him. "Let's go get the horses, Col," Alana said. "I want to leave right away."

Alana turned to head back to where the horses were. Colwyn watched her go for a moment before he started to follow her.

This is not going to go well for me, the ranger thought sourly to himself.

The Blademaster

Chapter VI
The Elven Woods

After four more days of hard riding, the party came to the edge of the Elven Woods. While Colwyn had been through the woods before, he was still nervous about guiding the party through. For while he was fairly certain that the elves would not give them any trouble, elves were still elves. And elves could always be counted on to dislike outsiders. Then, of course, there was his concern about seeing *her* again.

Still, decorum had to be maintained.

Colwyn held up his hand for them to stop just inside the woods. He turned to Alana and shrugged off his pack.

"Now we wait," he announced in response to Alana's questioning look. "To go any further into the woods without first receiving permission from Mirian Kovalani is to court disaster or even death."

Alana crossed her arms and glared at him. "Who is Mirian Kovalani?" she furrowed her brows at him.

"She is the queen of the clan of elves that live in those woods, the Forestwalkers." Colwyn explained as he took her in his arms. "Even if our lives were not at stake, it would be rude not to pay our respects to her."

"And how long do we have to wait?" Alana prodded, poking him in the chest for emphasis. "You know that I'm in a hurry to get on with this journey."

"It will take as long as it takes, Alana," he shrugged. "But I can tell you that there are warriors from the Forestwalker clan on their way to meet us as we speak."

Alana studied his face thoughtfully, "You've dealt with this Mirian Kovalani before, I hope," she asked. "It might make it a little easier for us to gain the passage we need if she knows someone in the party."

Colwyn turned from the woman he loved. "It may not be quite that simple," he breathed, unable to look her in the eyes. He took a few steps away from her.

Alana followed him and put two fingers on his cheek. She turned his face to look at her. "What is it my love?" she asked, stroking his cheek for comfort. "What is it that worries you about this Mirian Kovalani?"

"Before I met you, and before she became queen of the Forestwalker clan, Mirian and I were lovers." Colwyn sighed after a long hesitation. "We were forced apart by the clan's council of elders due to cultural biases. I have not spoken to her in three years. I do not know how she will react to my presence... or yours for that matter."

"Then we shall just have to make do and hope for the best." She smiled up at him. Over his shoulder, she saw some movement in the direction of the deeper woods. "At least we didn't have to wait too long."

Colwyn turned to follow her gaze. Two warriors from the Forestwalker clan were standing in the path. Colwyn recognized one of them as Mirian's brother, Otan.

"Colwyn Starseeker, you are welcomed back to the home of the Forestwalker Clan," Otan smiled, bowing. He clapped the human on the shoulder, "You have been away for far too long."

"Otan Kovalani, it is good to see you again." Colwyn grinned but only briefly. "I have been gone for so long because I did not think I was welcome any longer. The elders delivered their message all too well."

"You have always been welcome here Colwyn," the elf warrior chuckled. The hand on the human's shoulder gripped it tightly. "It was only as a love for my sister that the elders did not welcome you. And, if you recall, I had no such objections."

"How is Queen Mirian?" Colwyn asked "I have meant for some time to send her my congratulations on her ascension. It's well deserved."

"The queen is well," Otan bowed his head. "She knows that you are proud of her, just as she knows that your destiny must take a different path than the one that would have allowed you to be with her. She has been awaiting your party for some time now. I can tell you now that it is Lord Taelin's wish that you be granted passage through the woods."

"Thank you, my friend," Colwyn said softly as he clapped Otan on the shoulder.

"But Queen Mirian would speak with you first."

"Even if she was not planning on it, I would not expect to pass through these woods without first paying my respects to the Queen," Colwyn remarked. "I know the traditions."

"So few humans think that way," Otan sighed. "It is little wonder that you are one of the very few humans allowed free passage through the woods." He glanced over at Alana. "Who is this lovely lady, Colwyn?"

Colwyn's smile spread across his face as he put his arm around Alana. "This is Alana Steeldrake. She has agreed to be my wife, Otan. It is her quest that has brought me back to these woods."

"Welcome to the home of the Forestwalker Clan, Lady Alana," Otan bowed in her direction. "You humble us with your presence." Otan chuckled at the blank look he got from her. "Come, Queen Mirian is waiting."

"Lead on then, old friend."

The human ranger fell into step behind the two elf warriors. Alana fell into step beside him, her hand searching out his. When their hands connected, he smiled his special smile down at her. The rest of the party fell in behind the happy couple, gazing around in awe at the mighty trees.

They walked for several long miles before Colwyn caught sight of the first guard tower outside the Forestwalker city. It was a testament to elven architecture that Colwyn had such a hard time finding the guard towers despite the fact that he knew exactly where they all were.

Soon, the first tree bridges of the city came into view and Colwyn knew they were there. He felt a lump rise in his throat as he realized he would soon have to face the elven queen. It was not a task he was at all looking forward to. He did not know how she would react to him after three years. And he was even more nervous about showing up with the woman he was to wed.

But as he was climbing the ladder to reach the first of the three bridges, he realized that it was too late to worry about such considerations. Taelin himself had guided them here. They had no choice but to go forward. He had to trust in Taelin and that Taelin would continue to guide them.

After a brisk walk, they reached a house in the trees that Colwyn recognized all too well. And he knew that there would be no putting off this confrontation any longer.

"Colwyn, Queen Mirian has requested that only you and the Lady Alana enter," Otan announced with an ever so slight reverent bow at the waist. "The rest of your party shall remain out here with me."

"I understand." Colwyn nodded. Then the words fully registered, and he frowned. "I understand her wanting to see me, but why does she want to see Alana?"

"It is the Lady Alana's quest you are on." Otan raised his eyebrow. "Is it not?"

"Well, yes." Colwyn knitted his brows. "It is her quest."

"Then Queen Mirian would meet her." Otan chuckled as he clapped Colwyn on the back. "Besides, she would like to meet the woman who has taken her place by your side."

"Otan..." Colwyn trailed off unable to finish the thought.

The elf let out a booming laugh. "Oh, don't worry, my friend. She is happy for you. This is, after all, your destiny every bit as much as it is the Lady Alana's. Queen Mirian only wishes for you to be happy."

"For the most part, I am," Colwyn said. "Except for this bit about destiny. All this destiny nonsense gets tiring, especially with no explanations about what the destiny is."

"Understandable." Otan leaned forward. "Let me tell you a secret, Colwyn. Unlike what the mages, seers, and prophets of the world will tell you, neither destiny nor prophecy are fully set in stone."

"But prophecy is a vision of the future," Colwyn protested.

"Have you forgotten everything that I have taught you, ranger?" the elf lord admonished Colywn softly, thunking him gently on the forehead.

"What do you mean, Múinteoir?" Colwyn bowed his head to Otan.

"Prophecy rarely happens the way it sounds like it should. For example, a prophecy from our vaults that I believe is about you two reads: To stop the Lord of Chaos, she will be taken as a captive. Only her true love can blind the evil eye and set her free," Otan stopped for a moment and sighed. "I believe you two will learn what that prophecy means before too long."

"I wanted less prophecy and destiny in our lives," Colwyn grumbled. "Not more." He sighed. "But now, I think we should go see the Queen."

Otan nodded and motioned for Colwyn and Alana to enter the house. The ranger led Alana inside.

The living room of the little house had not changed in all of the time that Colwyn had been away. Tastefully decorated in rich greens and browns, the room featured artistically carved chairs and tables carefully placed throughout. The hardwood floors were bare and polished to a muted shine. A hall leading off to other rooms left through an opening in the wall to the right. On the wall in front of them was the room's only window. Queen of the Forestwalker Clan, Mirian Kovalani stood in front of the window, gazing outside. Even with her back to the door, she could tell who had entered the house.

"Colwyn Starseeker," she remarked, her musical voice low in the muted silence of the forest. "It is good of you to return to the home of the Forestwalker Clan after all this time." The queen turned to face the couple and granted them a warm smile. "Even if the circumstances of your return to my home are not as I might have wished."

Colwyn took Alana's hand and smiled at the queen. "While I am sorry that the council of elders decided to keep us apart, Queen Mirian, I am grateful as well. For if they had not come to such a decision, I would not have met Alana. I have come to accept that my destiny lies with her. It is my sincere wish that you would be happy for us."

"I am happy for you, Colwyn," Mirian nodded with a sigh. "And yet I am likewise deeply sad for the both of you. For I know what is yet to come for you two. And I know it will not be an easy road." She stepped forward to stand in front of Alana. Then she did the last thing that Colwyn expected her to do. She dropped to her knees in front of Alana and bowed her head in reverence. "The Forestwalker Clan pledges their lives and support to the Chosen One of Taelin."

Alana frowned as she looked down at the queen. "I don't understand."

"You will," the queen smiled sadly as she looked up at Alana. "When you get to the temple, all will be made clear. For now though, enjoy the hospitality of the Forestwalker Clan. Rest now. You can leave for the temple in the morning."

It had been a long time since Colwyn had spent any time alone in the Elven Woods and he'd needed some time alone to think. And that's what he'd told Alana. He just needed some time. Time to ponder about the nature of the journey ahead of them and their destination, which he now knew was a temple that he didn't remember ever encountering in the middle of the woods.

But he also wanted time alone to pray to Taelin and Laeyra, for he knew he needed a little wisdom and a lot of luck. As a ranger, he took Raeven as his personal deity.

But Alana prayed to both Taelin and Laeyra. He felt that he could use any help he could get in this situation.

And so, he found himself sitting in the branches of an ancient redwood tree looking out over the Forestwalker Clan's city. Although he didn't realize it before he chose this particular spot, he used to sit in this very spot with Mirian when they were courting. It was something that he would look back on and realize that he really should have recalled sooner.

He never heard Mirian arrive. Like the rest of the elves of her clan Mirian had perfected the art of walking and climbing through the trees of the forest without making any sound at all. And so Colwyn was slightly startled when the Queen was quite suddenly sitting right next to him. He recovered quickly, which was pretty much a necessity for he was sitting several hundred feet above the ground.

"It is only me Colwyn," Mirian laughed. "I'm not a monster. I'm just someone who still loves you."

"I still love you too, Mirian," Colwyn said after a few moments of thought. "But such can not be any longer."

"Colwyn, I'm the Queen." She laughed again, a twinkle in her eyes. "I can overturn the elders' edict. We could still be together."

"No." He turned away from her. "I am to be Alana's husband. My destiny is with her."

"I did not expect you to turn from your destiny." She laid a hand on his. "But I am afraid for you, Colwyn. What you two will go through at the temple will be extremely difficult. Not just for Alana, but for you as well. Perhaps even harder for you than her."

"You know what is going to happen, don't you?" He turned to face her, his gaze searching Mirian's. "You know what it is that Alana is expected to be?"

She nodded. "Yes. Of course I do."

"Then..."

She interrupted him. "But I can not tell you. Do not ask me what I cannot answer. For just as the sage Isaiah and the High Priest of Taelin were forbidden to reveal it, so am I." She sighed. It was Mirian's turn to turn away. "I am sorry."

Colwyn chuckled and patted her hand. "It's all right, Mirian. Honestly, I think I'd be a little disappointed if I got a straight answer at this point."

"So, you are determined to go through with this even though it could cost you your life?" Mirian turned back to him, her huge green eyes full of tears.

Colwyn nodded. "I am. I belong by Alana's side, no matter what it is she faces. And I have a feeling she is going to need me."

"Oh, of that I have no doubt." Mirian shook her head. She held a small red stone out to Colwyn. "Take this, Colwyn. It is a trap finder stone. It will come in very handy."

"What does it do?" Colwyn asked, raising his eyebrow.

"It is much like the finder stone I gave you. This stone will light up when a trap is about to spring on you and will light up the brightest when you are inside of a trap," she said softly. "You will find it very useful where you are going."

"I suppose," the ranger shrugged. "We're both actually very good at..."

"It is a very rare stone," she added, again interrupting him. "Not very many of my rangers even carry one," Mirian smiled. "I give it to you as a pledge of my fealty to you. And to Alana."

Colwyn smiled. "Thank you Mirian," he said as he took the stone from her. "Thanks for everything."

Mirian and Otan led the companions to the edge of the Forestwalker Clan's town. Brother and sister hugged Colwyn and bowed low in reverence to Alana.

"Go north on the path until you catch a glimpse of the temple," Mirian explained. "Once you do, you'll need to cut a trail to it. Once you leave the path, it will be next to impossible for you to be followed."

"Thank you Queen Mirian." Alana bowed. "For the hospitality and for the directions."

"Alana Steeldrake." Queen Mirian Kovalani bowed in return. "Be it known now that you and your companions may have free passage through these woods. While it would be polite for you to visit the Forestwalkers during your visits to these woods, it is no longer required. So mote it be." She clasped Alana's shoulders and gazed into her eyes. "May the wisdom of Lord Taelin and the luck of Lady Laeyra guide and protect you, my Lady."

Before Alana could respond, Otan and Mirian were gone.

There was nothing left for the companions to do but start down the path.

The Blademaster

PART II
Legacy of the Blademasters

Chapter VII
The Temple of the Blades

It had been a full two hours since Colwyn had first caught a glimpse of white through the trees. None of the others had seen it but, since he was their guide through the forest, they trusted his judgment. He had immediately altered their course towards the flash of marble he'd seen, for he remembered well Mirian's instructions on how to get to their destination. He worked slowly and methodically, cutting only where needed to clear a path through the dense undergrowth. Each cut of his sword resounded with a loud thwack and rustle of leaves. It was a fine line he had to walk between making sure the party could get through the path he was cutting and not trimming away so much of the undergrowth as to be easily followed.

He glanced back at Alana to say something then stopped. He stepped over to her and reached for a cluster of vines behind her, glaring at them in disbelief.

"What is it Col?" she asked as she looked over the vines in his hand.

"I cut through these vines so we could get through," Colwyn muttered as he lifted up one of the vines. "But look at it. It's as if it has never been touched."

"I guess that's what Queen Mirian meant when she said it would be hard to follow us once we turned off the path." Alana smiled broadly as she touched the vine. "Its hard to follow someone when there is no trail."

"But we are being followed through." Colwyn let go of the vine. "I haven't said anything because I didn't want to worry you. But I've caught glimpses through the trees."

"Elves?" Alana suggested hopefully, although she had a pretty good idea of what Colwyn would say to that even before she suggested it. *Still it is better than the alternatives,* she thought.

Colwyn shook his head. "Not elves. I would never had seen them," he reminded her. "Besides, it feels like whoever is following us don't belong in the woods. And malevolence. Definitely picking up malevolence. I daresay that I wouldn't sense either of those things if it were elves following us."

"Who then?" Alana demanded.

"If I had to guess, I would say that it's more of the people who attached us in Valendale." Colwyn trudged back to the front of the group where he'd been blazing the trail. "The last time I caught sight of them, there were fewer than when I first saw them. Hopefully the elves are keeping them sufficiently busy and buying us enough time that they won't catch up to us until after we reach our destination."

"Let's hope so." Alana breathed.

With that, Colwyn set back to the arduous task of cutting through the dense foliage. The muscles in his back and arms rippled as he worked. Although she had other concerns on her mind, such as the men following them, Alana was rather enjoying watching Colwyn's physical display. It took another full three hours for Colwyn to cut the rest of the way through the forest to the temple clearing.

When they finally broke through, they stopped short, mouths slacked open in awe. Before them was the largest and most ornate temple they'd ever seen. The temple was made of black and white polished marble. High marble parapets gave the temple a palatial feel. Banners from the parapets flapped in the breeze. Alana noticed that the banners were all the same: A dark blue background with a stylized gold shield in the foreground. The shield was crossed over at the center by two silver long swords.

As they fanned out around the temple, they saw the same stylized shield and swords inlaid into the walls. These inlays were made of silver and gold. The mottling in the marble seemed to be in constant motion, dancing in a pattern, although the companions could draw no meaning from the dancing.

Colwyn put his hand on the marble and was surprised to feel that it was warm to the touch, almost as if the marble had the blood of life running through it, and he felt oddly comforted by it.

He motioned for the others to go to the front of the temple. When he caught William's eye, he thought he caught a look of recognition for the briefest of instants in the mage's eye. "Do you know this place William?" he asked almost in a whisper. "I've never seen its like."

The mage said nothing for several long seconds as he gazed over one of the inlaid shield and sword symbols. Then shook his head with a sigh. "I will keep my own counsel as to what I think this place is, Colwyn," the mage said, his voice low and strained. "At least until I am sure. But I will say this, if I am right, our lives are about to get a great deal more interesting."

"More interesting?" Colwyn frowned in distaste as William joined the rest of the party. "I'm not sure I can handle our lives getting any more interesting," he muttered as he followed the mage.

When they got to the front of the temple, their mouths once more collectively dropped in awe. Five large white marble columns lined the entrance to the temple, each one as wide as Colwyn was tall. They held up a huge triangular frieze that depicted the ancient battle between Taelin and Thraal. Twelve white marble steps led up to the wide entry porch. Two large oak doors stood between them and entry into the temple. There was gold lettering to the left and to the right of the doors. Alana was drawn to the lettering on the left of the doors. She ran her hands over the words that she could not understand.

"What does it say, Col?"

"It's Elvish," Colwyn replied. He stepped over and wrapped her in his arms as he read the words aloud. "Ní mór di a rachaidh isteach anseo chun aghaidh a thabhairt ar ndán di dul isteach le croí glan. Ní mór sí ag troid i gcomhréir leis an idéalacha Taelin agus Laeyra. Ní mór di cloí le Dlí na lanna má ghlacann sí ndán di. Teip ciallaíonn bás." Colwyn turned to face Alana, his face ashen. "I think our lives are about to get a lot more interesting."

"Why?" Alana leaned her head against his chest and sighed. "What does it mean?"

"It means this. She who enters here to face her destiny must enter with a pure heart. She must fight according to the precepts of Taelin and Laeyra. She must abide by the Law of the Blades if she accepts her destiny." At this point he paused for a few moments before finishing the translation. He took a breath and added, "Failure brings death."

Alana grimaced. "That sounds pretty ominous."

"We can always turn back," Colwyn remarked, holding her protectively. "It's not like you've agreed to anything yet."

"We have to finish what we started, my love." She gave him a reassuring smile. She was touched by how much he cared for her. She kissed his cheek gently. "You are sweet to be so protective of me, but there seems to be bigger issues here than my own safety."

"As you say, my love," he kissed the top of her head affectionately. "Onward we go, then."

"But, before we go in," Alana interrupted. "What does this other writing say?" She gestured toward the writing on the other side of the doors.

Colwyn studied it. "I'll read it out loud," he said. "Sí nach bhfuil grá nach bhfuil a fhios Taelin chun é Taelin ghrá." He turned back to her, amusement dancing on his face. Before she could ask for a translation he provided it.

"It means, she who does not love does not know Taelin for Taelin is love."

Alana grinned. "Well, that's a little more positive. At least we know I love. I love you, after all."

"And I love you too," Colwyn chuckled. He mussed her hair. "Now, can we get this over with before I change my mind and turn us around?"

Alana tweaked his cheek slipped out of his arms. She stepped up to the doors and placed her hands flat against them, feeling the smooth hard wood underneath. Soundlessly, the doors swung open at her touch.

Before they could follow Alana and Colwyn into the temple, William grabbed Balaam by the arm and pulled him aside.

"You forget yourself, Mage of the White," Balaam glared at the mage's hand on his arm.

"You know where we are, priest," William snarled. "You know what will happen to them in there."

"As your ranger friend has said many times already on this journey, the way is the way," Balaam whispered. "I take no joy in what is to happen, William Stonehands. I want you to know that."

"I know that my friends are about to walk into one of the most dangerous situations they have ever faced," the mage growled. "No one has given them any choice in the matter."

"You know, now, what Alana is, mage. What has to happen next is beyond all of our control."

"What's going on, William?" Meryn asked. "What's about to happen?"

"Tell her nothing, William," Balaam held up a hand in warning. "That you know where we are is troubling enough. Any further foreknowledge of what is to come by any of you could prevent things from happening as they must."

"William, what is he talking about?" Meryn tugged at his robes.

"Not now, Little One," the mage shook his head. "You'll know soon enough."

"Now unhand me, mage."

"If any harm comes to them, priest..." William growled, his voice soft with warning.

"If any harm comes to them, you will do nothing, mage," Balaam snarled. "What happens to them happens according to the will of my Lord Taelin. You know that as well as I."

"If he dies, I hold you responsible," the mage hissed in Balaam's ear. "You know what I am capable of."

"Far better than you yourself know what you are capable of, mage," the priest growled. "The time soon comes when you learn what you are."

"What do you mean?" the mage's eyes narrowed.

"It is not for me to say," Balaam rasped. "I say again. Unhand me, mage."

"You are good at flaunting your knowledge without being at all helpful," William snarled.

The mage hurled Balaam away from him and the three of them followed Colwyn and Alana into the temple.

They entered a four foot square antechamber, the walls of which were made of the same black and white marble as the outside of the temple. Like the marble on the outside of the temple the mottling in the marble seemed to dance in a pattern. Even though he could not discern the specifics, Colwyn was convinced that the pattern was trying to tell a story. The only other door in the room was made of plain oak. The golden shield crossed by silver swords they had seen outside was displayed prominently in the center of the door. As they came further into the antechamber, the oak door swung open of its own accord, inviting them inside.

"I guess that means we're expected," Colwyn remarked. His eyes darted to and fro. Alana knew his mannerisms only too well. Colwyn was growing more uneasy by the moment. She did not dismiss his judgment easily. His uneasiness put her further on her guard.

"Indeed," the mage said, "We would never have found this temple were we not expected." Naturally, the mage's statement did nothing to ease Colwyn's sense of dread.

Alana raised an eyebrow as she turned to face the Mage. "You know more than you're letting on, don't you William? You know why we are here, don't you?"

William shrugged and motioned towards the far door. "Surely, your answers lie in there, Alana. Not with me."

Colwyn scowled at the mage then pulled his sword a few inches out of its scabbard to make sure it was clear. With his hand grasping the hilt of his sword, he led the way through the far door.

The doorway led into what had to be the temple's great hall. Reluctantly and just as carefully, the others followed Colwyn into an immense square room, one hundred fifty feet to the side. The ceiling cleared forty feet over their heads. Scores of banners hung in thirty feet below the ceiling of the hall. Each banner had a design, some sort of crest, on it. There was only one banner that had no design, and that banner hung directly over the altar. The banner was hunter green, the same shade as Alana's favorite dress.

The altar itself was a slab of obsidian. Someone had taken the time to carve a bas relief of women fighting shadowy creatures on the front of the altar. On the top, two plain long swords flanked a plain broad sword. The points of the three weapons were touching, as if pointing at the wall behind the altar.

"Welcome, Child of Taelin," a deep and rich female voice called out from the shadows behind the altar. "I have been expecting you."

The Blademaster

Chapter VIII
The High Priestess of the Blades

"I have been expecting you," the woman said again. "Although I must admit I had expected that you would arrive much sooner than this."

Alana whirled to look at the woman who had spoken. She was surprised to see how much like herself the woman appeared, right down to the armor. But there were differences. Whereas Alana's hair was auburn, the other woman's was black. Also, the other woman had dusky brown eyes that blazed with the same inner fire as Alana's green eyes. Still, they shared the same skin tone. The woman's armor, which featured a much lower cut neck than Alana's, just past the navel as opposed to the far more conservative amount of cleavage that Alana's showed, was black instead of the dark brown of Alana's. The woman wore her long black hair in a single braid which was slung over her left shoulder.

The Blademaster

"Who are you?" Alana demanded, "And what do you mean that you've been expecting me?"

Instead of replying right away, she paced over to Alana and ran her fingers over the armor on Alana's shoulder. "I see that you have received your birth right." She smiled at Alana. "And you have taken good care of it. May it serve you well in battle."

"Thank you." Alana frowned. "But that doesn't answer my questions. Who are you? Why am I here?"

"Ask the mage," the woman laughed softly as she looked at William. "He has known where you are for some time."

Alana glared at William. The young mage had a sedate and unreadable look on his face. His arms were tucked in the opposite sleeves across his chest, and his staff was notched in the crook of his right elbow. He shrugged.

"Unless I am very much mistaken," William finally said, "we are in the Temple of the Blades. You are at the end of this part of your journey, Alana. And I am afraid that you are at the beginning of a much more difficult one." He nodded to the woman who had addressed Alana. "That would, I believe, make you the High Priestess of the Blades."

"You studied well at the High Tower of the Inner Circle, William Stonehands. You will one day become a great Mage of the Inner Circle. Or a Sage, if your destiny lies in that direction. I cannot see what your destiny holds, only what Alana's destiny holds for her." With that, the woman turned back to Alana. "I am Solara Moonfire, the High Priestess of the Blades and the caretaker of the Legacy of the Blademasters. You, Alana Steeldrake, are here to learn what your destiny is."

"That would be nice." Alana grunted and stepped towards the woman. She pointed back to Balaam. "Neither this man, nor his predecessor, has been exactly forthcoming with that information, despite leading me along with half-truths."

Solara nodded and turned to Balaam. She glided over to him. "Where is my old friend, Caiaphas? I believed that he would be the servant of Taelin to bring this woman to me."

"Lord Caiaphas has gone to walk with Lord Taelin, my lady," Balaam sighed, unable to meet Solara's gaze. "Before he passed on, he named me his successor to the post of High Priest of Taelin, even though I am nowhere near the priest Lord Caiaphas was."

"My deepest sympathies," Solara bowed her head, tears running down her cheeks. "Caiaphas was a good and faithful servant to my Lord Taelin. And, to me, he was a good and dear friend. I will miss him greatly."

"Thank you my lady." Balaam bowed deeply.

Alana stepped forward. "Why am I here?" she demanded. "I have little more patience for all of this double talk. What is it that Lord Taelin wishes for me to do? What is it you have to tell me?"

"It is a long and, at times, sad story that has led you here Alana." Solara replied. She slipped into a chair at the back of the Great Hall and motioned for the companions to nearby seats. "The story begins many years ago. But perhaps I should start at the very beginning."

"That would be good," Alana agreed as she took one of the offered chairs. "It would be very nice to finally have answers to my questions."

"You know, of course, of the Blademasters," Solara began. She waved her hands and tea cups appeared next to everyone's chairs.

"Only what has been sung in the songs," Alana admitted. "Truly, I think they are just good stories to help children sleep at night. I have never put much stock in the tales."

"Oh, the Blademasters were real enough, Alana." Solara smiled. "But the songs omit a great deal of the rich Blademaster history."

"I see." Alana took a sip of her tea. "And this is what you would tell me about? Faerie tales?"

"Partly," Solara nodded. "For often one must understand the past in order to fathom the future."

"So it has been said." Alana crossed her arms. "But I am not a very patient woman, Lady Solara. And I've waited long enough. So, please get on with it."

"I can see that you are not very patient." Solara sighed. "I hope that that will not be your undoing."

"Get on with it," Alana repeated with an edge.

"Very well. When Calthea was first formed, each of the gods and goddesses created their own races to populate the world with. The region of Dracomyr was populated with peoples that Thraal and his minions had created. The Southern Dales and the other continents were populated by peoples that the other gods and goddesses had created. And so, Calthea was a peaceful world for a long time." Solara took a sip of her tea before continuing. "Thraal, the Lord of Chaos, was quiet for a great many years. Lord Taelin and Lady Laeyra thought that Thraal was content with the many races in the region of Dracomyr. They did not know that he had designs on controlling all of Calthea.

"Thraal created shadow warriors that he sent to fight all of the peoples of Calthea. He wanted to subjugate them as his slaves. The shadow warriors were terrible foes that struck fear into the hearts of the people.

"It was a dark and terrible time in our world's history. The shadow warriors were but the beginning. Thraal created the undead, ghouls, ghosts, zombies, vampires. The worst of all the undead were the liches, which Thraal favored above all undead.

"Lord Taelin and Lady Laeyra needed a solution to the problem. So they created the Blademasters."

"You know, I've heard mention of the Blademasters so many times," Alana said. "But no one has ever been able to explain just what a Blademaster is."

"The Blademasters, always women, are holy warriors dedicated to both Taelin and Laeyra." Solara explained, not at all upset about the interruption. "There is far more to a Blademaster than this, of course. Blademasters are a law unto themselves. Even the Kings of the Southern Dales themselves pledge their lives and their fealty to the Blademasters. However, you do not need to know all about the Blademasters to hear the rest of the story. The key thing you need to know is that a Blademaster is a master of all bladed weapons."

"If they are a law unto themselves, how did they keep themselves from abusing their power?" Colwyn asked. As a noble, he knew a great deal about the corruption that sometimes accompanied power in the Southern Dales.

"The Blademasters live according to the Law of the Blades, a sacred set of laws given to us by our Lord Taelin," the High Priestess of the Blades explained. She took a sip of her tea before continuing. "It is said that a Blademaster is an equal combination of Laeyra's luck and Taelin's wisdom. And before you ask, no one but Lord Taelin and Lady Laeyra know how they accomplished the creation of the Blademasters."

Alana nodded and took a sip of her tea. "So, what happened? I mean, they must have been successful, since we're not all slaves to Thraal."

"Oh, they were successful all right." Solara smiled. "The shadow warriors and the undead were driven back into Dracomyr. The people of Calthea were safe once more.

"However, with no definite enemy in their path, the Blademasters needed something to do. Taelin provided a new purpose for them. They were to oversee fair and equitable rule for all parts of Calthea. The Blademasters traveled far and wide. Although it was rare that they exercised such power, they could remove a tyrannical monarch or corrupt official. It was a time of peace and great prosperity that lasted for over five hundred years."

"So what happened to the Blademasters?" Alana asked. "If things were so good, where did they go?"

"Thraal was angry that his plan had been thwarted, but he could not act against the Blademasters directly. The Dark God had been banished to Limbo. From there, he could exert no real influence on the world. He still had his followers, though. And Thraal's followers preach hate. Hate in the right hands, is a powerful weapon. And that was the weapon that Thraal used to destroy the Blademasters." Solara sighed.

"How?" Alana furrowed her brow.

"Unfortunately, we'll never know what lies he whispered to people to turn them against the Blademasters. But just over three hundred years ago, the people rose up against the Blademasters. They were all thrown off the parapets of the Temple of the Blades."

"And Lord Taelin and Lady Laeyra never tried to create a new line of Blademasters?" Colwyn asked in disbelief.

"They were not needed," Solara shrugged. "Well, until now that is."

"Why are you telling me all of this Lady Solara?" Alana asked, although she had an idea of what the answer might be. "And why is it that you refer to the Blademasters in the present tense if they are all gone?"

"Because in order to stop Thraal, the Blademasters are needed once again." Solara explained. "You are the first in a new line of Blademasters."

"I see," Alana said softly. She glanced at Colwyn. "This is the only way then?"

"Only a Blademaster can keep Thraal from succeeding in returning to the world of Calthea." Solara nodded. "But you must accept this destiny of your own free will."

Alana searched Colwyn's eyes. He nodded once, telling her without words that he would support her no matter what choice she made.

"Very well," she said, turning back to Solara. "What must I do?"

"You must choose a husband." Solara smiled.

"What?" Alana blurted. It was the last thing she'd expected the High Priestess to say.

"You must have a husband." Solara repeated. "The powers of the Blademaster require balance. The balance required for the fighting and killing that you will do is the love you have for your husband. That is the most integral part of the Law of the Blades."

"I have committed myself to marrying Colwyn." Alana smiled at the man she loved.

"Speak not in haste, for he must pass the Test of the Blades, a test of his love for you." Solara held up her hand. "Should he fail, and live, he would be forbidden from ever seeing you again."

"May we have some time to discuss this?" Alana asked, watching Colwyn's eyes for any trace of hesitation. She found none.

"Of course, I will take you to a room where you can have some privacy." Solara nodded. "Call me when you have reached your decision."

The Blademaster

Chapter IX
Decision Made

 "I can't let you do this, Col," Alana insisted. Tears were streaming down her face. She was having a hard time looking at him. "You heard what Solara said. If you fail the Test, it would mean your death. Or that you could never see me again. I don't think I could bear for either to happen."

"I could not bear to lose you, Alana. If I don't do this, I will. She said as much." He took her in his arms and held her close, running his fingers through her hair and kissing her. He gently and tenderly kissed her hair. "There's no choice. I have to do this. I want to do this. This is the only way we get to be together."

Colwyn and Alana were in the little room that Solara had shown them so they could discuss the matter of the Test of the Blades. Much as the rest of the Temple of the Blades was, the room was built out of blocks of the finest white marble. Although he still did not understand how such a thing could be, Colwyn could feel a tremendous amount of warmth emanating from the marble walls. The same was true everywhere he went within the Temple of the Blades. He could not explain it, but it was as if the walls of the Temple were made of living marble. But that hardly made sense. There was no such thing as living marble.

Was there?

The room itself was simple. Eight feet by eight feet, it was fairly small. A padded iron bench ran along the wall immediately opposite the lone door. Other than that bench, there was no furniture to be found. Windows were also absent and, other than the door that they had entered the room by, there was no way out. Colwyn knew that they were under the ground level. They had gone down a flight of stairs to get to the little room. Four of the light globes that they had noticed throughout the Temple of the Blades were in the room, one in each of the corners just below the ceiling, providing enough light to fill the little room quite well. Despite the small size, the room was fairly comfortable. But such coziness was of little comfort to either Alana or Colwyn as they faced the grave decision that lay ahead of them.

It was a decision that would change both of their lives forever, no matter which way they decided to go.

Alana pulled away from Colwyn and sat down on the padded bench. She buried her face in her hands and wept again. Colwyn sighed and positioned himself next to her on the bench, gently wrapping his arms around her. She leaned her head on his shoulder and sobbed, her tears soaking his tunic. He stroked her hair lovingly. Comfortingly. He did not like to see her so upset, but he also knew that, until the Test of the Blades was complete, there was nothing he could do to fully comfort her.

"It's all going to be all right," he whispered softly. "I promise you that right now. It's going to be all right. I will make sure of it."

"How can you be sure of that?" her voice quavered. She turned her tear stained face back up to look at him. "What if you die in the Test? How could that possible be all right? I would not be able to go on if you were to die in the Test."

"I can assure you, my love, that dying is definitely not on my agenda, certainly not anytime soon," the young ranger chuckled. He kissed her on the forehead. "In all honesty, I am not at all worried about failing the Test. I will make it through just fine. You'll see."

"But how can you be so sure, Col?" she asked with a sniff as she wiped her eyes with the back of her hand. "What is it that makes you so sure that you'll be fine?"

"Because I know that you will be waiting for me at the end of the Test, my beloved." He grinned as he traced the trail of her tears down her cheek with one strong finger. "Your love will guide me safely through the test and get me back to you unscathed. There is nothing that will be in the Test of the Blades that will be able to hurt me because I am protected by your love." He ran his fingers across her cheek again, sending waves of electricity through her body. "And there is nothing that they can throw at me in the Test of the Blades that can stand against that protection. That, my love, is how I know that I will be safe during the Test. Nothing in this Test could keep me from you."

"There is no way that I can talk you out of risking your life for me is there?" She searched his face, half-smiling. It was a sad smile, just the same. Clearly, she was not happy about the situation. To be fair, he was not all too thrilled about it either. He really did not want to risk his life in this way any more than she wanted him to. He would, however, do whatever it took to get what he wanted out of life. He always had. And he had to be true to who he was. It was part of why she had fallen in love with him and why she continued to love him so much. He never backed down from a challenge to his beliefs or his wants. Most of the time, it was an endearing trait. At times like this, however, it was also very infuriating.

She knew that, no matter what, Colwyn was going to do this. All Alana could do was hope for the best and pray to Taelin and Laeyra that things went the way that Colwyn had promised they would. Alana wanted to be with Colwyn as much as he wanted to be with her. To that end, Alana would have to let Colwyn take the Test of the Blades. There was no way around it.

Colwyn would have to take and pass the Test of the Blades. And they both knew it.

"My love," Colwyn breathed. "This has to be. Everything that you and I have worked towards up to this point has led us to this one moment. All of our hopes, dreams and desires will either be fulfilled now, or they never will be. Don't you see? I have to do this. It's important to me that you and I end up together. And if I have to take this Test to prove to Lord Taelin just how deeply I am in love with you, then that is exactly what I will do. I love you, Alana. I always will. No matter what happens today."

"I love you too, Colwyn," she smiled at him again. But this time, the smile had real joy behind it. "I guess in the long run, that is all that really matters. I may not like this, but I know that it is what we must go through to be together. You've always said that the way is the way. And you're right. If this is the way it has to be, then so be it. I will tell you that I am not happy about it in the slightest, and I will definitely worry about you throughout the Test of the Blades. But I love you and I trust you to make it through in one piece. May Lord Taelin and Lady Laeyra guide you and protect you while you're in the Test. I tell you now that there will be a rather large kiss and hug waiting for you at the end of the Test."

"I am going to hold you to that," Colwyn smiled at her. He held her face between his hands and gently teased her lips with his.

Alana and Colwyn had kissed many times in the past, but there was something different with this kiss. Although it was a chaste kiss, there was an electricity that shot through both of them. It was as if that kiss sealed their bond to each other more completely than ever before. The both felt it. And they knew that neither of them would ever be complete without the other.

"You can count on it," she said breathlessly.

"I guess that there's only one thing left to be done then," he said with a smirk. He kissed her once more on the lips and she returned the kiss, although far more hungrily. After their lips reluctantly parted, the ranger stood and went to the door. "Lady Solara," he called, "we have made our decision. Let's get this over and done with before one or both of us change our minds."

"And what is your decision?" the High Priestess of the Blades asked with a raised eyebrow as she appeared in the doorway. Colwyn had a sense that she already knew what their decision was and that actually asking the question was a matter of formality.

"I wish to marry Colwyn," Alana said softly. She stood and came up beside Colwyn near the door. Her hand found his and she gazed up at the man she truly loved... the man she truly wished to marry. The man who now had to risk his life to prove to the world what the two of them already knew... that they belonged together. "As much as I don't like this, I know that it is the only way that Colwyn and I can be together. He will take the Test of the Blades."

"Lord Colwyn, in order for the Test of the Blades to proceed, the decision must be a mutual one between you and the Blademaster." The High Priestess of the Blades placed a hand on each of his shoulders and gazed deep into his eyes, as if she were trying to search his soul for the truth of how he felt about Alana. It was an uncomfortable stare, and Colwyn worked hard to fight the urge to flinch and turn away from Solara's stare. He took it as a true testament to how much he loved Alana that he was able to hold fast and not turn from the Priestess's gaze. "It must be of your own free will and for the love you have for this woman that you agree to take the Test of the Blades." She held up a hand to keep him from answering right away. "Do not answer in haste. Before you answer, you must realize that you risk your very life in the Test of the Blades. Only you can answer whether or not such a risk is worth it to you. Know also that should you fail the Test of the Blades and survive, you will be forced to leave the Temple of the Blades immediately. And you will never be allowed to see Alana again."

Colwyn stared back into Solara's eyes, his gaze fixed and unflinching. There could be no hesitation or doubt on his part, nor did he have any. He squeezed Alana's hand once to reassure both of them that the way was the way.

His only answer to Solara was one curt nod.

"Very well," Solara said. "Now that I know that you understand the risks and the consequences, I must ask you, Lord Colwyn Starseeker, heir to the title of First Lord of Arvendale, Blademaster Alana Steeldrake has named you as her Protector. Do you truly wish to marry Alana Steeldrake? Do you agree to the terms of the Test of the Blades and do you agree to accept the consequences of failure? Do you agree to this of your own free will without undue influence from anyone including Alana herself. Nothing has influenced this decision save for your love for this woman?"

"Nothing has influenced me save for the love of Alana, no," Colwyn said, his gaze steady on the High Priestess. "If taking the Test of the Blades is what I must do to prove my love for this woman, then so be it. Let us get on with it.

"Very well," Solara nodded. "I will prepare for the Test of the Blades. I will return in one hour to take Alana into the dungeons. You have until then to prepare."

Colwyn and Alana watched the High Priestess of the Blades leave the little room. Alana sighed, turned to Colwyn, fell into his arms and sobbed again. He put his arms around her and stroked her hair. It was almost amusing to him that she was agonizing over this decision for him to take the Test of the Blades when they both knew, and had known all along, that it was the only decision that could be made. They had grown far too close over the past few years to be able to live without one another. He knew that he would not be able to carry on without her. And he had no doubt in his mind that she felt the same way about him. He could see it in her eyes every time he talked to her. It was what gave him the strength to go through with it.

This made it that much more important to him that he not fail the Test of the Blades. Failure would mean not only his own death, but also, more than likely, the death of the woman he loved more than life itself. And, from what Balaam had told them about the situation in Tornith, they could not stop Thraal without Alana leading the fight against the evil High Priest. As much as he did not like the fact that so much seemed to depend on the woman he loved, he knew the truth of it. It wasn't just his life or

Alana's life on the line. The very continued existence of all of Calthea depended on his success at the Test of the Blades.

He would not let Alana down.

"Everything is going to be all right, my love," he assured her once more. "I'm ready to prove my love for you to you and to Lord Taelin. I'll be all right. And then we will be together for the rest of our lives. It is what we have wanted all along."

"Marrying you is all that I have wanted," Alana whispered. "But I have never wanted you to risk your life for me. Not in this way."

"Being with you is worth the risk," Colwyn smiled broadly. He held her tight. "But as I said, the risk really is minimal. Your love for me will protect me. I will be safe. I will come for you. I will always come for you. I love you so much that there's nothing else I can do but come for you. Your love will be my guide."

"I want you to do something for me," she said as she pulled back. "It would mean a great deal to me if you were to take my long swords into the Test of the Blades with you. They were blessed by Lord Caiaphas when he was the High Priest of Taelin. I add to that blessing on the swords the power of my love. That way, you will be doubly protected."

"I can't leave you unprotected," Colwyn said with a shake of the head. He pulled the baldric off his shoulder. The scabbard that was on his back came free and slipped to the floor. He picked the sword up and held it out to Alana. "I can only take your swords if you agree to carry this with you, Alana. This way, my love will also be there with you to protect you until the Test is complete."

"This is your father's sword, Colwyn. The one he gave you just before you left Arvendale for the Elven Woods. Even though he did not approve of your choice to be a ranger he knew that you would need this," Alana whispered reverently as she lifted the sword from him. She adjusted the baldric so that it would fit on her shoulder, for she had a much smaller frame, and slipped it over her head. She smiled as she fingered the hilt of the sword. "I would be honored to wear your father's sword in the dungeon, even if I really don't know how helpful it will be."

"And I would be honored to carry your swords into the Test with me," Colwyn declared with a grin. He helped her unstrap the sword belt and laid it along with the two long swords onto the floor. He sat back down on the bench and held his arms out to her. When she folded herself back into his embrace, she kissed him. "It will be good to have the reminder of your love with me. It will make it a touch better overall for me having that. For now, though, there is no more need to worry about the Test of the Blades. Worrying about it will not make any difference in the long run. Nor will it do anything to help the situation at all. I would much prefer to just spend the rest of the time holding you and reveling in the love that we share until the preparations are done and the priestess comes back to get you.

"That's a fine idea, Col," she breathed. She snuggled closer to his chest and closed her eyes. Much to Colwyn's amusement, she was asleep in a matter of seconds. He continued to hold her, gently stroking her hair as she slept. Colwyn was amused that she could fall asleep standing up like that. He would not let her fall, though.

He picked her up and gently carried her over to the bench. He sat her down, still sleeping. He pulled the baldric for his sword from around her and laid it onto the bench before he pulled her to him. Her soft slow breathing calmed him some, but his mind was still turning around and around about what was about to happen.

He wished that he could fall asleep also, but he knew that he was too wound up to get any kind of real rest. All he could do was hold Alana and try not to obsess too much about the Test of the Blades while he waited. He wasn't overly successful. After a few minutes of tortured silence, he knew what it was that he had to do. There was an old ranger technique that he had been taught by his ranger master, Otan Kovalani. It was an ancient technique designed to calm oneself in the face of great danger or challenges. It was not a technique that could be used all the time. In fact, it was pretty useless during a battle situation. It took close to an hour of intense concentration, far more time than a ranger would dare give during a life or death situation. But in a situation like this, when he knew he was about to engage in heavy combat, it could help to quiet his mind ahead of time so he would stand a better chance of surviving what was to come.

Colwyn closed his eyes, taking in and letting out several long, deep breaths. As he did so, he let his mind wander. He let all of his worry, apprehension, and nervousness about the Test of the Blades and how he was risking his neck in the attempt to finally win Alana for his very own and rolled it up into a small ball in his mind. He took the ball and locked it into a small box in the back of his consciousness, letting only the positive thoughts, feelings and energies remain. He focused on his love for Alana, letting the warmth of that feeling settle over him. This step had always been hard for him in the past, as he had never had anyone in his life that he had ever shared this level of love with. While he had loved Mirian Kovalani during the brief time he had been with her, and had been able to focus on that love for her for this purpose, the love that they had shared had never been this deep or all-encompassing. While he had been able to use this love for the early stages of the technique that the elves called stát ndoimhneacht na tsíocháin inmheánach, he had never been able to achieve the full benefit of the technique. This had been a point of frustration for the three of them, Colwyn, Mirian and Otan. For Colwyn, it was because he had never failed in any of the other ranger training he had received from the elves. For Otan, his teacher, it was because no matter what he did to help Colwyn, he was never able to manage to get Colwyn over the precipice into the full benefits of the technique. The elf lord felt that it was his own failing, not Colwyn's.

And for Mirian, it was the bitter suspicion that Colwyn was not able to succeed in delving into the deepest levels of stát ndoimhneacht na tsíocháin inmheánach because perhaps he did not love her enough. As with many other things in life, love was the cornerstone of the technique. Mirian knew this fact, which only fueled her suspicions. Of course, now the queen of the Forestwalker elves knew that she was perhaps not the one that Colwyn was destined to be with. But at the time, the thought that he did not love her as much as he could saddened her and had upset her to no end. Still, she never allowed it to show. And then, when he had been banished from the Elven Woods, the matter had become moot. But the seeming lack of love on his part had cut her deep. She had never told him, but Colwyn had known even without her telling him. He had tried to convince her that he loved her, but somehow his overtures always fell somewhat flat. To her, there was something keeping him from loving her as completely as she wanted him to. And now that she had seen Colwyn and Alana together, he hoped she could finally understand and find peace concerning the matter. When she had told him that she understood that his destiny was to be with Alana and that she knew she could never be the one he was to be with, it had been as if a great burden had been lifted. He cherished Mirian's forgiveness but it was Alana that he needed to focus on now. Living so far in the past would not help him to reach the deep states of stát ndoimhneacht na tsíocháin inmheánach that he now sought. Only his memories of Alana and their love could bring it on.

Colwyn renewed his focus. Peace and warmth flowed through his mind and body. In order for him to fully experience stát ndoimhneacht na tsíocháin inmheánach, it would be necessary to focus on one specific moment that would crystallize their love enough for him to trigger the technique. He was not sure which memory of Alana would be the one that would be able to trigger it, so he let his mind meander, touching on every memory he had of the two of them. This was the part of stát ndoimhneacht na tsíocháin inmheánach that took the longest and also the part he had never been able to master. He had never been able to land on a memory that would trigger the final phase of stát ndoimhneacht na tsíocháin inmheánach, but he had also not made the attempt to enter that state since he had met Alana. Somewhere in his mind, there had to be a cherished memory of Alana and himself that would trigger the technique. All he had to do was to let his mind wander until he came upon the right memory. Then he would slip into the deepest recesses of stát ndoimhneacht na tsíocháin inmheánach. He would finally experience what he had never been able to.

It wasn't that he had never gotten anything out of stát ndoimhneacht na tsíocháin inmheánach in the past, but until he finally experienced the deepest level of it, he would never know how much it could really help him. At least that's what Otan had always said.

Several long minutes later, Colwyn hit on the perfect memory. As he ran through the memory of the first time he had ever met Alana, he finally fell far more deeply into the deepest recesses of stát ndoimhneacht na tsíocháin inmheánach. Finally he knew what it was that Otan had spoken of...

Colwyn was in the sitting room of the small house he had built for himself before going to the Elven Woods. He had been back in Ravendale for two months, but he had spent much of that time in his own home. He also had not frequented the Lucky Minotaur at all. The tap room of the Lucky Minotaur had always been one of his favorite places to eat when he was in Ravendale. Albert, the proprietor of the Lucky Minotaur, had come by a couple of times to see how he was doing. Colwyn had suffered the visits with little enthusiasm. He knew that Albert was merely concerned, but the pain of having been banned from the Elven Woods was still too fresh. He could not tell Albert about what had happened, for although Albert cared deeply for him, the innkeeper would never understand the depth of the pain that the banishment had caused. It was a pain that no one should ever have to experience, and an anguish from which he felt like he would never recover.

And yet, he also could not just sit in his home for the rest of his life. If for no other reason, he knew that his duties in Arvendale would someday come knocking on his door. If he were ever to find a way to get on with his life, he would have to confront his pain. Somewhere along the line during his misery, he had begun to suspect that perhaps his life had some deeper meaning than he had ever thought it had. And somehow he had come to the realization that such a deeper meaning was the reason he had been banished from the

Elven Woods. Perhaps he could never have completed his life's greater purpose if he had stayed in the Elven Woods. There had to be something for him beyond the pain and misery he had been feeling.

Colwyn was determined to discover what it was.

Sitting in his house and feeling sorry for himself would not bring him any closer to this deeper meaning. And yet, he could not help himself, for he knew not what else to do. But feeling sorry for himself would only make him more miserable and he would only spiral downward from there.

Whatever the higher meaning and purpose for his life was, he suspected it would involve his skills as both a fighter and a ranger. Indeed, he would not possess those skills otherwise. Therefore, it only made sense to keep those skills honed... something could not do moping around the house.

So, after a month of sitting around and feeling sorry for himself, he began a daily routine of exercises in the courtyard of the small house he called his own. The exercises were designed to keep both his mind and his body sharp. In no time, the layer of paunch that had accumulated over his month long inactivity had withered away, but the fog that had been shrouding his mind since he had returned to Ravendale still remained. There was no level of physical exertion that could clear away the anguish and shame associated with his banishment from the Elven Woods. He hoped and prayed that there was something that would clear his mind before he sank too much further into despair. But so far, he had not happened upon any kind of cure.

Still, he continued to hope for one.

And so, until he could find whatever it was that would clear his mind, he spent his days in exactly the same way. His mornings and afternoons were dedicated to exercising his body to keep his skills sharp and his muscles honed. His evenings were spent in quiet contemplation in an effort to find the peace and the calm that had been eluding him since his banishment.

And so it was, on this particular evening, he was reflecting in the sitting room of his little house, his eyes closed. His breathing had slowed and he was searching for a memory that would bring on the state of *stát ndoimhneacht na tsíocháin inmheánach*. It had become something of a nightly ritual since he had come back from the Elven Woods. Each night, he attempted to enter *stát ndoimhneacht na tsíocháin inmheánach* and, as of yet, he had had no better success at entering the deepest states of that sacred ranger technique than he had while he was in the Elven Woods. He was frustrated at his lack of progress. He desperately sought that state of inner peace and calm and he was upset that he could not do so.

A knock on the door interrupted his thoughts. His concentration slipped. His eyes snapped open. He would never make further progress as long as there were distractions. Muttering, he padded over to the door and yanked it open.

Albert. Again.

Colwyn stepped aside. Albert came into the small house without a word.

"What are you doing here, Albert?" Colwyn wasn't really all that surprised. Albert had not visited him in a while. If he hadn't come on this night, it would have been the next morning or afternoon.

"I thought I'd see how you were doing, my friend," the old innkeeper said. He sat down, uninvited, in one of the large comfortable easy chairs that Colwyn had placed by the fireplace. "Gwen and I have both been very worried about you since your return to Ravendale. We haven't seen all that much of you. Mind you, neither of us wants to pry into your personal affairs, so I'm not going to ask you what happened to bring you back to Ravendale in such a state. But you should know that there are people who care about you and they're... we're really very worried about how you are doing." It was much the same thing that Albert said every time that he came to visit. "Gwen, especially, would like for you to come by the Lucky Minotaur tonight. I will make you a very nice dinner. What do you say, Colwyn? It would do yourself good to get out of the house for a few hours. I'll tell you what. If you do come to the Lucky Minotaur tonight for dinner, I will even pay for dinner myself. Now that's not something you often hear." The offer of a free meal, however, was something that Albert had never made during these visits. Albert giving away free food was completely without precedent.

Colwyn suppressed a chuckle and rolled his eyes. "Alright. You win. I can't promise that I'll stay very long, but I'll come by the tap room tonight. If only to have one of your special dinners. Besides, I don't want to pass up that price. Maybe then Gwen will see first hand that she can stop worrying about me. If that's even possible."

"I have a feeling that tonight will change your life, my friend." Albert stood from the easy chair, a smile plastered across his kindly face. "I have to get back to the Lucky Minotaur. The dinner crowd should be starting to show up soon. And, if you don't mind, may I suggest that you clean yourself up a bit. You smell like heavy sweat, and you know as well as I do that the less of that we have to deal with in the tap room, the better." He sniggered a little as he went out the door. "So, I'll see you tonight. Right, Colwyn? At the Lucky Minotaur for dinner."

Colwyn nodded and saw his friend out the door and then set to drawing himself a nice hot bath. While he was waiting for the steaming bath water to cool down just enough that he could immerse his body in it without scalding himself, he laid out a suit of his finest evening clothes. As much as he did not like wearing the fancy clothes that went along with being a noble, it was the expectation on certain occasions. And since he had not been out in public since he had returned to Ravendale, this would constitute one of those occasions, whether or not he liked it. And so, even though he would have preferred to go to the Lucky Minotaur in his beloved forest garb, he selected a more formal attire for the evening. Naturally, he would not go to the Lucky Minotaur unarmed. Although violence was greatly discouraged at the Lucky Minotaur, Colwyn had this nagging sense that he would regret not taking certain precautions. He hoped that he was wrong, but he had long since learned to trust his instincts. When it came to whether or not to wear weapons, his instincts were rarely wrong.

He sunk into the tub with a happy sigh. Soaking in a tub after his exercises had become one of the few pleasures that

Colwyn enjoyed these days. While he could not enter the final state of *stát ndoimhneacht na tsíocháin inmheánach*, at least soaking in a tub provided him with some of the peace and calm that he desired. He wasn't sure what it was about soaking in hot water that provided such peace, but he figured he would take whatever peace he could get whenever and wherever he could get it.

It was well over an hour later when Colwyn pushed open the door to the tap room at the Lucky Minotaur. Gwen tackled him in a hug as soon as his foot touched the floor of the tap room. Completely taken off guard by her overly affectionate greeting, Colwyn had no choice but to return it in kind. She smiled and, taking him by the hand, led him over to a table near the fire.

"It is so good to see you, Colwyn," she declared. "I'll bring you something to drink, and Albert will have your dinner ready soon."

"Thank you." Colwyn chuckled as he sat. "Thank you so much for your concern, Gwen. But, as you can see, I'm quite all right. It'll take a little time but I'll be fine."

Gwen nodded with an uncertain grin before flouncing back to the bar to get his drink. He shook his head, laughing to himself as he watched her dart off to the bar and then back to his table. She placed a flagon of ale on his table and then flitted off to another table. It was a crowded night in the tap room so Gwen was kept very busy indeed.

Colwyn's seat by the fire was right where he would have elected to sit and Gwen, having seated him before, knew of his preferences. Here, he could easily see everything that was going on without straining himself. His training as both a fighter and as a ranger had instilled in him the importance of knowing his surroundings intimately. Later on he would reflect on how happy he was with his seat that night.

As he scanned the room, Colwyn catalogued a list of who the likely troublemakers would be. As with any night in the Lucky Minotaur's tap room, there were more than a few patrons who looked a little worse for wear. Colwyn preferred to identify where trouble was likely to come from before it had a chance to sneak up on him so that should that trouble rear its ugly head, his response would be quick and decisive.

There was one table in particular that seemed like a candidate for a fair bit of trouble before the night was over. Four rather tough looking mercenaries were seated at the table. Colwyn took a sip of his ale as he scrutinized them. Things would get difficult if he had to take on all four men by himself, but he had faith in his own skills, and figured if push came to shove, he would probably still prevail. It was not cockiness, but rather just simple confidence and an honest assessment. He almost welcomed a fight. It had been awhile since he'd tested his skills and he could use a few thugs to take out his anger and frustration on. It could very well be the next step in moving on with this life.

The other good thing about where Colwyn was sitting was that it allowed him to see the door without having to move. This too, he would later recognize as a good thing when he looked back on the events of the evening.

That was when the young woman slipped in through the door of the tap room.

There was something about the young woman that Colwyn could not put his finger on. It was not simply that the woman was beautiful, although she was. Her deep auburn tresses were long and tied back in a simple ponytail. Her eyes blazed a dark emerald shade of green, and the dress she wore highlighted those eyes. They burned with an inner fire of intelligence and wisdom. Colwyn knew that she was no noble, but she bore herself with a grace that very few nobles could match. It only took one look at the woman to know that trouble danced at the Lucky Minotaur that evening.

Trouble danced with the tough looking men that the young ranger had noticed earlier.

Colwyn watched to see if the men spied the woman, and he looked on in distaste as they nudged each other and pointed. And it was then that Colwyn knew that he had indeed correctly foretold the trouble in the tap room on that particular evening. He was also glad he had heeded his instincts as far as his weapons were concerned. He watched as, almost as if it had been scripted, the rough looking men followed the young woman with their lusty gazes.

And just as these oafs had their role to play, so also did Colwyn. He knew without a doubt that he would intervene on her behalf. Colwyn did not like to kill unless he absolutely had to. But he suspected that, if it came down to a choice between the brutes or the woman, be would not hesitate to do so.

The young woman glided over to the bar. The brutes followed her with their eyes. It would only be a matter of time before they worked up the courage to approach her. Colwyn fingered the hilt of his father's sword. When these thugs made their move, he would be ready to act. He did not know who the woman was, and it did not really matter. He knew full well what kind of trouble men like these have in mind for young women like this one.

Colwyn could not sit idly by and allow such things to happen to her. It was not in his nature.

The woman placed her order with Gwen, seemingly oblivious to the drama that was playing out behind her. Colwyn decided it was time to study her as well. From the way she carried herself, he doubted that she was anywhere near as oblivious as she appeared to be. Indeed, he suspected that the young woman knew exactly what was going on both with regards to the brutes and also with Colwyn himself. It was clear that she was a warrior in her own right.

And yet she was also so much more.

Colwyn had a flash of insight that his higher purpose was somehow entwined with this woman. But he could gain nothing more.

He did not, however, think that would remain the way of it. It would just be a matter of waiting until the higher purpose for himself and this strange woman presented itself to the both of them.

It did not take all that long for the brutes to work up the courage to go after the young woman. They each knocked back the drinks they had and then they awkwardly stood, swaying like trees assaulted by the wind. As soon as the bunch started blundering through the tap room, Colwyn was in motion. Years of training as a ranger allowed him to move far more quickly and quietly than others. And so it was that, in no time at all really, he was positioned next to the young woman at the bar.

She glanced up at him, without a trace of surprise on her face. If anything, the spark of amusement danced in her eyes. She bestowed upon him a thin tight-lipped smile that seemed as if she were sharing in some big secret with him.

It was at that instant and with that one smile that Colwyn fell completely and hopelessly in love with her.

He only hoped he could one day win her love in return.

"My lady," he said with creased brow, "there are some men approaching who mean to cause you some trouble."

The young woman cocked her head in the direction of the brutes and then she turned her attention back at Colwyn, searching his face. "And?" The way she looked at the men confirmed his suspicions that she had known everything that had been going in in the tap room behind her.

"And..." For once, Colwyn did not know what to say.

"And you have come to my aid?" she finished for him. Her voice was soft and musical. The timbre perfect. But of course, Colwyn was biased. After all, he was already in love.

"Please don't mistake me," Colwyn asserted. "I know what men like those want of a beautiful woman." His hand reached up and gently covered hers. She did not protest, simply providing another of those tight-lipped smiles in return. "I would prefer it greatly if that did not happen to you."

"I see."

Colwyn flashed his teeth. "It would be my very great honor to stand as your protection."

"Your aid will be welcome, friend," the woman said with a nod. "My name is Alana Steeldrake. I have just arrived in Ravendale. I don't really know anyone in this city. And I would rather prefer not to make the acquaintance of those men at all. Thank you, kind sir."

"My name is Colwyn Starseeker," he replied. "And I daresay you're lucky that I even came out here tonight, Lady Alana. This is the first time I have been here at the Lucky Minotaur since I returned to Ravendale two months ago."

"I'm lucky?" she asked.

He smirked. "Naturally, I'm glad I did though."

"Have you considered that it is entirely possible that you were meant to come here tonight and meet me, Colwyn?" Alana smiled again as she laid her hand on top of his. "After all, nothing happens purely by chance."

"Well, well, well," one of the brutes snickered as the four of them sidled up to the bar. "Look at what we have here, boys. A pretty young lady has come to Ravendale to be my plaything. Isn't that just grand?" He shooed Colwyn. "You can go now, boy. We'll take it from here." Colwyn's hand found the hilt of his sword. The four men, as one, burst out in laughter.

In a blink, the sword was free. The distinctive ring of steel hit the air and killed all conversation in the tap room. All eyes were wide, taking in the scene at the bar. While many of the patrons knew Colwyn and understood him to be a chivalrous man, not one of them could say that they had ever seen him draw his sword in defense of someone. This was because, in truth, he never had done so before. The situation had simply never demanded it.

But now he had the chance to prove what he could do and he would do whatever it took to keep Alana safe.

"I think you boys should just back down," Colwyn remarked. The men all blinked at least once. So Colwyn clarified for them. "I'm not going anywhere. Therefore, you will have to go through me to get to her."

The leader of the brutes chortled. "The lady will be going with us." He sneered down his nose at the ranger. "The likes of you are not going to stop the four of us from getting what we want."

"I have other plans for this evening," Alana announced with a quiet air, patting Colwyn's arm for emphasis. "And they do not include the four of you."

"Change them!" the leader of the group of brutes ordered. He grabbed her by the arm. "You're going with us whether you want to or not."

Colwyn flicked his sword up, slicing through the man's arm at the elbow. Screams of agony and outrage permeated the room. But that didn't stop him for lunging at Colwyn, a knife at the ready in his remaining hand. Colwyn deftly stepped aside and the brute's eyes went wide in shock. He stumbled and then glared down at his chest where there was a knife handle protruding from his heart. A pool of dark red blood bloomed out from the wound. This time it was Colwyn's turn for surprise. He had not wielded a knife, nor had he turned the brute's knife on him. He faced Alana. She hid her emotions well, but Colwyn was an expert face-reader. There was no doubt that Alana had indeed killed the brute.

He had been right from the outset. Alana was someone special and not to be trifled with.

"I told you that I have other plans for the evening," Alana breathed. "Now, if you'll excuse me, I would like to get on with them."

The other three brutes shuffled off back to their table, mumbling incoherently. Perhaps they were deciding upon a new leader. Naturally, after that display, no one else in the tap room had any objection to Colwyn and Alana sitting together.

Two burly mercenaries that Albert paid to remove bodies whenever there was a fight collected the fallen man to take it wherever it was that they disposed of such bodies. One of the two mercenaries locked his gaze with Colwyn's and an understanding passed between them. There would be no inquiry into the man's death. It had been self-defense, after all. He was grateful for Albert's stance on the matter and appreciated that the old innkeeper continued to look out for him. It was nice to know that the people that you cared about the most held the same ideals that you did. Life was easier when you know you're not alone.

"So why don't you come sit with me, Alana?" Colwyn urged with a smile. "Albert is making my dinner now. If I know him, it'll be more than I can handle on my own."

Alana laughed softly. "I'd like that." Her laughter was like music to his ears. "I would like that very much, I think."

Colwyn took her hand and walked her over to the table. He held her chair out and helped her into it. Her own smile widened at the gesture. He could not have known it at that point, but Alana had never had a man show her that kind of respect. She had never thought she would ever be lucky enough to find anyone who would treat her that way.

"There are not many nobles who would have stood with me like that," Alana said as she took a sip of her kava juice, which she had brought from the bar. "You were very brave."

"I'm not like other nobles." He took a sip of his ale. "I am only noble by birth, not by choice. My occupation is that of a ranger. I love the woods and nature. I'm more at home there than I have ever been in my father's castle or in society."

"So I see," Alana chuckled. She took another sip of her kava juice and smiled again. "Well, it's good to meet a noble who doesn't act like one."

"I have news for you then," he said between sips of his ale. "Most nobles have times in their life when they just don't feel like acting like a noble."

The two of them laughed at that. It was a pleasing sound to Colwyn's ears, the combined laughter.

Gwen arrived with a tray of food. First she set a fresh ale in front of Colwyn and a fresh kava juice in front of Alana. Then she put an empty plate in front of each of them and started setting out the plates containing the food. Colwyn had been right. There would be far too much food for him to eat all on his own. Albert had prepared a bit of a feast. In fact, Colwyn began to wonder if Albert had known that he was going to end up with an unexpected dinner companion. Knowing the innkeeper as well as he did, Colwyn wouldn't have been surprised if he found out that Albert did know.

Whatever the case, the feast that Albert prepared looked and smelled wonderful to both of them. One plate had an assortment of fried strips of beef, pork and chicken, while another plate had a stack of Albert's famous sage infused sausages. A plate full of Albert's spiced potatoes completed the main course. Albert had also provided two of his personal sized chocolate pies. That was the clincher for Colwyn, and he knew he would have to talk to Albert about just how much he had known about the night's events beforehand. Even though he was a little annoyed by it, Colwyn was still touched by the old man's thoughtfulness.

"Alana," Colwyn ventured after a few moments of chewing on a strip of beef. "You said earlier that you thought that I might have been meant to meet you this evening. Were you referring to some sort of prophecy about our meeting? Or that it was destiny?"

Alana chewed in silence for a few moments before she responded. "Neither destiny nor prophecy are as absolute as we are sometimes led to believe, Colwyn," she replied.

It was not anywhere near the response that Colwyn had been expecting. It was, in fact, the very enigmatic kind of response that Colwyn might have expected from a mage or a sage. But certainly it was not something that he had expected from a swordswoman.

Alana continued. "Lord Taelin gave us all free will. By doing so, he allowed us all to choose our own paths. While prophecy can tell us of events that will happen, it can not tell us everything about those events, no matter how much some may wish that to be so. Yes, there was a prophecy about our meeting tonight. I was told by an old man they call the Dream Weaver in Talondale, my home city, that on the day I arrived in Ravendale, I would meet a man of sound moral character who would come to my defense. But he did not tell me anything more about the man than that. As soon as I saw you, I knew that you were the man the Dream Weaver spoke of. But still. It was your free will that led you to come to my aid. Not this prophecy. If it had not been you that rescued me, it would have been someone else." She took another sip of her kava juice and flashed him another of her broad tight-lipped smiles. "That being said, I am glad that it was you that came to my aid."

"So am I, my lady," Colwyn returned the smile. "Here. Try one of these." He offered her one of the chocolate pies. "Albert's chocolate pies are widely regarded as the best in all of the Southern Dales."

Colwyn came out of his meditative state caused by stát ndoimhneacht na tsíocháin inmheánach and glanced over at the sleeping form of the woman he loved. He felt the peace and calm of the depths of the ranger technique still spreading over him. Finally he had experienced the peace and calm of stát ndoimhneacht na tsíocháin inmheánach! He reveled in the confirmation of the total correctness of taking the Test of the Blades. He had no doubt that he was on the right path now. Someday, he would tell Otan that he had finally entered the final stage of the ranger technique. He looked forward to the elf lord's eventual approval.

A sound echoed in from outside the room. He suspected that it was Solara. Was he ready to take the Test of the Blades? Could he not have a few more minutes with Alana first? But that would be folly. The time had come.

He gently pushed on Alana's shoulder to wake her. He was rewarded with a smile and a questioning look as if to say, *Is it time?*

He only had time to nod once before the High Priestess of the Blades appeared in the doorway.

As if reading his mind, Solara answered for him. "It is time."

The Blademaster

Chapter X
The Legacy of the Blademasters

Lana stood up from the bench where she had been resting and fixed Solara with her gaze. But she quickly softened and nodded to the High Priestess before facing the man she loved.

"I just want to make certain that you are sure about this, Colwyn," she said. "If you truly want to go through with this, then I'm okay with that. But if you're not sure and you want to back out, then now is the time. As soon as the Test starts, there won't be any other choice."

Colwyn pulled his sword off the bench and placed the baldric of the scabbard over her head. He adjusted it so that it would hang off her left hip at just the correct angle for her to easily draw it. He smiled tenderly back at her and wiped a tear from her cheek with his forefinger. Her skin was cold. Like ice.

Fear does that to a person.

"I'm not backing out of this, Alana," he said with an earnest edge. He took her in his arms and kissed her hair. "Even if I were to die in the attempt to pass the Test, it would still be worth it. There is no doubt. This is the right choice for me."

Alana took his hands in hers and kissed them. She pulled away enough so that she could look over his face, but not so far that she could not feel the warmth of his body.

"Well then, since you're so sure about this, there's only one thing left to do," she said. She kissed him passionately on the lips and he hungrily returned the kiss. It was a kiss born of fear, desperation, and need. And it was, by far, the most passionate kiss they had ever shared. "Good luck, my beloved. I don't mind telling you that I'm scared to death about all of this."

"I'm scared too, Alana," Colwyn rasped. He gathered her back up into his arms. "It would be foolish of me to not be scared. After all, I am risking my life in this endeavor. The reward far outweighs any risk though."

"I love you, Colwyn," she breathed. "You have no idea how much it means to me that you are willing to risk your life for me. You know that you have never had to prove your love for me as far as I am concerned. I've known that I have had your love since the day we first met. But I'm sure you remember that day as well as I do."

He let slip a reassuring grin. "As a matter of fact, that particular memory has taken on a whole new meaning for me. There is a technique that is taught to elven rangers in the Forestwalker clan called stát ndoimhneacht na tsíocháin inmheánach. The technique requires a memory of the one that you love and channels that memory to provide a feeling of complete peace and calm. Tonight was the first time I have ever been able to successfully enter the deepest states of the technique. I had never been able to find a suitable memory to trigger the full effects of the technique but tonight I focused on the memory of the day we met. I can remember every detail of every minute of that day. Having never experienced the full effects of stát ndoimhneacht na tsíocháin inmheánach before, I did not know what it was that I should expect. And when I was finally able to experience the rich levels of peace and calm that goes along with those deepest states... Well, it was like nothing I have ever experienced before. I believe it has helped me to mentally prepare for whatever the Test of the Blades throws at me."

Solara took a step forward. "Am I to understand that you were able to enter the final state of stát ndoimhneacht na tsíocháin inmheánach by focusing on a memory of the Lady Alana?" Solara raised an eyebrow. When Colwyn nodded, she sighed softly and primly perched herself on the bench. "This changes things some. Only a memory that is shared with a person's true love can trigger that level of stát ndoimhneacht na tsíocháin inmheánach. Having lived in these Elven Woods for several hundred years and having dealt with the Forestwalker elves for all of those years, I have learned a great deal about their ways. Indeed, I have known a great many elven rangers from the Forestwalker clan, and they have told me about how the technique of stát ndoimhneacht na tsíocháin inmheánach is achieved. Lord Colwyn, there is just no way that you should have been able to trigger it unless the Lady Alana is your true love. And this would explain why you had never been able to trigger it until you met her. It's simply the way the technique works. There can be no doubt about it. The Lady Alana is your true love." She smiled at Colwyn. "This is very good news for you indeed."

Alana chimed in. "Does this mean that he is no longer required to pass the Test of the Blades?" A look of hope spread across her face. She wanted nothing more than for Solara to say yes.

Solara shook her head. "I'm afraid that Colwyn will still have to take and pass the Test of the Blades. Understand, it is not by my own choice that I would force Colwyn to do this, Lady Alana. It is a command from Lord Taelin himself that all men who would be the Protector to a Blademaster must take and pass the Test of the Blades. As much as I might now wish that it could be otherwise, there is only one way that our Lord Taelin will allow this marriage between the two of you. And that is for Colwyn to take and pass the

Test of the Blades. If it makes you feel any better, the very fact that Colwyn was able to enter a state of stát ndoimhneacht na tsíocháin inmheánach means that he is your true love. And as your true love, he is all but certain to pass the Test. That is why I said that it was good news."

"It does not make me feel any better in the slightest," Alana snapped. "Colwyn should not have to prove his love for me. Not to you, and not to Lord Taelin. And if he was indeed able to enter the final state of stát ndoimhneacht na tsíocháin inmheánach, that should be proof enough."

"Normally, I would not even think to disagree with you, my lady." Solara said with a frown. She stood up and crossed the room to where Alana was standing. She put her hands on the young woman's shoulders. "But in this case, I'm afraid that I must. You are no ordinary woman, Lady Alana. You are the first in a new line of Blademasters. The Law of the Blades must apply to every step of your journey, or we are all doomed to a life of darkness."

"Then I would choose to not be a Blademaster, Lady Solara," Alana growled. "I can not put Colwyn through this just to marry me. And I will marry no one but Colwyn."

"Please think carefully on this decision before you commit yourself to it, Lady Alana," Solara said, this time with a stern edge. "There is much at stake." The priestess slowly sat back down on the bench. "Also, consider this: If you do not accept the responsibilities of the Law of the Blades and thus do not take on the duties as the first in this new line of Blademasters, you will lose the abilities that are inherent in a Blademaster. Worse still, there will not be another Blademaster created and chosen in time to be able to stop Thraal from returning to Calthea. You would still have to make the attempt to stop him, but, as I said, without the abilities that are only inherent to a Blademaster. Faced with this scenario, it would be very unlikely that you could stop Thraal. Indeed, if you are to stop him at all, you will need every ability, weapon and trick you can spare. Please don't make this decision rashly."

Alana turned away from the priestess and faced Colwyn. Tears streamed down her cheeks. She loved him more than even her own life. She knew that he felt the same way. She wished things were different and they did not have to go through with this Test. But there was really no choice. They would have to go through with the Test of the Blades. Once she had realized what her destiny would entail, she had suspected that they would have to travel this path if they were to ever be joined. But her love for Colwyn was so great, that she would not have been able to live with herself without at least trying to find another way. She knew now that there was no other way. Especially if she wanted to be able to stop the Dark God from returning to Calthea.

Colwyn nodded to her. He clearly knew what was going through her head. And she knew that he had to go through with the Test of the Blades. She knew he would pass too. He had to. She realized that he had known all along what was really at stake, and he was willing to risk his life to see it all through to completion. Far more than merely a noble, Colwyn was a noble man. She admired, and at the same time was amazed by, his desire to fight the good fight no matter what the potential cost was to himself. And she loved him all the more for it.

"I'm sorry, Colwyn," she whispered. She ran her fingers down his face. The tears continued to stream down her cheeks. "I have tried so hard to find another way for us. I'm sorry. There's no other path. Can you forgive me, though, for trying to get out of our destiny?"

"There is nothing to forgive, my love." He took her back in his arms and held her. "You were only trying to protect me just as I have always tried to protect you. How could I ever fault you for that? But the priestess is right. There is far more at stake here than just my life and my safety. Thraal has to be stopped and you are the only one who can do it, my love. This is the only way that you will be able to do what must be done. The way is the way. This is my choice, my love. I must take and pass the Test of the Blades. And you must let me."

"I don't like it, Col. You should not have to prove your love for me." Alana leaned her head onto his shoulder, her tears soaking into his forest shirt. "I love you so much. I could not go on if you failed to survive the Test. But you're right. There is no choice in the matter. This is what has to happen. Not just for us, but for all of Calthea. But please be careful during the Test. Be careful and come back to me in one piece. I love you so much, Colwyn. You just have to make it through the Test."

"I'll be just fine, my beloved," Colwyn's smile bordered on cockiness. "I promise you. Your love will guide me and protect me through the Test of the Blades. You'll see. Everything will be fine."

"I'm going to hold you to that, Colwyn. I don't think I would ever be able to forgive you if you were to die on me in the middle of the Test," she chided him. It was a feeble attempt to inject a touch of levity into an otherwise tense situation. But it worked. Colwyn laughed. She peeled herself away from him and stood before the High Priestess of the Blades. "I am ready, Lady Solara. I know that this is the way things have to be. I suppose I've always known, but I have just had a hard time accepting the particulars. But Colwyn said it best. The way is the way. I will accept my post as the Blademaster. And I will go along with all that the Law of the Blades requires of me, although you should know that I do so reluctantly at times. I will just have to trust that Colwyn will make it through the Test of the Blades in one piece. I will tell you this now though. If he does not pass the Test of the Blades, I will not choose anyone else. I will not put any one else through the Test of the Blades."

"I understand," Solara nodded. She placed her hands on Alana's shoulders. "You have made a hard decision, Lady Alana. But it was the right one. You will come to see that in time. For now though, you must come with me." She turned her attention to the ranger. "Lord Colwyn, you will remain here until I return. I will take the Blademaster down into the dungeons to await her rescue. Once she has been secured, I will return and take you to the dungeon entrance. From there, you're on your own. You will have to discover the way to overcome the challenges of the Test of the Blades for yourself."

Colwyn nodded. "I understand," he said as he took Alana in his arms once more. He kissed her passionately. "I will see you soon, Alana."

"I'm counting on that, Colwyn," Alana said with a smile. "I pray that you will come for me and that you will come quickly."

Solara motioned for Alana to follow her out of the little room. Alana blew him a little kiss before exiting.

Colwyn watched the two women leave the room, knowing it was the last he would see of her until he passed Test of the Blades. He searched his mind for everything that he knew about the Blademasters and the Law of the Blades. Much to his chagrin, he did not know much. He was trying to find anything in what little information he had about the Law of the Blades that would help him as far as passing the Test of the Blades went. But as he searched back through his memory, he realized that he had never even heard of the Test of the Blades previous to this encounter. He had no knowledge that would be helpful. He would have to rely on his instincts as a ranger and the few little tricks he'd picked up over the years. He suspected his finder's stone and the trap finder stone that Mirian Kovalani had given him on their way to the Temple of the Blades would both prove useful during the Test of the Blades. He did not like going into a situation with so little advance knowledge of what he would face. But how was this any different than real life? He would just have to make do with what he had and hope for the best. As always. It would be difficult, but nothing worthwhile was ever truly easy. He would just have to stay the course and take the Test of the Blades moment by moment. He would have to be very observant to make sure he did not miss anything important. And he would just have to hope and pray for the best. After all, Alana would be waiting for him at the other end of the Test. He could not and would not disappoint the woman that he loved. He vowed it both to himself and to her. It was a vow he could not afford to fail to keep.

He scooped up the sword belt that had her two long swords on it and he buckled it around his waist. He checked to make sure that the swords were clear in their scabbards. It would not do for him to have trouble drawing the blades when the time came for him to use them.

When he was satisfied that the swords were clear in their scabbards, he set to the task of clearing his mind to prepare himself mentally for the Test of the Blades. Physically, he knew that he was pretty well able to take on anything the Test of the Blades could throw at him. Well, unless there was a dragon... He truly hoped that there would not be any dragons. He had fought against a dragon once before, and it was not an experience he was hoping to relive again anytime soon. Colwyn had gone with a group of twenty-four other rangers to the city of Solvendale three years before when that city had been threatened by a very old red dragon. They did succeed in severely wounding the dragon and getting it to agree to leave the city of Solvendale alone, but it had not been without great cost to the small group of rangers. In the dragon's first attack alone, he had incinerated seven of Colwyn's comrades with a tremendous burst of flame the likes of which he had never seen before, and he truly hoped to never see anything like it again. By the time all was said and done, Colwyn had been one of only six rangers left to help repair the damage that the dragon had done to the city. He could never forget what one dragon could do and he would never forget any of the men that he had fought alongside to subdue that dragon. Nor would he ever likely forget the screams of those who died during the battle as they burned alive, the flesh seared from their bones. It was a sound unlike any he had ever heard before or since. He still had occasional nightmares about that battle. It was one of the things that he had never told Alana about. He just didn't know how to broach the subject. It shamed him that he still kept secrets from the woman that he loved. But at the same time, he also knew that nothing he kept from her could ever hurt her.

He would not allow any of his secrets to hurt her.

The peace and calm that he had felt while in the deepest reaches of stát ndoimhneacht na tsíocháin inmheánach earlier had long since fled. There was not nearly enough time to put himself into the deepest recesses of stát ndoimhneacht na tsíocháin inmheánach before

Solara would return to take him into the Test of the Blades. But he figured if he focused on the memory of the day he and Alana had met, he still might be able to recapture some of the peace and calm that went along with the deepest states of the technique. If he were to succeed in passing the Test of the Blades, he would want to start as settled as possible.

Colwyn sat back down on the bench and closed his eyes. He focused on that memory and tried to feel the peace and calm flow over him. But it did not come easily. He knew he could not force peace and calm into his mind. That would only defeat the purpose of having peace and calm come into his mind in the first place, and it would make this a pointless exercise. To experience the benefits of that peace and calm, it had to flow naturally over him. It was hard for him to just let things flow. He had always been a take action kind of ranger, and he had always found it difficult to not force things his way. And while he knew that he would be in the thick of the action very soon, it was still not soon enough to suit him. He needed to act. And he needed to act now. Sitting and waiting was making him stir-crazy. On one hand, he was impatient for the Test of the Blades to begin. But on the other, he dreaded it. Even though it was worth the risk, he was not at all eager to put his life on the line, even for the reward of Alana as his bride. He just had to focus on the fact that he did find the reward worth the risk.

His eyes snapped open, for he sensed that he was no longer alone in the little room. He expected that Solara had returned but much to his great surprise, it was not, in fact, the priestess. A different woman entirely, one he had never seen before, gazed at him. At first he thought he was hallucinating. As he thought about it some more, he realized that, when someone hallucinates, the hallucination is of someone or something that he or she already knew. Such hallucinations were fabrications of the mind. That was not the case here. The woman had long blonde hair that was combed back into a loose pony tail. She had deep blue eyes and thin red lips. But the thing that interested Colwyn the most was that, despite the differences in eye and hair color, the woman looked a great deal like Alana. She also wore armor similar to Alana's. It was cut with a similar design, only it was red instead of Alana's rich brown. He studied her for a moment, knitting his brows. There was something that was disturbing about her, but at first he could not put his finger on it.

Then it came to him.

"You're a Blademaster," he blurted. But with the realization came the revelation of what had been bothering him about the woman. "But all of the previous Blademasters are dead. At least, that's what Lady Solara told us."

"Lady Solara was correct, Protector to be," the woman said softly. Even her voice reminded Colwyn of Alana. "But Lady Solara, as is her way, did not tell you everything."

Colwyn didn't like that. He was desperate for any information he could get. "What did she leave out?" He was tired of not being told the whole story. He knew Alana was tired of it as well.

"For instance, she did not tell you about the Legacy of the Blademasters."

"The Legacy of the Blademasters?" Colwyn asked, a frown creasing his rugged features. "What is that? I have never heard of the Legacy of the Blademasters."

"That is not all that surprising, Protector to be," the young woman chuckled. "It's generally not something that is discussed outside of the Temple of the Blades. In fact, other than Lord Taelin and Lady Laeyra, no one outside the Temple of the Blades even knows about it. It is something that we all think would be best kept secret for all of our sakes. If it were general knowledge that the Blademasters and their Protectors could talk to their dead predecessors, well, the people of Calthea might think they were crazy. If that were to happen, then the Blademasters would lose their credibility and thus their ability to work for the people. After all, if they thought they were crazy, the people of Calthea would not trust the Blademasters to work in their best interest, now would they?"

"I agree that you are probably right about what would happen if all of Calthea knew about this," Colwyn said after a long pause. He looked over the apparently dead young woman. "I admit that I'm having a bit of trouble believing it myself, to be perfectly honest." He rubbed his chin. "Who are you anyway? And how can I be sure that you are who you say you are?"

"My apologies," the woman laughed. She held out her hand in a gesture of friendship to Colwyn. "I forget my manners sometimes. It's been so long since I've talked to someone new that I forgot that you and I have not yet been formally introduced. My name is Raven Windrider. I am, or should I say rather, I was the first Blademaster. And you, I already know are the man who is to be the Protector for the new Blademaster. Welcome to my home, the Temple of the Blades."

"Colwyn Starseeker," Colwyn smiled, clasping her hand. He was surprised to find that, not only was her hand solid, but also it was warm to the touch. If she were truly a spirit, it should not have been either. He filed the information away, although he was not yet sure what use such information might be. "But I'm not her Protector yet. I still have not passed the Test of the Blades."

"I know," Raven sighed. She sat down on the bench and patted the spot next to her inviting him to sit with her. "And therein lies the problem. Since you have not yet passed the Test of the Blades, you should not be able to see me at all. It has never happened in the history of the Temple of the Blades that a Protector could experience the Legacy of the Blademasters before he passed the Test of the Blades. Not once. That you can speaks to the prophecies. A dark time is about to come upon the world of Calthea. I do not yet know if you and Alana will be successful in stopping it or not, but I do know that only you and Alana even have a chance. At least, that is what the prophecies say. The next little while will prove to be very dangerous for both of you."

"What do I have to do to keep the dark times from coming upon Calthea, Lady Raven?" Colwyn asked in a subdued tone. He sat down on the bench next to her and looked over at her. The resemblance to his Alana was even more striking from close up. He reached up and wiped a tear from her cheek with his thumb. She smiled up at the kindness he had shown her, but it was a smile tempered with sadness, just the same. "I will do whatever it takes to keep it from happening."

"Gentleness and wisdom," she said softly as she studied him. "Tempered with a strong desire to do what is right. The new Blademaster has chosen her Protector well. You truly do deserve to be among us, Lord Colwyn. I am honored to know you."

"And I am honored to have made your acquaintance, Lady Raven," Colwyn bowed toward her. "What is the Legacy of the Blademasters?"

"It is a long story, but it is an important one. It all started when the order of the Blademasters was first created," Raven started to explain. "Lord Taelin and Lady Laeyra decided that there needed to be some repository of knowledge for successive generations of Blademasters and Protectors. At first they thought of having the goddess Ana, the historian, to chronicle our journeys and house them in a special library in the Temple of the Blades. But there were two problems with this plan. The first problem was that Ana would not agree to take the time out from chronicling all of the events of the world to cull a selective history for use by only a subset of the world's people. The other problem was one of a more practical nature. Lord Taelin knew that the Blademasters and their Protectors would be people of action and would not be the type of people who would sit in a library doing research. Lord Taelin knew that there had to be some other solution to the problem. It was then that Lady Laeyra came up with the idea for the Legacy of the Blademasters."

"What was Lady Laeyra's idea?" Colwyn asked. He was getting very engrossed in the story, because he was fascinated to learn new things. And since this information would potentially be of use to Alana, he was even more motivated to learn it.

"Lady Laeyra decided that the best way for there to be a repository of information for successive generations of Blademasters and Protectors would be to have something of a living library," Raven said quietly. She sighed and looked away from Colwyn. Some of her hair somehow had slipped free of its pony tail, and it fell in front of her face. Colwyn could not tell if she would not look at him because she was upset or because she was embarrassed. "It was decided then that all Blademasters and Protectors would not go to walk with Lord Taelin when they pass into the afterlife. Instead, we would all return to the Temple of the Blades when we die. Here we will spend the afterlife until the time when the Blademasters and Protectors are no longer needed. Here we stay to help future Blademasters and Protectors as they fight the good fight in Lord Taelin's name. We each are responsible for the knowledge concerning the time that we served as Blademaster. And each of us have specific knowledge that we are responsible for from Lady Ana's collected histories. This way, any questions that a Blademaster or a Protector may have, such as the ones that I know you have right now, can be answered by the collected knowledge in the Legacy of the Blademasters. When you and the Lady Alana pass, you, too, will become a part of the Legacy of the Blademasters."

"That's a bit of an eerie thought," Colwyn grunted. "So, let me see if I have this correct. This Legacy of the Blademasters is, in essence, the collected knowledge of pretty much all of Calthea. And it is there for Blademasters and Protectors if they need information to help them complete whatever mission they are on. You are all here to help us. Do I have this right?"

"You indeed have the purpose of the Legacy of the Blademasters correct, Lord Colwyn," Raven nodded. She looked him up and down as if she were sizing him up for some reason. "And now, I sense that you want to ask some of the questions that are on your mind. I can't promise that I will personally have all the answers that you need, but you may ask me anything."

Colwyn rubbed his hands together. *Now we're getting somewhere!*

"I guess I should start with the most pressing concerns," He stretched his arms out in front of him then continued. "What can you tell me about the Test of the Blades?"

The Blademaster

"I can only tell you what my husband, Richard Kale, has told me in the past about the Test of the Blades from when he went through it." She paused before continuing. "And I can only hope that what I tell you will be of some help to you. I can tell you that there are four levels to the dungeons. The Lady Alana will be on the lowest level, so you will have to navigate through all four levels to rescue her. There will be all kinds of monsters in the dungeons that you will have to either kill or avoid. I know that you were worried about certain types of monsters and the monsters in the Test are different every time. I can tell you that there has not been a dragon in the Test of the Blades since the one that my Richard went on. And there are no undead in the Test of the Blades. Since those creatures are of Thraal, they are not able to be summoned to the Temple of the Blades for the Test. The most difficult monster you should have to face should be the one that will be guarding Alana. That one, you will have to kill. There is no way to avoid it. Once you kill that monster and release Alana from her bonds, the Test will be over. Make no mistake. All of the monsters in the Test have murderous intent. If they have an opportunity to kill you, they will take it. So don't feel guilty for dispatching one. Each of them are your enemy."

"I understand that I will fail the Test if I am killed before rescuing Alana," Colwyn nodded. "I promise you that I will not allow that to happen."

"There is a way that you can fail the Test and still survive, Lord Colwyn."

Colwyn did a double-take. This was news to him. Although, after thinking it over for a moment, he did remember Solara's admonition that, if he failed the Test of the Blades and survived, he would not be able to ever see Alana again. He should have realized from that statement that failure did not necessarily mean his death.

It might as well though. A life without Alana would be no life at all.

"You must guard against it," she continued. "There is a trap somewhere in the dungeon that will prevent you from completing the Test. I can tell you that there is a way out of the trap but I do not know what it is. You will have to find the solution for yourself if you end up in that trap." She sighed with a smile. "But I have faith in you, Lord Colwyn. I believe that you will find your way safely through the Test of the Blades. You and your Lady Alana remind me so much of my Richard and myself. I have no doubt at all that you and Alana will turn out to be everything that a Blademaster and a Protector should be. It is good to see fresh blood in the line."

"She gave me her swords so that I would have a tangible reminder of her love as I went through the Test of the Blades," Colwyn said softly. "It is going to be so strange to go into battle with someone else's weapons and not my own. But at the same time, it will be a comfort to have a reminder of her love with me."

"I did much the same thing for my Richard when he went through the Test," Raven chuckled. "It is fitting that your Alana has made the same decision that I did when I was in her position." She turned her eyes back upon Colwyn. "But be honest with me, Lord Colwyn. It is not really the Test of the Blades that is bothering you. You know as well as I do that you will pass the Test of the Blades."

"True enough," Colwyn nodded with a chuckle. "I know that her love will guide me and protect me. Still, a little extra advance knowledge can't hurt anything."

"What is it that is really bothering you, Lord Colwyn?" Raven asked softly. She smiled at him. "Perhaps it is something I can help with. That is, after all, the reason for the Legacy of the Blademasters."

"Very well. It is this mission that Lord Balaam has sent Alana and I on," Colwyn said as he stood and paced back and forth across the little room. "I know that we are supposed to be investigating the death of a young priestess of Taelin. But to be honest, I'm not even sure where to start looking for the answers. I have no idea where we are supposed to go to complete our mission. And besides that, I have this nagging feeling that there is a lot more to this mission than Alana and I are being told. I feel like a lot is being hidden from us."

"I know of your mission, and I can tell you a great deal about it," the young Blademaster said softly. It lifted Colwyn's heart a little bit to know that he might soon have some of the answers that he and Alana would need. Her face, though, bore something of a dazed look as she continued. "You need to understand that it will be a very dangerous journey for the both of you. And yes, there is a great deal more about your journey that you need to know than you have been told up to this point. I will tell you what I can about where you are going and what you will face when you get there. You will have to decide for yourself what you will do with the information. I will start by telling you that your destination is the city of Tornith."

"I know next to nothing about the city of Tornith," Colwyn frowned as he continued to pace. "What can you tell me about the city?"

"The city of Tornith is in the northern most reaches of the region of Calthea known as Dracomyr," Raven began. "The city is a stronghold for the forces of the Dark God Thraal. The Dark God has his largest ziggurat in all of Calthea in that city. It is where his High Priest lives and where he practices his demonic sacrifices to the Dark God. Tornith is a city sacred to the ideals of evil. Our Lord Taelin does have a small temple dedicated to him in that dark city. But for the most part, the only people who revere Lord Taelin in Tornith are the priests that live in the Temple of the White. You and the rest of your party will need to have your wits about you. And I think it would help you if you had a touch of the luck of the Lady Laeyra with you as well. Although she is as reviled as Lord Taelin is in Tornith."

"Wonderful," Colwyn grumbled. He ran his fingers along the hilts of the two long swords that Alana had given him to wear during the Test of the Blades. "This certainly sounds like a mission that I'm absolutely going to hate. What else can you tell me?"

"The woman whose death you are investigating was indeed sacrificed to Thraal," Raven continued after a few moments' pause. "But then, I think you already thought that would be the case. I won't tell you exactly what the High Priest of Thraal does during his sacrifices, because you would probably have trouble getting a good night's sleep. Let me just say this: It was not at all pleasant for the young woman who was sacrificed. After the sacrifice, something very odd happened. Thraal possessed the body of the young woman, and he spoke to the High Priest, using Merinda's voice to deliver his message. At that time, Thraal foretold the fact that there would be a Blademaster walking the world once more. Thraal did not know who the Blademaster is, so he could not tell his High Priest Alana's identity. I have learned, though, that the High Priest of Thraal has since discovered Alana's identity. Thraal has promised his High Priest that, if he were to be able to sacrifice the Blademaster to Thraal, he would help to free the Dark God from his prison. The Dark God would then be free to once more walk the world of Calthea and wreak the kind of havoc that only the Dark God can wreak. That is the goal, and the High Priest of Thraal is solely dedicated to bringing it to pass."

"That's not going to happen if I have anything to say about it," Colwyn snarled. "No one is going to sacrifice the woman that I love to Thraal."

"It will not be easy to stop it from happening, Lord Colwyn," Raven shrugged. "I will now tell you about the High Priest of Thraal. The High Priest of Thraal is a lich named Drakkhous. I do not know anything about his life before he became a lich. I am sure that one of the other Blademasters here does have that information. I'll be honest though. I don't know that having the information of what Drakkhous was before he became a lich would be of any help to you whatsoever. I am going to assume that you have not encountered a lich before in your travels, as they are very rare creatures. So I will tell you what I can about these foul creatures so that you will be as prepared as you can be to deal with this one. A lich is an undead creature that is the restored spirit of a mortal being, usually a human or an elf. Usually, the lich makes some sort of dark deal to have apparent immortality. The lich can be killed, but not through disease or old age. The only way a lich can be killed is for another being to physically kill it. Liches are the most brutal of all the undead, far more dangerous even than the mythic vampires. The touch of a lich drains the strength and vitality from the victim. But the touch of a lich has an even more insidious affect. The touch of a lich can drain off all the hope in a person. There are a number of recorded cases where the touch of a lich itself did not kill the person. But the person took their own life later, because they had no hope left inside to go on."

Colwyn paled as Raven described the lich. It was not a confrontation that he was looking forward to. And yet, deep down he knew he would not be the one to face off with the lich. It would be Alana who would be forced to face the lich when the time came. The thought upset and depressed him, and he vowed not to let her fight the lich on her own. Somehow, when the time came for that battle, he would find a way to make a difference, even if he did not yet know how he could be of use. His next thought was no less distressing for him, even if it seemed to be a way out of the predicament for the woman he loved.

"You said that the lich wants to sacrifice Alana to Thraal?" he asked, feeling a touch of guilt for even entertaining what many would consider a cowardly stance. When Raven nodded, he continued. "Well, then we won't have to face the lich at all. If Thraal needs Alana to be sacrificed to him in order to be freed from his prison, then the solution is simple. We just don't go to Tornith. If she's not there to be sacrificed, then she can't be sacrificed. Problem solved."

"If only it were truly that easy, Lord Colwyn, but I'm afraid that it's not anywhere near so simple." Raven stood from the bench and glanced over to where Colwyn was pacing. She shook her head sadly and sighed again. "The lich will keep coming for her, sending out groups of his followers to capture her as he has already done."

Colwyn nodded. "Like in Valendale."

"Precisely. If she does not go to Tornith voluntarily, one of the teams that he sends will eventually succeed in capturing her and they will take her to Tornith anyway, possibly without any of her companions.

"And if we go to Tornith on our own to investigate the sacrifice, at least we do it on our own terms," Colwyn finished. "And that way we will all be sure to be there for Alana."

Raven nodded. "Also, there is a member of your party who has a task in Tornith that only he or she can accomplish, and this task can only be accomplished in Tornith. I do not know what the task is, nor do I know who must complete it. What I can tell you is that this task is separate from the primary reason for going to Tornith. While I can not be sure, I can tell you that I do not believe that this task is for either you or Alana to complete."

"You spoke of Valendale earlier, Lady Raven. Do you know why the city was so empty when we passed through it? Only the sage Isaiah and the lich's men were in the city." Colwyn stopped pacing and looked at Raven. There was pain and sorrow in his eyes, and it was clear that he was grieving for friends who had once resided in the city. "It was very distressing to see the city so empty. I know a great number of the people who live in Valendale. Alana and I want very much to help those people out if we can."

"I'm afraid that I don't know what happened to them, Lord Colwyn," Raven said with a frown. "I do think that if you and Alana survive what is ahead of you in Tornith that it will become clear to you what happened to them. Perhaps then you can help the people of Valendale. In the meantime, I will ask the others if they have any information with regards to what has happened to them." Raven stopped and stood rock still. She cocked her ear, listening to a sound that was far off. Too far off for Colwyn to make out what it was. "Lady Solara is coming," she whispered. "I must go. She must not find out that you and I have been speaking, although I am sure she already knows. Nothing in the Temple happens without her knowledge. But it would cause a great deal of trouble for the both of us if she were to see us talking before you pass the Test. So I will go now. Good journey to you, Lord Colwyn. May the wisdom of Lord Taelin and the luck of Lady Laeyra guide you and protect you as you go through the Test of the Blades and during your journey to Tornith. We will not speak again until after you have passed the Test of the Blades and have married Alana. I know that you will be well and that you will pass the Test. Lady Alana is a lucky Blademaster to have you by her side. I will do my best to find the answers you seek by the time I see you next."

Raven stepped backwards and faded through the wall of the room, causing Colwyn to blink twice. He turned back towards the door, for he could now hear the foot falls that Raven had spoken of.

The time had come for the Test of the Blades to begin. There would be no more putting it off. Despite the fact that he had not been able to recapture the peace or the calm he had found while he was in stát ndoimhneacht na tsíocháin inmheánach, he knew that he was ready for the Test of the Blades. At least as ready as he was ever going to be. He also had a far better idea of what the consequences for failure would be, and he knew that he could not fail the Test. There was so much that rode on his ability to successfully navigate the four levels of the dungeon and find and rescue Alana. It was far more than just his ability to marry the woman that he loved that was at stake. He knew that he would not be able to protect Alana in Tornith if he were not allowed to continue to travel with her. He could not bear to think about what could happen to her if he were not there with her when she went to confront the lich in Tornith. He had given her his vow that he would protect her, no matter what happened. And while he knew that William, Meryn and Balaam were very capable as far as being able to help her, he also had to admit that it was deeply personal to him that he continue to help her. It would be different had he not given his vow, but the fact was that he had and it was a vow that he had no intention of breaking.

The door swung open and Solara Moonfire entered the room. She scrutinized the young ranger and nodded once, apparently pleased with what she saw. She glided across the room and placed her hand on his shoulder.

"It is time, Lord Colwyn," she said softly. "Are you prepared to risk your life to rescue Alana in the Test of the Blades?"

"I'm not ready," the ranger admitted with a sigh. He turned his raptor gaze to the High Priestess. "But let's get it over with anyway."

"Then follow me to the dungeons," she ordered. She turned and drifted out of the room, not even looking back to see if he was following her.

Colwyn took one more look at the wall that Raven had vanished through. He wondered if he had imagined all that he had seen and heard. He knew he hadn't imagined it, but that sill didn't mean that he truly believed it either. He shook his head in disbelief one more time before following the High Priestess of the Blades out of the room towards the dungeons where the Test of the Blades and the woman he loved awaited him.

The Blademaster

Chapter XI
The Test of the Blades

Large banquet table had been brought into the Great Hall of the Temple of the Blades. The table was heaping over with food. Solara had come back into the Great Hall about an hour before and told the three companions that Colwyn would be taking the Test of the Blades. She also told them that it would be some time before Colwyn and Alana returned to the Great Hall and that they should make themselves comfortable while they waited. The food was for them to enjoy until Colwyn and Alana returned... If they returned. There seemed to be some question on that matter. Still, she assured them that there would be plenty of food. As they ate the food plate by plate, the serving platters constantly replenished themselves. It was a magic that William had heard of, and had even seen firsthand on occasion. He wondered who in the Temple of the Blades might have been able to cast such a spell. Solara? Not likely. Casting spells of that nature were not among the normal abilities of a priestess. Of course, Solara was the High Priestess of the Blades and might have abilities beyond what he might expect. It was a line of thought that he found worthy of exploration and he decided to discuss the matter with Balaam at later time.

William was a tad concerned about Colwyn taking part in the Test of the Blades. His studies in the Tower of the Inner Circle had always indicated that the Test of the Blades was an especially dangerous undertaking. He was pretty sure that his friend was up to the challenge, but still, he was concerned. He truly hoped that the young ranger would pass the Test and therefore go on to marry Alana. He believed that the two of them were truly meant to be together. He could only hope that he would one day again experience that kind of love.

It was not that he did not love Meryn, for he loved the halfling very much. And he knew that he would be happy to be with her if that was his destiny. But there was still someone that he loved more than Meryn. He missed Silvestra Knightwing far too much for comfort. He did not know if he would ever see the fair maiden with the silver hair again, but he felt that only Silvestra could provide the depth of love and intimacy that he craved whenever he spied at Colwyn and Alana together. He hoped that he would one day see her again. But of course, that would hurt Meryn very much. It was unfortunate. But if Silvestra was to ever come back into his life, he would not wish to be with anyone but her. He was not entirely sure how the silver haired maiden felt, but he suspected that she did, indeed, feel the same way as he did. He wondered if he would ever know for sure. He pulled the small heartstone that he wore around his neck and looked at it once more. He glanced at it from time to time hoping beyond hope that it would change. And yet, it never did. Even now, it hung dull and lifeless on its chain. Even though he had been told that Silvestra had died during a mission – and surely the dead heartstone would seem to prove that to be the case – he still held out hope that, despite appearances to the contrary, she was still alive somewhere and that it was all a trick.

There was no chance at peace for the young mage until he knew for sure one way or the other.

William could still remember how it felt the day that he had first met Silvestra. There was something special about the young woman. Something deep and ancient in her blue eyes, a wisdom far beyond her apparent years. It was an ageless quality that William had found both endearing and enchanting. It was also a bit unnerving at first. But when he had first learned the truth about who and what she was, he had not been scared off as she had expected. Instead, his feelings blossomed. They flowed through him, making him stronger of mind and spirit. In essence, the love that he shared with Silvestra made him an even better mage than he already was. It allowed him to keep his focus on his magic. It was much like the way a Blademaster's abilities were bound up in the love she had for her Protector. Before Silvestra, his focus had always been prone to wander to less important things.

Even though she was not currently a part of his life, he was still able to use that love as a focus for his magic. He had felt all along that, if he held tight to that love, one day she would reappear. He had no basis for that feeling. But he still clung to it. It was a strange bit of circumstance though. By all rights, he should not have been able to still use the love he had once shared with Silvestra to focus his magic, but he was doing just that. If asked, he could not explain why he was able to do so. But he was thankful for the focus the love still provided. He suspected that, if he was right about the focus being similar to the binding of a Blademaster's abilities, it might mean that Silvestra was alive somewhere. He hoped so. Despite the love he still held close and the focus it instilled in him, William still longed to once again hold the woman he loved.

As hard as it was for him to do, he pushed the thoughts of Silvestra to the back of his mind as he watched the little halfling saunter over to where he was sitting on the altar's raised dais. She was carrying two plates of food. He assumed, naturally, that one of the plates was for him. With Meryn, it was hard to tell what was going through her mind at any given point, More often than not, her companions found this to be something of an annoyance. There were a great number of things in William's life that were far easier than trying to understand the mind of a halfling. Still and all, he was the only member of the party that even seemed to want to care about what the halfling might think about or want.

"Hello, Little One," William said softly to the halfling, a warm smile spreading across his face. He patted spot on the dais next to him, offering her a chance to sit down and talk to him. The halfling gave him one of the plates and sat down next to him. He knew that there was something bothering her, because she had been uncharacteristically quiet. William had a sneaking suspicion that it had to do with the Test of the Blades. "What is it that's bothering you, Little One?"

"I'm worried about Lord Colwyn and Lady Alana," Meryn admitted in a mumble. She nibbled on the end of a sausage, something that caught William's attention. She did not seem to have her usual appetite, another indication that she was deeply troubled. If things were normal, she would be scarfing down plate after plate of food from the banquet table. Yet, here she was still on her first place of food and she was only nibbling on the end of a sausage. She sighed before she continued. "Just how much danger are they in, William?"

William looked over the plate that she had handed him. She had collected a good selection of some of his favorite foods. He pushed some potatoes around the plate with the end of a sausage as he thought about how best to answer the halfling's question without causing too much concern. He shrugged and then bit the sausage in half, chewing thoughtfully in an attempt to gain a bit more time to think. It was somewhat distressing to see the usually talkative halfling so subdued. It almost forced him to rethink what he thought about how much danger Colwyn was in. Still, the young ranger was more than capable. He could handle whatever the Test of the Blades threw at him.

William put his arm around the halfling's shoulders. She buried her face in his side and started to cry. It was then that William truly realized just how worried and upset

Meryn was about Colwyn and the Test of the Blades. He wondered idly if the ranger would be at all amused to know just how much the little halfling was worried about him. He imagined Colwyn would be quite perturbed to know that she was crying over him. It was an amusing thought. He would have to tell Colwyn about how much the halfling was concerned about him. He would relish the look on the ranger's face.

"It is true that Colwyn is in a fair bit of danger in the Test of the Blades, Meryn," William said softly, measuring his words carefully. "But you have to know that with his ability to marry Alana on the line, Colwyn is going to do whatever he has to in order to make sure he pushes through just fine. Colwyn is a very resourceful young man, and you know as well as I do that he's not going to let anything stand in the way of his marrying Alana. I'm sure that Colwyn will be just fine. He and Alana will be back soon safe and sound. You'll see."

The halfling did not look up at him. Instead, she continued to sob into the fabric of his robe. The young mage wished there was something he could say to ease her worries. He suspected that Colwyn would successfully complete the Test of the Blades. He was also well aware that the stakes were higher than merely having the spouse of one's choice. He was now aware that some of the prophecies he knew were about his two friends. He would not tell them though, for he did not feel that hearing any of those prophecies would be of any help to them. If it turned out differently later on, he would tell them at that time. But not before. In all honesty, those prophecies scared him a little bit. He could only hope that the prophecies had a different meaning than what he and other mages thought they did. Such a thing was, in fact, a definite possibility. It was fairly common for prophecies to be misunderstood or misinterpreted. While it was true that prophecies generally came true, it was not always fulfilled in the way that was expected. William had once heard of a prophecy of a young woman, in which it was told that she would be killed by lions. The woman's city was captured by invaders, and the young women of the city were taken prisoner. It was widely known that these invaders had a tendency to feed their captives to their lions when they had outlived their usefulness. The woman had heard of the prophecy and had expected that the prophecy meant that she would be fed to the invader's lions if she remained captive. In an effort to prevent the fulfillment of the prophecy, she escaped. In the middle of the woods, not all that far from where she had escaped from her captors, she was surprised by a wild lion. The lion killed and devoured her. In this way, the prophecy had come true, although not in the way that she had expected it to. This, William had been instructed, was the danger of speaking a prophecy aloud to the people involved in the prophecy when it wasn't necessary. The woman could have, perhaps, lived a long time under her captor's rule. There were, he knew, exceptions to this rule, and if he knew that revealing a prophecy would be of help to his friends, he would certainly reveal to Colwyn and Alana the prophecies that pertained to them. For now, though, he was not convinced the knowledge would be of any help. And so, he would keep what he knew to himself. At least for now.

Besides these prophecies, he already knew what their destination was, although he did not believe that Colwyn and Alana knew what awaited them there. He did not like their destination one bit. And he did not think that Tornith would be a good a place to go. But he also knew that, regardless of his feelings, there was no escaping going to Tornith, for it was the only place where they had a chance to stop Thraal. It would be a very dangerous place for them, however. The prophecies did not actually reveal whether they would be successful in Tornith, but that actually did not bother him because he knew that there were probably a great many prophecies about Alana and Colwyn that he was unaware of. But he also knew that Alana and Colwyn were the best at what they did. So he would trust them to finish their mission and he would hope that trust was not misplaced.

He also knew that he would do whatever was required to ensure their success. He did not relish the alternative.

He gazed down at the halfling. She was still sobbing into his side, soaking the soft material of his robe with her tears. He gently patted her on the back, in an attempt to comfort her. As unsettling as it was for the halfling to not chatter on end about whatever it was that was on her mind, it was even more unsettling for William to see her cry like this. Thinking about it, he could not remember ever having seen Meryn cry in this way before.

"It's going to be all right, Little One," he whispered. She looked up at him with big wet eyes and smiled sadly at him. He reached over and messed up her hair. "You know everything will be all right with those two. If anyone can make things work, it's them,"

"I suppose that I shouldn't worry about Lord Colwyn so much," she said. "I just can't imagine what it would be like if he weren't here. I mean, think about it. First of all, Lady Alana would be so very sad if he were to die. I would not like for her to be sad like that. It would bring the rest of us down. That would not be good at all. I think that we need to make sure that she stays happy. I'm just not sure what we can do about that if Colwyn were to die in the Test. Besides. As much as he doesn't trust me, I would hate to not have him around. Don't ever tell him I said so, but I really like the big guy." She turned her face away from William and started to nibble on the end of the sausage again. "Do you see why I'm so worried now?"

"I can definitely understand, Little One," William nodded. He pulled her close to his side. "And I worry too. But if anyone can make it through this, it is those two. I have complete faith in them."

"I wish I did," Meryn sighed as she buried her face in his robes again. "I just wish I did. I hate worrying like this."

"I know, Little One," William nodded. "Not many people like it."

William took another bite of his sausage and continued to hold the halfling His thoughts were with Colwyn and Alana, of course, but he just could not shake the feeling that something was about to go wrong.

There were few things in life that Alana truly hated. One of the things that she despised more than anything was being tied up. It had always been so. When Solara had told her and Colwyn what would be involved in the Test of the Blades, she knew that it would be hard for her to submit to it. When Solara had taken her down to the room where she would wait for Colwyn to rescue her, she fought the need to bind her to the wall. But Solara had won out in the end, reminding her that if Alana did not submit, the Test of the Blades could not continue. And so Alana had allowed herself be bound to the wall of the little room. It was not something that pleased her by any stretch of the imagination. Nothing about this whole situation made her happy at all. She felt like a pawn on a chessboard about to be sacrificed for a king. She had no idea what she could do to make her life her own again. Being a Blademaster – and perhaps even more frightful, being the first of a whole new line of Blademasters – really did not seem to be something that would afford her any sort of a normal life. But she also knew that there was nothing she could do about it.

But her becoming the Blademaster could very well mean the difference between life and death for a great many people.

Wasn't that worth something?

The High Priestess of the Blades had left the little stone room without saying anything more once Alana had been tied up. The woman had likely gone to get Colwyn for the beginning of the Test of the Blades. There was nothing more that she could do for him to help now. The man she loved was on his own. All she could do now was wait for him to come bursting through that door.

But when the creature arrived to guard her, that's when she realized Colwyn would be in real trouble.

Said creature could be nothing else but a beholder, she decided. She had heard about beholders, but she had never seen one before. Many tales from her youth had described the creatures. And, naturally, she had heard just how powerful they were. She had hoped to never meet one in her lifetime. But that was not to be, it seemed. The beholder was an ugly creature with many eyestalks growing from its massive round body. Each eyestalk was capable of casting a different spell when it gazed at its enemy. Its body was spherical and grey and the eye stalks were red. Overall, it was a disturbing sight that Alana did not prefer to look upon. But this was to be her companion until Colwyn came for her.

"You must be the Blademaster," the beholder said in a voice that was as gravelly sounding as its body appeared.

"That is what they tell me," Alana grunted as she pulled at her bindings. "How about you just let me go and we call it a day?"

"That is not going to happen," the beholder said. "I am going to enjoy killing your so-called Protector. I hope he doesn't make it too easy. When I am done with him, I will devour you for dessert."

"It won't be anywhere near as easy as you think," Alana snorted. "Colwyn is very hard to kill."

"Things that may be hard for others come easy to a beholder," the creature laughed. It was not a pleasant sound at all, and Alana flinched when she heard it. "Killing people comes far too easy to my kind. Your so-called Protector will be nothing to me."

"You think you know my Colwyn, but you don't," Alana breathed. The calming influence of knowing what Solara had told them about Colwyn having to be her true love coursed through her veins. "Colwyn will come for me. And he will find a way to defeat you."

"That remains to be seen," the beholder chuckled. "For now, let us see how your so-called Protector does in the maze of the dungeons."

The largest of the eyestalks swiveled to a blank wall and a beam of light shot out from it and hit the wall. Alana could see the entrance to the dungeon. After a few moments, the High Priestess of the Blades and the man she loved entered the scene.

"The Test of the Blades is not an easy task, Colwyn Starseeker," the voice of the High Priestess rang out clearly from the image.

Alana watched in rapt fascination as the scene unfolded...

"The Test of the Blades is not an easy task, Colwyn Starseeker," Solara said from the entrance of the dungeon.

"I must ask you one more time if you are ready for this task and for all that it will entail, both if you succeed and if you fail."

Colwyn fixed the High Priestess of the Blades with his raptor-like gaze for several long seconds. He had followed her down from the little room where he and Alana had discussed the Test, without saying a word to her. It was silly, but he almost felt as if saying anything would drain the peace and calm that he had worked so hard to build up when he was in stát ndoimhneacht na tsíocháin inmheánach. The task would be difficult at best and he would need to keep his wits about him. In order to do that, he would have to retain the calm and focus he had achieved. But now, standing in the entrance to the dungeon located in the Temple of the Blades, he could no longer keep his silence.

"Yes, I am certain that this is what I wish to do," Colwyn said with a nod. "And I am sure that I am as ready for the Test of the Blades as I ever will be. The woman I love is counting on me. I shall not let her down."

"The dungeons in play in the Test of the Blades are four levels deep," Solara said softly. "You must fight your way through all four levels. Alana is on the lowermost of the levels and she is guarded by the toughest beast of all. Your task is to defeat her guard and rescue her. There is no time limit but the longer you take, the harder it will be to complete."

"I understand," Colwyn said. "I am ready."

"The Test ends when either you rescue Alana or you are incapable of continuing because you are either dead or incapacitated. The Test begins now."

Colwyn watched as the High Priestess of the Blades slipped back down the corridor and sealed the entrance to the dungeon. He turned to check down the corridor in the other direction and sighed to himself. He did not see anything in the hallway as far as opposition, but he knew that would not be the case for very long. He just had to keep his wits about him for the next few hours and try not to be surprised by anything that came at him. First things first, though. There were certain things he could do that would immediately increase his chances of success. He pulled two small stones from a pouch on his belt. One was his finder's stone, and the other was the trap finder stone that Mirian Kovalani had given him in the Elven Woods. He knew what to expect from the finder's stone, but he wished he had had time to experiment with the trap finder stone before he actually needed to use it.

"Find the most direct route to where Alana is being held," he said softly to the finder's stone.

The stone obediently leapt from his hand and orbited his head. After a few moments, the finder's stone settled in the direction that Colwyn had to go. Not that there was a whole lot of choice. From here, there was only one direction. Still, it was a comfort to know that there would be guidance for him when it came time to make a choice of direction. He knew that the finder's stone would help him out later on, at any rate.

The trap finder stone, on the other hand, he was not so sure about.

He sighed at the small red stone. As he turned the stone over in his hand, he thought about the conversation with Mirian Kovalani when she had given the stone to him

"So, you are determined to go through with this even though it could cost you your life?" Mirian turned back to him, her huge green eyes full of tears.

Colwyn nodded. "I do. I belong by Alana's side, no matter what it is she faces. And I have a feeling she is going to need me."

"Oh, of that I have no doubt." Mirian shook her head. She held a small red stone out to Colwyn. "Take this, Colwyn. It is a trap finder stone. It will come in very handy."

"What does it do?" Colwyn asked, raising his eyebrow.

"It is much like the finder stone I gave you. This stone will light up when a trap is about to spring on you and will light up the brightest when you are inside of a trap," she said softly. "You will find it very useful where you are going."

"I suppose," the ranger shrugged. "We're both actually very good at..."

"It is a very rare stone," she added, again interrupting him. "Not very many of my rangers even carry one," Mirian smiled. "I give it to you as a pledge of my fealty to you. And to Alana."

Colwyn smiled. "Thank you Mirian," he said as he took the stone from her. "Thanks for everything."

Sudden realization hit him hard. *She knew!*

She knew exactly what Alana and I would be going through when we got here. She knew and she didn't tell me. Why didn't she tell me? Colwyn's mind searched. *She probably was forbidden to tell us just like Balaam and Isaiah were. Still. I would have liked a little warning before coming here like this. Although, to be fair, if I had known, would I have let Alana come here?*

The question disturbed him so he focused on the red stone in his hand. He would have to depend on this gift from the elf queen. He could not be sure about her motivations, but he did not think that she would have given him such a valuable gift had she not intended for it to be of help to him. Still, he wondered how the trap finder stone was going to come in handy in a situation like this.

"Locate traps," he said softly, and the trap finder stone floated out of his hand to join the finder's stone. The stone pulsed gently and softly. He suspected that the calm throb of light was probably a good sign.

He took a deep breath before drawing Alana's two long swords from their sheaths.

With great trepidation, Colwyn Starseeker started down the corridor.

Balaam was struggling with his own turmoil. He knew what was happening in the dungeons, but he still had his doubts that Colwyn would be acceptable as a Protector. There was something about the young man that the priest found grating. But he also understood that the person that was to be Alana's Protector was not a choice for him to make. It was a choice that Lord Taelin would have to make, and he would have to live with that decision.

That did not mean that he had to like it though.

He stood in a corner of the Great Hall, away from everyone else. He did not partake of the banquet. Somehow it felt wrong to eat and drink while the Blademaster was down in the dungeons having her life's path determined. It was not something that he thought Lord Taelin would be happy to allow. Then again, a lot of things seemed to be happening that he did not think Lord Taelin would happily permit.

Such as Balaam becoming High Priest to Taelin.

Since Caiaphas had appointed Balaam to the post of High Priest, he had spent a lot of time wondering about why he had been named to the post. He had lost a lot of sleep trying to work it out. But second guessing the will of his god was not the most productive way to spend his time. Besides, Lord Taelin was the one who truly decided who would be his High Priest. Still, Balaam was one of those who needed to know the why behind things. It was a curse that had always plagued him. Most of the time, such concerns did not cause him too much trouble, but now it was plaguing him with sleepless nights. Most annoying!

What is it about me that Lord Taelin thinks is even remotely worthy of becoming his High Priest? Balaam asked himself. *There has to be some reason why I was selected to be the High Priest over, say, Naomi. I wish I knew what it was.*

"The will of the gods is not for mortal men to know, my dear Lord Balaam," a soft male voice said from the shadows behind him.

Balaam whipped around, too shocked that someone was able to sneak up behind him in the Great Hall like that to even grab for his mace. Standing behind him in a rose colored tunic and black breeches was an old man that no priest of Taelin could fail to recognize. He sank to his knees and bowed low to the old man.

"Lord Taelin," he breathed reverently. "I meant no disrespect to you, my lord. I only wished to understand why you chose me to lead your priesthood instead of others who are far more worthy of that honor."

"It is not wrong to question, my child," Taelin smiled at the priest. He motioned for Balaam to rise, and the young man reluctantly came to his feet. He kept his head bowed before the older man, not wishing to look his god in the eyes. "And rest assured that I have my reasons. It is not for you to know all of them, but I can tell you this: I have a task for you that you alone can complete. And you must do so as my High Priest."

"But why me?" Balaam asked softly. "Why couldn't Naomi or any of the others do it?"

Taelin looked the young man over with an amused expression on his face. The god put his hand on the young man's arm. It was a touch meant to comfort and show that Balaam was loved. Balaam recoiled a bit, shocked that his god would actually touch him in that way. He gazed down at the god's hand with a sigh.

"The reason that it has to be you is that you are the priest with the most vested interest in the situation," Taelin said quietly. The smile he turned on his High Priest was filled with sadness. "Do you know the First Law of the Blades, Lord Balaam?"

"Yes, my lord." Balaam nodded. "It is written that your priesthood must follow the Law of the Blades every bit as much as the Blademasters do. I do my best to follow the Law of the Blades."

"Very good." Taelin nodded in return. Then he sighed deeply. "Unfortunately, the First Law of the Blades, while straightforward, is also a double edged sword."

"I don't understand," Balaam said with a frown. "How could love be a bad thing?"

"You, of all of my priests, should be able to answer that the best, I think," Taelin replied. "How did you feel when Caiaphas told you that Merinda Delwyn had been sacrificed to the Dark God?"

"Miserable," Balaam muttered, his voice shaky. He looked down at his boots so that his god would not see the tears streaming down his face.

"I dare say that that is not all you felt," Taelin said. "You wanted to go to Tornith to tear the High Priest of Thraal limb from limb." He fixed Balaam with his gaze. "Am I not correct?"

"I did," Balaam grunted, turning away from his god. "It was not a feeling fit for someone who would be your High Priest, Lord Taelin."

"Of course it was and is," Taelin admonished. "I can't have someone guide my priesthood who is afraid of being human. Your feelings of anger and hatred and your lust for revenge are natural human reactions. What sets you apart from other humans is that you have to control your emotions so that the lust for revenge doesn't take over. I will tell you this one thing. You must learn the rest for yourself. You cannot give in to revenge when you get to Tornith. You must not seek out the High Priest of Thraal yourself. If you do, you will fail. And then we will lose the Blademaster. You must trust in me that revenge for Merinda's death is not the course of action I wish for you to take."

"I understand, my Lord," Balaam sighed. "I promise you that I will not seek to destroy him, although I still wish to."

"Use that righteous rage," Taelin urged. "It will come in very handy in the future. But do not give into your desire for revenge, regardless of circumstance. I know that you will find your true path."

"You have given me a great deal to think about, my Lord Taelin," Balaam whispered reverently.

"That is my job as your god, Balaam." Taelin laughed merrily. "But know this, my child. No matter what path your life takes, I will always be waiting for you at the end of the path where you will walk with me. And so will Merinda Delwyn."

"I will keep your words in mind, my lord," Balaam bowed.

When he stood back up, the old man was gone. Vanished without a sound. Balaam glanced around, sure that he had not imagined that the god was there, but at the same time, he still could not be sure that it was not his imagination. But then Lightbringer's words resounded in his head, and he knew that he would have to keep the promise he made to his god.

"Nothing is ever easy," the priest grunted.

Colwyn was slightly out of breath. He had run a good portion of the way through the first level of the dungeon, and had faced minimal resistance. He had run through two orcs before they had even had a change to attack and dispatched a wild boar that had charged him as soon as it had seen him. Colwyn had sidestepped the charge and sliced the boar open from head to tail, its viscera spilling out onto the stone floor of the corridor. But there had been no more difficult opposition than that. It bothered him that the monsters he was facing in the dungeon were fairly easily disposed of. The Test of the Blades should not be quite this easy. Perhaps there would be far more difficult opposition on the lower levels.

He only hoped that he was up for the challenge.

He turned a corner and skidded to a halt. He saw the entrance to a downward stairwell ahead. Blocking the way was a wyvern in flight. The wyvern had not yet seen him but as soon as it did it would be all over him. Wyverns were vicious and deadly. He would have to act fast. Although he could tell that this particular wyvern was young, the poison in its stinger would still be lethal enough to kill him. He ducked back around the corner and sheathed his long swords. Then he pulled the bow from his back and nocked an arrow to the string. Closing his eyes, he said a quick and silent prayer to both Taelin and Laeyra to guide his hand. He would get only one shot. He would have to make it count.

Quick as a wink, he rounded the corner again. This time, the wyvern saw him as he came around the corner, but Colwyn was faster. The shot was already lined up. As he let the arrow fly, he knew that he wouldn't even have to watch to see where the arrow hit. It was a perfect shot, and Colwyn knew it. The only question that Colwyn had was whether or not the shot would kill the wyvern instantly.

The arrow hit the wyvern directly in the heart, and the beast fell to the ground with a thud.

Colwyn waited for it to finish its death throes before he approached it. It twitched violently a few times before going still. He waited until the beast was still, because he knew that a sting from the wyvern as it thrashed about could kill him just as sure as if the beast had directed the sting at him. He dared not risk the possibility of getting killed by carelessly approaching the beast too soon. After the beast went still, he pulled the arrow out and cleaned it before returning it to his quiver. Then he stepped around the wyvern, passing it by the side where its head lay and stepped cautiously towards the stairwell.

He flattened himself against the wall by the stairwell and peered down the stairs. He did not see anything in view at the other end of the stairwell, but he could tell that the stairwell opened into a room rather than a corridor, which did not bode well. He imagined there was an enemy right around the corner from the stairwell exit. If he was right then the enemy would be in a perfect spot for an ambush.

And in Colwyn's experience, it never hurt to err on the cautious side.

Quietly, he slid his two long swords out of their sheaths and crept down the stairs.

The attack came without warning just before he left the stairwell.

A giant kobold, easily twice the size of a normal kobold and armed with a sword, leapt into the doorway of the stairwell and took a swing at Colwyn's legs. Fighting on a stairway is not the easiest thing to do, especially when your opponent is below. Colwyn grunted as he leapt over the strike. He kicked out with his right foot and caught the kobold square in the jaw, staggering it back. It wasn't a terrible blow but it was enough for Colwyn to slip down the rest of the stairs and face the kobold on more level footing. And once he was on the same level as the kobold, it was even more clear just how large his opponent was. Colwyn was not a small man, but the kobold easily had six inches on him. Kobolds were usually roughly the size of a halfling. Colwyn had never seen a kobold so large. As he blocked a clumsy attack from the beast's sword, he wondered for a moment how a kobold could grow to such a size before he decided he didn't really care. All he wanted to do was to defeat it and move on.

The kobold swung again at Colwyn, this time aiming for the ranger's arm. Colwyn leaned back and blocked the attack, catching the kobold's blade near the cross guard of his own. He flicked to the right, forcefully flicking the kobold's blade away and he followed it with a strike from his other sword, the blade biting deep into the kobold's forearm, drawing first blood.

The kobold screamed and launched an attack at Colwyn's head, a massive downward strike that, if it had connected, would have cleaved Colwyn's skull in two.

Fortunately, the strike never reached Colwyn. Instead, he caught the kobold's blade between his two blades and held it in place, his forearms straining with the effort. To break the stalemate, he lashed out with a wicked kick to the kobold's groin that connected solidly. The kobold dropped his sword and doubled over. Colwyn seized the opportunity and thrust his swords upward, puncturing through bone and muscle before cleaving the beast's heart in two.

He watched the kobold fall and slumped down to sit on the floor. It was by far the hardest combat he had faced so far during the Test of the Blades. He wanted to catch his breath before continuing.

"Search the kobold," a male voice whispered in the breeze. All he could tell about the voice was that it was male. He could not make out either the pitch or the timbre of the voice.

Colwyn glanced around, but there was no one else in the room. He frowned, wondering if he had imagined the voice.

"Search the kobold," the voice came again. This time, however, it said more. "There is something that the kobold has that you will need."

"Who are you?" Colwyn gasped. "And why would you help me?"

"If you are successful in the Test of the Blades, you will find out who I am," the voice said. Colwyn could swear there was a smile tucked in there somewhere. "As to why I would help you, my reasons are my own. Suffice it to say that I have good reason to want to see you succeed in the Test of the Blades. Now, do as I have told you. Search the kobold."

"You could tell me what it is that I am looking for," Colwyn grunted as he went over to the kobold and rifled through its clothing.

"I could," the voice chuckled. "But I rather think that you will know it when you see it."

Colwyn continued to methodically search the kobold's clothes. He grimaced at the bits of fuzz and lint in the kobold's pockets. It was several minutes before he made his way to the kobold's pants pockets. In one pocket, he discovered a green oval shaped gem. He thought it might be an emerald, but he wasn't completely sure. It certainly didn't look like any emerald that he had ever encountered. Nevertheless, he pocketed the gem. There was no confirmation from the mysterious voice regarding the gem so he continued to search through the rest of the kobold's pockets to be sure he hadn't missed anything. When he had completed his search, even down to the boots to be completely thorough, and had found nothing else that was even remotely interesting, he decided that the gem had been what he had been meant to find. He pulled it back out and looked it over.

The gem was rather large, about two inches long, and oval. It had an interesting luminescence about it, almost glowing in his hand. The shape was peculiar, almost eye-like but with no iris or pupil. He frowned at the gem, wondering how it might possibly be useful to him later on.

"What am I supposed to do with this gem?" he asked aloud.

"When the time is right, you will know," the voice replied, now little more than a whisper. "Trust me, it will keep you from failing the Test of the Blades."

"But..."

"Good luck, Colwyn Starseeker. I must leave you know. We will not speak again until you pass the Test of the Blades."

"Wait," Colwyn called. "Come back. I have so many questions!"

There was no answer from the voice. Once again, Colwyn was all alone. With a sigh, he scooped up his swords and made for the door on the other end of the room.

Alana was not the only one watching Colwyn's progress through the Test of the Blades. Although the High Priestess of the Blades may have considered it to be a violation of the rules of conduct for former Blademasters and Protectors in the Temple of the Blades, Raven Windrider was fascinated by this new Blademaster and her Protector to be. As she had told Colwyn, there were a great many prophecies that seemed to relate to this new Blademaster and Protector. And so she and her Protector had been watching the Test of the Blades from their room in the bowels of the Temple.

When the kobold had first appeared, her Protector had disappeared from the room. She did not know why he had gone, but she had her suspicions. He had returned not long after Colwyn had left the room where he had beaten the kobold.

"Why did you leave, my beloved?" she asked softly.

"You said prophecy spoke of this Protector," he replied. "I was simply making sure he has a chance to fulfill prophecy."

"Did you interfere in the Test of the Blades, Richard Kale?" Raven demanded. "You know that we are not allowed to interfere."

"I rather think that if Lord Taelin did not want me to do what I did, he would have stopped me," Richard shrugged. "Besides. The boy would have missed something very important had I not said something. Had he missed that, he would have likely failed the Test of the Blades. He still might, but now he at least has a chance."

"You are a very rare person, Richard Kale," Raven laughed.

Richard chuckled in reply. "I just know how much depends on these two."

The second level dungeon corridors had been a bit more difficult for Colwyn to traverse than the first level's had been. After leaving the room where he had killed the kobold, he had faced a band of seven orcs, another wyvern, this one fully grown, and a displacer beast. He had suffered a hard blow from one of the displacer beast's whip-like tentacles, and he thought that he might have cracked a rib. Drawing breath was painful at best, but he knew that he could not stop.

Alana was depending on him.

The walls of the corridors had been a plain white marble for most of his time in the dungeon, but now the walls had grown dark. He suspected this spelled trouble. He glanced at the trap finder stone. It was glowing slightly, more than it had been, so he suspected a trap near by. Avoiding it would be the trick.

He only had about a second's warning, still more than he would have had without the stone. The trap finder stone blazed a bright red just before walls slid down both in front of him and behind. He growled, upset at himself for not seeing that the trap was there before he was caught in it. It was too late for beating himself up about it though. And there would be nothing to gain. He needed to clear his mind and find a way out of the trap. Such traps could stop him from completing The Test just as easily as the creatures he had faced. He couldn't allow that to happen.

He took a deep breath, clearing his head, before carefully examining all four walls of his little prison. Three of the walls were dark. He ran his fingers along one of the dark walls. When he pulled his fingers away, he could see streaks in the darkness. He looked at his fingers and they were covered in a sooty substance. He frowned at that. He tried to recall any instance when soot residue was a good thing and failed. Soot was never a good thing. Soot meant fire.

He turned his attention to the fourth wall. The wall appeared to be a floor to ceiling tapestry made entirely out of gemstones. He studied the tapestry, which was of a hunting scene. Dogs were chasing a lone black wolf through the countryside. Men were behind the dogs with swords drawn. Something about the tapestry that tugged at the back of Colwyn's mind, but he could not place what it was. Again he scrutinized the tapestry. It took him several long minutes before he discovered what it was that was off.

There was a gemstone missing.

Upon reflection, he realized it was something he should have noticed right away. One of the wolf's eyes was missing. He studied the other eye. It featured a familiar sort of luminescence. He traced the socket for the other missing eye with his finger.

An oval.

He removed the stone he had taken from the kobold and fit it into the socket for the missing gemstone. It fit perfectly, so he pushed it in as far as it would go.

There was a deep rumbling coming from two of the opposing walls. Dust crumbled in on him and then the two walls that had entrapped him rose up into the ceiling, all evidence of the trap disappeared behind them.

With a grunt, he continued going down the corridor towards the stairwell that would lead down to the next level.

Alana cheered.

The beholder was not nearly as happy to see Colwyn make it through the tapestry trap. For Alana, it signified that Colwyn could make it all the way through to her. For the beholder, however, perhaps Colwyn would be far more trouble than was first assumed.

"I told you that Colwyn would be harder to kill than you first thought," Alana smiled broadly.

"He is not even halfway through the Test of the Blades, woman," the beholder growled. "He has a long way to go before you can gloat about how hard he is to kill."

But Alana could hear the worry in the beholder's voice. He had been surprised by Colwyn's competence.

What she did not understand was why a creature like a beholder should be so concerned with one ranger. But there was something more than concern here. It was clear that the beholder was quite afraid. Based on what she had heard about beholders, she knew that a beholder could inspire fear in its opponents. But she had never known that a beholder could feel fear as well. It was an interesting bit of information, and she filed it away for future reference.

It was a difficult thing to do, but Alana managed not to press her advantage over the beholder, choosing, instead, to continue watching the man she loved as he went down the stairs to the third level of the dungeon.

"Oh, hell," Colwyn grunted as he ducked under the blow from a club that had swiped at him as soon as he had emerged from the stairwell.

How he had not seen the ogre from the top of the stairs, he would never understand. Nevertheless, he was caught off guard. Even so, he still saw the club swinging at him before it hit, and he was able to step around it.

He swung one of his swords low, a good solid strike that severed one of the ogre's legs just below the knee. The ogre fell with a loud crash, and the floor vibrated with the fall.

Even on the floor like that, the ogre was still dangerous. The ogre swung the club again at Colwyn's head. But this time, Colwyn caught the ogre's wrist between his swords. With a grunt, he pulled the swords apart, slicing the ogre's hand off at the wrist. The club now out of the way, Colwyn plunged both swords deep into the ogre's chest, killing it once and for all.

Colwyn slumped down against the ogre's lifeless frame, deciding that a few minutes rest was in order before continuing the Test of the Blades. As he made more progress, the Test would become more difficult. He had to keep going but he would have to pace himself. *Just make it through the Test,* he decided, *and then I can be with the woman I love.*

With that thought, Colwyn continued the Test.

As he plodded down the corridor towards the next and final stairwell, he found himself wondering what life would be like with Alana. He imagined that they would live in his little house in Ravendale, which he preferred over his family estates in Arvendale. He did not know how his parents would feel about Alana, and he was not sure when or if he would even introduce her to them. He had not even spoken to his parents in over three years. They had not approved of his choice to become a ranger instead of remaining steeped in the noble traditions. They had yelled and screamed and carried on, but in the end, they had let him go. But when he came back from the Elven Woods, he did not even go back to his parents' house. Nor had he even sent them word that he had left the Elven Woods.

Nor did he think that they would have wanted to know that he had come out of the Woods. Although he was the heir to his father's title as the First Lord of Arvendale Territory, Colwyn knew that his father, First Lord Dargan Starseeker, did not approve of his son's choices. Colwyn suspected that his father knew that he had left the Elven Woods and that his father had been keeping tabs on him as he traveled about with his companions.

The situation with his parents was a bit of a shame, really. He loved his family, but as much as he loved his family, he could not handle their disapproval of his lifestyle. He was a ranger. He would always be a ranger. But even more so now, he would also always be the Protector to a Blademaster. He did not know how his family would handle that. He knew that his brother, Tyrus, resented that Colwyn received the family title as the oldest child. Colwyn did not want the title. He really wanted nothing to do with being a noble. All he wanted was to live his life with Alana in relative peace. But he knew that his parents would insist on his taking the title when his father passed. And he knew that his parents would insist on a noble wife for him.

He wished he knew a way that he could pass the title on to his brother without causing problems with his parents.

His thoughts were cut short by a sword swooshing by his face. Cursing himself for his lack of concentration, he let his instincts take over. He slipped back to put some distance between himself and his opponent. A lone forest orc stood before him, slashing back and forth with his sword. Colwyn was on the defensive at first, blocking each slash with one of his own swords. But it wasn't long before he lashed out with an attack of his own. The point of one of his swords caught the orc in the neck, ripping the carotid artery. The orc let off a gurgled scream as red bloody foam frothed from the wound and from the orc's mouth. The orc pitched forward, dead before it hit the ground, its sword almost grazing Colwyn on its way to the floor.

Colwyn kicked the body of the fallen orc and cursed himself again for his lack of concentration. *It is time to end the Test of the Blades*, he decided as he strode towards the stairs that would lead down to the lowest level of the dungeon.

Alana had winced when the orc had attacked Colwyn. The beholder had gloated when it thought Colwyn was about to be killed. But when Colwyn's instincts had kicked in, saving him from being slashed to death by the orc, the beholder screamed. Alana was amused by the beholder's reaction. She had the feeling that the beholder was actually afraid of Colwyn for some reason. She almost wished she knew what the source of that fear was. But then, it didn't really matter. Colwyn would sense the beholder's fear and somehow use it to his advantage.

Still, despite the brave face she was wearing, she was concerned about Colwyn's lapse of concentration. She had never seen him lose focus in that way and could only hope that it would not happen again. As good as he was, he might not be anywhere near as lucky next time.

"Colwyn is doing every bit as well as I expected him to," Alana taunted the beholder. "Even as distracted as he was there, he still managed to best that orc."

"It was pure luck," the beholder scoffed. "He still has a long way to go before he even reaches this room. There is a beast on this level of the dungeon that is more dangerous than anything he has faced yet. And it may be just the thing to best him."

"I think you are scared, beholder," Alana said quietly. "I think that you are scared that Colwyn will conquer all the little challenges that are a part of the Test of the Blades. And then he will storm in here and puncture every single one of your bulbous eyes before finishing you off once and for all."

"A noble boast," the beholder said with a shrill laugh. "However, I do not believe your Colwyn will make it through this level of the Test of the Blades at all, let alone come within striking distance of killing me. You are just wasting your time believing that he is going to come for you."

But Alana detected a shaky tremor in the beholder's voice. It was confirmation that she was right. The beholder was indeed afraid of Colwyn. The only question that remained was why. But she figured the answer to that would come in time. For now, all she could do was watch as Colwyn carefully made his way through the corridors of the lowest level of the dungeon.

Soon, Colwyn would burst through the door and rescue her.

A bead of sweat had rolled into Colwyn's eye, causing him to stop his forward momentum to wipe it clear with the sleeve of his tunic. Having stopped, he took the opportunity to listen carefully to his surroundings. A curious rasping sound was coming from somewhere ahead of him. He frowned. Was that sound familiar? Unfortunately, recognition was not forthcoming. He felt like he had heard the sound before, though.

He closed his eyes, concentrating on the sound. He tuned everything else out to the exclusion of the rasping noise. But even such careful concentration did not reveal the source of the sound. Perhaps some speculation was in order. It was likely the sound of something scraping against the stone wall of the corridor or perhaps the floor.

But what?

Unfortunately, it would have to remain a mystery until he encountered it.

Still, he was in the final level of the dungeon. It would only be a matter of time before his next encounter. And the sooner he got it over with, the sooner he could once again be with Alana.

Colwyn started back down the corridor towards the room where Alana was waiting for him. But with each step, the scraping noise grew a little louder. There would be no avoiding whatever was making the noise. Just ahead, the corridor he was in ended in a cross corridor. Instinctively, Colwyn checked the finder stone. It was veering to the right. He nodded to himself and stopped just short of the cross corridor. The rasping sound was very loud now. The source of the sound had to be just around the corner. He flattened himself against the left hand wall where he was able to look down the right side corridor enough to know that the creature was not coming from that direction. Then he backed down the corridor he had just come from a few feet so that he could surprise whatever it was.

He did not have long to wait. With his eyes focused on the cross corridor, he finally caught sight of the creature as it wandered across the cross corridor. Although it was dark, he was still able to discern that the beast had a lion's head. And, since he did not expect a simple lion in these dungeons, he suspected the creature to be a manticore. The thought of fighting a manticore by himself filled him with fear.

He almost gasped but caught himself. Pushing his fear away, he set himself for the battle. He would have to act quickly and immediately go for the tail. The spikes from a manticore's tail were widely known as one of the most dangerous weapons that a man could face from a beast. Hard as steel and shaped like a crossbow bolt, the spikes could either be flung at an opponent or could be rakde across an opponent's skin, flaying it like many sword slices all at once.

It was something Colwyn did not want to encounter.

Fortunately for Colwyn, the manticore had not noticed him in the corridor. So he waited until the manticore had crossed the entire corridor before quietly leaping into action. He launched himself at the manticore, making sure to keep far enough away from the end of the tail so as to not be raked by the spikes. With one powerful swing, his sword severed the tail right near the manticore's rear end.

The manticore screamed in agony and spun around to attack Colwyn. The ranger fell back to avoid the large paw. The claws were extended and Colwyn knew that a swipe from such a paw could rend his chest wide open. He sheathed one of his swords and flattened himself against the wall as the manticore charged at him. As the beast leapt, Colwyn slipped to the side and pounced onto the manticore's back, digging the fingers of his left hand deep into the creature's mane and wrapping his legs around the manticore's body for stability. From there, he would not have to worry about the manticore's claws. Now there was no way the manticore could reach him.

For his part, the manticore bucked and tried to throw Colwyn off its back, but the ranger would not be thrown. But he couldn't hang on forever. Nor did he intend to. With his free hand, he brought his remaining sword to bear again and again on the manticore's neck. Each strike drew blood and additional screams. It took fifteen hits, but eventually his sword blade had gone deep enough to damage the manticore's neck severely enough to hurt the beast. On the fifteenth strike, the manticore folded and Colwyn leapt off. He drew his other sword, ready to finish the beast off. But there was no movement. He scrutinized the body of the manticore.

But his swords were no longer needed here.

Tired and more than ready for the Test of the Blades to be over, Colwyn continued towards where Alana was waiting for him.

Alana was beside herself with glee. The beholder, however, was seething. She had always known that it would only be a matter of time before Colwyn burst through the door and rescued her from the beholder. The beholder was trembling now more from fear, Alana suspected, than from anger. There was something not right with the beholder. But whatever the case, she had no doubt that Colwyn would have no trouble dispatching this particular opponent. .

"You've lost, beholder," she declared. "There's nothing between Colwyn and you but that door. And he's going to burst through any moment."

"That's just not going to happen," the beholder rasped. "I'm not going to die. Your so called Protector is."

"We'll just see soon, now won't we?" Alana said with a smirk.

They watched as Colwyn neared the door to the little room. Alana was excited, but she could tell that the beholder was getting nervous. The scene on the wall was shaking slightly as the eyestalk that was showing the scene was quivering. Alana wondered again what was wrong with the beholder. She did not think a beholder should be able to feel fear in this way.

The door burst open and Colwyn skidded to a halt just inside doorway. He scanned the room and frowned at the sight of the beholder floating in the middle of the room.

The room was about twenty feet square. The ceiling was about thirty feet over their heads. Alana was tied to the wall but the beholder was between them. The objective was to free her. But from stories he'd heard, besting a beholder would not be the easiest task he had ever attempted.

Colwyn dove and rolled under the beholder. When he was directly under the beholder, he discovered that there was a cross hatch on the bottom of the beholder that seemed out of place. This was no ordinary beholder, if it was even a beholder at all. And if he was right about that, then he suspected that the end of the Test of the Blades would be a whole lot easier than dealing with a true beholder. Then again, almost anything was easier than dealing with a beholder.

He continued his roll and came to his feet on the other side of the beholder where he flung himself towards Alana. He sliced the ropes that bound her to the wall and pushed her down onto the floor against the wall.

Then, standing between her and his opponent, he turned to face the beholder.

"This ends now," Colwyn growled.

"Yes, ranger, it does," the beholder cackled. "For you, that is."

"I have been through hell and back during the Test of the Blades," Colwyn seethed as he took a step towards the beholder. "I have been afraid and I have come close to death. And when I burst into this room, I nearly fell over from fright with the thought that I would still have to fight a beholder." Colwyn flashed his enemy a grin. "But that's not the case, is it?"

"Of course I am a beholder, ranger," the beholder howled. "What else would I be?"

"I know exactly what you are," Colwyn nodded. "And you are no beholder."

"Colwyn, what are you talking about?" Alana asked.

"Isn't that right?" Colwyn finished.

"If you say so," the beholder sneered. He swiveled his eyestalks towards Colwyn.

But the ranger was no longer there. Again, he had dropped to the ground and rolled back under the beholder. With a quick flourish, he plunged his two swords into the beholder's body near the cross hatch. He braced his feet against the bottom of the beholder's body and pushed hard, propelling the beholder off of his blades.

The beholder shot upward, careening into the corner of the ceiling. Colwyn dove for and covered Alana with his body. When the beholder hit the ceiling, it exploded, raining fire over the room. Colwyn could feel the flaming shards hitting his back but he did not care so long as Alana was all right.

"You came for me," Alana said softly. "I knew you would." Colwyn nodded as he stood and brushed the ash from his tunic. Then he helped her to her feet.

"I told you. I will always come for you," the ranger smiled down at the woman he loved. "There will never be a need for you to doubt that ever again."

"So that was not a beholder then?" Alana glanced up at where the beholder had exploded. The wall had turned black with soot.

"Gas spore," Colwyn shrugged. "Their defense mechanism is that they resemble a beholder. But they're fairly harmless."

"Except that they explode when they die," Alana noted.

"Yes, except for that," Colwyn nodded. He stretched. "Lady Solara, the Test of the Blades is finished. I have found and rescued Alana."

"Yes, you have," Solara said as she entered the room. "Congratulations, Protector Colwyn Starseeker. You have passed the Test of the Blades. Only one thing remains. You and Blademaster Alana Steeldrake are to be married immediately. It is the Law of the Blades. Come, I will take you to a room where you can prepare for the wedding. I will heal your hurts and burns when you are there."

"But what of Alana? I'm not going to just leave her here."

Solara then swept out of the room without another word. Colwyn looked at Alana with a raised eyebrow.

"Go," Alana said with a giggle. "You've won. So go. But be quick about it."

With a nod, Colwyn followed the High Priestess of the Blades out of the room.

Alana watched the man she loved go, a broad smile on her face.

The Blademaster

Chapter XII
The Wedding

olwyn sighed loudly as he sat down on a bench in the little room he had been taken to prepare for the wedding.

"This is all happening too fast," the young man grumbled to no one in particular. "Don't get me wrong, I am happy that I am finally getting to marry the woman I love, but this is far quicker than I had thought it would happen when I proposed to her."

When he arrived in the small room, he had noticed the mannequin against the far wall. There was a suit of finely woven chain mail on the mannequin. Now that he was sitting on the bench, he noticed the note that had been left for him. He picked up the note and read it.

Lord Colwyn Starseeker,
This chain mail belongs to you now. By virtue of your becoming Protector to the Blademaster Alana Steeldrake, you

are required to wear this armor during the course of your duties. Put the armor on before coming out to the Great Hall for the marriage ceremony.
Solara Moonfire
High Priestess of the Blades

"What's with the chain mail?" he muttered as he fingered the finely woven links. "I'm a ranger. We don't wear chain mail. It makes too much noise and it interferes with the ability to fire a bow."

"You have a problem with the armor, Colwyn?" Solara chuckled from behind him.

"Yeah. Some. Why do I have to wear chain mail?" Colwyn whirled on her. He crossed his arms and fixed her with a glare. "It will interfere with my ability to protect Alana. I never had any trouble protecting her in my forest garb."

"Because it is required of you, Colwyn," Solara said softly. "Just as Alana is subject to the Law of the Blades as the Blademaster, so you too are subject to the same laws as her Protector. If you choose not to wear the armor, you do have the option to leave the Temple of the Blades now. No loss of honor will be recorded. But if you go now, you will never be allowed to see Alana again. It will be just as if you had failed the Test of the Blades. It is your choice to make. Choose now."

"I can't leave Alana," Colwyn turned away from the priestess. "I'll wear the armor," he spat. "I don't see that I have any choice."

"As I expected you would. You'll find that since the armor is elven made, it will still permit you to easily shoot a bow," Solara smiled. She went over and put her hand on Colwyn's shoulder. "Colwyn, I'm not trying to be difficult about this. Lord Taelin has entrusted me to make sure the Law of the Blades is fulfilled by the Blademasters and Protectors. And that is precisely what I shall do."

"I know, Lady Solara." He turned back to face her. "But that doesn't mean I have to like it. And I just don't like wearing chain mail."

"I understand. You need not wear the armor all the time, Colwyn. Only when you and Alana are journeying about in her duties as the Blademaster. You will find that this armor will not restrict your abilities as a ranger at all. Certainly not as you are expecting it will. This armor, as all armor worn by the Protectors over the years has been, was made by the Forestwalker Elves. I can't say that you will ever like the armor, but you will get used to it." Solara searched Colwyn's eyes for the answers to her questions. "You love Alana a great deal, don't you?"

"I would not have gone through the Test of the Blades if I did not love her as much as I do, Lady Solara." He smiled. "She begged me not the do the Test, you know. She was afraid that, no matter how much I loved her, the Test would not think it was enough and not allow me to pass and to save her. I held that since only her true love could pass the Test of the Blades, that meant that only I could do it."

"You will find that being the Protector to a Blademaster is not an easy job, Colwyn," Solara whispered. "Are you sure of this."

Colwyn shrugged. "Nothing in life worth doing is easy, Solara. Why should this be any different? Yes, I am sure. I have never been more sure of anything in my life."

"Then put the armor on," Solara urged, "and I will see you in the Great Hall in one hour's time. The Blademaster is lucky to have a Protector as dedicated to her as you are."

"I think I'm the lucky one," Colwyn replied.

Solara smiled again at him before leaving the room. He shook his head in amazement and started to pull his shirt over his head in preparation for putting the hated armor on when he heard gasps from behind him. He whirled to find two young Blademasters – one a brunette, the other a redhead – with their heads pressed close together.

"I told you that the new Protector was a sight to behold," the brunette whispered.

"You weren't kidding!" the redhead giggled. "The new Blademaster is very lucky indeed. My Michael was never such a specimen!"

"Do you two mind?" Colwyn grumbled. He covered his chest with his shirt. "I'm trying to get dressed here."

"Oh, we don't mind," the brunette giggled some more.

"Not at all," the redhead agreed.

"Please, don't stop on our account," they both pleaded in unison.

"Alyssa. Maria. Scoot!" a male voice boomed out from behind them. "Let the Protector prepare for his wedding in peace. You both remember how it was when it was your time for the bonding ceremony."

"Yes, Richard," the redhead sighed.

The two young Blademasters bowed their heads and slipped out of the room. A large older man strode into the room, chuckling and shaking his head.

"Congratulations! You made it through the gauntlet, Colwyn Starseeker," Richard said. "I know what that means. It was not an easy task. And I also know what it means to be able to marry the woman you love. That is why I helped you."

Colwyn's eyes went wide. "You're the one who warned me about the trap. You're the one who told me about the emerald."

"Yes," Richard nodded with a smirk. "I am Richard Kale. I am the first Protector. You and I are a great deal alike, Colwyn. I, too, did not want to wear the chain mail. Solara had to twist my arm just as she had to twist yours."

Colwyn pulled off his boots. "Can I ask you a personal question? I mean, you don't have to answer if you don't want to and I'll understand. But there's something I would like to know."

"It's all right," Richard grinned as he sat down on the room's only bench. "When I was in your position, I wished I had someone who had been through it before to answer my questions for me. Go ahead and ask what you want to ask."

"Were you and Raven happy?" Colwyn asked softly.

"Why do I suspect that you're really asking me a very different question than the one that you have asked?" Richard let out a sigh. "Look, you and your Blademaster will never have a normal life, Colwyn," Richard rubbed his chin in contemplation before continuing. "I'll be honest with you. You will be on the road for months at a time fighting and risking your lives on a daily basis. There will be days when it will hurt too much to carry on. But I will tell you another thing. No matter what else you two go through, so long as you love each other at least as much as you do now, you will also know great happiness in your lives. At least, that's the way it was with Raven and I. I suspect things will be good for you two."

"Thank you, Richard," Colwyn said. "That's what I wanted to know. And what I had hoped to hear."

"Enjoy your time with Alana, Colwyn," Richard advised as he stood, preparing to leave. "Even if you are saving the world, life is not worth living if you do not enjoy it."

"I understand," Colwyn nodded.

"Now," Richard smiled broadly, "why don't you focus on getting ready for the wedding? You wouldn't want to disappoint your beloved bride."

"I have no intention of disappointing her," Colwyn smiled back. "Ever."

"Good," the first Protector said with a nod. "I will leave you to it then."

Richard bowed and left the room, leaving Colwyn alone to prepare himself for the wedding. He turned the chain mail over in his hands as if it were a rotten fish. With a wrinkled nose, he sighed and slipped the chain mail shirt over his head.

Alana stretched. It had been a very long evening. Waiting for Colwyn to rescue her and the taunting of the gas spore had taken their toll. All she really wanted to do now was take a nap, but Solara had insisted that the wedding ceremony had to take place right away. And while Alana was thrilled to be marrying Colwyn, she just didn't see why it couldn't be done in the morning when everyone was fully rested. The last thing she wanted was to nod off during the wedding!

A yawn escaped her lips as she shuffled into the room that Solara had prepared for her.

The room was small and not much different than any of the other rooms in the Temple of the Blades. A bench ran along one wall and a mannequin stood in the corner displaying the dress that she figured she was supposed to wear.

And what a dress it was!

The dress greatly resembled the style of her armor, only in white satin instead of brown leather. The dress was more provocative than she would have worn. It was more like Solara's armor in that way then her own. Strips of satin ran from the shoulders down the front. The strips were about an inch wide at the shoulders and swept out to cover the mannequin's breasts. The V cut of the neck plunged dangerously low, almost to where the mannequin's navel would be. Instead of snapping to a solid back, the straps tied behind the neck, leaving the back exposed. Whereas the skirt for her armor was short and pleated, the dress was long, loose and flowing and stopped just shy of the floor. A long lace train stretched several feet behind the dress. The train was attached just above the waist and a large white silk bow covered where it connected.

She ran her fingers over the satin. It was soft and cool to the touch. It would feel very good against her skin. She hoped that Colwyn would like her in the dress. But then she took in the way the front of the dress displayed the mannequin's cleavage and laughed aloud. He would like the dress! She couldn't wait to see his face. She could just imagine how red the boy's face would be!

"I see that you had no problem finding the room," Solara said as she entered. "Is there anything you need?

"Lady Solara," Alana said, unable to pull her eyes from the dress. "This dress is worthy of a queen, not me. What did I do to deserve a dress like this for my wedding? I was just going to wear my favorite green traveling dress. After all, Colwyn likes the way that dress..."

"A woman of your importance cannot be married in a simple traveling dress, Alana," Solara interrupted with a laugh. "Whether you think you are worthy of this dress or not, it is yours to wear by right. This is the wedding dress of a Blademaster. It is the only wedding dress that would be acceptable."

Alana narrowed her eyes. "This is one of those Law of the Blades things isn't it?" For while she liked the dress, she was tired of being forced into things due to the Law of the Blades. It seemed like a much too convenient catch all for twisting her arm into doing things she wouldn't otherwise have done.

Lady Solara pressed her lips together before speaking. "As I told Colwyn when he was having trouble deciding whether or not he was going to wear the chain mail required of him by the Law of the Blades, Lord Taelin instructed me to make sure the Law of the Blades was followed to the letter. And that is what I intend to do," Solara's pressed lips curved ever-so-slightly into a smile. "Yes, it is a Law of the Blades thing, as you put it. So yes, I am going to force the issue. You will wear the dress."

"You're making Colwyn wear chain mail?" Alana was dumbfounded. "I didn't think that it was possible for anyone to make that man wear armor."

"Well, he was threatened with the one thing that was guaranteed to get him to wear the armor," Solara's smile turned sad. "I hated to do it, but the Law of the Blades must be followed."

"You told him that he wouldn't be allowed to marry me if he didn't wear the armor, didn't you?" Alana knew the answer before she even asked the question. Solara turned away but did not respond. Alana sighed. "Colwyn doesn't like being forced into doing things. I'd think that you'd be a better read of people after such a long tenure as the High Priestess of the Blades."

Solara turned back to Alana with a frown on her face. "What do you mean by that?"

"Sometimes, strict adherence to a rigid set of rules can be just as destructive as it is supposed to be orderly." Alana shrugged off the top of her armor and fingered the dress once more. "I know the Law of the Blades is important, and Lord Taelin is right to want the Law enforced. But perhaps the time has come for change. The Blademasters of old were killed because flexibility was not encouraged. I will not make that mistake. And neither should you."

"I see." Solara straightened. "Lord Taelin chooses his Blademasters well."

"Perhaps. But I don't feel any different than I did before, Lady Solara," Alana slipped the dress over her head and turned so Solara could tie the neck. "Except maybe a little happier knowing I'll finally be marrying Colwyn."

"I think you'll find that he's just as happy," Solara chuckled as she tied the dress together at the neck. "That's something you can count on."

"I hope so," Alana said wistfully. "Making him happy is important to me."

"Well, I think you'll do a good job at that," Solara laughed. "Are you ready?"

"How do I look?" Alana asked. "Think Colwyn will like it?"

"If he doesn't like it, I'll have to check for a pulse," Solara smiled broadly. "You, my dear Alana, are quite the ravishing woman in that dress."

"Thank you." Alana returned the smile. "I'm ready now."

"Then let's get you down to the Great Hall and marry you and Colwyn."

The Great Hall of the Temple of the Blades had been redecorated since Colwyn had begun the Test of the Blades. White banners now adorned the altar along all the edges. The hunter green banner above the altar that had previously been blank now displayed what Colwyn could only assume was Alana's crest: a stylized dragon in steel grey holding a silver long sword in each of its front claws.

Colwyn took in all of this as he strode into the Great Hall, now clad in the elven chain mail. Immediately, he located William, Balaam and Meryn loitering by a buffet table near the back of the Great Hall. His stomach rumbled and he realized that he was very hungry after the events of the evening, so he made his way over to the buffet table.

"You're in chain mail, Colwyn," William remarked with a smirk as the ranger approached. "It looks good on you. Even if it is a surprising turn of events."

"It's not by choice," Colwyn grumbled. "You should know how I feel about armor by now, William."

"The Law of the Blades," Balaam acknowledged quietly.

Colwyn said nothing as he scooped up a few sausages and some cheese. He wrapped one of the sausages and a slice of cheese in a piece of flat bread and took a bite, chewing thoughtfully. "The Law of the Blades," he confirmed. "Seems to cover a multitude of sins."

Balaam smiled. "If Lady Solara is forcing you to abide by the Law of the Blades, then you must have passed the Test of the Blades. I am glad to see that you survived. Congratulations, Protector Colwyn. So when is the wedding?"

"Wedding?" William raised an eyebrow.

"It's the Law of the Blades," Colwyn winked at William. "I am forced to marry the woman I love. It's an onerous task, but you know how it is. If the Law of the Blades commands it, I shall meekly submit."

"It is no trivial matter, Protector Colwyn," Balaam rounded on Colwyn. "Do not make light of this commitment you make to Alana."

"Balaam, I am all too well aware of the seriousness of my commitment," Colwyn growled. "You are not the one who just fought more creatures in the past four hours than in the previous three weeks. I am. You are not the one who had to prove his love to the world. I am. You are not the one who was almost trapped down in the dungeon and, as a result, almost forbidden from ever seeing the woman he loves again. I am. So before you get all high and mighty, remember that you've been less than helpful around here. You – and Caiaphas before you for that matter – could have told us what was in store long before now. Instead, you hid it from us. You sought to keep us apart when, as it turns out, we were supposed to stay together. So don't spout off to me anything about the seriousness of our commitment. You've lost any right to lecture me."

Colwyn stalked off to the other end of the table, where he nibbled on his flatbread. William watched him go with a look of amused surprise on his face.

Balaam just stared after Colwyn, disgust etched on his face. "I hadn't exactly finished," the priest said under his breath.

William closed the distance between himself and Colwyn and put his hand on the ranger's shoulder. "That wasn't very nice of you, Colwyn."

"I'm not apologizing, William," Colwyn fumed. "I'm rather tired of his delusions of superiority. I'm also greatly annoyed that he couldn't be bothered to just tell us what we needed to know. Instead, he sends us on this wild chase through the Southern Dales. We almost get killed in Valendale. I had to deal with Mirian Kovalani, and now I almost got killed again several times by the Test. No, I'm not in a mood to be nice to him right now."

"At least you get to marry Alana like you've wanted to," William grinned. "That's the bright side of all of this. Right?"

"True enough, my friend," Colwyn swallowed a mouthful. Then his lips parted in a smile and the shadow retreated from his face. The two of them shared a laugh and then Colwyn's granite face returned to more serious matters. "Will you stand with me?"

"Of course," William clapped his friend on the back. "When is the wedding?"

"Pretty much as soon as Alana is ready," Colwyn shrugged. "It is my understanding that she is putting her dress on as we speak." He took another bite from his flatbread and chewed thoughtfully. "Have you tried these sausages?"

"That soon?" William asked, his eyes wide. He would not be deterred from this line of conversation by sausages, no matter how delicious.

"Apparently that soon," Colwyn nodded. "Solara insisted we be married before we leave the Temple of the Blades. She said..."

"Let me guess. The Law of the Blades required it."

"Exactly!"

"You must be sick of hearing about the Law of the Blades," William chuckled. "It seems like that's all you've been hearing since you got here."

"You have no idea." Colwyn said with a chuckle. But as he absent mindedly continued to chew on his sausages, his thoughts wandered.

He wondered what would have happened had he failed in the Test of the Blades. What if they were not the Blademaster and Protector? What would it be like if they were just two normal people? Would they even know how to act with a normal life? Is there even such a thing as a normal life? What will it be like to be married to Alana?

All of these thoughts passed through his head as he waited patiently, though a touch nervously, for Alana to arrive in the Great Hall. He wished more than anything to marry Alana. And while he was willing to buy into the whole myth that their wedding was supposed to happen, he was still not willing to trust that it actually would happen until it had.

So he was ready to get the wedding over with and the marriage started.

When he saw the Blademasters and Protectors of old slip into the room and line up along the back of the Great Hall, he knew the time was upon them. Raven caught his eye and granted him a sly smile. Richard stood next to her and gave him a thumbs up. Colwyn smiled back at them and then turned back to William. He started to say something to him but lost all words.

Alana had just entered the Great Hall.

William followed Colwyn's gaze and his jaw dropped, a mere imitation of Colwyn's own reaction. William glanced at Colwyn and then back at Alana.

"Lucky bastard," William, chuckled.

Colwyn strode over to stand by Alana at the altar. He held his arms out to her and she stepped forward into them. She leaned up and kissed him tenderly on the lips. And when she pulled back from the kiss, she was smiling broadly.

"I guess this means that you like what you see?" she asked with a wide grin.

"You could say that," Colwyn gulped, his eyes wide. "You could say it twice."

"I like the chain mail on you, Col," Alana grinned, licking her lips, as she ran her fingers along the V neck of the chain mail shirt. "It's quite a look on you."

"I still hate it, but I'm willing to suffer through." He smiled roguishly as he looked her over. "Although I will say that seeing you in that dress makes it all worth it!"

They fell silent as Solara Moonfire entered the Great Hall from a door behind the altar. The High Priestess glided around the altar to stand before Colwyn and Alana. She looked them over appraisingly, and nodded her approval. Then she scanned over everyone assembled. A hush fell over the room.

"The Law of the Blades is unchangeable," Solara's soft voice reverberated throughout the hall. "And it has guided the activities inside the Temple of the Blades for ages." She turned and looked directly at Alana. "It is for you to understand why the Test of the Blades and this wedding are to happen. This is the First Law of the Blades. You are commanded to love. Love your friends. Love your enemies. Love without reservation. Love without hesitation. Love without condition. Love without expectation of return. If you must fight, then fight with love in your heart. If you must kill, then kill with love in your heart. Never kill or fight with hate or anger in your heart. Hate leads to impotence, but love brings power. This is the law a Blademaster must live by more than any other or else she will be powerless to serve as she should. It is the First Law of the Blades because it is the most important. Live by it, or you will die."

Alana nodded. "I understand." She reached over and gave Colwyn's hand a squeeze.

"This must be a marriage entered into by both parties of their own free will," Solara continued. "Blademaster Alana Steeldrake, do you enter this commitment of your own free will? Do you swear that you are not being coerced in any way into marrying this man? Would you have entered this commitment outside the bounds of the Law of the Blades?"

"I do so swear," Alana replied.

"Colwyn Starseeker," Solara turned to the ranger. "Do you enter this commitment of your own free will? Do you swear that you are not being coerced in any way into marrying this woman? Would you have entered this commitment outside the bounds of the Law of the Blades?"

"Marrying Alana has been my heart's fondest desire for over a year, Lady Solara," Colwyn said quietly. "Nothing would have kept me from marrying her."

"The Law of the Blades is satisfied that this marriage is being entered into freely by both parties," Solara announced with a smile. She put a hand on each of their heads and closed her eyes. Her hand was warm and they could both feel power flowing into them from her. "Lord Taelin, these two come before you as Blademaster and Protector, and as man and woman. You have commanded that the power of a Blademaster be bound up in love. Therefore, I demand that you bind this Blademaster's power to her love for this man, her Protector, who has passed the Test of the Blades."

The heat from Solara's hands intensified, and Colwyn knew something was happening. He wasn't sure what it meant, but it was a peaceful feeling that washed over him. Relaxation. Refreshment. And he could tell Alana was experiencing the same.

Solara's eyes snapped open. "It is done. Let the world know now that this Blademaster and this Protector are now bound for life. Let the forces of injustice quake with fear, for a Blademaster once again goes forth in full power and authority granted by Lord Taelin and Lady Laeyra."

There was a roaring in his ears, and Colwyn knew that the Blademasters and Protectors of old were showing their appreciation, but he was not able to turn to look at them. He was paralyzed, held enthralled by the feelings of warmth and peace running through him. After a few moments, the warmth subsided, and he and Alana were able to move once more. He glanced over at Alana, confirming that she too was experiencing the same thing.

He leaned in toward Solara. "What was that?" he asked quietly.

"Alana's power as a Blademaster is now bound up in her love for you," Solara explained. "What you felt was the bonding of that power. She is now bound to you and you to her for as long as you both shall live."

He scrutinized Alana to see if there were any signs that she felt any different. She smiled back at him. If anything, her smile was now even more radiant than ever before. He didn't know if it was an after effect of the bonding, but he hoped it would never change, for the light in her eyes blazed anew. He hoped she would always look upon him so.

"There is one last requirement of the Law of the Blades that must be done before the bonding is complete," Solara added.

Colwyn rolled his eyes. Again with the Law of the Blades? Naturally, the other boot had to drop.

Solara's eyes twinkled. "I don't think either of you will have a problem with this requirement. Colwyn, you must kiss her."

He signed with relief. "I think I can handle that one," Colwyn laughed.

He turned to Alana and smiled. She folded herself back into his arms and gazed at him with her large green eyes. He leaned down and gently brushed his lips against hers. Her lips parted against his and she kissed him back hungrily. The kiss seemed to last forever, as all good kisses should. When they finally pulled apart, the assembled Blademasters, Protectors, and their friends burst into applause and cheers.

Smiling, Colwyn led Alana to the buffet table.

After the day they'd had, they could both use the sustenance.

They would also need to refresh themselves for adventures to come.

Chapter XIII
Mergn's Discovery

Colwyn stood talking, with Solara Moonfire. His wife was hanging on his arm. The after glow from the wedding still filled him with joy. Love washed over his heart, drowning out any other feelings he might have been experiencing. Still, something did not feel quite right. He couldn't put his finger on it. But he wasn't about to let that nagging feeling ruin Alana's wedding day. So he chose instead to enjoy the time he could spend with his beloved. He and Alana each had a plate of food from the buffet that Solara had provided for the companions.

"Yes, indeed." Solara was saying. "I truly believe that this Blademaster is in very good hands. It has been a very long time since a Protector has gone through the Test of the Blades with such ease."

"You call that easy?" Colwyn rolled his eyes as he chewed on a strip of chicken. "I very nearly got caught in that infernal trap that would have kept me from Alana forever."

"But you were too smart for the trap." Solara replied. "And as a result, you are now the Blademaster's husband and Protector."

Colwyn took Alana in his arms, a feat that was made more difficult than usual by the fact that they both had plates in their hands. "For that," he smiled, "I could not be happier."

"Neither could I," Alana beamed. She snuggled closer in his arms, her food, for the moment, forgotten. "Can you believe it, my love? We're finally married. And to think, you weren't sure it was going to happen for a while?"

"It seems like a dream," he chuckled. The mirth faded from his face as, all of a sudden, Colwyn was able to place what was nagging at him, and his face darkened. He disengaged himself from Alana and peered about. "Where is she?"

"Who?" Alana asked.

"Who indeed?" Solara added.

"Where is the halfling?" Colwyn clarified. "I haven't seen her since before the wedding."

Alana scanned the Great Hall, her frown deepening. "I thought it was too quiet. Where could she have gotten off to?"

Colwyn's frown changed to a scowl. "I never should have taken my eyes off of her. She's trouble on two legs that one."

"She can not have gotten too far." Solara laughed. "I will help you look for her."

Meryn Swiftfoot had grown bored. Anyone who knew Meryn, or any other halfling for that matter, knew that nothing good could ever come from a halfling growing bored. There was a common saying in the Southern Dales. The only thing worse than a halfling saying she is bored, is a halfling saying nothing at all.

The trouble is, big people, as halflings referred to humans and elves, were rather boring creatures. While Meryn found great adventure and excitement in traveling with Colwyn and Alana (William was by far the most entertaining of her companions, having enthralled her with his magic, which is why she had fallen in love with him. But don't tell him that, she wouldn't want him to know how she felt!), she was nonetheless often bored with their tedious customs and ways.

Alana and Colwyn's wedding was an example of such wearisome insipid fare.

There was no question that Colwyn and Alana loved each other. She was even pretty sure that Taelin and Laeyra approved of such a match. So why did they have to go through an overblown, monotonous wedding to prove it? Or more accurately, to be told what they already knew? It made little sense to the halfling. But then, very little of the ways of big people ever really made sense.

And so she decided to pique her interest in other ways and explore the Temple of the Blades. She was specifically curious about the dungeons. After all, William had said that there was a possibility that there might have been a dragon as a part of the Test of the Blades. If there was a dragon anywhere in the Temple of the Blades, Meryn was determined to find it. That would certainly make things a touch more exciting. Dragons were fascinating creatures. She doubted she could ever be bored with a dragon around.

She did not know where her fixation with dragons came from, but they had always fascinated her. She had always wanted to meet a dragon. She wanted to talk to it. Learn from it. The legends told that dragons were extremely intelligent creatures. Perhaps they made excellent conversationalists. Of course, she had also heard tell that a dragon could be prone to fits of anger and might just as soon eat you as talk to you, especially if you argued with it. There was an old saying, do not meddle in the affairs of dragons, for you are crunchy and taste good with ketchup. She wasn't sure she believed the reports of such fiery dragon tempers but she was determined that, should she ever meet a real dragon, she would never anger him enough to find out.

And so it was with an odd mix of awe, excitement, and a little bit of apprehension (Not fear, though, because halflings don't feel fear per se, just a little bit of apprehension. Often, a healthy bit of apprehension has kept a halfling from killing herself by doing something stupid!) that Meryn charged down the corridors of the dungeons of the Temple of the Blades. She passed many doors as she went, but none caught her attention until she came to a locked door that seemed to call to the halfling.

Of course, a locked door means nothing to a halfling, especially to a halfling of Meryn's talents. She whipped out her lock pick set, and opened the door almost as quickly as if she had possessed its key. Too excited for caution, Meryn plunged into the room.

Colwyn cursed the halfling's disappearing act for they had decided Meryn was nowhere to be found in the Great Hall. Alana was secretly amused by the halfling's antics, although she would never admit it aloud, especially to Colwyn. William had refused to help with the search, stating that wherever she was, she would soon make her presence known. And thus, there was no point in searching for her. Balaam had been less vocal and therefore betrayed his indifference. And Solara only wanted to make sure that the Temple of the Blades was secure, although she commented that the she didn't believe the halfling could cause much serious trouble anyway.

"She has not left the Temple, I can tell you that for sure." Solara assured them. "I would know it if she had left. Perhaps we should search the dungeons."

"Probably looking for dragons." William remarked with a shrug.

"William, what have you done?" Alana rounded on the mage.

"What? I haven't done anything."

"What exactly did you say to Meryn?"

"Look, there was a good amount of time for discussion. So we talked about stuff to keep her mind off of the Test."

"What did you talk about?" Colwyn asked.

"All I did was mention that, you know, in the past dragons have appeared in the Test of the Blades," William shrugged again. "You know, historically. Or traditionally."

Colwyn rolled his eyes while Alana let out a deep breath. "That was probably enough to do it," she sighed.

"And you know how she is," William continued. "I've no doubt she's gone hunting for a dragon in the dungeons."

"There was no dragon in the Test of the Blades, William," Solara sighed. "In fact, there hasn't been a dragon in the Test of the Blades since the very first Test."

"Really?" he asked.

"There is no dragon for her to find."

William tried to conceal a smile but he failed.

"You knew that!" Alana accused.

"I was telling a story. Trying to keep her mind from what you two were going through. So I embellished? So what? The truth matters not to a halfling."

"You can say that again," Colwyn grumbled.

"She believes there is a dragon down there. And so she's probably gone off looking for it, even though there is none to be found," Alana concluded.

William nodded. "That is the way it is with the childlike curiosity of the halfling."

Before Solara could reply to that, the sound of a soft gong echoed throughout the Great Hall. Solara frowned.

"What's the problem?" Colwyn asked.

"The armory," Solara's breathed. "Someone has entered the armory without permission. Come, Blademaster Alana. I was going to take you to the armory in the morning anyway. But I guess now is as good a time as any."

"Sounds to me like it might be a better time than any," Colwyn remarked as he locked eyes with Alana.

"Meryn," they said in unison as Solara led them out of the Great Hall towards and into the dungeons.

Meryn had heard the gong sound as soon as she entered the room. It had been so long since she'd tripped any kind of trap or alarm in her exploits that she didn't know what to do at first. But, as is often the case, she figured it was probably too late to do anything about it. Besides, by all appearances she had stumbled into the armory. This required further exploration! And it would only be a matter of time before she was found anyway. In the meantime, she was determined to discover as much as possible before her fun was squelched. For being found in the armory would certainly squelch her fun. She was sure the big people would not want her in the armory.

Meryn found a small pewter statue of a dragon in flight. A delightful sculpture! She slipped the statue into a pouch on her belt. It wasn't exactly stealing. After all, she was simply keeping the statue safe and nearby until it was needed. She knew that it would be needed by someone someday. Maybe by Alana. You never know. And when it was needed, the statue would be safe and sound in one of Meryn's pouches.

She had just closed her pouch when Solara burst into the armory with Meryn's companions, William included, at her heels. They stopped short, all eyes upon the halfling.

"What are you doing Meryn?" Colwyn demanded.

"I was just looking!" the halfling protested. "I promise!"

"You should have stayed in the Great Hall." Colwyn snarled. The usual control he had over his frustration with the halfling was slipping.

"It's alright, Protector Colwyn." Solara laughed merrily. "As I said, I was going to bring you down here tomorrow any way. This is the armory of the Temple of the Blades. You are all welcome to choose any weapons as your own. Master Mage, I have something in here that I wish for you to have." She stepped to a dark corner of the room and produced a wooden staff. "This staff belonged to the Great Mage of the Inner Circle, Cirricus. It has not been used since Cirricus left it here. I believe it will help you."

"Thank you, my Lady." William bowed, taking the staff.

The others chose weapons as well. Alana took a brace of throwing stars and a pair of long swords that Solara told her had belonged to the first Blademaster. She left her own long swords in their place, thinking that, perhaps, a Blademaster years from now would take her blades as she now took those of the very first Blademaster. These swords were slightly lighter than the ones she had been using, and it would take a few swings to get used to the new weight. She did find that the balance was perfect for her, though. She attached the new swords to her sword belt and smiled.

Colwyn refused to replace his sword as it was his father's sword, but he put a new throwing dagger in his boot. Meryn found a new dagger she liked very much. And Balaam took a mace that had belonged to the High Priest of Taelin five hundred years before.

"Now that you are all well-armed, please rest for the night." Solara turned with a flourish. "Follow me and I will refresh your supplies so you can continue your journey in the morning."

The Blademaster

Chapter XIV
The Pewter Dragon

"Congratulations to you, Lord Colwyn," the melodious voice of the first Blademaster floated into the room just ahead of the ethereal form of the woman herself. "You and Lady Alana are to be commended for making it through the difficult process of becoming who and what you are."

"I think we're still working on getting through it, Lady Raven," Colwyn laughed. "In truth, I don't think I will ever be able to see her as more than the woman I love." He picked up her green traveling dress and lovingly folded it. "Being married to the Blademaster... well that will still take some getting used to."

"Just because she has embraced her destiny does not mean she has changed, Lord Colwyn," Raven Windrider chuckled softly. "Being named the Blademaster changes nothing about who she is. As my Richard learned when I was first named the Blademaster, the Blademaster is not actually chosen by the High Priestess of the Blades, so much as the High Priestess recognizes what is already evident in the Blademaster. Your Alana is certainly no exception to the rule. I have no doubt that she will prove to be every bit the Blademaster that Lord Taelin expects her to be."

Colwyn watched Raven for a few moments and was struck hard, not for the first time, by the great resemblance between Raven and Alana. And he found himself wondering, not for the first time if there was a reason that all the Blademasters he had seen so far had a similar look to them. He shook his head to clear it of the thought and turned back to loading Alana's pack. "I thank you for your vote of confidence, Lady Raven," he said under his breath. "But we still have a long way to go before we are even close to proving to Lord Taelin that he was right in his choice of Alana for the new Blademaster."

"Well, of her being the right choice, I am sure," Raven laughed. "Just as I am sure that you are the right choice for her Protector."

"I love her, Lady Raven," he said softly as he rolled up her bedroll. "That should be reason enough for me to be the right choice to be her Protector."

"Indeed," Raven nodded. She leaned against the wall, causing Colwyn to wonder how it was that she wasn't going through it. "I have seen the power of the love you and the Blademaster share, Lord Colwyn. Thraal should run and hide in fear from the power of it. I daresay that Lord Taelin himself has underestimated what he has wrought with you two."

"Somehow, I don't think the Dark God is quite quaking in his boots over us just yet," Colwyn snorted. "All we've managed to do so far is to prove that we love each other, and in doing so, we got to do something she and I have been wanting to do for some time; to marry each other. Now, when we take out the lich, it will be a different story. At that point, I believe we will have caused Thraal reason to quake in his boots."

"And I have no doubt that you will succeed," Raven smiled broadly. She reached out and touched Colwyn on the shoulder. A jolt of electricity coursed through his body. "You are both strong and good people. I have little doubt that fortune will follow you."

"To be honest, I'm more worried about the lich than I am about our fortune," Colwyn grumbled, still shaking off the static shock sensation from Raven's touch. "Frankly, I wonder if certain members of our party are up to the task at hand."

"I wouldn't worry about the halfling so much," Raven laughed. Her laugh was the sound of wind chimes tinkling in a breeze. He found it enchanting and even slightly alluring that someone could laugh like that. When the time comes, Meryn Swiftfoot will play the part she is supposed to play. And she will play it well."

"It's not the halfling I am worried about," Colwyn remarked with a shrug. He secured his bedroll to his pack as he continued. "I may not like the halfling. She's a thief and a liar. But for all her faults, she's fiercely loyal to Alana and she has certainly proven herself useful." He fixed Raven with his gaze. "No, to be honest, my problem is with Balaam."

"The High Priest of Taelin?" Raven's eyes were wide in surprise. "Lord Colwyn, he's here to help you and the Blademaster."

"Nevertheless, I don't trust him." The ranger shrugged again. He hefted his pack, testing its weight. "He kept all of this from us for far too long. And while I know the reasons why, I don't think I can forgive him for trying to keep Alana and I apart."

"It seems that you and my Richard have a great deal more in common than I first thought," Raven said after studying Colwyn's face for a long moment. She heaved a deep sigh. "He was much the same way with the High Priest of Taelin back in my day. He never got over it either. But Balaam is a good man. You will come to see that in time."

"I hope you are right Lady Raven," Colwyn sighed. He looked up from where he was tying Alana's bedroll onto her pack only to discover that he was talking to thin air. Raven Windrider had vanished once more. He shrugged. There had been other things he had hoped to address with the first Blademaster but his window of opportunity now seemed closed. And there was little he could do about it. He wondered if he would ever really be used to the way the former Blademasters suddenly appeared and disappeared at will. He decided that it really didn't matter because they were leaving and he wasn't sure if they would ever be back. He returned his attention to the packing, hoping to have it completed before Alana got back.

"You're not done yet?" Alana asked with a giggle as she popped into their room. "Here I've gone and spoken with Lady Solara about our mission, figuring you'd be all done with the packing by the time I got back. But what do I find when I return? You on your knees tying bedrolls to packs. You're usually much faster than this. What could possibly be taking so long?"

"I've been a little busy." Colwyn muttered. He tested the knots that secured her bedroll. "Between packing and getting the answers you need for this mission I've been busy."

"Yes, Solara told me you would have found some important information." Alana knelt down beside her husband and looked him in the eyes, taking his hand. "So how could you have gained this information? It's not like you've been able to ask anyone about it. We've all been here in the Temple of the Blades since we arrived yesterday."

"Part of my job as your Protector is to root out what you need to know." Colwyn remarked with a grin as he wrapped his arms around her. "I'll tell you what, when we're not being watched so closely by beings who can pop in and out on a whim, I'll explain what I've learned."

"Col, what are you talking about?"

"What you need to know for now is that our destination is the Ziggurat of Thraal in Tornith."

"Tornith?" Alana blinked. "Are you sure that's where we're going?"

"Far to the north, yes. All the way to the northern part of Dracomyr."

Alana sighed. "Tornith is a long ride to the north, Col," She shook her head and leaned against his shoulder. "Taelin's Light, it's a two week ride just to the border of

Dracomyr. We don't even have horses. Just how do you propose that we get there in time to stop Thraal?"

"Well, the way I see it, Thraal can't accomplish what he wants to without you there." Colwyn wrapped his arms a little tighter around her. "In order to enter the world of Calthea, you must be sacrificed to him. So, you need to be there, right?"

"Oh, there is no way I am going to be sacrificed to the Dark God," Alana snorted.

"Well, obviously this is what we have to keep from happening," Colwyn agreed. She pulled out of his embrace and started pacing as he continued. "I can tell you for sure that I am not going to finally get to marry you only to lose you to something stupid like a demonic sacrifice."

Alana smiled at Colwyn. "We really did get married didn't we?" she whispered. "This hasn't just been a dream?"

"I'm pretty sure most of this would qualify as a nightmare over a dream," Colwyn grimaced. Alana frowned so he went to her. "But yes, we really did get married."

"True enough." Alana sighed as she folded herself into his arms once again. "We just have to find our way through this nightmare, Col. That's all. We've been through worse. Right?"

"Sure we have," Colwyn said. But he could not recall a single instance that he would classify as worse than their current predicament. Not that he would tell her that, of course.

"I think you will find that you will have a great deal more help than you expect, Blademaster Alana." Raven said softly from behind her.

Alana spun on the voice and lunged. Raven had taken two steps back, she still found the point of Alana's blade at her throat.

"Very impressive." Raven whistled in appreciation. "None here at the Temple of the Blades have reflexes that honed."

"And you are?" Alana demanded. The blade at Raven's throat did not waver.

"Alana Steeldrake," Colwyn intoned regally, "may I present Raven Windrider, the very first Blademaster." Colwyn bowed in Raven's direction. "I believe that is her sword you have pointed at her throat."

"Indeed, it is," Raven said.

"But how is this...?" Alana frowned but lowered her sword nevertheless. "She should have gone to walk with Taelin many years ago."

"And so I did." Raven bowed to the current Blademaster. "Lord Colwyn will explain it to you in detail soon, but suffice it to say that I am the source of his information."

"All right then," Alana sighed. "Then we know where to go, and I assume I know what to do." She looked at Colwyn. When he nodded, she continued. "Col, finish our packing. I'll get the rest of the party moving. I want to be on the way within the hour."

Colwyn nodded. "As you say, my love." He watched Alana leave the room and then turned to thank Raven only to find she had left as well.

"I really hate it when they do that," he grumbled to himself.

Solara had made sure that the supplies in their packs were replenished before they left the Temple. Even though the first two days of their journey out of the Elven Woods had been uneventful, Colwyn was certain they were being followed. It was such a pervasive feeling that Colwyn gave little thought to what the halfling might be up to. That didn't mean that he wasn't worried about Meryn. He always worried about Meryn. But in this instance he would let Alana handle whatever it was that the halfling was plotting, for he was sure she was plotting something.

She was always plotting something.

It was the second night out from the Temple of the Blades. They had just settled in for supper in the middle of a clearing when Colwyn took Alana aside and asked her about Meryn.

"She's up to something," Colwyn muttered as he handed Alana a bowl of rice with some slices of dried meat scattered on top. "I tell you, Alana, she's up to something."

"You always think she's up to something, Col," Alana sighed.

"That's because she's always up to something."

"Not always. More often than not, you're wrong."

"Not when it counts, I'm not. And I'm telling you that she's up to something. Ever since we left the Temple of the Blades, she's been avoiding me."

Alana shrugged. "So? You always think she's up to something so she always tries to avoid you."

"Even more than usual. She looks guilty about something."

"I think you're reading too much into things, Col." Alana took a bite of the meat and chewed thoughtfully. "She's a halfling. They always look guilty about something."

"That's because they always..."

"Lady Alana," the halfling's squeaky voice interrupted them as she entered the circle of firelight next to Colwyn. She was carrying the statue she'd taken from the armory. She put it down at Alana's feet. "I'm feeling a little guilty for taking this."

Alana glanced briefly at Colwyn who mouthed "See?" before she turned her attention to the statue. It was a pewter replica of a gold dragon in flight. Alana looked from the statue to the halfling and back again. "Where did you get this?"

"From the armory of the Temple of the Blades," Meryn squeaked.

"Interesting," Alana mused.

For a moment, Colwyn let go of his issues with Meryn and joined Alana's train of thought. "What would a pewter statue of a dragon be doing in the armory of the Temple of the Blades?" Colwyn wondered.

"I was wondering the same thing," Meryn said sheepishly. "That's why I took it. I figured that it was probably important. And then I figured that if it was important, it should be kept safe. The next thing I knew it was in my pouch. And now I feel guilty about taking it, because that priestess lady was so nice to me and let me have that dagger that I really liked..."

There really was no stopping a halfling when she got going.

Chapter XV
Codalthaxillius

The great gold wyrm lay sunning himself, great wispy tendrils of smoke drifting up from his nostrils. Even sleeping, the great wyrm was completely aware of his surroundings. And so it was that he was completely unsurprised by the old man who approached. Nor was the dragon at all surprised by the identity of his visitor. After all, the old man was the only visitor the dragon had ever had in over three hundred years. He would have been happy had the old man stayed away.

"What do you want?" the dragon asked without opening his eyes. "I'm busy."

"Busy dying, it looks like," the old man snorted. He crossed his arms as he frowned at the old dragon. "Or busy feeling sorry for yourself. Take your pick."

"Why shouldn't I feel sorry for myself?" the dragon rumbled. "You've kept me in exile for three hundred and seventeen years. Give or take a day or two."

"I didn't realize you were keeping count, dragon" the old man chortled out between chuckles.

"Well, I am." The dragon blew a puff of smoke at the old man. "I only have a few years left I want to spend them sleeping. Go away, old man. Leave me in peace."

"And what if I were to tell you that the end of your exile is at hand?" The old man raised one furry eyebrow at the dragon.

"I would say that the Draconic Council would never agree to it," the dragon remarked. "As you recall, I am sure, they wanted me killed for that incident at the Temple of the Blades. Eliazar went so far as to claim that gold dragons that act like red dragons should not be allowed the luxury of life. I doubt his opinion has changed in a mere three hundred years."

"You forget that the Draconic Council answers to me, Cobalthaxillius," the old man admonished. "I am Taelin, the Lightbringer. I have deemed that your exile is to be at an end. And therefore, it is so."

"Touching, old man," the dragon snorted, plumes of smoke puffing from his nostrils. "But I am too old and too apathetic to be of much use to anyone. Why now?"

"Desperate times call for desperate measures, Cobalt," Taelin said. The god sighed softly and put a hand on the dragon's neck. "Thraal has put events into motion that must be stopped."

"I'm too old to become embroiled in your godly battles, Lord Taelin," the dragon rumbled. "I'm afraid you need a younger dragon for that. One that is, decidedly, not me." With that the great ancient wyrm closed his eyes and laid his great head on the ground.

"A Blademaster walks the world once more, Cobalt," Taelin said, his voice a mere whisper on the wind.

The dragon's eyes snapped open, and he roared with fury. "A Blademaster?"

"Yes, I thought that would get your attention."

Cobalt raised his great head. "What have you done?"

"No more than was necessary." Lord Taelin shrugged. "It seemed the best solution. Laeyra agrees."

"Do you realize the trouble that you could have caused by creating a new Blademaster?" Cobalt thundered. "Do you not remember what happened the last time a Blademaster walked the world?"

"I remember full well what happened," Taelin snapped. "But only a Blademaster has the ability to prevent what Thraal has set into motion. I should think you would be happy. Here now is your chance at redemption."

"You want me to serve as the Blademaster's nathair an aeir a chosnaíonn." the dragon snorted. "Well, too bad. I believe my summoning statue has been destroyed."

"Don't you think me capable of solving that particular problem, Cobalt?" Taelin laughed. "I put your summoning statue in the armory of the Temple of the Blades some time ago."

"And just how do you expect the Blademaster to acquire my summoning statue?" Cobalt asked, amused.

"The Blademaster has a halfling in her party." The god shrugged brandishing a broad smile. "I rather expect the halfling to steal the statue from the armory."

"What?" the dragon bellowed, a font of fire exiting from his throat. "You are leaving something of this importance to chance? Laeyra is starting to have a bad affect on you, old man. There's no way to guarantee that this halfling will steal the statue as you expect."

"Actually, I'm pretty certain that the halfling will do just exactly as I suspect." Taelin laughed some more. He patted Cobalt on the side of the neck. "You see, dragon, not only does this halfling have the usual halfling love of shiny objects, but this particular halfling has something of an infatuation with dragons. A shiny metal dragon will be just too much for her to resist. I would be surprised if the item in question has not already been pilfered."

Cobalt shuddered. He unfolded his wings and flapped them twice as if making sure they still worked. "It seems that you have thought this adequately through, Lord Taelin," the dragon remarked. "The Blademaster has the statue. I feel its call now."

"Then you must go to her, Cobalt," Taelin affirmed. "My wisdom go with you."

"Thank you, Lord Taelin," Cobalt bowed his head. "For everything." Cobalt launched himself into the sky, his giant wings beating slowly as he soared away.

"I do believe that the Blademaster is in good hands," Taelin sighed as the dragon soared off into the distance.

"The dragon is right." Laeyra said as she appeared next to Taelin. "You took a big risk on the halfling. The stakes are too high to be taking gambles like this."

"You should know by now my dear, that even a wise man needs a little luck sometimes." Taelin said. He took her hand in his. "You know I depend on your luck every bit as much as I depend on my wisdom to get through. Besides, I think the Blademasters are proof enough that my wisdom and your luck are a very powerful combination."

"True enough." Laeyra nodded. "This new Blademaster intrigues me."

"How so?" Taelin raised his eyebrow.

"Her traveling companions for one." the goddess replied. She sat on a boulder and yawned ever so slightly. "I know that you like the halfling. You've always had a soft spot for them as a race. But I guess I'm just not used to a Blademaster having friends. Usually, save for their Protector, Blademasters are solitary beings."

"Perhaps that was our mistake the last time, Laeyra." Taelin said. "Maybe this time, we learn from the past."

"We can hope." Laeyra shrugged as she stood. "The stakes are too great to test whims though."

"Agreed." Taelin nodded. "Thraal has gone too far this time."

Alana held the statue that Meryn had given her. She looked at the statue and then looked at the halfling, disbelief at what the halfling had said all over her face.

"Where did you say you got this?" she asked, her voice dangerously soft. She was willing to forgive a great many of the halfling's sins, but this may have been one sin too many.

"Don't be too hard on Meryn, Alana," the mage interjected softly. "The halfling is only doing what comes naturally to her race. You knew this was her nature when you agreed to let her travel with us."

Alana ignored William and continued to glare at the halfling, demanding an answer.

"I said that I got it from the temple," Meryn grumbled as she shrunk further away from Alana's rage.

"Please say that one more time," Alana thundered. She took a step towards the halfling. Her eyes blazed with anger.

"She said..." Colwyn tried to clarify. Normally, Colwyn would have been reveling in the halfling being caught as a thief and being yelled at. But Alana was angrier than he had ever seen her, so he could take no joy in the halfling's misfortune.

"I want to hear it from her, Colwyn," the Blademaster whispered, and Colwyn knew that it was the Blademaster talking and not Alana. It was a difference he did not necessarily like. She never took her eyes off the halfling. Her look was one that would brook no falsehoods from the halfling.

"I took it from the Temple of the Blades," Meryn whimpered. "Lady Alana, please don't be mad at me. I couldn't help myself."

"How could you do this?" Alana bellowed. "I felt bad enough taking weapons and armor that were offered. And you repay the High Priestess's hospitality by stealing from the temple? Meryn, you don't steal from any temple, let alone the Temple of the Blades."

Alana glared hard at the halfling, but Meryn was staring at the statue in Alana's hands, which had completely captured the halfling's attention. Curious about what had Meryn so transfixed, Alana glanced down at the statue as well.

It was glowing.

The statue had lost its pewter cast and now appeared as if it were made of pure gold. The golden glow was growing in brilliance with each passing second. Soon enough, it was much too bright to look at. Still, all the companions, save for Meryn, were regarding the statue with expressions of confusion, curiosity and awe.

But Meryn, ever alert, was no longer interested in the statue. For something else had caught her attention and it was far more interesting than a glowing statue. Something danced in her periphery, far off in the night sky. It was too distant to make out exactly what it was, but it was moving and coming in fast towards the clearing where they were camped. Meryn had her own ideas of what the flying object was.

"A dragon," the halfling breathed.

The others turned their attention to Meryn's line of sight and followed her gaze.

The dragon quickly came within visual range of the clearing. Meryn had been right. The creature was a gold dragon. A very large gold dragon.

"Probably ancient," Alana remarked under her breath to no one in particular.

As the dragon approached, they could feel the wind from its beating wings.

Alana glanced from the dragon to the statue. There was more than a passing resemblance.

"Get clear, everyone," Colwyn ordered.

Everyone scattered as the dragon swooped into the clearing and buzzed the trees on the perimeter once before setting down in the soft grass.

Alana scrutinized the statue again, shaking her head. Clearly this dragon was the model for the statue. And she was certain the dragon's arrival coinciding with the statue's glow was no coincidence. But she had no idea just what it all meant. She had a feeling she was about to find out though.

"Blademaster Alana Steeldrake," the dragon rumbled as he bowed his head in reverence. "I pledge my life to your defense. As per the Law of the Blades, I am to serve as your nathair an aeir a chosnaíonn."

"That Law of the Blades might come in handy after all," Colwyn whispered.

The dragon regarded Colwyn for a cold moment before turning his attention back to Alana. "My life is yours to command."

Alana bowed in return. "Noble dragon, what is your name?"

"I am called Cobalthaxillius, Blademaster Alana," the dragon replied. "But you may find it easier to call me simply Cobalt."

"Very well, Cobalt," Alana replied with a smile. She reached out tentatively. At her side and just behind her, she could sense Colwyn tense. But Cobalt made no move against her. So she scratched the dragon's neck. "How did you find us?" she asked.

"The object in your hand is my summoning statue," Cobalt said, showing rows of razor sharp teeth. Alana assumed she was perceiving the dragon's smile. "When you are in need, simply hold the statue and concentrate on me. I will always come to your aid." The dragon scanned the companions and stopped on Meryn. "And do not be angered at the halfling for taking the statue from the Temple of the Blades. It was placed in the armory specifically for her to find. She has played her role well."

Alana glanced over at Meryn, whose spirit seemed defeated. She gave the halfling a tiny nod. Meryn perked up at that which warmed Alana's heart. Then she turned her attention back to the dragon. "May I ask who put the statue in the armory, Cobalt?"

"Yes," Colwyn added. "Who meant for Meryn to steal it?"

"The same entity who assigned me as your nathair an aeir a chosnaíonn, Blademaster Alana," Cobalt said softly. His dark blue eyes met her deep green ones. "It would seem that Lord Taelin has indeed taken a special interest in his child."

"Fascinating!" Balaam exhaled.

Alana frowned at the dragon's phrasing. She knew that Taelin looked on all created beings as his children. But did the way the dragon said 'his child' in reference to her almost imply something more? Before she could ask him about it, she noticed the dragon's ears twitching. She cocked her head to look at him quizzically.

"What is it?" she asked softly.

"Company," the dragon snarled. "Everyone, give me room. I will take care of this."

Alana hesitated for a moment but William took her by the arm and led her and Colwyn toward the outskirts of the clearing with Meryn and Balaam right on their heels.

The great dragon oriented his ears, then turned to face the southern entrance to the clearing. He lowered his head and rested it on his front paws.

It took only a moment or two for the intruders to arrive. They were on foot and they skidded to a halt after entering the clearing, the sight of a giant gold dragon glaring at them was probably the last thing these three followers of Thraal had been expecting. Still to their credit, the Thraalish minions were not of a mind to give up so easily.

"Who are you?" the dragon thundered.

"We're here for the Blademaster," the man in the lead replied. "Give her to us, and there will be no trouble." Colwyn was impressed that this man's voice did not so much as waver. Having faced a dragon, he knew that he would not be nearly as calm as this man was if their positions were switched.

Cobalt narrowed his eyes at the three intruders. "What do you want with the Blademaster?" As an afterthought, he added, "As if I had any intention of turning her over to you."

"Lord Thraal requires her for a sacrifice." The leader sneered.

"Well, at least this one's honest," Colwyn muttered from where he was crouched in the underbrush at Alana's side.

"I don't think that is going to happen." Cobalt punctuated his boredom with a yawn. He took advantage of the yawn to suck in a great quantity of air. Then he exhaled it in a great font of flame, completely engulfing the three followers of Thraal, incinerating them immediately. But, Alana noted, the nearby trees remained in pristine condition.

"There will be more where those came from," the dragon sighed. "Perhaps we should go."

"You think?" Colwyn asked. By his tone, Alana knew he didn't expect an answer.

Alana brushed herself off before approaching the great dragon and placing her hand on his neck. "I think we have a little time. Time enough for you to answer a few questions. There are things that I want to know from you."

"You Blademasters are all the same," Cobalt sighed. "Always wanting to know why. It's all a tremendous waste of time. But go ahead and ask your questions."

Alana flashed Colwyn a winning smile and was rewarded with a shrug before she continued. "So exactly why did Lord Taelin assign you to be my nathair an aeir a chosnaíonn?" she asked. She rubbed a spot on the mighty dragon's neck and based on the way his ears lolled back, she figured that she had located a sweet spot. She filed that information away for future reference.

"Lord Taelin, in his wisdom, has offered an old dragon a chance at redemption," Cobalt replied in a low rumble.

"Redemption?" Alana arched a brow. "For what sin do you require redemption, noble dragon?"

"I have... how should I say it? Not always been noble." Cobalt turned away from her, great tears welling up in his eyes. "I assume you know the story of the Blademasters."

"Yes." Alana nodded. "Lady Solara imparted to me the full history. Including the end of the line when the Blademasters were lynched and thrown off the Temple of the Blades."

"It is good that I do not have to recount that part. I was the nathair an aeir a chosnaíonn for the last Blademaster, Crystal Sapphire. She was the only Blademaster that had her summoning statue with her that day. It was the very statue that you now hold in your hands, Blademaster Alana. I suppose it was just her bad luck that I was her nathair an aeir a chosnaíonn." The dragon stopped and sniffled. Tears threatened to flow.

"What happened?" Alana prodded gently, still rubbing that special spot on Cobalt's neck.

"She used the statue to summon me. I had just caught myself a herd of displacer beasts, and was settling down for a nice dinner when I felt the summons. But it had been days since I had last eaten. I wrongfully ignored it until I had finished my meal," the dragon explained, still unable to look Alana in the eye. "When I reached the Temple of the Blades, the mobs had gone. Blademaster Crystal lived only long enough to ask me why I hadn't come to help her. But I had no answer. I tried to heal her with my magic, but I was just too late." Finally he turned back to Alana. "So, I will understand if you wish another nathair an aeir a chosnaíonn, Blademaster Alana."

Alana set her jaw. "Noble dragon, Lord Taelin has assigned you to be my nathair an aeir a chosnaíonn. If he feels you are the dragon for the job, then I am honored that his wisdom has seen fit to have you fighting by my side."

Cobalt blinked but said nothing. Then he sighed and a great plume of smoke puffed forth. "Thank you, Blademaster Alana," the dragon said. "You do me a great honor by not holding my past against me. And I vow that I will not lose another Blademaster on my watch."

"I believe you," Alana said.

"And I'm going to hold you to it," Colwyn added.

"Cobalt, why did you refer to me as Lord Taelin's child?" Alana asked. "I mean, I know we're all children of Taelin. But I got the feeling that there might be more to it than that."

"There is indeed," Cobalt nodded. "It is said that a Blademaster is an equal mix of Taelin's wisdom and Laeyra's luck. That is true, although it is true in a way other than what most people think."

"What do you mean?" Alana frowned. "I don't quite understand."

"When you were conceived your mortal parents were imbued with Taelin's wisdom and Laeyra's luck to pass along to you during conception," Cobalt explained. "In essence, you are a product of a union of the two gods. It is that way with all the Blademasters."

"I don't understand," Alana said again. "How could Lord Taelin have known that a Blademaster would be needed now in time for my birth?"

"Thraal," Cobalt spat the name out with distaste, "has not exactly been secretive about his plans. Lord Taelin has known this was coming for well over thirty years. He had more than enough time to prepare a defense."

"I see." Alana continued to stroke the sweet spot on the dragon's neck. "Well then, as you so astutely pointed out, we should probably get going. Thraal won't be stopped by himself."

"What is our destination?" Cobalt asked softly.

"Tornith," Colwyn replied. "That is where the High Priest of Thraal is trying to bring the Dark God back to Calthea."

"It has been many generations since I have done much of anything," the dragon admitted. "I am not as strong as I once was. I suspect that I will not be able to take you all the way to Tornith but I will take you as far as I can before I must rest."

"I understand." Alana assured him. "That will do. You will still save us time on our journey."

"Then climb aboard." Cobalt declared as he flashed a brilliant row of razor sharp teeth.

His smile, Alana reminded herself. *It's only his smile.*

The companions scrambled up onto Cobalt's back. Alana found the seating to be surprisingly comfortable and watched as her companions settled in among the folds in the great dragons scales. When everyone was settled, she patted the dragon on the neck.

"Before we take off, I have one final question," Alana whispered into the dragon's ear.

"I will answer, if I can," Cobalt said.

"Why did Lord Taelin wait over three hundred years to bring the Blademasters back?"

"Because," Cobalt chuckled as he stretched forth his great wings. "Until now, they were not needed."

Any reply that Alana had was lost in the rush of air as the dragon took to the sky.

The Blademaster

Part III
Showdown in
Tornith

Chapter XVI
Dracomyr

Cobalt flew on through the night. He'd cast an enchantment over the companions so that they would sleep through the trip, otherwise the wind, cold and altitude would prevent them from sleeping. He knew that they would need their rest. Dracomyr was ruled by the minions of Thraal and the other evil gods. The companions, who were faithful to Taelin and Laeyra amongst others, would find no help there. And so it was imperative that they were well rested when they arrived so they would be at the best of their abilities. If they were not well rested, they might make mistakes that could get them caught or killed. And then Cobalt would have failed his duties as Alana's nathair an aeir a chosnaíonn.

Cobalt would not fail another Blademaster.

As he drifted over the clouds, his thoughts reflected back to that day over three hundred years prior when he had failed Crystal Sapphire. It was something he dwelled on often over the years of his exile. Indeed, he thought of little else during his exile. The memory of the death of his Blademaster had haunted him. It was not easy for a dragon to deal with such an event, especially when said dragon blamed himself.

Great dragon tears rolled down from his eyes, cascading over his golden skin and falling to the ground far below as he again ruminated on his past failure…

Cobalt had been trailing the herd of displacer beasts for hours. They had led him on a merry chase through the Wilds, the borderlands between the Southern Dales and Dracomyr.

The displacer beasts were Cobalt's favorite meal. Black four legged furry animals, displacer beasts were about halfway between the size of a dog and a horse. A pair of whip-like appendages attached to the creature on its rump just forward of where a tail would have been if displacer beasts had tails, which they did not. Although the two tentacles could whip out in any direction to attack or to defend, they did not possess any poison or barbs or anything of that nature to make them overtly dangerous. However, they could be whipped in any direction with such a force that they could easily break bone. The tentacles, though, were not even the primary defense mechanism at a displacer beast's disposal. As dangerous as they were, the tentacles could not defend the beasts against something as large as a dragon. Dragons were a major concern for displacer beasts as many dragons enjoyed hunting them for food.

To defend against dragon attacks, displacer beasts had developed a defense mechanism unique to their species. A displacer beast had the ability to make itself appear as if it were several feet away from where it actually was, displacing its appearance sufficiently to cause confusion to a would be attacker. This ability is what gave displacer beasts their name. Because of this ability to displace themselves from an enemy, displacer beast hides were widely sought after by magic users to make cloaks that would give their wearer the same ability to shift his appearance. Even in death, the hide of a displacer beast retains its ability. Cloaks of displacement were exceedingly rare, however. And there were those who believed that wearing such cloaks would erode the wearer's soul. Such a claim had never been proven, though. A cloak of displacement tended to sell for a great sum of money whenever one was made available to purchase, so the common adventurer could ill afford to purchase one.

Cobalt, however, did not care about making a cloak of displacement for himself. Such a cloak would be impractical at best for a being of his size. It would take the hides of all of the displacer beasts in the largest herd that Cobalt had ever seen in order to make a cloak of displacement large enough to displace a whole gold dragon. Cobalt was one of the largest gold dragons that existed on Calthea. The protection that such a cloak could offer him was not all that great especially when compared with his own natural defenses.

No, he was far more interested in this herd of displacer beasts because he was hungry.

He had not realized it, but he had flown all the way across the part of the continent between the Southern Dales and Dracomyr that was commonly just called the Wilds. Even now, the Stonegate Mountains were coming into focus. That was a very good thing as far as Cobalt was concerned, for if it turned out that the displacer beasts did not sate his hunger, he could always ferret out a few dozen goblins from the nearby mountains as a second course. Goblins were no displacer beasts, but they came in a close second.

The herd of displacer beasts had been running for hours, leading Cobalt on a wild chase. He had enjoyed the chase, though, almost as much as he would enjoy his dinner when he finally caught and slaughtered the herd. It was a relatively small herd, only about eight beasts. But it would make a good dinner. All he really had to do was to wait for the herd to stop and then he would attack. At the moment, he was gliding on a current of warmer air, so he was not really expending a great deal of energy in the hunt. Which meant that when he did finally catch his prey, not only would he be fully able to enjoy his meal, but also he would be able to get the fullest energy and vitality out of his meal as well which was something that was always important for a creature his size. He had learned long ago to get as much out of each meal as possible in order for him to survive.

He watched the displacer beasts charge along the ground. From his vantage point, he could tell that there were no other predators anywhere near the herd. It was all his. No sharing required, which was just the way he liked it. He also hated to waste his kills, so he was glad that the herd was small enough that there would be no waste. He circled lazily overhead, watching as they slowed and came to a stop in prime grazing grounds.

He came back around, taking his time, savoring the view of the herd below. As he dipped towards the herd, he lurched.

His summoning statue!

But he was so hungry. And he had chased the herd for so long. It hardly seemed fair to have to abandon all of that hard work. He could scoop them up quickly and feast upon them within minutes. He had always replied to a summoning on time. A few minutes would not make a difference.

It was not easy, but he was able to shake off the pull of the summoning statue by sheer force of will.

With a deafening roar, he launched himself into a dive, gliding over the displacer beasts that would serve as his meal. Teeth and claws slashed and gashed at the displacer beasts and it was over soon enough. he was curled up in the warm grass munching on the flesh of the beasts. It was a good dinner, and he was very satisfied. He did not expect to require a second course of goblins to finish off his hunger.

But then the pull from the summoning statue returned. But he wasn't yet finished! He had worked so hard for his meal. Why couldn't he at least finish it in peace? With a burst of effort, he ignored it once more. He would be delighted to go see what his Blademaster wanted.

When he was finished his meal.

He could tell by the pull that she was far to the south, probably at the Temple of the Blades. What harm could she be in at the Temple of the Blades?

As he ate, he let his mind wander to his service to the Blademasters. He did not know how he had been selected to be a nathair an aeir a chosnaíonn. It was an honor that he had never wanted. And yet the Draconic Council had seen fit to bestow such an honor upon him. Most of the time, he felt as if he was being punished for something by having such responsibilities piled upon him. The leader of the Draconic Council, Eliazar, had always said that it was a great honor. He had been selected for his courage and his fierce determination. But Cobalt found that he no longer wanted the honor. He wished there was a way out of it, but he knew that so long as he was a nathair an aeir a chosnaíonn, there were only two ways out of his position. One was that his Blademaster was killed, in which case, he would be disgraced. The other was that he was killed. That option also did not appeal to him for obvious reasons. He wondered if there were perhaps a loophole, another alternative for ending his service to the Blademasters.

But for now, all that he was truly concerned with was his dinner.

As he finished off the last of the displacer beasts, the pull from the summoning statue became more insistent. But he found that he was now more easily able to ignore the statue's pull, having been able to ignore it twice already.

So he took his time on the last few morsels of his dinner, savoring the flavor. He did not bother to cook his meat first. Most dragons did not bother to cook their meat. Stripping the meat from the bones was the real trick anyway. If not stripped off properly, the bones could turn into painful slivers that could get into the dragon's jaws and cause unbelievable pain.

Cobalt was a master of stripping meat from bones, though, and he never got such a sliver during his meals. And this was a source of pride. One of his last, for that matter.

For this reason, among others, he did not rush his dinner, but it came to an end nevertheless. He did not allow himself the luxury of an after dinner nap as was his custom because he did not wish to get more of a tongue-lashing from his Blademaster than he was already likely to get for being so tardy. He was late enough, as it was.

With a resigned huff, he launched himself into the air and flew south towards the Temple of the Blades as fast as his wings could carry him.

The Elven Woods stretched below Cobalt. He had no real way of knowing what had been going on but he somehow sensed that something terrible had happened. The pull of the summoning statue had ceased over an hour before. He did not know what that meant. He hoped it meant that the danger had passed and that Crystal no longer needed him. But that was looking at the bright side and he knew all too well that there was also another side. One he didn't wish to entertain.

Had dinner been so important?

He urged himself to fly faster but he was at his top speed. In the distance, the spires of the Temple of the Blades poked up through the tree tops. It appeared he had surmised correctly. The Temple of the Blades was ground zero for whatever had happened.

But how was that possible? After all, only the Blademasters, their Protectors, and the High Priests of both Laeyra and Taelin knew exactly how to get to the Temple of the Blades. Of course, the Forestwalker Elves knew how to get there too. But the Elves were notorious for making it difficult for even the Blademasters to get to the Temple of the Blades.

It seemed to take an inordinate amount time for Cobalt to reach the Temple of the Blades. The spires did not seem to be coming closer, although Cobalt knew he was going just as fast as he could. He watched as the spires came agonizingly slowly closer to him. He urged more speed. He prayed to Taelin and Laeyra and any other god that might be listening that he was not too late.

Finally, after what seemed like hours from when the spires first came into view, he found himself over the clearing that was home to the Temple of the Blades. He was intimately familiar with every inch of the clearing. He had walked the Temple of the Blades in his human form many times. That was the one benefit of being the nathair an aeir a chosnaíonn to Crystal Sapphire. He was able to spend time exploring the Temple of the Blades. The temple fascinated him and he spent much of his spare time there.

Cobalt circled around the edge of the clearing, gazing down at the view of the temple grounds.

He did not like, nor could he believe, what he saw.

The broken bodies of Blademasters were sprawled out upon the ground. Dead. At least he was pretty sure that they were all dead. He scanned the bodies for Crystal but failed to locate her. He circled the clearing again. She was not present. His heart began to hope that she might have somehow survived. Again, he circled, preparing to land but then he spied her, not far from the temple door.

With a roar, he hit the ground and lunged toward the temple, shifting to human form midstream. He knelt down next to where she lay. Her body was broken in many places, and there was blood smeared over her face and arms.

She coughed.

She was alive!

He turned her over.

"Cobalt?" she asked weakly as her eyes focused on him.

"I am here, Lady Crystal," he assured her. He gently lifted her head and stroked her hair. She was weak. "What happened?"

"The people of the Southern Dales..." she started. Crystal fell into a fit of coughing before she could continue. He continued to stroke her hair gently, hoping to comfort her. "...said they were tired of living under our rule. Said that they would not allow a single Blademaster to live. Forced us up to the top of the Temple of the Blades and drove us off."

She started to weep.

"What of the Protectors?" Cobalt asked. Surely the Protectors would not have allowed such a travesty.

"Killed in the dungeons."

An outrage!

"And the other dragons?" Cobalt asked. He could not believe that he had been the only one summoned.

"None of the other Blademasters had their summoning statues with them," Crystal whispered. The light started to fade from her eyes. Her time was upon her. "But I had mine. I summoned you..."

Cobalt shook his head but could not speak.

"But you never came."

"I am sorry, Lady Crystal," he rasped. *It was all he could get out. He could not admit to her that the reason he did not come sooner was because he was eating.*

"I waited for you," she breathed, her voice weaker with each word. *"I watched. And when they pushed me off the top of the temple, I prayed that you would catch me before I hit the ground."*

Cobalt's eyes welled up with tears.

"But you never came."

"I... I'm..."

"Why didn't you come?"

But Cobalt could not answer her. He could only hold her, weeping softly. He had failed in his duties as nathair an aeir a chosnaíonn. The other dragons that served as nathair an aeir a chosnaíonn to the other Blademasters had an excuse. They could not have been summoned. No other summoning statues had been present. But his had. And his Blademaster had used it.

And he had ignored it.

He would have to face the Draconic Council. They would punish him, perhaps even kill him. But he did not care what they did to him. He could never forgive himself for failing his Blademaster. There was nothing that they could do to him that would even compare to the guilt that now rested on his shoulders.

"Stay with me, Blademaster," Cobalt cried. He closed his eyes and reached deep inside. He wasn't without resources. He had his own draconic magic. If he could just use it in time...

But try as he might, he could not access his magic to heal her. His guilt blocked the way.

It pained him to watch as the light and the life left Crystal's eyes and the last of the Blademasters passed away in his arms. He continued to sit there long after she had passed away. There was nothing else for him to do but sit there and hope for death. It would hurt too much to even attempt to do anything else. He could not live knowing that he had been able to save his Blademaster. If he had only heeded the pull of his summoning statue.

Instead, he had acted like a red dragon and had let his stomach guide him.

He did not know how long he sat there watching Crystal. He knew time was passing. He perceived the setting of the sun. He simply did not care. He would sit there forever. He would sit until death claimed him. And the sooner, the better.

It was many hours or many days later when he felt a hand on his shoulder. Cobalt wasn't sure. He looked up to see a stocky old man gazing down at him. Cobalt, of course, knew exactly who the old man was. He'd been in Lord Taelin's service for centuries. He shrugged off the old man and turned his attention back to his fallen charge.

After several more silent minutes, Cobalt spoke. "I failed her," he croaked. "She summoned me and I ignored the summons. I have failed."

"I know," Taelin said softly. "I have been watching. I know what happened. And I know how you feel about it. Nothing can be hidden from me, Cobalthaxillius. But do not pass judgment on yourself. The Draconic Council will fulfill that role."

"I understand," the dragon nodded. He did not look at his god, but he could feel that Taelin was watching him. He did not know what the god thought about his failure but he felt as if he was being judged, even though he knew that Taelin did not judge people based on one or two mistakes. Nor did he judge dragons for that either. He figured that one day, Taelin would give him a chance to redeem himself.

But he was not certain he would welcome such a chance when it was offered.

"I never wanted to be a nathair an aeir a chosnaíonn, Lord Taelin," the dragon said softly. He turned his pain filled eyes towards his god. "Even so, this is not how I would have chosen to end my tenure nathair an aeir a chosnaíonn to Blademaster Crystal."

"I know, Cobalt," Taelin said softly. "Come now. The Draconic Council is gathering and they will be expecting us."

The god waved his hands in a circle and the very air shimmered, seeming to fold in on itself. A void formed in the fold as it drew the two of them into it. Then it folded back in on itself.

In a blink, the void was gone, taking Taelin and Cobalt with it.

The Isle of Dragons did not appear on any map. It was located roughly three hundred miles southeast of the port town of Lovendale. No ship from the Southern Dales or Dracomyr ever made port on the Isle of Dragons, for no man not born of dragons could walk the island's shores. The gods Taelin and Aram had made that a decree when they had set aside the isle for the dragons. They had known that the peoples of Calthea would never be totally accepting of dragonkind, and so they had set aside a place for the dragons to live. It was their home. It was also where the Draconic Council met.

Only the Draconic Council could pass judgment on a dragon.

The Draconic Council was made up of the eldest of all fifteen different varieties of dragon native to Calthea. There were the good dragons: gold, silver, bronze, brass, and copper. Then there were the more neutral-tending dragons: the diamond, sapphire, emerald, amethyst and ruby. And then there were the evil dragons, the red, blue, green, black and white. These dragons had aligned their tendencies since the beginning of time and it had long been felt that the only way that there could be fair and equitable decisions concerning all of dragonkind would be if all fifteen dragon types were represented in council.

The Draconic Council had been formed and met only when needed in the Temple of Dragons near the center of the Isle of Dragons.

Taelin and Cobalt materialized about three hundred feet away from the Temple of Dragons, just off the road that led up to the temple. The two of them stepped onto the road and slowly made their way towards the temple without saying a word. They were passed only one time by a young amethyst dragon that Cobalt did not know. She bowed to Taelin and the god bowed back to her. Cobalt watched the dragon as she approached the temple. His stomach sank. A large group of dragons would have gathered for his judgment.

He expected that the end result of such a gathering would be his death.

He followed Taelin silently into the Temple of Dragons. This would perhaps be the last time he would walk these steps. Each step was painful to take. There was no doubt in Cobalt's mind about his guilt. He therefore fully expected the Draconic Council to sentence him accordingly.

It wasn't that he wanted to die, but he was responsible for the death of not only his own Blademaster, but all of the others as well. He could not live with such guilt weighing on his soul. And all for a herd of displacer beasts.

He felt sick.

As he entered the Great Hall of the Temple of Dragons, he glanced around. It was the first time that he had ever been in the presence of the entire Draconic Council. It was an imposing sight, and one that he hoped never to see again. There were five great tables arranged in an arc around the seating area. Three dragons perched at each of the tables, none of them in their human forms. In order to accommodate the council, the room had to be huge. It was also open to the sky, and the late evening sunlight lit the room with an orange tint.

Each of the five tables hosted one of each of the three alignments of dragons: one good, one evil, and one neutral. The Council was arranged in such a way so as to prevent undue alignment influence. It was a practical solution, one that the dragons had come up with on their own.

The center table concerned Cobalt the most for in the center of the arc were the leaders of the three respective alignments of dragons: the great gold wyrm Eliazar, the ancient red dragon, Shakaaris, and the oldest diamond dragon that Cobalt had ever seen, Mintakis. It was these three dragons that would preside over the Draconic Council and it was these three dragons that would be the primary source of the questioning. Eliazar was the dragon that concerned him the most. Cobalt had, unfortunately, engaged in dealings with the great gold wyrm before and the results had not been favorable for either of them. They did not exactly like each other. Perhaps it was Cobalt's disdain for his position of nathair an aeir a chosnaíonn, but there was something about Cobalt that Eliazar had never liked. Cobalt did not believe that the older dragon would let personal feelings interfere with how he ran the hearing, but it was a possibility nevertheless.

It was not as if Cobalt planned to lie about what happened though.

Even the thought of lying to the Council felt like a further betrayal of his Blademaster. He could not betray her memory in that way, so he would admit the terrible truth to the Draconic Council and pray for their mercy. In this case, Cobalt felt that death might just be a mercy.

"Now that the accused is here," Eliazar rumbled, "we can begin." The old wyrm narrowed his eyes at Cobalt. "Would the accused please assume his draconic form for the Council?"

"I do not feel worthy of the dragon form," Cobalt said replied. He let his arms fall to his sides. "But if the Draconic Council insists, I have no choice but to comply."

'It is required of you," Mintakis said gently. "So naturally, we insist. I would, however, ask why you do not feel worthy of your draconic form."

"It is the reason I am here, Lady Mintakis," Cobalt said. He shifted into his draconic form and turned to face the lead table of the Draconic Council. "We all know what I have done that has placed me before the Council. And we all know without doubt that I am guilty of what I am accused of. I suppose that the only real question is what is to become of me?"

"What is it that you feel you are accused of, Cobalthaxillius?" Eliazar croaked as he fixed the younger dragon in his gaze.

"I have failed in my duties as nathair an aeir a chosnaíonn to the Blademaster Crystal Sapphire," Cobalt said simply. He could no longer look at the three dragons at the head table. "And my failure has shaken me to my core."

"Then where are the other dragons that served as nathair an aeir a chosnaíonn to the Blademasters?" Shakaaris scoffed. "They should be here as well if that is all that you are accused of, gold dragon."

"*They did not fail in their duties as I did, Lord Shakaaris,*" Cobalt rasped. His voice was breaking with the great dragon tears that were falling from his eyes. "*They were never summoned. I was. But I ignored the pull of my summoning statue. Had I not ignored the summoning, then perhaps I could have saved not only my own Blademaster, but also the others as well.*"

"*Why did you ignore your summoning statue, Cobalthaxillius?*" Mintakis asked. Her voice was gentle, but all Cobalt could hear in that gentleness was the edge of accusation. Or maybe it was the edge of his own guilt cutting at him. "*What was so important that you could not go to your Blademaster when summoned?*"

Cobalt thought for a moment and rejected hunger as an excuse almost as quickly as he thought of it. "*I suppose I had grown complacent,*" Cobalt sighed. "*Mostly the Blademaster had summoned me to fly her around the Southern Dales. I figured it was another ride that she wanted. Since I felt that was what it was, I believed that it could wait until after I had finished the meal I had just caught. Had I known the truth, I would not have delayed.*"

"*Cobalthaxillius,*" Eliazar growled. "*Yours was a sacred duty. And you ignored it. And for what? To fill your stomach. You act far more like a red dragon than a gold dragon.*"

"*Objection!*" the red dragon, Shakaaris, blurted. But he was ignored.

"*Gold dragons who act like they are red dragons should not be allowed to continue to live. I have nothing but contempt for you. You shame the rest of your kind.*"

"*That is a bit harsh, Eliazar,*" the red dragon remarked. "*And the bit about red dragons is uncalled for.*"

"*If I may address the Council?*" Taelin said softly from where he stood at Cobalt's side. In his shame, he had forgotten that Taelin was standing next to him. His voice, though soft, cut through the room as only a god's voice could. "*There is something I would like to say.*"

"*Of course, Lord Taelin,*" Eliazar bowed his head towards the god standing next to Cobalt. "*Of all of the deities of Calthea, you are the one who holds the causes of dragons* closest to your heart. You are always welcome to speak to the Draconic Council."

"Very well." Taelin stepped forward. "It is true that this dragon failed in his sacred duties to the Blademasters. Of all in the room, I am the one who should be the most upset. And yet, I can find it in my heart to forgive Cobalt. Do I think he should not be punished? No. What he did was a grave offense, and it may yet cause a great deal of trouble for our world. But what he has done is not worth his life." Taelin glanced up at Cobalt. The dragon could hardly believe his ears. "Instead," Taelin continued, "I would see him exiled from the Isle of Dragons."

Gasps echoed through the chamber.

"But where would he go?" Eliazar inquired. "We can't have him simply roaming about, escaping the consequence of his actions and eluding the rule of this council."

"I would have him sent to the Wilds. There is a place there that I can keep him separated from the rest of the world. There he should serve out his days in quiet contemplation of what he has done. Consequence enough, I think, considering how he has taken his failure to heart. And perhaps one day, there might even be an opportunity to make amends."

"You make a good argument for exile over death, Lord Taelin," Shakaaris snorted, a plume of smoke curling from his nostrils. "And perhaps it is an alternative that we should seriously consider. As bad as what this gold dragon did was, can any of us on the Council say in truth that we have never at times let our baser nature take precedence over what we were pledged to do? I say now that if any of the dragons on this Council says they have never done so, then that dragon is a liar. And so if we condemn this dragon to death, we really must condemn all dragons to death."

"It is settled then," Eliazar growled. "As much as I think that Cobalthaxillius should be put to death, I will abide by the suggestion of our Lord Taelin and commute the sentence of death in favor of exile. Cobalthaxillius, you will remove yourself from the Isle of Dragons. And you are never to return. Lord Taelin will take you to the place he has selected for you. There you will live out your days in contemplation of what you have done, or as it turns out, have not done on this day. We, the Draconic Council leave it up to Lord Taelin as to whether you may one day redeem yourself. On a personal note, I must say that I am most displeased that it was a member of my own species that failed the Draconic Council in this manner." Eliazar huffed. "Unless there is objection, the matter is closed. The Draconic Council is adjourned."

The dragons that made up the Draconic Council filed out of the room leaving Cobalt alone with Taelin. Cobalt shifted himself back into his human form so he could talk with Taelin more comfortably.

"Lord Taelin, what you have suggested is a fate worse than death," the dragon said quietly. "Do you expect me to be grateful?"

"I expect you to do your duty. That is all I have ever expected. Now you must commit yourself to a different kind of service," Taelin chided him.

"But Eliazar is right. I do not deserve to live. This sentence is more than I can bear."

"Only time will tell if that is true or not, my dear Cobalt," Taelin smiled warmly. "I can only tell you that there will come a time when you will have a chance at redemption. It may well take many years, but your opportunity will come. I suggest that, when the time is upon us, you take it, because your next chance will surely be your last."

Cobalt nodded. "Take me to my new home," the dragon said, turning away from his god. He could not bear to think about redemption when all he could think about was Crystal Sapphire's broken body. He knew that her accusations would ring in his ears for as long as he lived. "I can't bear to be on this island any longer. I no longer belong here."

"As you say," Taelin nodded. "I will come and visit you often. I promise you that."

The old man waved his arms and dragon and god disappeared from the Isle of Dragons.

True to his word, the old man had visited regularly over the next three hundred years. It was only the final visit, three hundred and seventeen years from the beginning of Cobalt's exile, that had been the visit to finally change his life.

The Blademaster

Once again, Lord Taelin had requested his service as a nathair an aeir a chosnaíonn. Cobalt had not dared to believe that it was true, but the truth of it had been made clear to him.

Once again, he was a nathair an aeir a chosnaíonn. He would not fail again.

Cobalt emerged from his reminiscing to find himself over the same clearing where he had caught the herd of displacer beasts so many years before.

Tears welled up and threatened to fall. It would not be safe to go further, he decided. Not with his new Blademaster and her companions at risk. He circled around the clearing, each pass lower to the ground than the one before. Finally, he touched down, his great feet churning up the dirt as he landed. The jolt of landing after the smooth sensation of flight jostled the companions and jerked them awake.

"Sorry about the landing," Cobalt grumbled. "I'm not used to flying with people on my back anymore.

"Where are we, noble dragon?" Alana asked, stroking the dragon's neck lovingly.

"We have flown all the way through the Wilds. We are now on the edge of Dracomyr," the dragon replied. "I can take you no further."

"Very well," Colwyn hopped down from the dragon. "You've taken weeks off our journey. There is nothing more that we can ask of you."

"Colwyn is right, noble Cobalt," Alana agreed. She stroked the dragon's neck. "Go and rest. If we need you, we will summon you."

"Very well," the dragon bowed his head towards the Blademaster and her Protector. "I will come if you need me. You need only hold the summoning statue and think of your need."

"Go and relax," Alana chuckled softly as she slid off the dragon's back into Colwyn's waiting hands. She waited until the rest of her companions had joined her on the ground with all of their stuff. Then she rubbed the dragon's neck again. "We will try to muddle on without having to call upon you."

"Call on me if you need," the dragon urged. "I will not fail you as I failed Blademaster Crystal."

Alana knew what it was that had been bothering Cobalt at that point, and she knew that there was really nothing she could do to comfort the dragon. She watched as he launched himself into the sky, quickly becoming a small speck of gold in the distance.

"I guess we should get going," she suggested to her companions. "We're pretty well rested and we still have some sunlight left. We can probably make the Stonegate Mountains before dark. We'll camp in the mountains."

"Better than being out in the open," Colwyn remarked.

The companions scooped up their packs as Alana led them towards the distant mountains.

The Blademaster

Chapter XVII
Goblin Attack

Colwyn stood atop a rock outcropping that overlooked the valley below. He had a good view for miles around. It had been a fairly peaceful watch; only a lone wolf came anywhere near the camp. He had let the wolf go about her business of finding food for her young, for he knew that the wolf could sense the wards that William had put up around the camp and would simply pass the companions by.

The peace and tranquility of the uneventful watch gave the young ranger some time to think. It had been a very strange few weeks since Colwyn had found Alana at the inn where she had gone to after running away from him. He was not at all sure he hadn't imagined at least some of it. Although he was quite happy to have married the woman he loved, he felt that the rest of it was not much more than a very bad nightmare, and he had a feeling that Alana felt much the same way. She had not said as much, but he knew her mind well.

Turning his thoughts to Alana only served to make him smile. Ever since he had met her, he had felt that there was something truly special about this warrior woman that had captured his heart. She was strong and exceedingly smart. And she possessed a singularly clever wit. That she loved him too was something that amazed him beyond what words could express. That she was a Blademaster terrified him beyond all contemplation, for it was said Blademasters often died young and their deaths were often unpleasant. He vowed, as he figured every Protector before him had, to keep his Blademaster from dying until she could die peacefully of old age, preferably in her own bed. His only hope was that he would be more successful than his previous counterparts had been. The thought of losing Alana, especially now that they had finally been wed, was just too much for him to bear. He had never felt this kind of deep and abiding love for anyone. It was something for him to cherish and to fight for, if necessary. He would never allow any one or any thing to take her away from him.

It was because of that very love for her that he had been able to finally understand what it was that love is. He remembered a passage from a letter that he'd once read. The letter had been sent by the first High Priest of Taelin, a man of great faith and courage named Apollos, to members of the early Church dedicated to Taelin in an effort to bolster their belief and faith. It had been one of many letters Apollos had sent to the early Church that had been designed to teach and edify believers of Taelin. Those letters had been later collected to form a large part of the Book of the Word of Taelin. During his studies of the Book of the Word of Taelin as a younger man, Colwyn had first come across a passage that had stuck in his mind, a passage in which the High Priest discussed the very nature of what love is in the eyes of Taelin.

If I speak in the languages of men and of angels, but I have not love, I am only a resounding brass or a clanging cymbal.

If I have the gift of prophecy and I can fathom all mysteries and all knowledge, and I have a faith that can move mountains, but I have not love, I am nothing.

If I give all I possess to the poor and I surrender my bed to the flames but I have not love, I gain nothing.

Love is patient. Love is kind. It does not envy. It does not boast. It is not proud. It is not rude. It is not self seeking. It is not easily <u>agreed</u>. It keeps no record of wrongs. Angered?

Love does not delight in evil, but it rejoices in the truth. It always protects, always trusts, always hopes and always perseveres. Love never fails.

But where there are prophecies, they will cease. Where there are languages, they will be stilled. Where there is knowledge it will pass away. For we know in part and we prophecy in part. But when perfection comes, the imperfect disappears.

When I was a child, I spoke as a child, I thought as a child and I reasoned like a child. When I became a man, I put childish things a ways behind me. Now we see but a poor reflection as in a mirror but then we shall see face to face. Now I know in part but then I shall know fully even as I am known.

And now, these three remain; faith, hope, and love. And the greatest of these is love.

Even though he'd heard the words many times before, he had never fully come to understand them until he'd met Alana. Since he had met her, everything just seemed to make more sense. It was amazing to Colwyn that something as simple as the love of a good woman would make such a difference in a man's life. He had quite literally turned all of his perceptions around because of his love for Alana. No matter what, he would never be the same for the touch of her love in his life. And now that he was married to her, the impact on his life would be even more profound.

And he would not have it any other way.

A rustling sound from behind him interrupted his thoughts. He whirled around, his sword out and at the ready.

But he sheathed his sword and relaxed when he saw that it was only Alana stepping up onto the rock to stand the last of his watch with him. Even though he preferred her asleep in their bedroll because he knew that she – as did they all – really needed some sleep, the sight of her climbing up the rock to spend the last few minutes of his watch with him made him smile broadly. He opened his arms wide to her and she happily folded herself into them.

"You should be sleeping, my love," Colwyn admonished quietly. "We still have a long way to go before we reach Tornith, and you will most certainly need your strength when we get there."

"I tried, Col." Alana heaved a deep sigh. "But I just couldn't sleep with you out here. I don't recall ever having this problem before."

"I know. Of late, I seem to be having much the same problem." He chuckled softly as he held her. "I can certainly think of worse problems to have."

"So can I," she sighed softly as she nuzzled closer into his chest. "A life without you would definitely be a much worse problem to have. I hate to think how close we actually came to that. I'm just glad that you were able to pass the Test of the Blades."

"I did have a little help," Colwyn smiled wryly. "It seems that the good spirits wanted us to be together. The first Protector, Richard Kale, helped to guide me through. I don't think that could have happened unless Lord Taelin himself approved of our union. I think that we just need to face the facts, Alana. We were obviously meant to be together."

"I think you might just be right about that." She looked up at him with love in her eyes. "How did you get to be so wise, Col?"

"It goes with the job of being your Protector, Alana." Colwyn smiled sadly, for the things he'd learned about their mission brought him little joy. "Such as getting you the information you need for us to successfully complete our mission."

Her face darkened. It was obvious that she caught his change of mood. "Alright Colwyn, what is it? What else do I need to know about our mission that has got you so down?"

"Merinda Delwyn was sacrificed to Thraal." Colwyn sighed and hesitated a few moments as he decided whether or not to tell her the rest.

"And?"

"And it is what Thraal has in mind for you as well. He believes that sacrificing the Blademaster will be what's required to allow him to walk the world once more. His High Priest is a lich named Drakkhous. He is, from what I have been given to understand, very much in Thraal's favor. I won't tell you what this lich does to his sacrifices but suffice it to say, it is profoundly not pleasant."

"Profoundly not pleasant? What kind of phrasing is that?"

"Look, I will not allow this Drakkhous to do what he wishes to do to you."

"Well, I would certainly hope that that would be your position Col," Alana said with a laugh, sufficiently lightening the mood. "You are my noble Protector, after all. You're supposed to keep me safe from him. You heard Solara Moonfire. That's your job now."

"I will always do my best to keep you safe, Alana," he mumbled gently, pulling her closer to him. He tenderly kissed her lips. "I vow to you that, as long as there is breath filling my lungs, I will always do whatever I can do to make you safe."

"How touching this is," William smirked as he leapt up onto the rock to take his turn on watch. "Now why don't you two lovebirds go back to camp? It's my watch and I'm not going to spend it watching you too make lovey dovey eyes at each other. Don't get me wrong, I'm very happy that you two have found true love against all odds, etcetera, etcetera, but I'm telling you right now that if you two kiss again, I'm going to throw up." The mage rolled his eyes and made for the front of the rock, turning his back on the two lovers.

It would be something he would regret, turning his back on Colwyn. The ranger shot Alana a particularly conniving look before lobbing a small rock at William's. The rock hit square in the back of William's head, causing the mage to whirl around, but by that time, the lovers had already slipped off the rock and were well on their way back to camp.

"You know, throwing that rock at William wasn't very nice Colwyn," Alana admonished as they strode back to camp. It was hard for Colwyn to take the admonishment seriously though, for it was with a smile that she had said it. "Really, I'm pretty sure that he was only joking with us."

"And I was only joking with him," Colwyn protested with a grin. "Besides, if I'd really wanted to hurt him, I would have thrown a much bigger rock at him."

"True enough," Alana laughed. She put her arm around him as they returned to the camp.

Being in each other's arms like this seemed to replenish both of their strength in addition to the comfort that it provided. Although he was not a mage, Colwyn was aware that Alana drew strength from the comfort he provided whenever he held her. It was something that was unheard of from someone who did not practice magic, however he suspected that the bond between them from the point of their wedding may be responsible for the connection. It was not something that he had heard from the songs and stories about the Blademasters of old. It was turning out that a great deal was missing from those songs and stories. Whatever the reason, he would happily provide a strength boost to her this way whenever possible. After all, he took a great deal of comfort from her closeness as well.

The two of them quietly and carefully made their way to their bedroll, trying as best they could not to wake up the priest or the halfling. Although, as Colwyn would remark later, there wasn't all that much that would wake up the farking halfling. Still it would have been rude to wake the others. Neither Colwyn nor Alana had any desire to annoy the others by waking them and would have appreciated the same courtesy if the roles were reversed.

Privacy was hard to come by in a camp setting. And so the couple had taken their bedroll to the far side of the camp where they were able to spend some time alone. When they got to their bedroll, Colwyn could not help but look at his wife with desire and longing in his eyes. Alana, for her part, reflected the look back at him. They were glad for the appearance of privacy, for they both knew that this night would definitely be one that would warrant privacy. She placed her hand on his cheek and brought his face down to hers. Their lips touched, just barely. The gentle graze of the kiss sent a wash of yearning through them both, electrifying their longing and pushing them further in their desire.

He brought his hands up to her shoulders and released the snaps that held the top of her armor up. The armor slipped down to her waist and she gasped aloud at the cold air biting at her breasts. He placed his hands over her breasts, gently playing with her nipples. The cold of the air and the warmth of his hands waged war over her flesh, sending goose pimples rushing over the flesh around her nipples. She gasped again.

She helped him out of his chain mail and ran her hands over his chest, running her hands over the taut muscles and sinews. She slipped the bottom of her armor off and stood before him, naked. She was a sight to behold. She leaned into him, pressing her breasts against his chest and kissed him full on the mouth, letting her tongue dance against his. She ran her hands down his back and sent shivers through them both.

Alana laid down on the bedroll, gently pulling Colwyn down with her. She circled her arms around him and held him close to her. He enjoying the warmth of her body next to his. They kissed long and passionately and his hand roamed over her breasts to her stomach. She looked at him longingly, her eyes pleading with him to enter her. But he could not give her what she wanted.

At least not just yet.

He kissed down her body, little kisses and licks all the way down her front. She arched her back and barely contained a loud moan when he ran his tongue over her sex.

"Please Colwyn," she gasped. "Please, I want you inside me now. I can't wait any longer."

He smiled and moved back up her body, kneeling between her legs. He placed just the tip of himself inside of her and gazed longingly at her.

"You know, you don't have to be gentle, Colwyn," she said breathily. "I promise I won't break."

Nevertheless, he was gentle when he entered her. Their lovemaking was quiet. But what it lacked in noise, it more than made up for in passion. They went slow to ensure that they both got the maximum pleasure out of it. If there had been any questions about how the other felt, this first lovemaking of theirs answered them all. It was everything that they could have hoped for and more. They clung to each other under the blankets when they were done, and fell asleep in each other's arms, each of them flooded with peace and love.

Colwyn awoke to the sound of Balaam tripping over a branch not too far from the couple's bedroll. He had always been the lighter sleeper of the two and so he was not surprised that Alana did not wake up at the sound. The priest had a worried and harried look on his face, and the ranger came fully awake in a heartbeat. He could sense it.

There was danger close by.

"What is it Balaam?" Colwyn asked as he started pulling on his armor. "What's wrong?"

"Trouble, Colwyn," the priest gasped, trying to catch his breath. "We have big trouble."

"I figured that much out just by the look of you," Colwyn grunted. "You still haven't answered my question. What did you see during your watch?"

"Goblins," Balaam panted. "There are goblins on the way." The priest slumped onto a nearby log to compose himself. "A large group of goblins. I have never seen such a large group of goblins in my life."

"Have you ever seen any goblins in your life?"

"Well..."

"Look, goblins aren't that much to worry about unless there are an awful lot of them," Colwyn added. He pulled the chain mail tunic over his head and then shrugged at Balaam. "How many could there possibly be anyway?"

"Colwyn, there are easily enough goblins for whatever their purposes are, and I can only imagine we won't like whatever their purposes are." Balaam gritted his teeth.

"Again, you haven't answered my question."

"There are hundreds, if not thousands of them."

Colwyn stopped strapping his sword on and frowned at Balaam. "Ok, that might pose a bit of a problem then." He finished strapping his sword to his back, his mind racing. He shook Alana awake and motioned for her to get dressed. When she shot a questioning look his way his only response was one word. "Trouble."

"Trouble?" she murmured, but the look on his face told her he wasn't joking. She got up and started putting her own armor on. "How much time?"

Colwyn fixed the priest with a questioning look.

"By the way they were moving," Balaam replied, "I'd say that we only have a few minutes before the goblins start hitting the wards." Balaam grimaced. "I'm afraid that there's not enough time to get you out of here without a fight, my lady."

"It's all right, Balaam," Alana grunted. "I'm not the type to turn tail and run."

"But if we become prisoners of the goblins then we can't complete our mission," the priest protested. "Then Thraal will win and my Merinda will not be able to walk with Taelin. Her soul will be trapped in Tornith forever."

And there it was.

Colwyn and Alana had both presumed that there was more to Balaam's desire to accompany them than simply his expressed statement to help guide the Blademaster along the right path and to help her remain in service to Taelin and Laeyra. Colwyn had known in his heart that the priest was out for revenge. Colwyn could not really blame the man. If someone ever managed to kill Alana, he would hunt them down. Death would be too easy for anyone who hurt Alana. He would make them suffer, and he would make them beg for death. That is of course, if he were not killed before Alana was, which he had sworn would have to happen. So long as he was breathing he would not allow her to be killed.

But he did not think he would put revenge before his duty. And it appeared that the priest was doing exactly that.

"Thraal can't win if we don't show up, Balaam," Alana smiled softly as she put a hand on his arm. "If he is to win, his High Priest must sacrifice me."

"But still," Balaam continued to protest angrily, "Merinda is stuck in Tornith. She can't be freed without our help. We must set her soul free to walk with Taelin."

"And we shall," Alana smiled at the priest. "Don't you worry."

Balaam looked unconvinced as he stormed back over to his bedroll. Time was of the essence so they all worked to break camp as fast as they could. The whole party was now wide awake and about. Alana was in danger and keeping her safe was the priority. They would do whatever had to be done to keep Alana from being taken by the goblins.

Colwyn glanced over at Alana as he finished tying their bedrolls to their packs. She looked nervous, which unsettled him. He'd always thought of her as a strong woman and her nervousness seemed out of place.

"Whatever happens, Alana, we're going to be all right." He flashed her a reassuring smile.

She returned the smile but Colwyn could tell that it was just a tad forced.

Colwyn led Alana to the front of the camp, nearest to where the goblins would be expected. The couple stood side by side, weapons at the ready. Each had set their face in a look of grim determination. The battle before them would not be an easy one. But they were both determined that it would be far more costly to the goblins than it ever would be to them.

It was a few minutes longer than Colwyn had expected before the first goblins arrived. Colwyn tightened the grip on his sword. He stole a glance at the rest of the party and was reassured that they were just as ready for the coming battle as he was. Balaam had his mace in his hands and was uttering a silent prayer to Taelin. Meryn had two daggers ready to attack with. William had a look of intense concentration on his face and Colwyn knew that the mage was getting ready to loose some kind of heavy attack spell. Alana had her swords crossed in front of her, seemingly at rest, with the points on the ground. This was her preferred and most dangerous ready to attack position. He had seen the result of underestimating her many a time, usually with disastrous results for the one underestimating her.

The first group of goblins to arrive, a small advance scout of twenty, stopped just a few feet shy of the wards. The leader of the group stepped forward and scrutinized the party. It was to Alana that he finally tried to address, his words coming out as something of a sibilant hiss. The goblin's voice did nothing to alleviate Alana's feelings of worry.

"Four humanssss and one halfling," the goblin hissed. "You are far from home. You should not have come into Dracomyr. It wassss a misssstake. It will be your lasssst."

"I think someone's a little full of themselves, Col," Alana said through clenched teeth.

"Don't antagonize the goblin, dear," Colwyn chuckled softly. Louder, he called out the goblins. "Who are you to challenge and threaten us? You're nothing more than orc spawn."

"Sssilence human," the goblin roared. "I am Legate Altassss of the goblin kingdom. The Sssstonegate Mountainssss are off limitssss to all outsssidersssss. Assss ssssuch it issss my duty to inform you that you are now my prisssssonersssss. I would ssssuggesssst that you do yoursssselvessss a favor and come with ussss peacefully. You wouldn't like the other option, but you are coming with ussss one way or the other."

"I really don't think I feel like going with you," Alana snorted. "Orc spawn!"

"You don't have a choice," the Legate roared. "Sssseize them! Sssseize them now!"

The rest of the goblins in his group launched themselves towards the party's camp. As the goblins hit the wards around the camp, they burst into flame. Acrid smoke rose from where each goblin hit the wards. The only goblin left standing was Legate Altas who gazed daggers at the party. Colwyn, for his part, returned Altas's glare with nothing short of contempt. His moment of triumph was short lived though. A much larger group of goblins, this one numbering close to a hundred, came scrambling into view.

Altas ordered the new group forward, and once more, when they hit the wards, they burst into flame. Colwyn could almost see Legate's blood boil.

"Ha!" Meryn taunted. "The rate you're going, you'll to be a Legate without a kingdom! You're never going to catch us so long as those wards are in place. You may as well just crawl back to the skirts of whatever spawned you. The day they made you Legate must have been a black day in the Goblin Kingdom. I know there must have been better candidates for the job than you. Why you're not just an orc spawn, you're lower that. You're their excrement. I'd spit in your face but I wouldn't want to waste good spit on orc poo like you."

There was more to Meryn's diatribe but it was drowned out by Balaam's hand over her mouth. Colwyn wished the priest had gotten her mouth covered just a few moments sooner. It had been a long time since he'd heard Meryn taunt someone like that but he knew that such taunting never ended well. Meryn's taunting always seemed to end the same way, with the party getting into some kind of serious trouble. At the moment, though, Colwyn couldn't think of how they could be in much more trouble than they already were. He wasn't really ready to find out how, either.

"It'ssss true," the Legate nodded thoughtfully. "We can't take you captive with thosssse wardssss up. Fortunately for me, our magessss know how to take wardssss down. Assss ssssstrong assss thessssse wards are, I doubt our magessss will take more than a minute or two to have them down. You sssseem to have underesssstimated ussss. That will be your lasssst misssstake."

"William, is what he says possible?" Alana asked the mage without turning.

"I've never seen wards as strong as the ones I put up broken." William shrugged. "However, I have heard that if a mage is strong enough, then it is theoretically possible. And if several mages work together in concert, then yes, it is quite possible that they could succeed in bringing down the wards. I am afraid we are in for a great deal of trouble if they succeed."

"I think we are in trouble then." Colwyn declared as he pointed towards the path.

When the rest of the party looked to where Colwyn was pointing, they saw another group of goblins coming up the path; this one numbering several hundred strong. At the front of the group of goblins was a small group of goblin mages. Colwyn had never seen goblin mages before but he had always known that there were such a thing. What he didn't know was if the goblin mages together had the power required to bring down William's wards. He wasn't willing to find out.

As the party looked on in horror, the goblin mages began to writhe and chant dark incantations. Colwyn wasn't sure but he didn't think the incantations were doing anything to the wards. At least he hoped that nothing was happening to the wards. Legate Altas was sure that something was happening though as he sent a hundred of the goblins against the wards. Like the goblins before, they burst into flames as they hit the wards. The Legate cursed at his spell casters and threatened to skin them alive if they failed to bring the wards down.

The mages writhed and chanted more and more frantically knowing that failure meant death. After a few more minutes the Legate sent another hundred goblins against the wards. The results were the same. The Legate cursed some more, jumping around to emphasize his displeasure to the mages. Were it not for the dire seriousness of the situation they were in, Colwyn might have found the whole thing funny.

Then there was a sudden burst of light from the wards, followed by nothing. Colwyn turned to William with a raised eyebrow. The mage, eyes closed with a look of grim determination on his face, shook his head, confirming what the ranger already suspected.

The wards were down.

They were in a whole lot of trouble.

Colwyn readjusted the grip on his sword, determined that, if they were going to be captured, then it was going to be as costly for the goblins as possible. A quick glance in Alana's direction told him that she had come to the same conclusion. It was now a pure numbers game. And the numbers were not in their favor. No matter how good the five of them were, they were not good enough to take out the huge number of goblins that they were facing. All they could do was kill as many of them as possible now so that when the opportunity came to escape they would have that many less goblins to deal with later on.

The first of the unimpeded goblins rushed through where the wards had once been, and they were met by flashing steel. The companions fought valiantly but, in the end, the numbers were indeed too many for the party to overcome. One by one, they fell to the advancing horde of goblins. Colwyn tried to back his way over to Alana after she received a blow to the head from behind and subsequently fell, but there were just too many goblins between him and his wife.

"You should have jusssst ssssurendered," Altas cackled. "It would have been far eassssier."

It was the last thing that Colwyn heard before he felt a sharp pain to the back of his head.

He briefly saw stars spinning about.

Then the world went black.

Chapter XVIII
Prisoners

Colwyn woke up to a raging headache. His eyes popped open and he braced himself for even more pain as the light flooded into his vision. But that didn't happen. All he could see was darkness. It was as if he hadn't opened his eyes at all. Colwyn opened up his other senses. From the feel of the air, he suspected that he was in a cave, probably deep in the mountains that the goblins lived in. He remembered the attack, the feeling of being ultimately enveloped by the overwhelming goblin numbers. And he suspected that his companions had fared no better.

He stood slowly and carefully made his way to the nearest wall. Using the cool rock wall as a guide, he slowly worked his way around the room. Eventually, he discovered that the only way out of the room was an iron door. He tried to open the door but it was locked. Of course. He suspected that even Meryn would have a hard time of it. Since he could not get out of the room, he decided to explore the contents of the room, turning his attention first to the issue of his companions. He was hoping that they were all being held together and set about to find out if that was the case.

He slowly crawled across the room. If he happened upon one of his companions, he didn't want to run the risk of hurting them. Especially Alana.

A thought crossed his mind and he reached for his pouches to see if they had been taken. Luckily, all they had removed were his weapons. He grinned to himself as his hand found the pouch that he kept his finder's stone and the trap finder stone in. He pulled the finder's stone from the pouch and laid it in his hand. It pulsed with a soft green glow. The glow was far from enough to light the cavernous room that they were in, but it could still help him find Alana. Besides, a little light in this room was far better than the darkness in which he'd been floundering.

"Find Alana," he commanded softly to the finder's stone. His voice was unnaturally loud in the stillness of the room, despite his attempts to keep the volume down.

The finder's stone pulsed brightly and leapt from his hand, orbiting his head in a vicious circle. He watched the stone in fascination, knowing that it would eventually settle down and point him in one specific direction.

After what seemed like hours, but was really only a few seconds, the finder's stone settled down to one direction, and Colwyn smiled to himself. The finder's stone had never failed him. The elven made stone had been quite predictable in that way. And it was a comfort to know that he could always depend on the gifts he received from the elves.

He slowly crawled in the direction indicated by the finder's stone. He still could not see where he was going so he slowly picked his way across the room, deciding that time was not a critical thing in this situation. They were prisoners, and they would continue to be prisoners whether or not he found Alana quickly.

It took Colwyn about a quarter of an hour to crawl across the room at the pace he was going. The light cast from the finder's stone was enough so that if he had come across any of his companions while he was moving across the room, he would have known it. He did not have any such luck until he came to where the finder's stone had been leading him. He found Alana lying face down on the floor. Her back was moving up and down ever so slightly, so he knew that she was still breathing. It was a small comfort, though, as she was still unconscious. He hoped that she wasn't badly hurt.

He rolled her over so she was on her back and propped her neck over his knee so that she was almost sitting up. He gently ran his fingers through her hair and traced the curve of her cheek with his fingers. Slowly, he leaned down and kissed her on the lips. The kiss had the desired effect. Her eyelids flickered and she awoke. Her green eyes darted around the room, finally settling on the man she loved. She smiled weakly up at him.

He was relieved. Alana was alive and well.

"Where are we?" she breathed. "Last thing I remember was a large band of goblins... "

"We've been taken prisoner, Alana," Colwyn said softly. "We are somewhere in their caves. I don't know for sure what they have planned for us, but whatever it is, it can't be good. In fact, it would not surprise me in the slightest if they were going to deliver us to the High Priest of Thraal. Nothing about our situation would surprise me anymore and a bunch of goblins turning us over to our enemies would seem to fit with our luck."

"What of the others," she asked.

"I haven't found them yet. You were my first priority after I searched for a way out."

Alana pulled herself upright. "How long do you think we've been out?" she asked. "And, is there any water? I'm parched."

"I haven't come across any water," Colwyn admitted. "As to how long we've been out, I couldn't tell you for sure. My internal clock doesn't like constant darkness so I have no reference from which to make a guess. If we were being held somewhere in the woods, I could probably tell you to the minute. But here in a cave? Your guess is as good as mine, better probably."

"It's all right," Alana insisted. "All that matters is that we're together. The others are probably somewhere nearby as well. How big would you say this cavern is anyway?"

"I measured it to be about a hundred feet to a side," Colwyn shrugged. "It's a very large room. And it's dark. This finder's stone does not give off a lot of light. We have no torches, and even if we did, neither of us has a way to light them because Meryn has the flint and steel with her." Colwyn had a thought. "You know, if we could find William and wake him up, he might be able to shed some light on our situation."

"So, either way, we need to find our friends if we want any light." Alana said. "So let's find our friends." She started to move, but Colwyn placed a hand on her shoulder. "What? You don't have to be so over-protective, Col. I can move. We'll work as a team. Let me help you."

"You just woke up from having been knocked out, Alana," he replied. "And I only have the one finder's stone. I'll leave one of my other stones floating over you so that I can find you again without having to use the finder's stone, but you will stay here while I find the others. If you were to pass out while looking, it'll make it so much harder to find you after I've found the others."

Alana nodded. "You're right, of course, Colwyn," Alana said with a sigh. She placed her hand over his. "Just be careful. I don't intend to lose you in these caves. I know you're not very comfortable in caves like these. Come back to me soon, my beloved Protector."

"Wild dogs wouldn't be able to keep me from coming back to you," Colwyn laughed. He kissed her again, this time with passion instead of gentleness. It was a promise to return and a promise to find the others. And she returned it hungrily, promising to be there when he returned. They parted finally. "You know, when you kiss me like that, it's hard to do anything but keep whatever promise you want me to make to you. I promise you, I will be careful. I'll be back with the others before you even realize I'm gone."

"I'm counting on that, my beloved."

Colwyn kissed her again before laying her back down on the ground. Then he removed his cloak and rolled it up so that she could use it for a pillow. He produced one of his ioun stones and released it into the air over her. It pulsed a pale blue light as it slowly orbited her. With her position so marked, he felt a bit more comfortable about striking out into the large room.

He worked slowly, using the finder's stone to pinpoint each missing individual. It was slow going, because he did not wish to trample any of the others. He came across Meryn first and dragged her back to where he had left Alana, thankful that the little halfling was so light. The mage was next, his thin frame not that much heavier than the halfling's shorter and stockier one. The mage's robes kept catching on the rough floor of the cave floor, and Colwyn had to keep stopping to free the robes whenever they caught on something lest they tear. William would never forgive Colwyn for tearing his robes. Soon, he had the two companions lying next to Alana.

The priest of Taelin was the last one that he found.

Balaam was just coming around when Colwyn found him. The ranger pulled the priest to his feet and accompanied him over to where Alana was watching over the others. He helped the priest back down to the floor and then he sat down himself next to Alana. He gently took her hand, hoping to provide some comfort to her.

"So, what's next?" she asked.

Colwyn gave the matter some thought. To his way of thinking, it was only a matter of time before they figured out how to get out of their predicament.

Their companions were still groggy, but now awakening. Colwyn was relieved to see that all of the companions would likely make a full recovery from their injuries.

Colwyn used the light from the finder's stone to scrutinize his companions well enough to run a catalogue of their injuries. Nothing seemed too serious. It was mostly some bruising on their heads and shoulders. They were all battered and worse for wear, but it seemed that they would be all right. Of course, he was not a healer so he couldn't be completely sure. Perhaps, once the priest was up to snuff, Colwyn would have him look over everyone just to be on the safe side.

Once William had cleared his head, he addressed their situation with his own questions. Colwyn explained about how the party had been captured by the goblins and presumably taken as prisoners to their stronghold in the Stonegate Mountains. William listened intently as Colwyn described what he had found when he searched the room.

"So escape will not be easy then," William noted softly,

"Agreed. Escape will be very difficult," Colwyn said. "I think it likely that we will be taken somewhere, rather than held as guests for the next goblin feast, if you know what I mean."

William rolled his eyes.

"What?" Colwyn asked.

"I guess your jokes can't all be clever, dear." Alana remarked.

Colwyn huffed. "Fine. Well, if we're to be delivered somewhere, we'll have a better chance of escaping once the goblins take us from this room and are en route to our destination. If we can agree that this is likely the case, I will work up a plan of escape. Just remember, we'll probably only get one chance to escape. So be ready when the time comes."

The others nodded in agreement. Colwyn glanced over at Alana. The young warrior woman had a frown on her face. Colwyn suspected that she was not happy about the thought of having to wait for their chance to escape. He knew she did not like being confined, and the thought of being stuck in one room for a long period of time without the chance for escape was likely too much for her. She would prefer to act. Colwyn wished he had a way to make that happen. For now, they would have to bide their time and wait for the right moment. He didn't like it any more than she did, but it was the best he could do.

He studied Alana's face a bit more. There was pain and anger over the situation that they found themselves in that face. He knew her moods and expressions, in many ways, better than he knew his own. It was part of why he had been able to survive the Test of the Blades. Had he not known Alana and loved her as well and as much as he did, there was no way he would have survived and been allowed to marry her. But with that marriage came the responsibility of being her Protector. And with that responsibility, he knew that he could not just let their current situation stand. It was incumbent upon him to come up with a way out. Already, the beginning of a plan was forming in his head. In time, the rest of the plan would come. All he would need was the right opportunity.

As he had pointed out to Alana, however, such a plan could not succeed while they remained in their current predicament. Logistically, it was just a very bad tactical situation for them to try to fight their way out of the room. First there was the fact that they could not see in the dark little room. Beyond that, there was the matter of not knowing the layout of the caverns and tunnels that made up the goblin kingdom inside the Stonegate Mountains. Without knowing where they were going once they left the room, there was no way they could plan a full escape. Plus there was the matter of not knowing where their weapons were being held. All in all, there was no way Colwyn could justify an escape attempt, as things stood. It would be far better for them to wait until they were being moved. At that point, they could have the light and open spaces of the outdoors and the companions could work according to their strengths. Certainly, Colwyn and Alana would both be able to fight better in the open.

The real trick to planning an escape was not so much timing it as it was ensuring that the plan utilized all of the companions best talents. He knew that his archery would come in handy, as well as Alana's swordsmanship. Meryn's lock picking skill would also come in handy, as they would have to find a way out of whatever cage they would certainly be bound or caged in transit. And he was fairly sure that both Balaam and William had a good offensive spell or two that could be used in the escape attempt, although Balaam's abilities were likely more defensive and healing-related than offensive. Still, the priest knew how to cast a binding spell, and Colwyn had seen that binding spell put to great use in the past. When totaled up, the party's skills were formidable. But even so, they would be no match for the goblins in the mountain caverns. It would be both futile and foolhardy to try to battle out of their prison on the goblins' terms. It would take an act of divine providence to ensure that they all made it out safely. Whereas if they waited and struck when the party was being transported, they would have a greater chance of successfully escaping the goblins. Especially since the odds were good that there would be far fewer goblins present during the transport.

There just was no other way around it.

Colwyn whipped his head towards where he remembered the door to be, motioning the others to be quiet. Something had caught his attention. After a few moments of quiet, he grimaced, sure that he had indeed heard what he had thought he had... footsteps coming in their direction. He slipped the finder's stone back in his pouch, once more plunging the room into total darkness. Colwyn kept watch, glaring at the door even though he could not actually see it, as if the very act of staring at it would keep the door from opening. But with each footfall that came, the goblins were creeping closer to their little room.

Who were they coming for? One or all of them?

Could it already be time for the party to be moved?

It did not matter if the party was ready to attempt an escape or not if the goblins were coming to take them away already. He ran through his plans in his head, hoping beyond hope that there would be something in there that would be useful to get them out of their situation. Unfortunately for Colwyn, all that he could think of involved them being out in the open. Colwyn had never lived inside of a mountain before, and the lack of knowledge of tactics used inside of a mountain now annoyed him greatly.

The fact was that it was too early. They weren't ready!

He watched the door, dread in his heart. He was not afraid for himself, but rather he was afraid for the woman that he loved. He did not want her hurt and he was afraid that she would be if the goblins had their way. He had to find a way to protect her from the goblins, but he was not sure how he could do that here and now. Not like this. He felt naked without his sword and his bow. It was rare that he found himself unarmed, and it always unnerved him. Being held prisoner in a cave, someplace where he was far outside his comfort zone, only added to his discomfort. Until now, he had never realized how much he hated enclosed spaces and caves.

The sooner they found a way out, the better!

He longed for a forest. The life force present in the forest, he found to be rejuvenating in ways that no other environment could ever hope to be for him. This was why he had become a ranger. To protect the forests.

But things had changed for him. Now, instead of protecting the forests he loved, he had turned into a Protector of another kind. He had given his life over to protecting one life instead of all of the life force found in a forest. It was an interesting trade, and one that he had never expected to make. He would not have it any other way though.

The sound of the footfalls grew louder. Colwyn figured they had less than a minute before the goblins would burst into the room.

His desperate mind searched for salvation. The dragon? Could they summon the dragon? No. Cobalt would be unable to get into the mountain caves. But he filed the thought away for the future. They would have to make summoning the dragon a priority once they were free of the caverns. Besides, Cobalt would appreciate a meal of fresh goblin meat. He just hoped that he would not have to watch the dragon eat the goblins in person. He was afraid that such a show might actually make him kind of sick. He did not need to deal with that while protecting the Blademaster.

The footsteps came to a halt. The goblins had to be just outside the door. Keys jangled and he heard one key scrape into the lock of the door. The door creaked open, grinding against the stone floor as it slowly swung. The light from the corridor outside was not very bright, but after the near total darkness of the room they'd been in, even the dimmest light was painful and blinding. They had all turned their faces away from the door but Colwyn, who squinted defiantly into the light.

Two dozen goblins streamed into the room, heading straight for the party. Without even thinking about it, Colwyn positioned himself between Alana and the goblins. But without his weapons, there was really nothing he could do to prevent the goblins from taking Alana if that was what they wanted to do.

The goblins did not say anything as they raced over to where the party was huddled together. Colwyn tried to punch one of the leading goblins, but he was whacked in the head with the butt end of a spear for his trouble. His vision swam as the goblins swarmed around Alana and dragged her out of the room. He tried to stop them, lunging and flailing, but the pain in his head made him clumsy and the nearby goblins beat him to the ground before he took two steps.

The door clanged shut behind the goblins. And then Alana was gone.

Colwyn heard the sound of the key in the door and grimaced as he sat up, rubbing the lump on his head. It was the second time that a goblin had been able to put him down. He swore it would be the last time. His reputation as a ranger, a warrior, and as the Protector to a Blademaster couldn't handle any more of that. Twice now, he had let Alana down as a result of goblins.

He vowed not to do so a third time.

Balaam shuffled over and placed his hands on Colwyn's head. The ranger felt warmth flowing from the priest's hands into his skull, and he could hear the priest chanting healing words. Colwyn knew that healing was not one of the things that priests of Taelin were best at, but some were better at it than others. As it turned out, Balaam was one of the better ones. The headache was gone almost immediately, and Colwyn's vision soon returned to normal. He smiled weakly at Balaam, even though he knew the other man could not see him.

"What do we do?" William asked quietly, asking the question that every one of the companions had been thinking. "Alana is gone. What do we do? How are we going to get out of this? And how do we get Alana back when we do get out of this?"

"We wait," Colwyn shrugged. "There's really nothing else that we can do at this point. We wait for them to bring her back and we hope that she's all right when they do bring her back."

"We can't just wait, Colwyn," Balaam protested. "She's too important. We have to do something to get her free."

"What do you propose we do, Lord Balaam?" Colwyn raised an eyebrow. He brought the finder's stone back out and the pale green glow faintly lit the others' faces. "We have no weapons and no way to get out of this room. There is nothing that we can do to change our own situation, let alone free Alana from hers. I'm sorry, Balaam."

"I don't like it, Colwyn," Balaam crossed his arms. "It feels like we're letting down the Blademaster. You're her Protector. You know better than anyone that we can't do that."

"Do you think I like letting Alana go off into danger like that, Lord Balaam?" Colwyn said crossly. "This is the woman that I love more than anything. I want to go running to her rescue more than you could ever know. And yet, I understand that I can't do anything. You need to understand that too. Futile action is still futile. The time will come when we can escape. But that time is not now. Alana knows that too. We're working on how to get out of here, but it will have to wait until we're moved from this room." Colwyn crossed his arms to match his stance to that of the priest. "I'm sorry if you don't find that acceptable, Lord Balaam. But it is the way that it has to be. You must accept my leadership in this matter. There can be no further discussion between us about it."

Balaam faced away from Colwyn, obviously upset with the ranger. Colwyn could do nothing to make the priest any less upset. Alana was his primary concern, and he could do nothing to help her. He wished things were different. He ran through all of his escape plans, but they remained in the same predicament.

So they waited. There was nothing else to do. But they did not do so patiently. William rifled through his spell book. Meryn emptied her pouches and was rummaging through her treasures. Balaam had entered a meditation state. And Colwyn, the least patient of the companions, was pacing the little room.

The companions waited for over an hour in silence. No one wanted to discuss the matter any further. The waiting bothered each of them in different ways, but no one would expound on it. Colwyn continued to pace, slowly tracing his way around the room's perimeter, taking about five minutes to make each circle. He stopped every few minutes to listen to the corridor outside. He did not hear anything in the corridor for over an hour. Finally, he heard the sound of goblin foot steps and of a body forcefully dragged down the corridor. He gritted his teeth in anger but kept quiet. There was also the sound of a struggle. Someone grunted and he knew it was Alana. He could not help but smile at the sound of the woman he loved fighting against the goblins. He turned to face the door so he could join in when she arrived.

When the door sprung open, he covered his eyes so that he would not be blinded by the light from the hallway. The goblins threw her into the room and then turned without saying a word. Colwyn was tempted to go after them, but Alana came first. He raced to where she was lying on the ground and knelt down beside her.

"Are you okay?" he asked. He pulled the trap finder's stone from his pouch so that he could have a little light and brushed some hair out of her face.

She nodded. "I'll be alright."

"What did they want, my beloved? Why did they take you? And where?"

"They took me to see Legate Altas," Alana locked eyes with him. "He gloated that he would be responsible for my being taken to Tornith. That's what they want us for. They're taking us to Tornith so I can be sacrificed."

"You know that I will not let them sacrifice you, Alana. No matter what it takes."

Meryn stepped forward. William stood by her side. "None of us will," the halfling declared.

Alana blinked but a smile did not appear. She squeezed Colwyn's hand. "They're going to take us there in the morning, my love."

A smile spread across Colwyn's face. "Then in the morning, we will make our escape."

The Blademaster

Chapter XIX
Escape from the Goblins

"The goblins have left the Stonegate Mountains, my lord," Adouon announced after entering the private sanctuary of the High Priest of Thraal. "She is with them."

The lich did not look up from his meditation, nor did he acknowledge his assistant's presence. Adouon edged closer to his master, but did not dare touch the lich for fear of what the reprisal would be. Seeing that his master was not going to acknowledge, Adouon gave a tight bow and turned to leave the sanctuary. He had only taken a step before he heard a soft wheeze coming from his master.

Adouon slowly turned to face the lich.

"How long?" the lich rasped quietly. "How long will they take to bring her to me?"

"The journey from the Stonegate Mountains is long and somewhat treacherous, my lord," Adouon shrugged. "I

The Blademaster

estimate it will take them six days to arrive. But goblins are not reliable, my lord. You leave much to chance."

"I leave nothing to chance, Adouon." The lich let out a throaty, raspy laugh. "You, of all people, should know that by now. I will tell you now that even if she were somehow able to escape the goblins, she will come to me anyway. I have foreseen it. She does not yet know that she dances to my tune."

"It will be quite the highest insult to that accursed Taelin that you are using his own chosen warrior to return Lord Thraal to the glory that should be his," Adouon remarked.

"Yes, it will be glorious," the lich agreed. "It will be the most glorious sacrifice that I have ever had the pleasure to participate in. Our Lord Thraal will be greatly pleased."

"I will go have a cell prepared for the Blademaster and her companions, my Lord Drakkhous," Adouon said softly. He turned. "I envy you this sacrifice, my lord. It will be the most glorious sacrifice to our Lord Thraal to date."

"Yes, Adouon," the lich grinned at his assistant's back. "It will be indeed."

The room was as dark as it had been since they had been thrown in there, and Colwyn was grumpy about sitting on the cold floor. It was hard on his haunches and his back. He had given his word to Alana that he would not allow her to be sacrificed to Thraal, and he intended to keep his word. Even before he had become her Protector, it was not in his nature to break his word. He didn't intend to start doing so now.

His companions were still in the room with him. He took some comfort from that. And since Alana was here with him, he would be present when the goblins came for her. He was still unarmed though, and that would limit his fighting ability. Sure, he could kill a few goblins with his bare hands, but the sheer number of goblins that would be coming would be far beyond what he could handle.

He made a mental checklist of the things that they needed in order to make an escape. But everything hinged on being free of the mountains.

For now, all they could do was wait. Waiting wasn't really the problem. The goblins would likely be there soon to take the companions. He did not know exactly how much time had passed since Legate Altas had brought Alana back to the locked cavern after gloating to her, but they had been given three meals since then, so he figured that it was the next day. And since it was the next day, he suspected that it would be sometime in the next few hours that the goblins would come to take them.

They would have to be ready when they came.

He patted himself down. He knew that they had taken his bow, quiver and sword, but maybe they had missed something. He was not sure what he was looking for, but there had to be something. When he got to his boots, he smiled broadly. Somehow, they had missed his boot knife. It gave him an escape related idea. It would involve Meryn, the halfling, which did not bother him nearly as much as he thought it should. This would be something best suited to her talents. He may not particularly like the halfling, but he would be a fool not to use her talents when they were needed.

He shuffled himself over to where he could hear Alana softly praying to Taelin. Gently, he put his hand on her shoulder. She would know his touch. He could not see her in the darkness, but he could tell she was smiling at him. It made him happy to know that his touch was enough to make her smile. Marrying her had been the best moment of his life, and he wanted to make her as happy as she had made him. It was important to him that she stay happy. It was also important to him that she remain safe. He was expected to keep her safe. It was the biggest part of his vows as her Protector. It was not always going to be an easy thing. He vowed one more time that Zish, the god of death, would not claim her until Colwyn himself had succumbed.

"Alana," Colwyn said softly. "They're going to bind our hands when they take us out of here. When they do, I won't be able to do what I need to do to free us by myself."

"What do you want me to do, Colwyn?" she asked just as softly. For all they knew, there could be a goblin hiding in the dark room.

"When the time comes, I want you to grab the knife from my right boot and cut my bindings," Colwyn explained. "I'll tell you when. I'll free you and the halfling. At that point, you need to grab your summoning statue and bring Cobalt to us. He won't be able to resist such a tempting feast anyway."

"Why the halfling?" Alana asked. Her voice was laced with surprise.

"Because the halfling is the best for picking locks and stealth," Colwyn grinned. "Trust me. I've got this worked out now."

"You'll be putting her in danger," Alana remarked. It was not quite a protest, because she trusted Colwyn and knew he wouldn't use Meryn unless he needed her exclusive talents. "But I guess it will be dangerous for all of us when you come right down to it."

"I made a promise in the Temple of thee Blades to keep you safe, Alana," Colwyn sighed. He gathered her up in his arms. "If I am going to do that, I need to be able to use all of our companions' skills to accomplish that goal. This plan uses Meryn's skills. You're the one that keeps telling me that I need to trust her more. So I'm trusting her. I'm trusting her with your life. If she succeeds, we'll be free and I will be able to get you to Tornith to kill the lich."

"And do you trust the dragon?" Alana asked softly. "We haven't talked about what you think about Cobalt."

Colwyn shrugged. "I trust that Lord Taelin knew what he was doing when he assigned Cobalt to you as your nathair an aeir a chosnaíonn ." Colwyn paused. "Look, I'm not used to following the tenets of Taelin. I'm a ranger. All my life I've dedicated my life to Lady Raeven of the forests. But I know that, as your Protector, I will need to trust Lord Taelin and Lady Laeyra as well. I believe that Lord Taelin knows what he is doing, and that's good enough for me. I will give Cobalt the chance to prove himself."

"I see," Alana snuggled her head against his chest. "Then I leave you to your plan. I will do my part."

"I'm glad you agree, Alana," he kissed her hair. "All I want is for you to be safe."

"Then I am in the wrong profession," Alana laughed softly. "I don't think that I'll ever be truly safe as a Blademaster. But, as long as I have you beside me, I'll be safe enough."

Colwyn pulled her close and squeezed her hand as he ran the fingers of his other hand through her hair. He loved the feel of her against his body, and he treasured every moment they had to be together. He knew that such moments would not always be easy to find. His marriage to Alana would never be what many would consider normal. Being married to a Blademaster guaranteed that he would be spending a great deal of time on the road. And not just on the road, but on the road with weapons brandished. Learning to trust gods other than the one he held sacred was going to take getting used to. But, with Alana, he had been doing work for the Temple of the White for many years anyway. Working to further the tenets of Taelin would not be as large an adjustment as furthering the tenets of Laeyra would be.

For Alana, though, he would adjust to anything.

He wondered how this woman had managed to worm her way into his life to the point where he would abandon his duties as a ranger and his dedication to Lady Raeven of the forests for a life as a Blademaster's Protector and a new dedication to Lord Taelin and Lady Laeyra. It was an odd set of circumstances, and he wondered if Alana knew just how much he had changed for her. He suspected that she did, but she had the grace and love for him not to say anything about it. He loved her deeply and he would do anything for her. Whatever happened, it would be the two of them together for the rest of their days. Even if that meant only a few more hours.

He had never thought he would find true love, and yet here it was right in his arms.

He was a very lucky man, indeed.

And yet, Alana continued to claim that she was the lucky one. He had finally persuaded her that both of them were lucky. He truly felt that was the case. Lady Laeyra had indeed been keeping them in her favor. Then again, if the rumors about the Blademasters were to be believed, then

Alana was, in a way, Laeyra's daughter. If that were the case, Laeyra would be watching Alana closely and luck would naturally influence her life and decisions. Therefore, luck had more to do with the two of them finding each other than destiny did. This thought amused Colwyn. For all of Solara's talk about Colwyn and Alana being destined to be together, what if it were just pure luck that they had found each other? It was certainly a line of thought worth pondering. Whatever it was that had brought the two of them together, he felt lucky to have her in his life, and he knew she felt the same way.

So he continued to hold her, his thoughts of his love for her and of how lucky they were to have found each other flowing through his head. He did not want the moment to end, but end it would. Any minute, the goblins could arrive to fulfill their nefarious plans and he steeled himself for the intrusion. Alana shifted against his chest as if she sensed his change in mood. He sighed, displeased that she had picked up on his demeanor. He pulled her closer, tightening his embrace to let her know that he would not let anything happen to her. Of course, it was a little late for that kind of gesture since they had already been taken captive, but at least he could assure her that he would not let anything worse happen to her. Besides, he had a plan for their escape, and she trusted him that the plan would work.

There wasn't going to be any time for stát ndoimhneacht na tsíocháin inmheánach before the goblins arrived. He suspected they would be heading to Tornith. Perhaps they should just let the goblins take them there. After all, it was where they were going anyway. No. It was better to arrive at Tornith on their own terms. If they arrived as goblin captives, then the priests of Thraal would be in control. There would be no element of surprise and there would be no chance to get into the ziggurat of Thraal undetected. They would enter the ziggurat as prisoners and there would be little they could do at that point.

No, in the ranger's mind, the best way was to escape. And the best way to escape was what he and Alana had already laid out. Even if it meant depending on Meryn.

Naturally, it galled him to think that everything depended on the halfling, but that was the way things were. Even so, he knew that the halfling would be able to do what was expected of her. As much as he did not like her, even he had to admit that, when it came down to it, she could be depended on when it came to this type of thing. He still did not understand why Alana liked the little one so much, though. He suspected that, no matter how long she was a part of their party, he would never understand that. He figured that Meryn would always leave him perplexed.

And maybe a little crazy.

It was nice to know that some things would probably never change.

He felt the touch of a hand on his shoulder. Meryn. No one else's hand was so small. He could never get used to how silently the halfling could move. She was, perhaps, the only one in the party that could slip through the forests quieter than he could. It surprised him whenever she snuck up on him, and he suspected that she reveled in the surprise. However, from the feel of her insistent touch, he deduced that this was not an attempt to surprise him.

She would have some important information to relay.

Naturally, she'd had no problem finding him in the darkness. Of all of the party, she was the only one with any kind of darkness vision. Of course, her vision was nowhere near as sharp as those of elves or goblins, but halflings were one of the races that were gifted with the ability to easily make things out in the dark. When he had first started living with the Forestwalker Elves, Colwyn had been jealous of their ability to see in the dark. It was something that he had always wished he could do himself, but as a human, it was not an ability he ever expected to develop on his own. Over the years, he had become less jealous of those who could do what he could not. Instead, he had come to welcome and depend on their abilities. He wished he had thought about her darkness vision when he had originally searched their prison. It might have been far easier for him to find the door had she helped him.

But that was neither here nor there. Whatever it was that she had to tell him was very important, or she would not have searched him out. Especially since he had not made the same mistake twice. As sharp as her eyes were, Meryn's hearing was even sharper, so he had positioned her by the door so they would know when the goblins were coming.

"What is it, Little Bit?" he asked. He felt Alana stir. Clearly she had not heard Meryn arrive either. At least he wasn't the only one.

"Colwyn, I was sitting near the door as you asked me to," the halfling started.

"The short version, please," Colwyn prodded.

"Right. There are footsteps coming. Probably about five minutes away."

"Thank you," Colwyn said with a nod. "Get the others up. May as well be ready to go when the goblins arrive. And remember. Everyone is to follow my lead."

"Right," she replied as she disappeared back into the darkness.

"Five minutes,' Alana breathed. "That's not much time."

"Nope," Colwyn admitted. "But we're not going to escape now anyway. It's just not the right time. But the right time will present itself soon enough. Trust me, Alana. We'll get out of this in one piece, and I'll get you to Tornith. On our terms."

"I'm counting on it, my beloved."

That was all they had time to say or do before the door to the room was flung open. Although the light in the hallway outside the room was muted, it flashed bright when compared to the total darkness of the room. Alana shielded her eyes. A headache wouldn't do now. As their eyes adjusted, the companions could all see a large number of goblins spilling into the room. Legate Altas was at the head of the group.

"Ssssecure their handsssss behind their backssss," the goblin leader sneered. "Bring them to the cage."

Colwyn and Alana both flinched as the goblins tied them up. They gave a convincing show of resistance, but it was only a show, never intended to actually succeed. They knew that it would look suspicious if they did not at least try to fight off the goblins, but at the same time, it was not the right moment to escape. They would have to fight the entire mountain's worth of goblins to escape at this point. It would have been a losing battle, and one that made no sense to even attempt.

From the force of the shove the goblins gave them to move once they were tied up, Colwyn suspected that their act had been convincing enough.

The goblins led the party through the corridors. The walls were no different from those of their prison. Small globes of light lined the walls, separated by several feet of wall between them. The lights were not very bright, but compared to the darkness of their prison, they seemed like small suns to the companions. The walls were rough stone and from time to time, a stalagmite rose up from the floor. The goblins expertly led the party around all of the stalagmites as they encountered them.

Alana tried to map out the corridors in her head, thinking that she might one day have a need to navigate her way back through the Stonegate Mountains. But she was not able to keep an accurate map in her mind, and after several long minutes, she gave up. Still, she never admitted defeat. She merely chose to use her concentration on other matters. So she focused on the plans that she and Colwyn had formulated for the escape. She knew what they had to do, and she knew that it would work.

She glanced back at Colwyn, as if to reassure him that she was not going to do anything to jeopardize their escape plans. She knew that even the simplest plan could be screwed up by seemingly innocuous actions, and this plan was not as simple as she might have liked. Still, she liked that Colwyn was using the halfling. Perhaps he had softened toward her. She shook her head. No. He would never soften towards the halfling.

She hoped that things would go the way that Colwyn had planned, but she was also keenly aware that things never quite went to plan. She prayed to her Lord Taelin and Lady Laeyra that this time would be different. Something still didn't sit right with her.

Perhaps it was just the fact that they were prisoners.

Or maybe it was that there was so much at stake.

The party rounded one more corner before entering a large room where they found two large steel cages. One cage held all of the party's possessions. That was one problem solved. They'd just have to keep track of that cage for their escape attempt. The lock shouldn't be a problem for Meryn. They just needed the right opportunity... the right moment.

The goblins shoved the party into the other cage and sealed the cage shut. The cage was already mounted on a wagon for easy transport. The goblins goaded the attached horses and the wagon pulled forward. Another wagon that carried the other cage followed suit.

The two wagons and flanking goblin escort emerged from the caverns into utter brightness. The companions squinted their eyes against the harsh sunlight. The light burned against their eyelids, causing them to turn away.

But they would get used to it.

They rode throughout the day, jostling with each bump. There was not much that they could do as they travelled. They had no way of knowing just how long they would take to get to Tornith, but they weren't planning on being in the cage long enough to reach their destination. They would have to act at the right moment and in the right ways. The plan was sound, but it required that they act in concert. Alana knew that timing was critical or else it would never work.

So all they could do is wait for that perfect moment.

When the sun went down, the goblins stopped their march towards Tornith. They left the party in the cage.

Colwyn noted the layout of the camp. The goblins would likely camp every night in a similar manner. Knowledge of the camp layout would be to their advantage when the time came to make their escape.

They managed to get a little sleep that night, but it was not easy. The cage floor was hard and the cage itself was cramped. None of them were able to get very comfortable. Still, they all knew that it was important for them to be well rested when it was time to make their move. So they had to make do with the cramped conditions.

The next morning, it was more of the same. They traveled all day in the hot sun. The road was rough and with every bump, the companions were further battered. By the time the goblins pulled up for the night, all of the companions had a dozen new bruises, and they were all very sore.

Colwyn peered out of the cage after the goblins camped for the night. He watched the sentry pace back and forth around the cages, making note of the pattern of the sentry's movements. His suspicions were confirmed. The sentry would be out of sight of their cage long enough for the halfling to act. And yet, he was not yet ready for action. Acting prematurely would only cause failure and they could not afford to fail. He needed just a little more time to make sure he had the sentry's patrol schedule down.

A half-hour later, Colwyn smiled to himself, now certain they were ready for the escape. He inched over to where Alana was resting against the bars. She picked up on his grin.

"Is it time?" she asked.

"It is," he said with a nod.

Alana wasted no time. She maneuvered herself and slid the knife from Colwyn's boot. With a quick flourish, she sliced through the ropes around Colwyn's wrists. Colwyn took the knife and did the same for Alana before he moved over to the halfling. He smiled at Meryn. Meryn returned the smile. It was her turn now.

"Meryn," he said as he cut the bindings from her wrists. "Do you think you can retrieve my bow from that other cage? My bow and my quiver first. Then, while I'm taking care of the sentries, you can go get the rest of our weapons."

"No problem, Colwyn," Meryn grinned broadly. "No problem at all."

Meryn let herself out of the cage and deftly crossed the camp to the other cage completely unseen. Colwyn shuffled over to William and made short order of the mage's bindings, all the while keeping a close eye on Meryn's progress. By now, she had picked the lock on the other cage and was rifling through the stack of weapons for his bow. By the time he had freed Balaam, she was on her way back to their cage with his bow and quiver in hand.

She clambered back into their cage and handed the bow and quiver to Colwyn. He smiled at her and messed up her hair.

"Good job, Little Bit," Colwyn grinned as he strung the bow.

"I also brought this," Meryn chuckled as she dropped a pouch in Alana's lap.

Meryn beamed and slipped back out of the cage to go and get more of the party's weapons. Colwyn chuckled. Alana pulled the summoning statue out of the pouch Meryn had brought. While she worked at summoning Cobalt, Colwyn nocked an arrow on his bow and tracked one of the sentries. Silently, he let the arrow fly. As usual, his aim was true. The arrow thudded into the goblin sentry's chest. He quickly nocked a second arrow and tracked a second sentry. A moment later, the second sentry joined the first on the ground. There was no doubt that they were both dead.

There were two sentries left, but they were out of range, so he had to wait for them to come into his aiming arc.

They were also nowhere near Meryn, who seemed to appear from nowhere, more weapons in tow. Silently, she distributed them while Colwyn waited patiently for the sentries.

It wasn't long before the two sentries came into his aiming arc. Seconds later, the two remaining sentries were also dead. With all of the sentries handled, the party burst from the cage, weapons flashing and spells flaring at the goblin camp.

Goblins were cut down quickly, and soon, a wide swath was cut around the cages. The party was careful with how they cut down the goblins, never expending too much energy on any one kill.

Then, the party felt a breeze that grew in intensity with every passing second. That's when the dragon came overhead, snatching the goblins' attention.

Cobalt blew a large plume of flame ahead of him, singeing a good number of goblins. The dragon put himself down between the goblins and the party. He turned his great head towards Alana and a great dragon smile crossed his face.

"You called for a rescue?" Cobalt said.

"Yes, noble dragon," Alana nodded. "And none too soon!"

"These goblins wanted to hold the good lady against her will," Colwyn added.

Alana agreed. "I didn't much care for that idea."

"Well, in that case, all of you get on my back," the dragon roared. "And we shall leave this place."

The five companions scrambled up onto the dragon's back and he waited for them to secure themselves. Each time the goblins got too close, he unleashed another plume of flame at them, keeping them at bay. When he was sure that the party was all secure, he launched himself up into the sky with a harrowing roar before pointing himself toward the city of Tornith.

The Blademaster

Chapter XX
Tornith

The great gold dragon circled high around the city of Tornith, allowing Alana and her companions a chance to see just what lay ahead for them. As they flew over the ziggurat of Thraal, they could see some of the priests pointing up at them. Spells came tearing through the air towards them, but Cobalt was able to dart through the air in such a way as to avoid such attacks. Cobalt continued his slow lazy circle of the city, finally settling in a clearing outside of Tornith on the opposite side of the city as the ziggurat.

Alana slid off the dragon's back to the ground. She motioned for the others to join her. When they were all on the ground, she ran her hands lovingly over the dragon's neck. Cobalt leaned down and put his nose right next to hers so that he was looking her right in the eye.

"I must leave you now, Blademaster," the dragon said softly. "I know that you are going into deep peril. I would come with you if I could, but I have used up all of my energy reserves in the past two days and would be of little help. I must find a good meal and rest for some time. I will still come if you call, but I must rest or I will not be able to help you."

"I understand, noble dragon," she replied with a smile. "I do not think that even Lord Taelin himself could ask you to do more for me than you have in the past two days. You truly are a good friend. I am honored to know you. Go and rest, my friend. I will be fine."

"I am the one who is honored, Blademaster Alana," Cobalt bowed with reverence towards her. "You know my past and yet you have not held it against me. Indeed, you have done your best to make me feel once again like a trusted friend to a Blademaster."

"You are a trusted friend, Cobalt," Colwyn smiled at the dragon. "I trust Alana's judgment. If she trusts you, then so do I. And you have been very helpful. I, too, am honored to know you. Go and rest, my friend. This is unsafe territory. The time will likely come when we will need you again."

"Colwyn Starseeker, you truly are a Protector in every sense of the title," Cobalt smiled back at the ranger. "I trust you will keep my Blademaster safe."

"It is what I am here for, Cobalt," Colwyn chuckled. "Now go. And don't waste your time or energy searching for a meal when you know right where we left you one. Don't worry about us, but stay alert for your summoning if we do need you."

"I will," the dragon nodded. He waited for the companions to move away so that he could take off without knocking them to the ground.

The five companions watched Cobalt take to the sky. The dragon circled above them several times before finally zooming off into the distance. The companions watched as the dragon became nothing more than a speck in the distance.

"Now what?" William asked.

Colwyn looked to Alana. They both shrugged.

"It's up to you, Alana," Colwyn said. "You are the Blademaster. Where do we go from here?"

"I think that the most logical place to start would be visiting the Temple of the White here in Tornith," Alana said thoughtfully. She turned and pointed to a building not far from where they were standing. "And the Temple of the White is close by. Cobalt saved us the time of traipsing through the city, even without knowing exactly where we were going."

"I am starting to truly like that dragon," Colwyn remarked. "Maybe we can leave our gear at the Temple of the White so that we don't have to carry anything but our weapons into combat."

"Probably not a bad idea," Alana nodded.

Colwyn and Alana set a fast pace towards the Temple and the others followed. An assault on the ziggurat would involve a great deal of planning and a good amount of rest prior. Both could be had at the Temple of the White. Colwyn would have liked to have kept Alana from Tornith altogether so that there was no chance that she could be sacrificed to the Dark God. But the lich would stop at nothing to put the Blademaster on his altar. Colwyn would never allow the lich to sacrifice Alana. He had come too far to lose everything to a sacrifice like that.

He could only hope that the planning that was to come would help to prevent such a sacrifice from happening.

As he walked, he glanced over at the woman that he loved. Somehow, he had been lucky enough to meet the one woman who would complete him. He could not suppress the smile that thought brought with it. He was lucky. He saw that every time that he looked into her eyes. And when he looked into her eyes, he could also see that she felt the same way.

Love like theirs was a rare thing on the world of Calthea. It was something to be cherished. And cherish that love he did. It was the most important thing in his life, and he was determined to do everything in his power not to lose the love he shared with Alana.

It did not take long for the five companions to reach the Temple of the White in Tornith. Like all Temples of the White that the companions had ever been to, the one in Tornith was made of white marble. On the front door, there was a small crest of Taelin. The crest was much smaller than they were used to. In fact, the entire temple was much smaller than they were used to.

Alana decided that it was a result of the fact that they were in lands that held Thraal sacred as their deity. A temple and a priesthood that were dedicated to Thraal's sworn enemy probably was not well frequented in Tornith. She suspected that the Temple of Laeyra, if there even was one in Tornith, would be even smaller.

Alana did take a bit of comfort from being near a Temple of the White. She'd never thought much about who her patron deity would be before the revelation of who and what she was. But now, as a Blademaster, she did not have all that much choice as to who her patron deities were. All Blademasters held both Taelin and Laeyra as their patron deities. Alana had always been comforted by the beliefs held by the followers of Taelin, so it was not that much of an adjustment for her. It was why she had always been so willing to sell her services as a sell sword to the Temple of the White. Since she was most in line with the teachings of Taelin, she felt most comfortable working for that god and his temple.

Her life as a sell sword was over though. She still did not know the full scope of her responsibilities as a Blademaster, but she knew enough to know that a Blademaster never sold her services to whoever could pay for them. Such an act would go against what Taelin and Laeyra had intended the Blademasters to be. Now that she had accepted the position and duties of being the first in a new line of Blademasters, she did not wish to do anything to screw up the honor of her office. A lot depended on her and her companions. She felt the pressure, but she knew that she was up to the challenge.

She knew Colwyn would be as well. For Colwyn, she knew it would be easier than it was for herself. As the heir to one of the First Lords of the Southern Dales, Colwyn already had to hold himself to a much higher standard.

She cleared her mind of such thoughts and went up to the front door of the Temple of the White. The door was locked. She frowned, because no Temple of the White ever locked its doors. Shrugging, figuring that it was because of the city they were in, she pulled her dagger from her belt and used the hilt of the dagger to pound on the door, knowing, as she did, that the priests would likely not be in the adjacent room and might not hear a simple knock.

Alana glared at the door, willing it to open. She wanted nothing more than to be on the other side. Standing out in the open in the middle of a city dedicated to the Dark God was not her favorite place to be. The longer she waited outside in the middle of the city, the better the chance that followers of Thraal would recognize her for who she was.

She did not want to think about the consequences if that were to happen.

It seemed to take forever, but finally, the door to the Temple of the White opened a crack, and a red hooded face peeked out at the companions. The eyes behind the hood went wide in surprise.

"I'm sorry, we're not seeing anyone today," the woman under the hood said softly. "No audiences today. Come back tomorrow."

"My companions and I have come a long way," Alana said quietly. Her foot darted forward and caught the door before it closed. "We would like to say our prayers to Lord Taelin to thank him for getting us through our ordeals on our journey to Tornith."

"I am sorry, but the Temple of the White is closed today," the woman reiterated.

"Closed?" Alana asked.

"Is that even possible?" Colwyn echoed.

"I'm sorry," the woman continued. "We are seeing no one today. You will have to come back tomorrow if you want to say prayers of thanksgiving to Lord Taelin. I'm afraid that is my final answer."

"Let me handle this, Lady Alana," Balaam remarked as he pushed his way to the forefront of the party. To the young woman, he raised an eyebrow and raised his voice ever so slightly. "What is your name, Priestess of Taelin?"

"My name is Olianna Tencis," the young woman replied. "I have been assigned to teach the acolytes at the Temple of the White here in Tornith."

"And do you recognize me, Priestess Olianna Tencis?" Balaam asked.

"I recognize by your garb that you are a Priest of Taelin as am I, my lord," the priestess nodded. "I am very sorry that I cannot accommodate your party today. If you will just come back tomorrow..."

"I am more than simply just another priest, Priestess Olianna," Balaam's voice went cold. He held up his hand displaying his ring of office. "Do you recognize this ring?"

"Of course, my lord High Priest," she said, going pale. Alana could tell that she was fighting the urge to kneel. "Forgive me, my lord, for not recognizing you on sight."

"Then you will allow us to enter," Balaam ordered. "No Temple of the White is closed to the High Priest of Taelin. Or to a chosen warrior of our Lord Taelin, as this woman is."

"You mean she is a..." the woman trailed off, not wanting to say the word for fear of what it would mean if the wrong person overheard her say it. "Lord Taelin be praised!"

"Yes. But this is better discussed inside where prying ears cannot hear."

"Of course, my lord," the woman bowed and disappeared behind the door.

Slowly the door creaked open and she ushered the five companions inside. She led the companions to a small anteroom and offered them something to eat. Each of the five companions took some of the dried meat and cheese that the woman offered. She looked over the five of them before silently leaving the room, presumably to get the highest-ranking priest to attend to them.

The five companions were each left with their own thoughts as they waited for the priestess to return. Balaam's mood had turned darker than normal when he had seen that the Temple of the White had closed and barred its doors. Alana could only wonder what was going through the young priest's mind, but the fact that things had gotten to the point to closing the Temple of the White meant that things were extremely bad in Tornith. If the priesthood of Taelin had been forced to turn its back on the citizenry, she knew there would be little help coming from these priests.

She wasn't surprised. She had not expected much in the way of help.

All she had really hoped for was information about the layout of the city and about what she might be able to expect at the ziggurat of Thraal. She did not expect them to help her fight the lich. That would have been nice, but it was definitely too much to ask. All she could really ask of them was to pray for her. There were some things that she needed to know, and she could only learn those things here at the Temple of the White. It was the only place in the entire city that would be even the least bit friendly to her and her companions. She only hoped that they were more forthcoming with information than they had been with their hospitality.

She scrutinized the small anteroom where they had been left and sighed. She had not seen such a plain anteroom in any of the Temples of the White that she had ever visited. It was totally devoid of any decoration, simple plain white marble walls. After the pure opulence of the Temple of the Blades, this Temple of the White truly left a lot to be desired. But then, as she thought on it, most of the Temples of the White that she had ever been in had been less ostentatious than other temples. Just not quite as boring and plain as this one was. She did not want to make such a comment to the High Priest though. She did not want to upset him any more than he already was.

It was the death of Merinda Delwyn that had him so upset.

Not for the first time, she wished she could do something to help the young priest. She knew that what he was going through was difficult at best. At worst, she knew that he would be looking for a way to join his Merinda. She did not want to contemplate his taking that path.

The success of her mission in Tornith depended on Balaam as much as it did her. She did not know how she knew this, nor did she care. The truth was the truth. She did not have to understand it. She only had to accept it. Somewhere along the line, she had learned that Balaam would be integral to the coming task. The High Priest must remain safe. She did not even know how she had come to know this. Perhaps the insight came from another Blademaster ability she had yet to learn about?

She just was not all that sure how she could do that without excluding him from the party. And if he were as integral to the task at hand as she had come to believe he was, she could not do that.

The priestess returned with the highest ranking priest in the temple and Alana was forced to retreat from such thoughts. This higher ranking priest was a slightly stooped older man who had the medallion around his neck that marked him as the highest ranking priest on site. He possessed a kindly face and next to no hair and looked completely out of place in a city like Tornith. From the gleam in his eyes, he had no idea, really, as to what to expect concerning the temple's guests.

"Taelin bless us," the man bowed towards Alana. "A Blademaster at last. I am Arthais, the highest ranking priest in this temple."

"Alana Steeldrake," Alana smiled. "I am a Blademaster, as you have said. These are my companions, Colwyn Starseeker, my Protector. The halfling is Meryn Swiftfoot, and the mage is William Stonehands."

"Greetings to all of you. You are all, of course, welcome in the Temple of the White in Tornith, such as it is." He greeted each of the companions in turn. He turned towards Balaam. "And, of course, our High Priest. You indeed honor us with your presence."

If it had been anyone else other than Alana that the old priest had greeted before him, Balaam would probably have been upset. But it wasn't every day that a priest of Taelin encountered a Blademaster. Balaam seemed to be pleased that Alana had accepted her destiny and that she had a man that had passed the Test of the Blades as her Protector. The Blademaster was important for the coming events. None of them knew quite what to expect in Tornith, but Balaam was quietly relieved that the Blademaster had chosen to start with a visit to the Temple of the White.

"Thank you, Lord Arthais," Balaam smiled. His smile turned cold though. "You know the tenets of Taelin. Perhaps you can tell us why you closed the doors to the temple."

"It is a long story, Lord Balaam," Arthais sighed. "Come to my study and I will explain. I suspect that our story has something to do with why the five of you are here."

Balaam gestured to the door. "Lead on, then."

The old man bowed and turned. He hobbled from little anteroom with the companions in tow. The old priest led them through the corridors of the temple. The maze of corridors wound through the temple, belying the size that the temple appeared to be from the outside.

Alana glanced around, wondering how the size of the temple could have been so deceptive. It appeared to be so small on the outside, and yet there seemed to be so much to the temple. Somewhere along the line, Alana figured, the temple had been the recipient of some magical enhancements to allow it to be larger than it appeared from outside. But she did not know what kind of enchantments could do that.

But she did not need to know how it was the case; she only needed to understand that it was true. It was the way, she found, that she had to deal with most of the things in her life. She knew the truth of a great number of things, and she realized that when it came to each of those things, she did not need to understand the reasons why they were the way they were. She only needed to accept that things were the way they were and go on from there. It was not always an easy thing to do, but, as the first in a new line of Blademasters, she knew that she would have to accept a great many things she never would have accepted before.

She hoped that it would get easier in time.

And she hoped that someday Colwyn and Balaam would be able to work together as part of her team. She knew that the priest would not always be with them on missions, but as long as he was the High Priest of Taelin, she would always have dealings with him. As the Blademaster, she would have to deal with the priesthoods of both of her patron gods. She'd never worked with the priesthood of Laeyra before, and she wondered how that would be. She had heard that the priesthood of Laeyra was a far more fun loving bunch than the priesthood of Taelin. Many considered the priesthood of Taelin to be stuffy at best. At worst, they were considered to be the most rigidly intractable of all of the pantheon's priests. Taelin was, after all, the god of Wisdom and Justice. It was not all that surprising that the priests of Taelin were as they were.

Still, Balaam had shown moments when he could be flexible and maybe even a little on the fun loving side.

Just a little.

Alana did not understand why the two men, Colwyn and Balaam, were possessed of such animosity towards the other, but ever since their first meeting, the two men had been at odds. Once Colwyn had passed the Test of the Blades, it had been less pronounced, but Alana could tell that the two men still did not like each other. It bothered her, because the two men should be working together, not sniping at each other with every opportunity. Not for the first time, she promised herself that she would talk to Colwyn about being nicer to Balaam. But every time she promised herself that, something happened to sidetrack the party, and she never got to have the talk she needed to have with Colwyn. This annoyed her to no end. She needed to voice her concerns soon but she did not really see how they would have time to squeeze it in before they would have to assail the ziggurat of Thraal. Still, she promised herself that she would find the time to talk to Colwyn about Balaam.

But first, she would have to talk to the priest, Arthais, and get the story about the temple and what was going on in Tornith.

The stooped little priest led them to an oak door at the end of a long corridor. Again, the crest of Taelin was displayed prominently. She suspected that they had arrived at Arthais' study. As was usually the case in these matters, the elder priest, in this case Arthais, would be the only one with access to the room.

Arthais removed a key from a pouch he wore on his belt and unlocked the door, pushing it forward and motioning for the five companions to enter.

As Alana entered the room, she looked around, impressed by both the size of the study and by its appointments. The room had red leather furniture, one long couch along one wall and several overstuffed sitting chairs scattered in a semicircular pattern around a fireplace that was built in the wall opposite the door. The fireplace itself was a thing of beauty. An oak mantel and red brick hearth were the main components. A fire was raging merrily and Alana could feel the warmth from the fire throughout the room. Along the wall opposite the couch, bookshelves stretched from one wall to the other, each one full of leather bound books. She could not tell what they were from where she was standing, but each book had golden lettering on the binding. She assumed that they were diaries or holy books and dismissed them as unimportant for the moment, although she suspected that important information about a number of things might be contained in the books.

Only time would tell if she would even get a chance to ask.

"Please, sit," Arthais said to the companions, indicating the large, overstuffed chairs. "We have a great deal to discuss."

The priest's eyes never left Alana, as if he expected her to disappear the moment his gaze turned away from her. He need not have worried. She wasn't going anywhere. She intended to hear the whole story. Something in what he was about to tell them could very well be helpful in stopping the lich. Therefore, she intended to listen to every word with rapt fascination.

"You seem surprised to see me, Lord Arthais," Alana remarked as she sat upon one of the chairs. "Surely our Lord Taelin told you about me and about my mission. You had to know that I would be coming to see you when I got to Tornith."

"Just because my Lord Taelin informed me of a Blademaster and that she would be coming to Tornith did not mean that I should expect you," Arthais replied. He toppled onto the couch and stretched his legs out in front of him. "To be honest, I did not think I would ever be lucky enough to meet a Blademaster in my lifetime. I thought I would have to wait until I went to walk with Lord Taelin in order to meet one. I have a great deal that I would tell you, but I would hear of your journey first, Blademaster. I am sure that you have travelled long to get to Tornith, and I would like very much to hear all about it."

Alana looked to Colwyn and got a shrug for her efforts. She settled in her chair and sighed. The other companions followed suit, each settling into one of the nearby chairs.

And so, Alana told Arthais about their journey. She started with Colwyn's proposal and how she had run. She told him about the merchant in Ravendale that she suspected was more than he appeared to be. She told him about the trip south to Valendale and how they had found Valendale devoid of life and about how they were ambushed there.

The priest frowned deeply at this, but did not interrupt.

She told him about the sage Isaiah and about how he told her to go to the temple in the middle of the Elven Woods. She told him about their stay with the Forestwalker Elves. And she relayed to him the events at the Temple of the Blades. She went on to tell him of her meeting Cobalt and their escape from another ambush. And she continued the tale by relating to him the details of their capture by goblins and about their ultimate escape including their flight to Tornith and how she had decided that she should seek more information before they could assault the ziggurat of Thraal and kill the lich. She told him about her mission. She told him everything until she ran out of words, and the priest listened with rapt fascination, his attention never wavering.

"A fascinating and sad story, Lady Alana," Arthais said softly. He sighed deeply as he looked her over. "And one that I am afraid I am going to make sadder. It is as you say. Merinda Delwyn was sacrificed to Thraal over a month ago. It was a terrible night in Tornith. The Dark God appeared that night by animating her body and speaking through her. It was a terrible sight to behold, or so my sources have told me. The Dark God indeed knows that a Blademaster walks the world, and he is after you. The High Priest of Thraal is to sacrifice you in order to release the Dark God from the prison that our Lord Taelin has kept him locked away in for centuries."

"We know all of that," Balaam waved impatiently. "Let us get back to the reasons why you have closed the temple, an act that is in clear violation of the tenets and laws that our Lord Taelin has set down for generations. By closing the Temple of the White to supplications, you deny the citizens of Tornith the wisdom and guidance of the Bringer of Light. A city like this can ill afford to be denied that wisdom and guidance, Lord Arthais. Explain yourself."

"I was forced to close the Temple, Lord Balaam," Arthais sighed. "Believe me, it was not without a great deal of personal anguish that I came to that decision. But the fact is that the temple could have only remained open at great personal risk to every priest that resides here."

"Please, spell out your reasoning," the High Priest demanded.

"I'm afraid the danger comes from those very citizens you are so quick to defend, Lord Balaam. How do you think Merinda was taken to be sacrificed in the first place?"

"It was my intention to ask you how you let one of your priestesses be sacrificed to the Dark God," Balaam snarled. "Thank you for saving me the effort."

Clearly the High Priest's anger had not abated when it came to the matter of Merinda Delwyn. Nor had she expected that it would have. Could she blame him? How would she feel if it were Colwyn that had been sacrificed?

Balaam continued. "The very fact that one of your priestesses was sacrificed to the Dark God is reason enough for me to replace you if I so chose. Surely you realize this."

"Yes, my Lord Balaam," Arthais sighed as he lowered his head in shame. "I was not here when it happened."

"That does not excuse you, Arthais," Balaam said under his breath. "You are still responsible for the well being of the priests and priestesses who reside in Tornith."

"I know, Lord Balaam," Arthais replied sheepishly. "Believe me, I know." He stretched his left leg again and folded it under him. "That is precisely why I closed the temple. Perhaps it would help if I told you what happened to Merinda and what occurred after she was taken."

"That would be best, yes," Balaam crossed his arms. "I want to know exactly what happened to Merinda Delwyn. Not only was she one of my priestesses, she was one I trained personally. She was also the woman I intended to marry."

"Your anger and impatience makes sense then, Lord Balaam," Arthais bowed his head again. The priest made a religious gesture and said a silent prayer for his lost priestess. "Merinda attended to a couple that came in supplication. No one could have known that they were followers of Thraal looking for a sacrifice. I suppose I would have been able to tell had I been present. Maybe that's why they waited until I was not here to visit. They came in with a story about needing counseling for their marriage. Of course, Merinda was only too happy to help them. You know her, Lord Balaam. You know she was quick to help, and slow to harm."

"Yes, I know, Arthais," Balaam's lips twitched. "That was, in fact, one of the reasons I fell in love with her." The High Priests's voice quavered slightly with sadness.

"I suppose I can understand that, Lord Balaam," Arthais chuckled. It was a rare sound for the old man, and the companions were not sure at first that the noise was actually a laugh. But one look into his sparkling eyes told them that it was definitely a chuckle. "But it was the very fact that she was so trusting that caused her to be taken."

"What happened?" Alana asked softly.

"I thought you weren't here," Colwyn said. "How exactly do you know what happened?"

The old man blinked at Colwyn. "I assure you, my sources are reliable." He then fixed his gaze back on his High Priest. "From what we can tell, the couple was a pair of priests of Thraal," Arthais continued. "One of them cast a binding spell on Merinda and they carried her right out of the temple. No one saw them leave. But we do know what happened from there because there were other eyewitnesses. She was taken directly to the ziggurat of

Thraal and held there for three days. Then, on the night of the full moon, she was sacrificed."

"And that caused you to close the temple?" Balaam raised an eyebrow. "One incident hardly seems to justify such an action, even if it resulted in the death of a priestess."

"No, it wasn't just that incident that forced my decision, Lord Balaam," Arthais sighed. He pulled a cup of tea from the small table next to the couch and took a deep sip. "Since the sacrifice, violence against followers of Taelin has gone up exponentially. None of us can walk about the streets of Tornith without the very real fear of being attacked. If we left the temple open, the people of Tornith would storm it. We would be under attack."

"I see," Balaam nodded. He stood up and went over to the small bar near the couch and poured himself a glass of wine. "Very well. Your point is well-taken. We'll keep the temple closed for now."

"Thank you, my Lord Balaam." Arthais turned to Alana. "And so, what can I do to help you in your mission, Blademaster?"

Alana decided not to mince words. "Do you have any intelligence on the layout for the ziggurat of Thraal? Specifically, I need to know where to find the lich and the best way to get out after I kill him."

Arthais nodded. "We do indeed have a map of the ziggurat of Thraal available for your use. I will have a room prepared for you and your companions to study the map and to plan out your strategy."

"Thank you, Lord Arthais," Alana said. She stood and Colwyn stood with her. "We'll go to the planning room now."

The companions worked late into the night on their preparations for the assault of the ziggurat of Thraal. But they decided to wait until the next morning to start towards the ziggurat.

They were given a room to sleep in for the night, and they slept well for the first time in weeks, bathed as they were in the light of Taelin.

Alana was glad when they all woke completely refreshed. It was the main reason that she had wanted to visit the Temple of the White. She knew that they would have the chance to get some restful sleep there.

It was restful sleep they would need. And chances are they would get none until the mission was over.

After they ate with the senior priest, they left just before noon and wandered through the city. They were not bothered by any of the inhabitants, although Alana expected that they would be if anyone learned who and what she was. It took them several hours to wind their way through the city and arrive at the ziggurat of Thraal.

Eventually, they found their way to the forests that surrounded the ziggurat. From there, they were able to watch the activity and plan their attack.

Chapter XXI
The Ziggurat of Thraal

Black robed priests of Thraal were climbing all over the ziggurat. To Alana, they appeared to be nothing more than insects crawling over a tasty morsel. The way they moved over the ziggurat made Alana's skin crawl. Getting into the ziggurat would not be easy. And getting out would be even more difficult. But get in and get out she had to do. At least, if worse came to worst, she could count on her companions to help get her out of the ziggurat alive. She would rather not have to depend on them for that, but it was good to have them.

As Alana watched the priests of Thraal, Colwyn silently crept up beside her. He watched with her for a few moments but said nothing. She knew he was working out his own plan of attack as a contingency. She wanted so much to tell him not to worry about her and that she would be fine. But saying as much would just be wasting her breath. Colwyn would worry about her no matter what. He had before they were married. Things would be no different now that they were bound together for the rest of their lives.

They watched in silence for a time. The others had held back, letting Alana and Colwyn canvas the ziggurat to get a feel for the place and to develop their plans. The Blademaster and her Protector were the best suited for this work, so the others just let them do what they needed to do. It was, after all, their mission. No one else could plan it for them. Alana knew that the others would be delighted to help them if it were possible. Somewhere deep inside, she wished they could help as much as they wanted to. It would certainly make her life a little easier. But such was not to be. She was the one who knew her abilities and her limitations. She was the only one who could plan for this.

The priests of Thraal did not seem to be in a hurry as they scampered up and down the steps of the ziggurat, and Alana assumed they were just going about their normal daily routines. They did not seem to be in any state of heightened alert in any case.

But that would change as soon as she entered the ziggurat.

She still wasn't all that sure what she hoped to accomplish by assaulting the ziggurat. As much as she would like to, she was pretty sure she would not be able to just go in and kill the lich. That would be too simple. Too easy. If she were honest with herself, she would admit that the most she would be able to accomplish would be to get a feel for an escape route for their actual assault. However, much more likely than being able to get in and out of the ziggurat cleanly was the likelihood of being taken prisoner and held for the sacrifice. It was a possibility that she did not relish.

At least she had some backup in case she was taken prisoner. Colwyn would not let her be sacrificed to Thraal, no matter what happened. Also, her four companions were determined to make sure that she completed her mission. She knew she could depend on them if the need arose.

She preferred to keep them out of it, if possible. Naturally, she couldn't control them. If they felt she needed help, they would go in whether she wanted them to or not.

There was no question that they were totally devoted to her. Such devotion could and would probably lead them to disregard her orders if her safety was at stake. It was the price she had to pay for her friends. It made her feel about as safe as she could in her position. But that did not mean she had to like the situation.

And she most certainly did not like the situation at all.

Colwyn glanced sideways at her. She had a feeling that he knew what she was thinking, but he had the good grace not to speak. He no doubt disliked the situation as much as she did, and there was no way he would be dissuaded from helping her if he decided she needed him. It was part of why she fell in love with him. And part of why she was so happy to have him at her side.

She searched her mind for everything she knew about liches. Unfortunately for her, what information she had about the creatures was sadly lacking. They were undead creatures that trapped the soul of a human in the decaying body. Their touch could cause extreme pain, and, in some cases, death. She had heard that a fight with a lich would be dangerous at the least. It could prove to be fatal to her. But she was determined that, if she was going to die fighting the lich, the lich would go down with her. Of course, this was assuming that a creature that was already dead could be killed. Destroyed was perhaps a better word. Unfortunately, she could recall nothing about how to destroy a lich. Perhaps decapitation. That was always a good solution. Very few creatures survived after the head was removed. And she could remove the lich's head fairly easily. Two swords would be good for that. Just cross her swords at its throat and pull. She could do that.

She absently checked that her two long swords were clear in their scabbards. It was an unconscious gesture that she used when she was about to go into a dangerous situation. Nothing stopped an assault as fast as not being able to get her swords free for battle. And many a swordsman had died because his sword was stuck in the scabbard. It was not a good way for a warrior to go, and she had determined a long time ago that she would never die as a result of that. Therefore, she always checked her swords before going into a situation that might warrant drawing them. No one had ever died by being too cautious, and, in Alana's mind, there was really no such thing as being too cautious.

It would not be an easy assault, she knew that. But it was necessary. She sighed softly, not nearly loud enough to grab any of the priests' attention as far away from the ziggurat as she was. Colwyn raised an eyebrow. Apparently, a sigh was not what he expected from her.

Alana motioned for Colwyn to follow her back to where the others were waiting. It was time to discuss strategy.

The companions crouched down together. Their features were all grim. The situation was not ideal and Alana was comforted to have the other three with Colwyn and her. At least they were all on the same page.

"We all know what we have to do," Alana said quietly. "I'm about to assault the ziggurat of Thraal."

"Perhaps we should start by talking about the priests," Colwyn suggested.

"I'm going in alone." She fixed Colwyn with her gaze.

"Like hell," Colwyn spat. But it was a token argument. He couldn't let her go in alone without some show of opposition. "I'm going in with you."

"You know that I can't let you do that, Colwyn," Alana smiled sadly. "If anything happens to me, I need you to make sure that the mission is carried out. I am depending on all of you for that."

"Of course, Alana," Meryn said.

Colwyn nodded. "But do you have to go in by yourself?" He gestured toward the halfling. "At least take Meryn with you. I'd feel better if you went with someone by your side."

"I'll be in and out before you even know I'm gone, Colwyn," she smiled at him. "Meryn will be of more use to you if you need to come in after me. It'd be better for me if I just went in and out, without having to worry about anyone but myself. I am no stranger to sneaking around. I may not be as good at sneaking around as you or Meryn is, but I'm not so bad."

"I'm not saying you are, Alana," Colwyn replied. "I just don't like you going into a dangerous situation by yourself. I am sworn to be your Protector after all. How can I protect you if I am not with you? "

"You're cute, Col," Alana chuckled. "It's sweet of you to be so concerned for me, but this time it's just not necessary. I fully expect to be in and out of the ziggurat before I'm even discovered."

"I hope so," Colwyn grunted. He knew full well what she was planning, but he wasn't convinced she could pull it off, especially alone. It would be difficult. And, naturally, he wanted to go with her. But she could not allow it.

Alana placed her hand on Colwyn's shoulder and smiled before turning and starting off. Colwyn watched her go as she made her way all the way to the ziggurat. When she slipped inside, he turned back to the other three companions and flashed them a weak grin.

"Okay," Colwyn said softly. "This is what we're going to do..."

The lich Drakkhous paced back and forth in his sanctuary. He was agitated. Ever since the Blademaster and her companions had escaped from the goblins, he had been unable to track them. He was concerned about having lost them, but he would not let such annoyance show to anyone but his closest associate. He was even careful about telling Adouon about his agitation and apprehension for fear of looking weak to him. That was something that he could not allow to happen.

But in the privacy of his sanctuary, he was free to react as the situation afforded. And so he attempted to burn of his frustration with pacing.

His biggest concern, of course, was that losing the Blademaster would bode ill for the remainder of his tenure as Thraal's High Priest. This task was extremely important to the Dark God. The lich did not want to disappoint his god by failing to secure the Blademaster for the sacrifice. Of course, he knew that he was well loved by Thraal, so he did not think that such a disappointment would necessarily be fatal. But he did not wish to test his status. He did, after all, value his life, such as it was. He also valued the fact that he would one day be with his Lilliana. He knew that it would not happen without Thraal's favor and that he had to make this sacrifice happen before he could be reunited with his Lilliana. It was important that he make it happen. Failure was not an option.

This was the source of his frustration.

All he could do was to pray to his god that the Blademaster would somehow reappear. If she did, she would be his. And when that happened, it would only be a matter of time before the sacrifice that would bring his Lilliana back to him would happen.

He quieted his breathing and stopped pacing, forcing himself to focus on the noises beyond his sanctuary. The movements of dozens of priests hustling about the corridors caught his attention. None of the priests sounded like they were heading his way, so he let slip his concentration and turned back to the wall that held his book shelves. He looked them over, sighing softly to himself. He slipped over to a nearby shelf and pulled one of the books off, running his fingers over the worn spine. This was the first book that he had been given when he had first joined the priesthood of Thraal. It was a book of prophecy written by one of the first High Priests to Thraal. The book of prophecy had been fascinating reading at first, but now he knew that some of those prophecies were, in fact, coming true. One prophecy in particular was about to be fulfilled. He opened the book and flipped to a page in the middle. He found the passage he was looking for and started to read.

"In the year when a Child born of the Light walks the world after three hundred years without one, the Dark God will rise once more. He will be freed from his prison in Limbo by one who wears the red of his enemy. But not before a swath of blood stains the altar of the ziggurat of Thraal. The Great Fire will run red with the blood of the faithful."

Drakkhous had never really understood the prophecy. In truth, he still did not understand it. He was fairly certain that it meant that the Dark God that he served would rise again before the year was out. That much was clear, as a Child born of the Light, a term often used in prophecies to refer to a Blademaster, was walking the world. But he still questioned the part about a swath of blood staining the altar. He assumed it meant that there would be a great fight before the sacrifice happened. He had not been able to isolate any useful information from any other texts about what it might mean. There was nothing in any of the texts that would further explain the prophecy. He disliked going into something so important with so little information, but there was nothing he could do. He could only proceed with the information he had.

Frustrated, he set the book back on the shelf and turned to his meditation area, hoping that a little meditation might clear his mind or even give him some insight into the prophecy.

Or at least wisdom as to where the Blademaster might be.

Before he settled into his meditation chamber, he focused his hearing again on what was happening outside his chamber door. There was the same hustle and bustle he had heard previously, but this time, in addition, he heard one set of footsteps that he knew all too well. And they headed towards his sanctuary. He smiled to himself. Surely, Adouon would only dare to interrupt him if he had vital information.

He turned to face his sanctuary door, keeping his focus on the footsteps. They came closer and closer, and Drakkhous chuckled to himself as he listened to the cadence of the footsteps. The lich licked his lips in anticipation of the information, whatever it was. With the way that Adouon was racing towards his sanctuary, the information must have been very important.

When the footsteps reached the door, the lich's smile had morphed into a purely sadistic grin. He sauntered across the room to the door and waved his hand in front of the nearby metal plate. The plate of magic only responded to the hand of the High Priest. Someday, he knew, the plate would respond to Adouon's hand and not his. But for now, he was the High Priest, and he was happy to be so. It was a joy he found to be second to none in his life to date. And it was a joy he would not easily give up.

The door slid open at his wave, revealing a clearly startled Adouon standing in the doorway. The younger priest raised both eyebrows in surprise as the lich ushered him into the sanctuary. Clearly the young human had not expected Drakkhous to be awaiting his arrival.

"You have information for me?" Drakkhous said softly. He pointed to his sanctuary's meditation area. There were a couple chairs that Drakkhous used when someone visited his sanctuary. "Please, have a seat, my friend."

Adouon moved over to the meditation area and sat down in one of the chairs. He smiled broadly at the lich as the High Priest also seated himself. The lich gestured for him to begin, knowing full well that whatever it was that the young man had to tell him was something that he wanted to hear. He had every hope that it had to do with the Blademaster and her location. If that was the case, then it was even more important that he hear what Adouon had to tell him. It could mean the chance to bring his Lilliana back to him. If so, he would have to take the chance given to him, no matter what it would cost the ziggurat in minions.

"My Lord, your wait is over," Adouon said softly. "The Blademaster and her companions are in Tornith as we speak. My sources in town say they are headed here to the ziggurat. I do not doubt that the Blademaster will try to storm the ziggurat soon. I suggest that we be ready for her when she does. We might not get another chance to capture her."

"I quite agree, Adouon," Drakkhous replied with a nod. "Prepare your men. I want her taken alive and unharmed. When she has been captured, I want to see this Blademaster with my own eyes. I want to see the living door that will bring our Lord Thraal back to the world of Calthea."

"It shall be done as you say, Lord Drakkhous." Adouon stood. "I shall go rouse the warriors. We shall be ready for her when she arrives. She will be yours to sacrifice soon, my Lord."

"I expect it to be so, Adouon. See to it at once."

"I shall look forward to the sacrifice with glee, my Lord," Adouon said as he crossed the sanctuary "The warriors will catch her as soon as she enters the ziggurat."

The priest left the sanctuary, his steps light with the anticipation of a good battle. The lich hoped that Adouon would not underestimate the battle prowess of the Blademaster and that he would take appropriate measures to make sure that there were enough warriors in the attack parties to ensure a successful capture. Really, it was only important that there be enough warriors to distract her long enough for a priest, presumably Adouon himself, to initiate a binding spell on the young warrior woman. Once the Blademaster was bound, she could be easily taken to a dungeon. Once in a dungeon, it did not matter if she stayed bound. She would not be able to escape. And then she would belong to Thraal.

The lich looked over at the skull that he used to communicate with the Dark God and smiled wickedly. He sat the skull on the floor in front of him, dusted it with a powder and closed his eyes.

"*Shakthala revinthos*," he rasped. "Lord Thraal, I call upon you now. Come to me, Lord of Chaos. Come to impart your wisdom."

"I am here, my friend," a liquidly evil voice came from the skull.

Drakkhous opened his eyes. He picked up the skull and held it in front of him so that they were eye to eye. The lich's features contorted into a cruel smile as he gazed at the blue flames in the empty eye sockets of the skull.

"Lord Thraal, the time is coming soon," Drakkhous rasped. "The Blademaster has arrived in Tornith. It is only a matter of time before she has been captured so that she can be sacrificed to your glory."

"You have done well, my High Priest," the god's voice said softly. "I am well pleased. This will be a glorious sacrifice. My time is coming soon. And with it, I will keep my promise to you. You will be reunited with your Lilliana very soon."

The eyes of the skull glowed brighter, presumably in joy. A course dark laughter issued from the skull, and

Drakkhous joined it with his own cackles. Both god and High Priest laughed wickedly in the muted silence of the sanctuary.

Alana slipped through a small door in the side of the ziggurat of Thraal. And there she was. Inside. She was disturbed by how easy it was that she was able to sneak into the ziggurat. There should have been at least a couple of guards near the entrance. The ease of her entrance raised her guard. It was very likely that her entrance had not gone unnoticed, and she braced herself for the inevitable resistance.

She slid her swords quietly from their scabbards and prepared for the worst.

Not for the first time, and not for the last time, she wished that Colwyn had come with her. But she knew that it could not be. For some reason, she felt she had to do this on her own. It was what she was used to despite the companions she now had. She did not like to depend on others, and she never had. As the Blademaster, though, she would have to depend on her companions. Besides, she knew that the completion of her mission depended every bit as much on her companions as it did on her. Especially on Colwyn and Balaam.

Knowing that the mission depended on her companions did not make it any easier for her to rely on them. And that was why she found herself creeping through the corridors of the ziggurat of Thraal alone, knowing full well that she was probably walking into a trap that would lead to her capture. In a way, she almost hoped she would be captured. While avoiding the sacrifice would be more difficult if she were captured, being captured would also bring her closer to the lich. He would not be guarded during the sacrifice, after all.

That would be her best chance to kill him.

She crept further down the corridor, taking her time so as to make as little noise as possible. She kept herself up close to the walls, trying to make herself as unobtrusive as she could. It was not easy because she had never been fully trained in such techniques of stealth. But she did her best.

As she slinked towards a cross corridor, she frowned. She would be most vulnerable crossing such an intersection, but she wasn't about to turn around now. She stopped and listened. It was quiet. But just because there was no noise did not mean that there were no priests in the area.

She took a quick glance around the corner, taking a quick peek to each side to make sure there was no one in the cross corridor. Unfortunately for Alana, there were a pair of priests just down the corridor. One of them gave a shout of recognition when he saw her. She cursed and ducked back into the corridor she was in, but it was too late.

She had been seen!

Swearing again, she sprinted back down the original corridor, trying to put as much distance between herself and the inevitably pursuing priests as she could. She ducked down a side corridor, one she had not yet investigated, and put on a burst of speed. After another couple hundred feet, the corridor split off to the right. As she made the turn, she skidded to a halt.

The corridor ended in a door.

She tried the handle and found it to be locked. She spun around and searched for another way out. But there was nothing. She was effectively cornered. So she slumped against the door. The priests would burst around the corner any time. When they arrived, she would be ready. But she would be severely outnumbered. Of course, that had never stopped her before. She promised herself that, if she were going to be caught, it would be more costly to the priesthood of Thraal than it would be to her.

Very costly.

She said a silent prayer to Taelin as she adjusted the grip on the hilts of her swords. She gripped the hilts of her swords tighter, hoping beyond hope that she would be ready for them when they came.

She heard footsteps coming from around the corner. She did not have to look to know that it was the priests that had detected her presence in the corridor. She readied herself, holding steady with her swords in hand. She exhaled and waited patiently for the priests to come around the corner. She was going to meet them with steel in her hands and she was going to teach them what it meant to go up against a Blademaster.

She would not go easily.

The priests rushed her and the dance began. Alana's swords seemed to move of their own accord, thrusting and parrying with surprising speed and accuracy. She ducked a blow from one of the priests and threw a thrust in his direction. It struck true, cutting a deep gash in the man's arm.

While she was focused on fighting off the priests, she did not hear the previously locked door open behind her. A priest slipped up behind Alana and placed a hand on her back. There was no time to react before she was immobilized. The only thing she could move was her head.

"That was almost too easy, Blademaster." Adouon laughed at her as he stepped around her paralyzed frame. She watched every move that the priest made. "I expected it would be much harder than that to capture you. Lord Drakkhous will be most pleased."

"I hate to disappoint you, priest," she spat at him. "But I'm not going to be sacrificed to your god. Not now or ever."

"Go get the High Priest," Adouon barked to one of the other priests. He spun on the young warrior woman with a smile. "Oh, I think you will find that you really have no choice in the matter, Blademaster. It will be a glorious sacrifice indeed. It will be the most glorious sacrifice that I have ever been a part of. I look forward to hearing you scream as the High Priest climbs on top of you to do his duty to our Lord Thraal. And you will have no way to stop him."

"You are full of bluster, priest," Alana cackled. "Do you really think that I am alone in Tornith? You will find that those who have accompanied me to Tornith will ensure that I am not sacrificed."

"I think you will find that your friends won't be anywhere near as much help to you as you think, Blademaster Alana Steeldrake," a raspy voice cackled from around the corner. The lich strode into view, and the priests shuddered involuntarily. "They will die just as surely as you will."

"So you say, lich," Alana scoffed. "Oh yes, I know who and what you are, lich. And I know that you will never sacrifice me. I promise you now, lich, that it will be you that will die on top of the altar, not me. I swear it by my Lord Taelin. And by my Lady Laeyra."

"Your pathetic belief in your gods cannot help you now, child," the lich said through an evil grin. He reached up and ran his sharp fingernail along her cheek. "Take her down into the dungeons. Make sure you do not release the binding spell until she is safely inside her cell, Adouon. I do not want any mistakes. You know the penalty for failure."

"Yes, Lord Drakkhous," Adouon replied with a nod. He motioned for the priests to lead the way, dragging Alana along with them as they headed towards the nearest downward stairwell. "It shall be done as you say. There will not be opportunity for escape, and I will order extra tight security over the dungeons while she is our guest. I will report to you in your sanctuary after she has been secured."

Drakkhous nodded and watched the younger priest fall in behind the others as they dragged the Blademaster off to the dungeons. He smiled wickedly to himself. Soon, he would have the privilege of sacrificing the hated Taelin's champion and the Dark God would return. And soon, he would be rewarded for his hard work with the return of the woman he loved. Only that made all his hard work worthwhile. Soon he would be reunited with his Lilliana and his life would be complete once again.

Still smiling, Drakkhous turned and stalked off towards his sanctuary.

The Blademaster

Chapter XXII
Orakkhous

The stone floor was cold on Alana's back. No matter which way she turned, she could not get comfortable. She was pretty sure her discomfort was part of the lich's plans to break her spirit before the sacrifice. And even though she was determined that there would be no sacrifice, she was nonetheless disturbed to find herself starting to lose more and more of her spirit as the hours wore on.

She found herself asking the same question over and over again.

Where was Colwyn?

She hoped he was all right. But she wasn't sure. She hadn't seen him since she had entered the ziggurat. What were he and the others doing? Had they come into the ziggurat to rescue her? Or were they seeking additional help? Did they have a plan for what to do if she actually was sacrificed? For that matter, did they have a plan to prevent her from being sacrificed?

"Alana?" Colwyn's voice called from just outside her cell.

Alana jumped.

She hadn't heard him come down the stairs. She wondered if she were imagining him.

"Are you all right?" he asked.

"Better now." She sighed. "I'm as all right as I can be, considering I have a lich that wants to sacrifice me to his Dark God," she replied. "It's good to see you, Col," Alana smiled broadly. Then her smile turned into a look of shock when she saw how he was dressed. "You look like a priest of Thraal!"

"That's the idea," Colwyn laughed softly. "How do you think I was able to come down here and check on you?"

"Good point," Alana chuckled. "But what happens if you're caught?"

"Then I am in a world of trouble," Colwyn shrugged. "The others are here too. We're working on a plan to get you out of here."

"I suppose that I will have to just have to let you do your thing and pray to Taelin that, whatever your plan is, it's a good one," Alana laughed. "Just... Promise me you'll be careful."

"I promise," Colwyn nodded. "I have to get back upstairs. The lich is going to visit you a little later on." He came forward and put his hands against the bars. "You be careful too. The lich is very powerful."

"I'll be careful, Colwyn," Alana smiled. "You and the others have to find a way to get me out of here though."

"We're working on that," he smiled back. "I promise you. You will not be sacrificed. I love you."

"I love you too. Now get out of here before they discover you."

Colwyn nodded and hurried back up the stairs. Alana watched him go and sighed softly to herself. She wished he could have stayed, but it wasn't worth the risk. Slumping back down on the ground, she wondered when or if she would even see him again. She wanted to hold him in her arms and tell him that she loved him. She wanted to forget about the whole mission. She just wanted to go home and live a somewhat normal life. Even if she knew such a thing would never be possible.

She found being stuck in a dungeon utterly annoying. And boring. There was nothing for her to do but wait. And Alana hated waiting. She just wanted this whole thing to be over and done with. She wanted the lich dead and to be home with Colwyn to enjoy their lives together. Even if she had a sneaking suspicion that they would always be working on some mission for Taelin.

The wonder of her situation was that the lich had made the mistake of leaving her weapons. Somewhere along the line, she intended to make them pay for that mistake.

She just hoped that an opportunity would present itself before she was sacrificed to Thraal.

She lay down on the cold stone floor, opting to try to get some rest. After all, if she was going to have an opportunity to kill the lich, she would need to be well rested to take advantage of it.

She tossed and turned for a time before settling rather uncomfortably into a light sleep. Faint shadows drifted by in front of her as she drifted off into the fitful sleep...

The corridor seemed to go on forever. Alana had been walking for hours, it seemed. She knew that she had to keep going, because it was the only way she was going to escape from the lich. Just continue to walk straight ahead and not look behind. She hoped that Colwyn was following her. She wanted him to get out of the ziggurat alive too. She had already seen the other three killed in front of her. Drakkhous had used them in order to force her to submit willingly to the sacrifice.

It hadn't worked.

But when they'd seized Colwyn, her determination had wavered. She realized she would probably submit rather than lose Colwyn. And that thought scared her. She would allow the world to fall into darkness rather than lose the man she loved. Alana wasn't sure she could live with that. But then, she wouldn't live through the sacrifice, would she?

Somehow, though, they had gotten away and started running down this corridor.

The corridor stretched on ahead. There were no doors on either side and no cross-corridors. She could only go forwards or back. And back was not an option. She could hear the scraping of weapons against the corridor walls. Hundreds of followers of Thraal slowly pursued her and Colwyn.

"Hurry, Colwyn," she called to her husband. But she didn't look back to see where he was in relation to her.

"I can't run anymore, Alana," he grunted between huffs. "You go on. You're the Blademaster... the one who needs to stay safe. Go. I'll slow them up enough to keep them off you."

"I can't let you sacrifice yourself for me, Colwyn," Alana cried as she whirled around. "If we go down, we do it together."

"Together then," Colwyn agreed, his jaw set.

They stood side by side with their weapons out as the horde of followers of Thraal charged towards them...

Alana awoke with a start. She was still in the dungeons, but she was still a little disoriented from the dream. She slumped back against the stone floor with relief that it was just a nightmare.

"Bad dreams, Blademaster?" a raspy voice came from outside her cell. She leapt up and whirled towards the voice.

Sitting on the ground outside the door to her cell was the lich. She pulled a throwing star from the bandolier around her chest and whipped it at the lich. It got to the door and promptly fell to the floor as if it had hit an invisible wall. The lich just laughed at her.

"Silly woman," the lich said between chuckles. "Did you think I would sit in your line of sight if I had anything to fear from you? No weapon can come out of your cell to strike me. I would not have allowed you to keep your weapons if they were a danger to me."

Alana did not respond, she simply stepped closer, maintaining eye contact. Then she bent down and scooped up the throwing star, reattaching it to the bandolier it belonged to. Then she made her way toward the door, watching the lich with her arms crossed about her chest. "How long have you been watching me?"

"Long enough, my dear," Drakkhous smiled. "Long enough to know that you are having difficulty sleeping."

"It's a cold and hard floor. It's not exactly comfortable," Alana scoffed.

"It's more than that. You are having nightmares."

"You are a nightmare, lich," Alana growled. "Your face is enough to inspire bad dreams. But I intend to make sure you are not a nightmare to anyone ever again. I'm going to run you through that cold stone you call a heart."

"Such spirit." Drakkhous smiled even wider. "Too bad it's wasted. There is nothing you can do to stop what's going to happen. This sacrifice is your destiny."

"Is that why you're here? To gloat?" Alana raised an eyebrow. "Because if it is, then you should go away. I don't want to hear it."

"No, I am not here to gloat," Drakkhous snorted. "I wanted a chance to appraise my prize."

"So, I am your prize now, huh?" Alana crossed her arms even tighter.

"You are the greatest prize I have ever collected for my Lord Thraal, Blademaster," the lich rumbled. "And you will be the key to my salvation."

"Your salvation?" Alana quirked an eyebrow. That was the last thing she had expected the lich to say. "What do you mean by that?"

"I mean that you are the way by which I will be saved, of course," Drakkhous snorted. "Since you are about to be sacrificed to my Lord Thraal, it is only fair that I tell you my story."

"What if I don't want to hear it?" Alana snorted as she dropped back down to a sitting position. She crossed her legs and pulled one of her long swords out of its scabbard and started to polish it. "I mean, you're not exactly the most interesting person I've ever met."

"Perhaps that's because you don't know my past. I think you will find my story to be rather interesting," the lich rasped.

"Just tell me what you're going to tell me and get on with it," Alana yawned loudly. "I'm rather bored. I think I'd rather sleep up until you try to kill me."

"You will be sacrificed soon enough, my dear," the lich chuckled as he shifted his weight. "Honestly, I do not know why I have this burning desire to tell you my story, Blademaster. But I feel that I must tell it to you before I sacrifice you. You should know that the main reason you are being sacrificed is not to free my Lord Thraal, but for love."

"What do you know of love, lich?" Alana scoffed. "You serve the Dark God. The Dark God does not believe in love."

"That is just what you have been told, child," the lich said softly. There was a tenderness in the lich's voice that Alana never expected to hear. "I was not always a priest of Thraal. Before I became a lich, I wore the White robes of Taelin."

Alana had no idea what she had expected the lich to say. That wasn't it, though. It piqued her curiosity to the point where she had to hear the lich's story. And maybe, just maybe, she would find something in the lich's story that she could use against him.

"Very well, lich, tell me your tale," Alana said, adjusting her legs so she was more comfortable. "I'll try to stay awake, but I can't promise that it will change my mind about you."

"I don't expect it to." The lich shrugged. "For neither will it change the fact that you are to be sacrificed. Nevertheless, my story really begins in the Wilds..."

There were towns in the Wilds that formed the border between the Southern Dales and Dracomyr. The people who lived in these towns claimed fealty to neither of the bordering regions, making the Wilds the third region of Calthea. Each of the towns in the Wilds was, in essence, its own little kingdom, for each town in the Wilds was self-governing. Unlike the Southern Dales and Dracomyr, there was no central council or government for the region and, for the most part, the region was the better for it. That was not to say that there were no squabbles between the towns. But, for the most part, the setup of the Wilds worked for everyone that lived there. The only times that the Wilds were not an ideal place for the people who lived there was during the times of active war between the Southern Dales and Dracomyr. Many of the battles in those wars were fought in the Wilds. But such periods of war were exceedingly rare. It had been several centuries since the last war between the Southern Dales and Dracomyr, and the Wilds had been a good and peaceful place to live that entire time.

Most, if not all, of the gods in Calthea's pantheon had at least one temple somewhere in the Wilds. For the gods Taelin and Laeyra, their most prominent temples in the Wilds were located in a tiny village in the middle of the Wilds called Vikerin. It was small even in comparison to other villages in the Wilds, nevertheless, for the priesthoods of Taelin and Laeyra, Vikerin was an important village.

The Temple of the White in Vikerin was the largest of all of the temples dedicated to Taelin in all of the Wilds. It was small when compared to the Temples of the White that were scattered throughout the Southern Dales. The Vikerin temple was home to a good number of priests of Taelin. The leader of the Priests of Taelin in the Temple of the White in Vikerin was a young and unassuming priest named Darius Redwind. He had risen quickly through the ranks of the priesthood, and there were many who thought that he was on the fast track to becoming the High Priest of Taelin. But Darius had no ambition for becoming the High Priest. There was only one ambition that Darius Redwind had any desire to pursue. And he intended to pursue it with all the energy he had.

And that was marriage.

Marriage to the woman that he loved.

Lilliana Marant was devoted to Laeyra, the goddess of luck. She had come to Vikerin not long after Darius himself had arrived. Since the priesthoods of the two gods tended to work together a great deal, it was no matter of great coincidence that the two came into close contact. Ironically, it was at a village festival that they met, not a function sponsored by either of the temples.

The attraction was quick and mutual.

It was from their very first dance at the festival that the two fell in love. They danced for hours that very first night, and they remained inseparable throughout their time in Vikerin. They worked hard to bring the Vikerin temples of Taelin and Laeyra together. The two temples worked far closer together than ever as a result of their relationship. It was a happy time for both of them, and they were together for two very good years. Darius and Lilliana enjoyed their time together. And the priesthoods of Taelin and Laeyra enjoyed their being together because it made the rest of the priests just as happy.

Two years into their relationship, a wasting disease wound its way through the Wilds. When it reached Vikerin, Lilliana and Darius did everything they could to help the people. But their help just was not enough. Terra, the goddess of healing, had next to no presence in Vikerin. And without Terra's guidance, nowhere near enough healing could come to Vikerin to stop the wasting disease.

The disease struck quickly and without mercy. The only merciful part with regards to the disease is that, once contracted, it did not take long to kill those who were infected. But it was a painful and hard death, not only for the one dying, but also for those who loved that person and had to watch him or her go through it.

It was one morning three months after the wasting disease came to Vikerin that Darius went to the temple of Laeyra. As a member of the priesthood of Taelin, he was allowed access to any part of the temple of Laeyra. He traversed the temple without being questioned. He knew where he was going, having been there many times in the past. But when he pushed open the door to Lilliana's room, he fell to his knees in quiet supplication. The pungent aroma of death had greeted him as soon as he opened the door to her room.

Taelin did not often answer such prayers for it was not Taelin's dominion to heal. Still, Darius hoped that, just this once, Taelin might make an exception and heal the woman he loved.

Lilliana was lying on her bed clearly afflicted with the wasting sickness that had been ravaging Vikerin. Darius could tell that the sickness had already spread through most of her body and, based on his experience with the disease, she did not have more than a day or two to live. It broke Darius's heart to see her lying on the bed so clearly dying. He wanted to do something... anything... to help her. But there was nothing he could do at this point. The wasting sickness had taken her past the point where any priests but those of Terra might be able to save her. He wasn't even sure that priests of Terra could help her at this point.

He shambled over to her bed, each step as if he were dragging through mud. The sight of Lilliana was constricting his heart and making it hard for him to move. When he reached the bed, he dropped to his knees once more and he gently took her hand.

"I'm here, my Lilliana," he said gently. "I'm here."

She slowly turned her head to look at him, a weak smile playing across her delicate features when she saw him. She squeezed his hand with every bit of strength she had. It was not much. The squeeze was just enough to tell him that she was still alive. It was all that he could hope for, but he still prayed for a way to save her. Instead of some kind of divine inspiration, however, he felt his heart breaking. There was nothing he could do to alter the ultimate outcome.

"Do not grieve, my love," she breathed, her voice devoid of the musical qualities that he had come to love. "I die so that others may live. I made a bargain with my lady Laeyra that my death would stop this plague. I would rather die knowing that my death will save so many lives than watch those lives perish when I know I could have done something to stop it."

"I can't bear to lose you, Lilliana," he said weakly. "I love you. I have loved no one else but you."

"I know, Darius." She smiled again. This time the smile was genuine and deep. It touched his soul. "I know how much you love me, and I love you just as much. That is what made this decision so difficult. And believe me, it was difficult. But life will go on for so many more because of this decision."

"But I need you," he protested weakly. "I will always need you, Lilliana. What will I do without you?"

"You will live your life, my love," she said weakly. "You will continue to serve your Lord Taelin as you always have. And you will remember me. As long as you remember me, I will never truly be gone."

"Lilliana, I don't know if I can carry on without you," Darius cried. Any control that he had over his composure was gone. He could not help but let the tears flow freely. "You mean too much to me."

"You will find a way," Lilliana smiled one last time. "My time is near. I will see you when you come to walk with Lord Taelin."

Lilliana closed her eyes. Darius watched her with concern. He gripped her hand tightly as if that act alone would keep her from slipping into the next world. He watched her as she fell into what appeared to be a deep sleep.

One from which she would never awaken.

He watched her all day and into the night. He did not leave her side to eat, drink, or sleep. To his mind, he had to be there for her no matter what. These would be the last moments of her life, despite his fervent wishes and prayers to the contrary. He could not allow her to spend her last moments alone.

Day stretched into night, and the shadows cast by the sun through the window of the room lengthened and covered the entire floor. Still Darius stayed by the bed. It was late in the night hours when he finally heard the death rattle that was her last breath.

He buried his head into the blankets on her bed, wailing in misery. He wished he could join her in death. He did not want to live without her.

It occurred to him that he would have to build a pyre for her body. Still, he could not bring himself to do so. All he could do was to mourn for her in his own way. Memories of all the time they had spent together flooded through his mind. He remembered every moment that the two of them had spent together. And he cherished them all. It was all he had left of her.

The flood of memories brought on a flood of tears. There was no way to stop it. He did not want to cry. He did not want to mourn. He did not want to lose her. But it was too late for all of that.

It was several hours before he could even move. His memories had paralyzed him, preventing him from doing anything other than cry. But he could not put off any other activities any longer. He scooped up her body and carried her outside to where the funeral pyre would be built to burn her body and send her spirit off to her goddess.

He gently placed her body down and started working on the pyre. It was a long and painful process, both emotionally and physically. It tired him out, but he kept moving because he had no choice. Even though he was not a priest of Laeyra, his relationship with Lilliana made him the only logical choice to perform the funeral rites for her. Even though it was the last thing he wanted to do.

He took his time building the pyre. When he was done, he placed her body gently on the top of the pyre. Standing back, he set fire to it and watched the pyre consume her body. No one sat watch with him. It was a lonely vigil as he watched her body burn, releasing her spirit to walk with her goddess in the afterlife. As he watched, a glowing version of the woman he loved rose up from her body and came over to him.

"Do not grieve for me, my love," the spirit said. "I go to walk with my goddess whom I love. When the time comes, you will join me there."

"But..." he trailed off.

"There are no buts, my love," she smiled. Her spirit hand touched his solid cheek. He felt a spark of electricity at her touch. "It is the way things are."

"I will miss you," Darius cried.

"I know," Lilliana smiled. "You and I will be reunited in time. It will be all right. I have loved you since the first."

"And I have loved you, Lilliana," Darius replied with a sad smile.

"Good bye, my love," Lilliana said softly as her spirit started to fade. "We will be reunited at the end. Our Lord Taelin and Lady Laeyra will see to that. Trust in your faith."

Darius watched her go, tears streaming down his face. He turned away from the pyre when her spirit disappeared from view. When he turned, he spied a figure dressed in all black. The figure's hood was up, preventing him from seeing who or what the figure was. Darius stepped towards the mysterious figure and slowly walked around it. The figure did not move or speak.

"Who are you?" Darius asked softly.

"Someone who can give you what you want," the figure remarked in a sibilant voice. "Someone who can bring the woman you love back to you. But you have to do something for me."

"No one can bring someone back from the dead," Darius grunted. He stopped in front of the figure again. "No one can do that. It goes against the gods' design."

"Oh? Even a god can't bring someone back from the dead?" the figure laughed. It was not a pleasant laugh, and Darius had a bad feeling about the figure based on that laugh. "Your lack of faith in the gods is disturbing for one in your position, priest."

"I am a priest of Lord Taelin," Darius said quietly. "Lord Taelin would not do something so evil and chaotic as bring someone back from the dead. Only a god from the evil side of the pantheon would do such as that. Why would I do anything for such a god when I serve Lord Taelin? You must think me a fool. I have just laid the woman I love to pyre. Leave me, Evil One, for I now know who you are."

"Oh?" the figure cackled. "And who do you suppose I am?"

"You are the Dark God, Thraal," Darius said calmly. "You are the Bringer of Chaos and the enemy of my Lord Taelin."

"And what makes you say that, Darius Redwind?" the figure asked.

"Because what you have said qualifies as chaos," Darius replied. "Only the Lord of Chaos would come to me with such claims. And do you truly expect me to forsake my vows to my Lord Taelin just on the outside chance that you might be right about being able to bring my Lilliana back?"

"Not only do I expect you to forsake your vows to Lord Taelin, I fully expect you to become my High Priest," the Dark God sneered. "I assure you, I can give you your Lilliana. I believe that you will do whatever you have to do to bring her back."

"You don't know me that well then, Evil One." Darius started to push past the god towards the Temple of Laeyra. "Go away."

"I will not," the god replied. "You will come to believe me. You will become my High Priest. I will give you powers beyond that which you could ever imagine. You will become immortal. And it will all be for your Lilliana. I have foreseen it."

"Your foresight is lacking then, Dark God," Darius snorted. "I will never turn to you. Not for anything. Not even for the empty promise of the return of the woman I love."

"Not even for this?" the god asked.

The god waved his arms and the body on the pyre started to move. The body stood, its form complete and unharmed by the flames. She walked over to Darius and ran her fingers along his chest.

"Hello, my love," the body's mouth moved, speaking in Lilliana's voice. "Now I can be with you once more."

"No," Darius said, pulling away from her. "You're dead. I watched you die. I burned your body on the pyre. I watched your spirit leave your body. I will not believe."

"I am your Lilliana in all of the important ways," the woman said.

She leaned up and kissed him just the way Lilliana always had kissed him. He tried to resist, but the kiss was too powerful and too real for him to succeed. He could not help but to kiss her back, a desperate and hungry kiss.

And Darius knew at that moment that he would do whatever it took to get her – the real Lilliana – back.

And yet his Lord Taelin either could not or would not return Lilliana to him. Was he serving the wrong master? Was everything he had ever learned – everything he had ever believed – been false? At that moment, something inside of Darius died.

When the kiss broke, Darius turned to Thraal and bowed his head. The Dark God cackled as he watched Darius shuffle over to him and drop to his knees. The Bringer of Chaos placed his hand on Darius's head and said a series of *words that the priest did not understand. Darius could feel things changing… shifting in his body. More importantly, he could feel things altering in regards to his spirit. He could feel his spirit being locked deep inside of his body. He knew that he would never be the same after this, and he knew that it was far too late to change his mind.*

He was changing into something new.

"Arise, Drakkhous," the Dark God ordered. "You are now my High Priest. If you serve me well, I will bring your Lilliana back to you."

"I will not fail you, my Lord Thraal," Drakkhous rasped.

"That is my story, Blademaster," the lich said. He stood up and lurched forward to the bars. "What do you think?"

"I think that you are a sick and twisted individual." The Blademaster stood. She took three deliberate steps to join him mere inches from the bars. "There is no way that your Lilliana would return to you for anything. Especially not when you have broken your vows to Lord Taelin to follow the Dark God."

"Infidel," Drakkhous roared. "You will suffer terribly for what you have said."

"You already are planning my suffering which is to conclude with my death, lich. Do you really think that you could do any worse?"

"I will indeed make your death far more painful than is necessary," the lich smiled wickedly and his face seemed almost to crack apart at the effort. "Worse for you and for those who love you. You will rue the day that you mocked me."

Drakkhous turned on his heel and stormed away. Alana watched him go, a smile on her face.

She had just learned a most valuable piece of information. She had just learned the lich's one true weakness.

Now she only had to figure out how best to use the information. She would have to keep her eyes open for the right opportunity.

Chapter XXIII
The Sacrifice

Drakkhous rose from his meditation as Adouon entered the chamber. The lich smiled at his assistant, his thin skinless lips drawn back to reveal his rotting teeth.

"Everything is ready for the ceremony, my lord," Adouon informed him mid-bow. He held the ceremonial dagger out to the lich. "We only await the appointed hour."

Drakkhous picked the dagger from his assistant as if it were fruit from a tree. He would do this slowly and deliberately. It was a testament to his desire to please Thraal that he did not immediately race downstairs to the dungeons to drag the Blademaster up to the altar by her hair. But nothing would be served by rushing things. He did not want to ruin the sacrifice in his haste. That would, displease Thraal to no end. Drakkhous knew better than anyone that people had a way of twisting in agony for all of eternity when they displeased Thraal. And that was not the fate he wished for himself.

No. He had an entirely different fate in mind.

So instead of rushing down to the dungeon, Drakkhous nodded and lowered himself back down onto the rug. Adouon sat opposite from the lich.

Drakkhous appraised his assistant with a raised eyebrow. "Something bothers you, Adouon?"

"My lord, I assure you that it was not one of my men, but..." he trailed off.

"But what, Adouon?" Drakkhous said softly. "What are you so upset about?"

"The sacrifice is not pure, my lord," Adouon paled. "She has known a man."

"Yes, I know. Lord Thraal has already told me," the lich replied. "It matters not. She is still the key to our Master returning. He has found her acceptable, even if she is impure."

Adouon breathed an audible sigh of relief. "As long as our Master still finds her acceptable, I am relieved to no end. I was afraid that he would not be pleased. I feared for the repercussions if the sacrifice were to displease him."

"You were wise to fear such failure." Drakkhous rasped. "Lord Thraal would not make it easy on either of us had we failed him."

"But we've not failed him, my lord," Adouon declared.

"No we have not."

"Our lord Thraal will rise once more this very evening!" Adouon's smile widened.

"It will be glorious to behold," the lich added.

"I must go prepare myself, my lord," Adouon stood. "I am looking forward to tonight's festivities. Tonight will be a night that the whole of Calthea will not soon forget."

"No, you're right, Adouon." The lich smiled wider as he watched his assistant leave the chamber, his heavy bootfalls fading quickly down the corridor. "Tonight will be a night the whole of Calthea will remember for ages to come."

Drakkhous reached over to a nearby shelf and pulled a skull down from its resting place. He sat the skull on the floor in front of him, dusted it with a powder and closed his eyes.

"*Shakthala revinthos*," he rasped. "Lord Thraal, I call upon you now."

"I am here, my friend," a liquidly evil voice came from the skull.

Drakkhous opened his eyes. He picked up the skull and held it in front of him so that they were eye to eye. The lich's features contorted into a cruel smile as he looked at the blue flames in the empty eye sockets of the skull.

"My lord Thraal," he bowed his head ever so slightly. "All is as you have asked of me. Tonight you shall be returned to your rightful glory on Calthea."

"You have done well, Drakkhous," Thraal said. "You have but to ask me for anything as your reward, and I shall grant it. Name it."

"There is only one thing I want, my lord, aside from the pleasure of seeing you returned to your glory," the lich said quietly.

"Name it and it shall be yours my friend," the Dark Lord replied. "For you have been faithful to me."

"Return my Lilliana to me," the lich rasped desperately. "Return to me my true love."

"It is done," the skull channeling Thraal laughed, an evil throaty laugh. "Tonight after I return to Calthea, you and your Lilliana will be reunited at long last."

"Thank you, Lord Thraal," the lich bowed his head. "You honor me by allowing me to serve you. And you further honor me by granting me such a simple request."

"And you have honored me by providing the means of my return to rule Calthea, as is only fitting." Thraal laughed wickedly. "I will not soon forget what you have done."

"It has been my pleasure to serve you, my lord," Drakkhous smiled, his rotting teeth bared to his master. "Far more than that accursed Taelin."

"I am overjoyed to hear you say that," Thraal said, his voice fading. "My time is short for this session. We will not speak again until I am once again walking the world of Calthea."

"I understand," Drakkhous nodded.

The lich watched as the light went out of the skull's eye sockets. Reverently, he put the skull back on the shelf and returned to his meditation.

His thoughts were full of his Lilliana. He longed to hold her again.

And it would not be long.

The cold floor had sapped a lot of Alana's strength and she had not been given any food. She was thankful that she still had her pack, because she had dried field biscuits that had allowed her to avoid hunger. The lack of water was more troublesome. There had been a little water in her canteen, but it had been hard for her to ration her meager supply. She had run out earlier in the day. Now she was thirsty and had no way to slake her thirst. Most dungeons she had been in – and, unfortunately, there had been many – were damp, often with dripping water. While not the best of solutions, she could have at the very least sloughed the water off the stones or caught drips in her mouth had the dungeon been a moist one. But not this dungeon. Since they were just going to kill her anyway, perhaps her captors had decided that they didn't need to work too hard to keep her alive. Just alive enough to kill. She also figured that it was important to them that she was weakened enough so she couldn't fight back too hard when the time finally came to sacrifice her.

Alana was determined to fight them even if it took every last breath she had. It probably would.

Where was Colwyn? She had not seen him since his brief visit the night before. She was comforted by the fact that her friends were there in the ziggurat. And she hoped that when the time was right they would be in a position to help her. She had to assume that they had some kind of plan to help her end the threat that this sacrifice represented to all of Calthea. She believed that Colwyn and the others had the depth of strength and determination to see their plan through to the end.

And she hoped she was right.

But Alana hated depending on others. Especially in such important matters. Perhaps her feelings of helplessness were getting the best of her. She searched her memory for the songs and stories told by the bards of the Blademasters of old. She couldn't recall them telling of a Blademaster's companions. She knew that the magic of the Blademasters was bound to the love she shared with her husband, but she did not even remember Protectors being mentioned in the songs of old. Which is why that particular part of the Law of the Blades had caught her so much by surprise. She could still remember what Solara had told her during the wedding.

"This is the First Law of the Blades. You are commanded to love. Love your friends. Love your enemies. Love without reservation. Love without hesitation. Love without condition. Love without expectation of return. If you must fight, then fight with love in your heart. If you must kill, then kill with love in your heart. Never kill or fight with hate or anger in your heart. Hate leads to impotence, but love brings power. This is the law a Blademaster must live by more than any other or else she will be powerless to serve as she should. It is the First Law of the Blades because it is the most important. Live by it, or you will die."

She still found the concept of the First Law of the Blades somewhat surprising, but she understood it a little better now. It was, after all, her true love for Colwyn that drove him to protect her just as his love for her had guided him to her during the Test of the Blades. She had been so afraid for him during the test, and her fears were only made worse as she listened to the gas spore go on and on about the various challenges Colwyn had to face to get to her. She had been so afraid to lose him to the test that she hadn't wanted to believe it when he'd burst through the cell door.

But all the fear had been worth it the first time he had kissed her as her husband. That kiss in the middle of the Great Hall of the Temple of the Blades would be permanently etched in her memory, and she knew Colwyn would never forget it either.

The one wish she had for her companions was for Meryn and William to get the chance to experience the same sense of blissful euphoria that she and Colwyn had experienced when they finally married.

One day, those two would marry. Or at least she hoped they would.

For Balaam, she simply felt sorrow that he had not been able to marry Merinda Delwyn before she had been sacrificed to Thraal. She could only hope that helping to release her soul to walk with Taelin would ease the man's sorrow somewhat. And, perhaps in time, Balaam could find someone else to eventually take Merinda's place in his heart. However, she would not be surprised if he never fell in love again.

The thought saddened her.

The sound of an iron door clanging open shook her from her thoughts, and forced her attention to her surroundings. Heavy footfalls made by boots thudding against stone steps echoed through the dungeons and assaulted her ears. What little light there was from the one small window in her cell had long since faded. Soon it would be time for her to be taken up for the sacrifice. She was still not quite sure how she would keep the sacrifice from happening, especially since her hands and feet would likely be bound to the altar.

More and more, she realized, that her very life and the welfare of Calthea rested in Colwyn's hands and whatever plan he had devised.

A man in black robes appeared in front of the doorway to her cell. There was something familiar about the man, but his hood was up, so she could not see who it was. He raised a finger to cross his lips, gesturing for silence. it was then that she saw the lock of hair that formed the ring around his ring finger.

It was her hair!

The finger across his lips kept her from telling Colwyn that she loved him. She knew the danger that he was in just by being there. If they knew he was impersonating one of their warriors, he would be a dead man. She blinked twice to let him know that she recognized him and he nodded once to acknowledge her.

"It is almost time," he said, perhaps a little too loudly. "You will soon be taken up to the altar for the sacrifice. You will go willingly or you will be dragged up there by your hair." He dropped his voice to a whisper. "When the time is right for you to act, you will know. William will make sure you are free to act at that time."

"You'll have to kill me to get me up there," Alana roared. "But then your god wouldn't like that so much, would he?" She too then dropped her voice to a whisper. "I'll be ready. But the lich is mine."

"Insolent bitch. Lord Thraal will rise again over your corpse." She could tell that he was having trouble saying the words, even though it was just an act. He lowered his voice once more and added. "Just don't die."

Alana didn't answer; she simply turned her back to him dismissively.

Colwyn gave a small chuckle and headed back out of the dungeons.

At the top of the stairs, he met up with another black robed figure. The two men fell into step with each other and began walking towards the upper levels of the ziggurat.

"How is she?" William asked softly.

"Angry and defiant," Colwyn chuckled softly. "They'll have their hands full with her. That's for sure."

"Did she understand the message?" William asked.

"Yes. She had a message for all of us in return," Colwyn smiled. "And I suggest that we all pay heed to it. The lich is hers to kill."

"She's welcome to it. I'm certainly not going to stand in her way," William snorted. "Who's going to tell Balaam though?"

"I suppose that I'll have to do that," Colwyn said with a sigh.

The two men walked off in silence. Neither had seen the thin black robed woman following them. Before they could get a glance of her, she slid off down a side corridor and kept going.

They never knew she was there.

Back in her cell, Alana waited.

The followers of Thraal would come soon. At least now she had an inkling as to Colwyn's plans and she could be ready to act. She was resolved that if she were to die today, it would be in battle, and not at the point of a ceremonial dagger.

She closed her eyes and centered her consciousness, allowing her mind to clear.

"Lord Taelin, if ever you have listened to my prayers, then please listen now," she said quietly. "Give me the strength and determination to do what must be done. Guide my steps. Guide my blade. Make my aim true. By your grace and light, I will survive this day to serve you for years to come. But if I must die tonight, then let it be in service to you. Let me not be sacrificed to Thraal."

"Praying to Taelin will not save you, my dear," the lich's raspy voice mocked from behind her. "In just a few hours, your soul will be trapped in the Great Fire to twist in torment forever, and my Master will walk over your dead body to rule Calthea once more."

"You're deluded if you think that I'm just going to roll over and let you sacrifice me, lich," Alana spat through gritted teeth. "You won't succeed and I'll fight you with every breath I have." She slowly opened her eyes and glared at the lich, her gaze boring holes through the dead man's skull. She mentally chided herself for letting him sneak up on her. "You will lose and your master will never return to Calthea. And just how do you think that your Lilliana would feel about your bringing Thraal back to Calthea just so you can bring her back to life? I rather doubt that she'll appreciate the gesture."

"What would you know about it, you insensitive bitch?" Drakkhous snarled.

"I know that no woman in their right mind would be pleased to be reunited with the man she loves if it meant that the Dark God were allowed free reign over Calthea as a result," Alana snorted. "I know that if Colwyn were to do what you are doing, then I would never be able to forgive him for it. And I would be sure to make the rest of our lives together miserable for him so that he would never forget his mistake."

"Lilliana is not you, Blademaster," Drakkhous wheezed. He took one step toward the barred door of her cell. "She will be happy with what I've done."

"Have you forgotten that Lilliana was a priestess of Laeyra?" the Blademaster scoffed. "She serves a goddess who is no less an enemy of Thraal than Lord Taelin is. There is no way she could forgive you for this. Stop now while you still have a chance to prove you truly love Lilliana. Don't go through with this."

"Enough!" the lich roared. "I have heard enough of your blasphemies. The sacrifice will happen in short order, as planned. Then you will see the power of my Master. And then we will see who is right about my Lilliana."

The lich did not give the Blademaster a chance to reply as he stormed from the dungeons. She could hear his dark mutterings echo about the walls for several minutes after he left.

"Seems I struck a chord," Alana mused.

Adouon had his eyes closed and his arms crossed in front of him. He was deep in meditation, but he still easily detected the woman as she entered his private sanctuary. The woman stood, waiting, knowing enough to not interrupt Adouon during his meditation.

After a few minutes, Adouon opened his eyes and glowered at the woman.

"You have something for me, Mariska?" Adouon asked quietly, his eyes hooded.

"We have imposters in our midst, my lord Adouon," the young acolyte answered. "I know the identity of two of them, and I can find them. I assume there are others, but I have yet to detect them."

"And who are these imposters?" Adouon asked, a note of amusement in his voice. Mariska had always been known to have flights of fancy. He felt that this might well be one of those times, but he humored her anyway. A little amusement before the seriousness of the ceremony would do him well.

And if she were right...

Well, if there were imposters, they would have to be dealt with quickly and quietly. Before the sacrifice. Nothing must interfere with the sacrifice.

"The two that I saw and followed are some of the Blademaster's companions," Mariska reported through a wicked grin. "One was named Colwyn. The other was named William."

This news caught Adouon up short. "You have done well, Mariska," he said quietly. "Nothing must interfere with the sacrifice. Capture them immediately. If there are others, they will tell us if properly motivated."

"Of course, my lord," Mariska nodded. "That is why I came to you right away."

Adouon stood and led the acolyte from his private sanctuary. He knew Mariska would follow without having to be told to. The woman may have flights of fancy, but she was also fiercely loyal to Thraal. That made her a good acolyte. One day she would even make a good priestess. And, although he would deny it if asked, Adouon had something of a special place in his heart for Mariska. It was the closest Adouon had felt to love his entire life. And maybe someday, he would even tell her.

Always careful to keep his thoughts guarded from others, Adouon said nothing to Mariska as they walked. He let Mariska lead him along the corridors of the ziggurat.

Mariska did not try to engage Adouon in conversation either, for she knew how he was. She knew a great deal about Adouon. After meeting him, she had made a point of learning everything that she could about him. And in time, she had grown to love him, although she'd not told him so.

Soon, they came to a sparsely crowded part of the ziggurat. Mariska increased her pace in the direction of a pair of black robed figures that were just now rounding a far corner of the corridor.

"Those are the imposters then, Mariska?" Adouon asked, punctuated by a raised eyebrow. He lengthened his stride to keep up with the shorter acolyte.

"Yes, my lord," Mariska replied, slowing slightly so he could catch up.

"You still haven't told me how you discovered their identity," Adouon chided. "I would very much be interested to know how you found them out."

"There seemed to be something odd about the one who called himself Colwyn," Mariska said with a shrug. "I set a spell up to let me know when he went down to the dungeons to speak with the prisoner. He spoke with her earlier this evening. When he came back up from the dungeons, he met up with the other one. I overheard them talking about stopping the sacrifice. Colwyn said that the Blademaster had said the lich was hers to kill, and they both had a good chuckle over it."

"Interesting indeed," Adouon noted. "And that is when you came to find me?"

"Yes, my lord," she nodded again. "I couldn't let them interfere with the sacrifice, and I knew you or the High Priest would have to deal with it quickly. Quite frankly, I'd rather deal with you than the High Priest. He terrifies me, to be honest."

"He terrifies me too, sometimes, Mariska," Adouon laughed. "And that is as it should be." He stopped short and put his hands on Mariska's shoulders. "You have proven yourself today, Acolyte Mariska. This night, you are no longer an acolyte. This night, you may take your rightful place among the chosen as a priestess of Thraal. You shall even be given the honor of casting the binding spell on the Blademaster when we bring her to the sacrificial altar. I will inform Drakkhous of this decision and of how you helped to preserve the sanctity of tonight's sacrifice."

"I am honored, my lord," Mariska bowed. "I promise not to disappoint you." Mariska skipped a step in joy. "But before anything else, we must catch the imposters."

"My thoughts exactly," Adouon nodded as he sped up slightly, Mariska kept pace with him.

It took them several minutes to catch up to the two black robed figures. Adouon placed his hand on the shoulder of the stockier of the two men. The man spun around to face Adouon, a look of surprise on his face.

He immediately fell to his knees.

"Lord Adouon," the man said softly. "Forgive us. We did not hear you come up behind us. What is your bidding, my lord?"

"It is time to bring the Blademaster up to the altar for the sacrifice," Adouon declared as he helped the man back to his feet. "You two will go and bring her up to the altar. Do not forget the binding spell."

"Yes, Lord Adouon," the man said. "We will see to it at once."

The two imposters turned around and started down the corridor. Without looking to see if Mariska would follow his lead, for he knew she would, he placed his hand on the man's shoulder and released his power into him. The man froze, bound in place as if held by invisible ropes. When he glanced over at the other man, Adouon smiled to see that he had been similarly incapacitated.

"Summon some warriors, Priestess Mariska," Adouon sneered. "These two, Colwyn and William, are to be brought up to watch their precious Blademaster be sacrificed to Thraal before they are cast alive into the Great Fire to burn in torment for eternity for their crimes against our Lord Thraal."

"It will be done as you say, my lord," Mariska bowed.

He watched with satisfaction as she raced off to follow his instructions. He laughed wickedly to himself over the easy dispatch of the two imposters.

When Mariska returned, she brought several warriors with her. He watched in satisfaction as the warriors carried the two imposters away, and then he and Mariska headed down to the dungeons. They did not notice the small figure materialize out of the shadows as they left.

"What would those two do without me to save them?" Meryn sighed softly as she watched Colwyn and William carried off.

The waiting was getting the best of Alana. She didn't understand why they didn't just come and take her up for the sacrifice already. Time seemed to be dragging on, but she knew that it must be beyond time for it. Unless their plan was to drive her crazy before they sacrificed her. She couldn't see how Thraal could be pleased by the sacrifice of a crazy woman, but if they didn't come to get her soon, that was pretty much what they would get.

She didn't know when it happened, but she had started pacing. It was an annoying habit, she decided. She hated pacing. But she hated sitting inactive even more. She was getting more and more restless the longer she waited for something to happen. The desire to act consumed her. It was all she could think of. It was all she wanted. She prayed for Taelin's light and peace to fill her with purpose and calm. She would need to be centered if she were to stop the sacrifice.

The sound of people scrambling down the stairs towards the dungeons assaulted her ears. She steeled herself for what must be done. Soundlessly, she slid her long swords from their scabbards. She was happy to finally have cause to draw them, and she had been afraid for a moment that the inactivity might have caused her to forget how to draw them in anger.

Backing up to the back wall of her cell, she coiled herself for a strike. She was as ready as she was ever going to be. She gripped the hilts of her swords tightly, her knuckles white, the bands of wrapping dug into her palms.

"Unlock the door and bring her out," a gruff male voice ordered. "I want her unharmed. But be careful. She still has her weapons."

The door to her cell flew open and six burly warriors in black robes burst through the opening. She waited until they were all in the cell before uncoiling.

"Only six of you?" she scoffed, raising an eyebrow. "I killed more than twice that number in Valendale. The lich continues to underestimate me and it will be the last mistake he ever makes."

It was with that witty retort that she launched her attack. There was nothing fancy about it. She simply thrust her sword through the first man she came to then sliced through a second. She had run a third one through before the remaining men realized they were under attack. But they had no chance for they were unarmed. And even if they had weapons, they were under strict orders not to harm her.

Alana was fully armed and had no such restrictions on hurting them.

Two of the men tried to flank her while the third rushed her from the front. Alana dropped back a step, putting an extra second or two between her and the man rushing her.

An extra second or two would be sufficient.

She sliced to the left and right, catching the two flankers across their necks. Both men dropped, gagging on their own blood. Alana continued the slices until the points of her swords were touching. Then she thrust forward with both swords. The man rushing her effectively skewered himself.

The battle was over almost before it had begun.

When she felt the hand on her back, she suddenly realized that the lich had not underestimated her at all. The attack had been meant only as a distraction. With that unfortunate realization, she also found herself trapped in a binding spell.

She was caught!

There was no way Alana could fight her way out of a binding spell. Her eyes were the only parts of her body that could move. And move her eyes did. A man entered her cell and her eyes tracked his every movement.

"Very good, Mariska," the man said quietly. "I'm very impressed. Not only are you maintaining the binding spell on two fairly powerful people, but you managed to get the binding spell on her on the first try. I don't know that I could have done as well were I in your position. Lord Thraal will be well pleased."

"Thank you, Lord Adouon," Mariska said as she stepped around from behind Alana. She looked the Blademaster up and down. "She doesn't look so powerful now."

"Need I remind you that she just dispatched six of our best warriors without even breaking a sweat?" Adouon raised an eyebrow. He took a step towards Alana. "She is not to be underestimated, even like this. She will be bound to the altar, and you will maintain the binding spell on her until the sacrifice is complete. Do you understand me, Mariska?"

"Of course," Mariska nodded. "So long as I am alive, I will not release either binding spell, Lord Adouon. You can count on me for that."

"Oh, I know I can count on you, Mariska." Adouon doled out an approving smile to his follower. He reached over and grabbed Alana's chin in one hand. She tried to flinch away from his touch, but the binding spell prevented her from moving even a smidge. "Listen to me well, Blademaster. There is no one to come to your rescue. We have already captured two of your companions. It is only a matter of time before we find the others. They will all be there to watch your death and the rise of our Lord Thraal. And then they shall be cast into the Great Fire to burn for eternity."

She wanted to shout that it wasn't the truth. She wanted to slap him across the face. She wanted to rip the head off Mariska. She wanted to tell them that there was no way she was going to be sacrificed to Thraal. But the binding spell kept her from doing any of those things. Adouon laughed at her inability to respond, which only served to make the anger boiling up inside Alana to roil more.

She added them to her list of those she would kill when she was free, right under the lich.

He pried the swords out of Alana's hands and sheathed them.

"Take her up to the top of the ziggurat and bind her to the altar," he ordered. Several warriors as they entered the cell and split into two groups, each flanking Alana. "Mariska, go with them to make sure that everything is prepared for the sacrifice. It would not do for anything to go wrong at this point. Our Lord Thraal will rise soon."

"Yes, Lord Adouon." Mariska bowed slightly. She turned to the warriors and motioned for them to pick Alana up and carry her out of the cell.

Alana tried to will herself to fight the men, but the binding spell had her powerless to resist. She felt her shoulders grabbed roughly and her legs pulled from the floor. The walls flew by as she was hurried up the stairs. The trip seemed to take forever, but finally, they burst through the door to the roof altar of the ziggurat. The heat from the Great Fire licked at Alana's flesh, and she caught sight of Colwyn and William standing unmoving by the Great Fire. Alana and Colwyn locked eyes. A tear rolled down Alana's cheek as she felt herself being placed on the altar.

We can't have lost! She thought sourly as her wrists and ankles were tied down to the altar.

But Balaam and Meryn weren't there. Maybe they could still keep the sacrifice from happening.

Taelin, help us! She screamed silently.

Adouon found the lich adjusting the scabbard for the ceremonial dagger. He had never seen the lich this nervous before. But then, they had never had a sacrifice of this magnitude of importance before. Unlike the previous sacrifices, there was just no margin for error with it. Everything had to go exactly as Lord Thraal had required it to go, or the Dark God would not be able to break free from the prison that the accursed Taelin had put him in and once more walk the world of Calthea. Adouon knew that Drakkhous feared failure. The lich had a great deal riding on this. Even more than simply seeing their Master returned to his rightful glory. Adouon didn't know what deal Thraal had made with Drakkhous to ensure success of the sacrifice, nor did he really care or want to know. But, whatever it was, it was even more important to Drakkhous than anything.

So he knew that Drakkhous would do whatever it took to ensure that the sacrifice went as required. It was a relief to Adouon to know that the High Priest was so dedicated to the cause. It meant that, overall, there was a greatly reduced chance of failure.

"It is time, Lord Drakkhous," Adouon said softly. "All is ready."

"The Blademaster has been taken up to the altar?" Drakkhous asked.

"Mariska is removing her armor as we speak," Adouon nodded. He took a deep breath before continuing. "My lord, we have two of her companions. They were impersonating our faithful. They are held in binding spells and will be made to watch the sacrifice before they are themselves killed. I have promised them that they will be thrown into the Great Fire after the sacrifice has been completed."

"Excellent," Drakkhous rubbed his hands together in fiendish glee. "Which of our faithful discovered the imposters?"

"It was Mariska, Lord Drakkhous," Adouon smiled broadly, proud of the new priestess. "I have promoted her from acolyte to priestess for her work in preserving the sanctity of the sacrifice. She is the one who put the binding spell on the Blademaster. She has done Lord Thraal proud this day."

"Very well," Drakkhous replied. He slid the dagger forward an inch or two on his hip, then nodded in satisfaction. "You care deeply for Mariska, do you not, Adouon?"

The human paled. "My lord, I have done my best not to show it, nor to show her any favoritism. How could you have known?"

"You have done well in concealing your feelings for her, my friend," Drakkhous laughed, slapping him on the shoulder. "I doubt that she even knows. But it is still quite obvious to me. You forget, Adouon, that Lord Thraal has gifted me with powers of perception far beyond that of a normal human. I see things that none of you can. And I have seen your feelings for Mariska. But do not fear. I do not see those feelings as a weakness."

"Thank you, Lord Drakkhous," Adouon whispered, bowing slightly. "For a moment, I thought I had failed or displeased you. I am glad you are not disappointed in me."

"Adouon, do you know why I serve Lord Thraal when I was once a priest of Taelin?" the lich asked, catching Adouon's eyes in his own gaze.

"No, my lord." Adouon turned away. "I never thought it was my place to ask that. I always figured that our Lord

Thraal could give you something that the accursed Taelin could not. And I figured that was the reason."

"Yes, there is something I want very much that Lord Thraal will give me this very evening when he returns to power on Calthea." Drakkhous smiled but this time there was genuine warmth behind the rotting teeth. It was the first time Adouon ever seen a smile of pure joy and happiness from his high priest instead of the usual malicious grin. "My Lilliana," Drakkhous breathed.

"Lilliana?" Adouon frowned, puzzlement staining his features.

"Tonight will be my last sacrifice, Adouon," Drakkhous continued in a soft rasp. "After Lord Thraal returns to Calthea and he returns my Lilliana to me, I will be resigning as High Priest."

"But my lord..."

"He has already approved. At that time, you will be my successor. Thraal is quite pleased with you."

"I am honored, Lord Drakkhous." Adouon shook his head. "But I am not ready."

"I did not think that I was ready when I took over the position, Adouon." Drakkhous placed his hand on the human priest's shoulder. "Trust me on this one, my friend. You are ready."

"Thank you for your confidence in me, my lord, even if I think it is misplaced." Adouon sighed. Then he smiled wickedly as a thought crossed his mind. "Shall we go up to the altar now?"

"Yes," Drakkhous agreed. "It is finally time to see our Lord Thraal rise once again."

It seemed like every priest in the ziggurat was on hand, waiting for the sacrifice. It was a sea of black robed men and women as far as the eye could see. There was a good ten feet clear around the altar and the Great Fire in every direction. Alana could not see the lich anywhere, but he would show up sooner or later.

And the sacrifice would happen just as soon as he arrived.

The stone of the altar had been heated by the Great Fire and was warm on her bare backside. She was not embarrassed to be naked in front of all the assembled priests of Thraal. It did, however, intensify her rage towards them. She could tell by looking into Colwyn's eyes that he too was equally as angry about it. At the moment, though, there did not seem to be anything that either of them could do to change the situation.

When the priestess had come to the altar a half hour ago, Alana had tried, once again unsuccessfully to break free of the binding spell. It was clear to her that, unless she found a way to free herself from the binding spell, she would not be able to prevent Thraal from returning to Calthea. She had locked her eyes with Colwyn's as the priestess had stripped off her armor and placed it to the side of the altar with all of her weapons. Her swords were still within her easy reach. If only she could move her arms! The anger blazed in Colwyn's eyes, and Alana knew that he would have killed the priestess with his bare hands had he been able.

We still have time to figure this out, Alana thought dourly. *Somehow we will prevail. The Dark God can't win. I won't let him.*

Their time was short though. The priestess had told her that Adouon was going to get Drakkhous, so the lich would arrive shortly. And she was no closer to figuring out how to get free. There had to be a way to break the binding spell. She just had to figure it out! Well, she knew from conversations with William about magic that if the priestess that had cast the binding spell were to be killed, then the binding spell would be released. Unfortunately, she didn't have a ready way to kill the priestess. Was it possible that the spell could release on its own somehow?

In the end, it didn't really matter. Her hopes sagged when Adouon and Drakkhous stepped through the door to the roof of the ziggurat. The lich smiled at Colwyn and William standing unmoving by the Great Fire, then he turned his gaze to Alana, and she felt her flesh prickle when he took in her naked body, a lecherous grin spread across his decrepit face.

How could he look at another woman like that when he is supposedly so in love with his Lilliana? She asked herself. *Or is it just that he sees me as the way to get her back by raping and murdering me? Is he trying to work up that much lust for me?*

The lich strode forward and ran his fingers along her body. His fingers left a trail of coldness wherever he touched her. He ran his fingers over her breasts, tracing around her nipples and down to her freshly shaven sex. That had been the final indignity that Alana had been forced to suffer through. Since the lich did not like his sacrifices hairy, Adouon had ordered Mariska to shave the hair from Alana's sex. It did not even allow her the appearance of privacy, leaving her sex extremely visible for all to see. As he ran his fingers over her folds, sending a chill up her spine, he licked his thin skinless lips in lustful anticipation of what was about to happen.

"Mariska, release the binding spell from her neck up," Drakkhous ordered softly. "I want to hear her screams as she is sacrificed."

"As you command, Lord Drakkhous," the priestess nodded. Mariska closed her eyes and whispered several words in another language that Alana could not make out. Then there was tingling from her neck up and she could move her head around, for whatever that would profit her. "It's done, my lord."

Mere seconds after feeling the tingling sensation, Alana felt another odd sensation. The bindings on her wrists and ankles felt as if they had been removed. She glanced up at the bindings on her wrists and saw that they were still there. She glanced over at William and Colwyn. William was smiling, and she knew then that he was the other person that Mariska held in a binding spell. She realized with a jolt that the bindings were, in fact, now only illusions cast by William. When Mariska released that much of the binding spell on her, it must have released the same on William too.

Now, if only she could get the rest of the binding spell released.

"It is time," the lich announced as he lowered the hood of his robe from his head. "Those of us who are assembled here represent the core of the faithful followers of Thraal. We have been waiting for an opportunity to return our Lord Thraal to the glory that he so richly deserves.

"Tonight, Lord Thraal will rise once more.

"This woman lying naked before you is a Blademaster, one of those mighty warriors of old created by the accursed Taelin and his equally accursed consort Laeyra as a bastion of truth and justice and to keep our lord Thraal out of power.

"The truth is that this Blademaster is the key to Lord Thraal's return. With her sacrifice, the gates sealing Lord Thraal in Limbo will be rent open and our lord will be free to walk the world once more."

"Like hell he will," Alana spat out, unable to keep quiet any longer.

"Ah, how I love my sacrifices to have spirit," Drakkhous laughed. He stepped over to the altar and put his face right next to Alana's. She could smell the dry rot of his teeth and wrinkled her nose in disgust. "You have failed, Blademaster. There is no way to stop this from happening. I'll do my best to make sure you enjoy the sex though. I would hate for your last time to be less than pleasurable."

"Taelin will not allow me to be sacrificed to Thraal," Alana spat in his face. "Thraal will never be released from his prison in Limbo."

"As I said," Drakkhous rasped as he wiped her spittle from his face. "There is nothing you can do to stop this."

"I think you'll find that I can do more than you think I can, lich," Alana sneered. "One way or another I am getting out of this binding spell. And when I do, you will be reunited you with your Lilliana. But it'll be my way."

"Brave words from the doomed," Drakkhous countered. "But alas, you are out of time. The time for Lord Thraal to rise is upon us."

Drakkhous rose back up to his full height and drew the ceremonial dagger. He laid the dagger on Alana between her breasts with the point pointing up at her chin. Then he let his robe slip to the ground and took his place on the altar between her spread legs. He leered down at her as his phallus grew erect.

She shuddered at the sight of him, but she did not give him the satisfaction of a scream. She swore to herself that, no matter what, she would not scream.

When she felt the touch of his phallus against her sex, she closed her eyes.

She felt the dagger lifted from her chest. She could hear his raspy breathing as he raised the dagger.

Time seemed to slow.

The tip of his phallus was ice cold against the folds of her sex. She started counting the seconds until she would feel the knife plunge deep into her chest.

She heard a scream then felt her whole body tingle. Then she felt a body land across her. When she opened her eyes, she saw confusion dancing in the lich's eyes as the dagger was pulled out of the body that was laying across her.

The body was Balaam's.

With a grunt, he shoved the dead priest's body off of her. In doing so, he also managed to pull the tip of his phallus out of her and freed her enough so that she could move. With the binding spell released, she could easily move her arms enough to draw her swords from the pile of her armor and weapons.

Before the lich knew it, she had both of her swords crossed at his throat.

With the lich immobilized by the threat of his imminent decapitation, Alana took the time to assess what had happened. Balaam's body was dumped to the side of the altar, his white robes stained with red from the hole in his chest. It had been his scream she had heard as he had launched himself at the lich to prevent the sacrifice from happening. And it had worked, although it had cost Balaam his life. He had taken the dagger's thrust in her place. And Drakkhous had been so surprised that he had not even fully entered her.

She felt great sorrow for Balaam's sacrifice for her.

As she continued to glance around, she noticed that the priestess Mariska was lying in a pool of her own blood. Adouon was kneeling next to her, his hands on her chest. He had a look of intense concentration on his face, and his eyes were closed. He was mumbling a whispered prayer to Thraal, and she knew that he was trying to heal her. With a smirk, she realized that Meryn must have appeared out of nowhere and stabbed her.

And that was what had caused the binding spell to fail. The lich had underestimated her companions.

She looked over at William and Colwyn. William had just cast a dispel magic spell on Colwyn to release him from the binding spell he was under. The two men were racing over to the altar. Meryn joined them as they arrived.

"Nice timing, Little Bit," William smiled as he mussed the halfling's hair.

"Good job, Meryn," Colwyn smiled. It was the first time that Alana could ever remember Colwyn commending the halfling. But she figured since Meryn had just saved her life, Colwyn had a right to be very happy with the halfling for a change. "Good job indeed," he continued. "For once, I am very glad you're around."

Alana nodded and smiled at the halfling before turning back to the lich.

"I told you what would happen to you if I got free of the binding spell," she said quietly. "I truly hope that your Lilliana is far more forgiving a woman than I am."

With a great grunt, Alana yanked the two swords apart, slicing the lich's head from his body. The head rolled along the ground to stop by the unconscious form of Mariska. Adouon stared at the head in disbelief before glaring at Alana in hatred.

"You bitch!" Drakkhous' successor roared. "You will pay for that!" He turned to face the assembled priests and warriors of Thraal who all looked notably shaken. "What are you all just standing there for? The bitch just killed your High Priest. Kill her and her companions. Kill them now!"

"You know, Alana," Colwyn chuckled as he moved closer to her. "You really need to stop killing our hosts. I can't seem to take you anywhere."

"Colwyn, shut up and keep them at bay long enough for me to get my armor back on."

Her companions circled about her while she put her armor on.

The Blademaster

The assembled followers of Thraal attacked en masse.

It was dark and slightly cold when Balaam awoke. The darkness kept him from making out his surroundings, but he could tell that he was lying on something hard. The soft touch of a hand on his face restored him fully to his senses.

"Balaam?' a tentative female voice asked softly. "Balaam Otakis? Is that you?"

"Merinda?" Balaam asked, raising an eyebrow. He recognized the voice. It was a voice that he would never forget. "I was told that you were dead. Killed by the lich in a sacrifice to Thraal."

"I am afraid that what you were told is quite true, my love," Merinda smiled sadly at him. "I am afraid that you are also dead. You must have been killed by the same dagger that killed me." Her face was finally coming into focus, and it was indeed his beloved Merinda. "That's the only way you could have ended up here. While I'm happy to see you once more, I wish things were different."

"What is this place, Merinda?" Balaam asked, still confused at seeing her. "What am I doing here? Did I succeed in saving the Blademaster?"

"This place is a prison of sorts," Merinda sighed. "Our souls are trapped here until we can free ourselves or be freed. There is an exit, but it is guarded by a great beast. It has been said that only a High Priest of Taelin can get the beast to move. But I don't think Lord Caiaphas would ever come here to save us."

"Merinda, Caiaphas is dead," Balaam said quietly.

"Then... who is the High Priest of Taelin?" Merinda asked.

"Well, I'm not sure who it is now, but I was High Priest when I died," Balaam grunted as he sat up.

She looked surprised at first but then her face lit up in a broad smile. "I'm very proud of you, Balaam."

Balaam was glad of that. But there wasn't time for such pleasantries. 'Merinda, I need to know if the Blademaster is safe."

"A Blademaster walks the earth?"

"Yes. Is there any way to find out from here?"

"No, my love," Merinda said with a shake of her head. "We have no way of seeing what occurs on Calthea from here. We would have to escape this place first. What happened to cause you to end up here, Balaam?"

"The Blademaster was about to be sacrificed," Balaam sighed deeply. "I jumped on top of her as the dagger was coming down. I guess it killed me instead of her. Merinda, we have to get out of here. Can you show me to this beast?"

"Of course, Balaam," Merinda nodded. She took his head and helped him up. "Follow me, and I will take you there."

The two lovers hurried off in the direction of the exit.

Alana's sword sliced a nearby woman's head from her shoulders. Alana grunted as the woman fell forward on top of her. She shoved the body off and glanced toward Colwyn. He and the others were closing in on the door that led to the downward stairs. She was far behind them and fighting for every inch. But if they could all get to the door, they would likely be all right. Alana regretted that they had to leave Balaam's body behind, but there was just no way that they could take the body and escape. Maybe when they got free she could summon the dragon and he could rescue the body. She really didn't want to leave it behind. He deserved better. Who knew what priests of Thraal, especially angry priests of Thraal, would do to the body of the High Priest of Taelin?

And that's when it hit her.

The dragon!

Why should she wait until she was free to summon the dragon? Surely this was just the kind of situation that a nathair an aeir a chosnaíonn was specifically designed for! It was a life or death struggle against an overwhelming force. A good bit of dragon flame would surely even the odds. Then again, even some mage fire would be useful, Alana thought with a chuckle as she tossed her sword to her other hand and reached for the summoning statue in her pouch.

As if in response to her thoughts, a giant ball of fire erupted past her, presumably from William. The flames trickled around her, leaving her untouched by them. But the followers of Thraal that were closing in on her were not so lucky. Indeed, dozens of them were incinerated, opening up a clear path to her companions. When she reached her friends, she had both of her long swords in one hand and the summoning statue in the other. Colwyn grinned at her when she arrived.

"You looked like you could have used a touch of help, Alana," William laughed.

"A few too many suitors for my taste, I'll admit. Thanks." The Blademaster took a deep breath. "Great timing."

"Maybe they just don't like that you've already been spoken for," Meryn added.

"They're probably just upset that you put your clothes back on" Colwyn remarked with a mischievous grin. "I know I am."

"Colwyn Starseeker," Alana chided. "Now is not the time for that!"

"Sorry dear," Colwyn laughed. "But you know what I like!"

"What I'd like is to be on the other side of that door with those fellows still on this side of the door," Alana announced. "Think you can help with that?"

"Your wish is my command," Colwyn replied soberly.

The ranger turned and threw his weight against the door. But the door didn't budge. Again, he railed against it. But to no avail. On the third time, his shoulder hit the door and it popped open. The four companions scrambled through the door and Colwyn slammed it shut behind them. William said a few words of magic over the door, locking it with a mage's lock. They all knew that the mage's lock would only hold until a mage came along to unseal the door.

Alana stopped to sheath her swords and secure the summoning statue back in her pouch. The statue had gone warm, so she knew that Cobalt was on the way.

"Out," she ordered with a smile, answering all of their unasked questions. "The quickest way possible." She smiled. "The dragon is on the way."

They all scrambled down the stairs towards freedom at the fastest possible speed.

Balaam was starting to get a little nervous. Perhaps being dead did that to a person, but he didn't know, having never been dead before. It felt like they had been going in the same direction for hours without really getting anywhere. The walls and floor all looked the same. Drab and grey. The wonder of seeing Merinda once more had faded somewhat in the anxiety of not knowing whether or not the Blademaster had survived. With the Blademaster still held in a binding spell, it would have been a simple matter for the lich to just throw him off her body and still proceed with the sacrifice. He hoped that Meryn had indeed done her part and incapacitated the priestess responsible for holding Alana in the binding spell.

He truly hoped his sacrifice was not for nothing.

"How much farther, Merinda?" he asked quietly.

"Not much, Balaam." She smiled back at him. "It's just around the corner."

"Merinda, how many people are here?" he asked.

"Drakkhous has been High Priest for over a hundred years. He sacrifices someone at the new moon and again at the full moon. Plus he made other sacrifices whenever he felt like it or one of the followers of Thraal displeased him," Merinda explained. "There are a couple thousand souls that are roaming these halls. We all want to go to walk with our gods, Balaam."

"And by getting the beast to let us all leave, I will allow that to happen?" he asked.

"Only the High Priest of Taelin can accomplish it."

"I'm afraid that I don't know what to do," Balaam whispered in despair. "I wouldn't even begin to know how to make this beast let us leave."

"You must only command it to leave. It will recognize your authority over it as the High Priest of Taelin."

"How do you know all of this, Merinda?" Balaam asked. Something was not right. "Are you really my Merinda?"

Merinda sighed. "I can understand your suspicion, Balaam. I have been here for well over a month, and I have talked extensively to the beast. As for knowing if I am really me or not, I will tell you something that only I would know about our relationship. The first time you and I met, I slapped you very hard across the face because you were so arrogant that you thought I would just fall in love with you. And because I did fall for you but I didn't want you to know it."

"I'm sorry, Merinda." Balaam shook his head and turned away from her so that she wouldn't see the pain in his eyes.

"For what, my love?" Merinda asked, putting her hand on his shoulder. Her touch was still electric to him. He felt her undying love for him in that touch.

"For doubting you now," he said weakly. "And for failing you before. If I had only been able to get Caiaphas to transfer you back to Ravendale, you might not be dead now. And maybe I wouldn't be either."

"Things happened as they were meant to happen, my love," Merinda leaned up and kissed his cheek. "We were not meant to be together in life, but we will be together in the next world when we both go to walk with Taelin. And there is no need to be sorry for doubting me. I know how disorienting it can be to find yourself in this condition."

"Especially on finding the woman I love, whom I know is dead, there with me," Balaam said half to himself. "Disorienting doesn't even begin to cover it."

"How do you think I felt when I saw you lying there, Balaam?" she asked softly. "I knew you had to have been killed by that dagger in order for you to be here. I was happy to see you again, but sad to know that you were dead."

"I know." Balaam wrapped his arms around her. "It's good to hold you in my arms again, my beloved Merinda. I have missed you so much. Now. Let's go talk to this beast and get him to free all of our souls."

Merinda kissed him again before extricating herself from his arms. She grabbed a hold of his hand and led him the rest of the way to where the beast was. As disorienting as it had been to see her again, he marveled at how good it felt to once more hold her hand. He had done his best to shove the pain of her loss deep inside the recesses of his mind. Seeing her again had both released the pain and healed it. He was once more amazed by how powerful the emotion of love was. It was no wonder that Taelin and Laeyra had used love as the focus for the Blademasters' power. It was the one force that Thraal could not stand against, for Balaam had heard it said that even Thraal's own High Priest had loved. It was his understanding that Drakkhous was actually acting to restore his true love to him. Looking at Merinda once more, Balaam knew he would have done anything to see her smile once again.

Perhaps he and the High Priest of Thraal were not so different after all.

That was something of a sobering thought.

As they continued toward the beast, Balaam's considered what he was in for, wondering not for the first time about the nature of the beast he would soon face. If Merinda was right, and he did not doubt that she was, then only he had the power to get the beast to let them go. But how was he to do so? He doubted it was as easy as merely telling it to let them pass. As they rounded the last corner and he caught sight of the exit and its guardian, his hopes faded.

It was a dragon.

And not just any dragon either. It was a giant of a dragon with five heads. Each head was the head of one of the five different metallic dragons: gold, silver, bronze, copper, and brass. Balaam had heard that metallic dragons were fairly independent so he had no idea how it was that he would be able to get the dragon to listen to him.

He said a silent prayer to Taelin for guidance.

"You've been gone a long time, Merinda," the gold dragon head remarked as it snaked towards them. "We have missed your company."

"And you have brought a friend," the silver dragon head added. "How lovely."

Balaam realized for the first time that the dragon was a female. He wondered if he could use that information to his advantage.

"This is Balaam," Merinda bowed to the dragon. "He is the one I was to marry before I was sacrificed to Thraal."

"Balaam," the copper dragon head bowed to him. "We are Mahumet."

"It is an honor to meet you, Mahumet." Balaam bowed in reverence. "But I wish to leave this place along with the rest of the souls that are trapped here."

"Only a High Priest of Taelin can make that request of us," the brass dragon head noted. "Are you a High Priest of Taelin?"

"Before I was killed, that was indeed my position on Calthea. So, yes."

"You said that you were killed," the bronze dragon responded. "You mean sacrificed. Correct? Only sacrifices to Thraal end up here."

"I was killed preventing a sacrifice," Balaam replied. "I gave my life freely to save another. I must know if I was successful in saving her. In order to do that, I must leave this place. I implore you, let us pass."

"Only a High Priest of Taelin who died in such a manner can ask that of us," the gold dragon said quietly. "We will stand aside and let you pass if that is what you wish. However, you should be aware that there are consequences."

"What consequences?" Balaam asked, his brow furrowing.

"We are not permitted to say," the silver dragon said. "You must accept the consequences without knowing them. That is the condition placed by the gods."

"I accept the consequences of my actions," Balaam agreed. "Please, let us pass."

"Very well," the gold dragon replied. "Tell Lord Taelin when you see him that we beg his forgiveness for what must now transpire. We have fulfilled his every command and ask that we not be held accountable for what is to be."

The great dragon lumbered aside and the lovers walked through the exit.

Adouon held Mariska's head in his lap as he watched the Blademaster and her companions escape through the door that led down into the ziggurat. He couldn't believe that the Blademaster had succeeded in killing the lich and preventing Thraal from returning. It wasn't fair. They had done everything right. They could not have failed.

And yet... they had.

He knew that since Drakkhous was already dead that it would fall on him to take the punishment from Thraal. He deserved whatever came for his failure. He should have been more diligent in finding the Blademaster's other companions.

At least he could take comfort in the fact that Mariska would be all right. He had successfully accomplished her healing and she was now sleeping comfortably in his lap as she regained her strength. He turned his eyes from the door, wishing to no longer focus on his failure. His gaze stopped on the lich's head.

The eyes were glowing.

Adouon leaned over and picked the head up frowning as he gazed at the skull. If the lich was dead... How could the eyes be glowing?

"Adouon, you have pleased me," a deeply resonant male voice issued from the lich's mouth. "As did Drakkhous before you."

"Lord Thraal?" Adouon asked tentatively. "I am sorry to have failed you."

"You did not fail," the Dark God laughed. "It was never the Blademaster that needed to be sacrificed to me. The High Priest of Taelin needed to be killed by the dagger so that he would be sent into Limbo with the rest of the sacrifices. Only a High Priest of Taelin who freely gave his life for another could ask the guardian to move from the exit."

"You mean..."

"I have been freed, my new High Priest."

"Then... you are not displeased with me for failing you?" Adouon raised an eyebrow.

"No. I walk the world once more," Thraal laughed. "It will take some time to regain a form and my power, but I am free. Now come. We must get inside quickly. The

Blademaster's dragon is on the move. If you are still on the roof when he arrives, you will die."

"The mage has sealed the door, my lord," Adouon replied.

Two bolts of energy shot forth from the lich's eye sockets and blasted into the door. Splinters erupted and scattered everywhere as the door burst apart.

"Hurry now," Thraal urged. "We have preparations to make."

Adouon scooped Mariska up in his arms and carried her through the door. He was halfway down the first flight of stairs when he heard the beating of a great dragon's wings and the roar of dragon fire. He did not look back as he charged down the stairs towards the High Priest's sanctuary.

The companions had not stopped running until they were halfway across the city of Tornith. They did not want to take the risk of being caught by the followers of Thraal even knowing that many of them had been locked behind the door to the roof altar. Alana drove them onward until they had some semblance of a safe distance from the ziggurat. She did not think she would feel safe, though, until they were safely in the Southern Dales.

Then they continued to wind their way slowly through the city towards the White Temple. Alana's thoughts returned to Balaam and the sacrifice that he had made for her. She wondered if her life were really worth his. Who was more important? Blademaster or High Priest? She knew that Balaam had believed he had done the right thing. But she didn't agree, and that thought saddened her.

Before she knew it, Alana found herself face to face with a priest of Taelin on the doorstep to the White Temple. By the shocked look on the man's face, she suspected she had looked better.

"It's the Blademaster and her companions," the priest called out. "Come in. We have been expecting you. We are overjoyed to see you alive."

Alana followed the priest inside, still numb from the loss of Balaam, who she had come to regard as a friend.

The priest led them into a small anteroom off the great hall. There was someone sitting in a chair close to the fire in the small room, but he had his back to the door, so Alana could not make out his identity. Upon closer inspection, however, she realized that the man was very old.

The old man addressed the priest who had led them into the room without turning to face them. "Arthais, please go and bring the Blademaster and her companions some food. They must be quite hungry after their ordeal."

She had not thought about it, but now that the old man had mentioned it, she realized that she was famished. She flopped, uninvited, into a chair not far from the old man. She looked him over blankly, stricken by the unmistakable feeling that she should know him.

Realization dawned on her suddenly.

"Yes, child," he said softly when he saw the light of recognition on her face. "I am Taelin."

Alana fell to the floor, bowing to the god. "I'm sorry for not recognizing you on sight, my lord," she whispered reverently.

"Please sit back in the chair, Alana," Taelin said quietly. "Now is a time for rest, not for reverence."

"As you wish, Lord Taelin," Alana agreed as she scrambled back into the chair. "Is it over? Has Thraal been defeated?"

"Nothing is ever really over, Alana," Taelin smiled. "But for now, it is."

"The cost was high," Alana said bitterly.

"Ah, yes," Taelin nodded. "You refer, of course, to Balaam. His death was necessary."

"Necessary?" she cried. "What's that supposed to mean?"

Taelin smiled wistfully. "You can ask him yourself. He has been waiting for you for some time. He and Merinda Delwyn both."

"Alana, don't be sad," Balaam said softly as he came into the room. He was holding hands with a woman who Alana assumed was the priestess Merinda Delwyn. "My death allowed you to escape from the lich, but it also allowed me to free Merinda and the rest of the souls that

Drakkhous had trapped during his sacrifices to Thraal. It was something that only I could do."

"I am relieved that you and Merinda have been reunited, Balaam," Alana smiled. "True love is a wonderful thing."

"Which is why Lord Taelin and Lady Laeyra were wise to use it as the focus for the Blademasters' powers," Balaam explained. "Long life to the Blademaster and her Protector. We will be watching. Keep her safe, Colwyn."

"You have my word, Balaam," Colwyn said. "Peace to you, my friend."

"It's a shame that it took my death for you to call me friend, Colwyn," Balaam said sadly. "We both only had the best interests of Alana at heart. I would like to think that, in time, we could have been friends in life as well."

"The shame is not that it took death for me to call you friend, Balaam," Colwyn turned away, a tear running down his cheek. "The shame is that my anger towards you blinded me to any possibility of seeing you as a friend. For that, I am sorry."

"Something we were both guilty of," Balaam nodded. "I accept your apology if you will accept mine."

"Done." Colwyn smiled. 'I will see you both again when I go to walk with Taelin. May that be a very long time from now."

"Agreed." Balaam returned the smile. He turned to Taelin. "We will wait for you, Lord Taelin. I know you have other things to say to the Blademaster."

"I will be along shortly," Taelin said.

Balaam and Merinda both bowed to Taelin before heading out of the room. Alana watched them go, realizing that her sorrow for Balaam had been replaced somewhere along the line by joy.

"I am happy for them," she said softly.

"I am too," Colwyn agreed.

"There is one more person who wishes to speak with you before he goes to walk with me," Taelin smiled.

A young man walked into the room and glanced nervously at Alana before going over to Taelin and bowing to him. He turned back to Alana and smiled sadly.

"My name is Darius Redwind," the man breathed as he bowed to her. His voice was barely audible. "I am the man who became the lich Drakkhous. I wanted to thank you for freeing me from the lich's body. I don't know if my Lilliana will forgive me or not, but at least I no longer am in service to Thraal. Lord Taelin has granted me his forgiveness and will allow me to walk with him. Thank you, Blademaster, for making it possible."

"You're welcome, Darius," Alana said with a smile. "May the luck of Laeyra guide you in your quest for forgiveness with Lilliana."

"Thank you, Blademaster." Darius bowed again. "I must go to her now."

"Good journey, Darius," Alana said to his back as he turned to leave.

"To you as well, Blademaster," Darius said softly. "You truly are worthy of the title of Blademaster. Lord Taelin chooses his Blademasters well."

Alana watched as he left then turned back to Taelin, who was watching her with great interest.

"What will happen to him?" she asked.

"That depends largely on Lilliana." Taelin smiled. "But I believe she will grant him forgiveness."

"And what of me?" Alana asked.

"Well, that is a bit more complex." Taelin sighed. "For now, I wish for you to wait here. Cobalt will bring Balaam's body along in short order. Wait here for instructions from my new High Priest. When you have received those instructions, carry them out without question. Then, I think you have earned a bit of a rest." He stood and walked over to her. Then, without warning, he embraced her in a solid, tight, hug. His warm smile was infectious. "You have exceeded my wildest expectations, Blademaster. You have done yourself proud."

With that, the Lightbringer left the room, leaving Alana to wonder about what she had just seen and heard.

The Blademaster

Chapter XXIV
Burial at Sea

The landing this time was much smoother, although the companions knew better what to expect from a dragon landing this time around and were prepared for the worst. Perhaps it was because they were carrying the cairn with Balaam's body in it that Cobalt took greater care in his approach. Whatever the reason, Alana was grateful for the gentle landing.

Colwyn and William carefully and reverently took the cairn from the dragon's back. They followed Alana over to where a group of priests of Taelin were standing near the stone. Alana stepped in front of the leader of the Priests and bowed.

"We have brought the body of the High Priest to be buried in accordance to the traditions of our Lord Taelin," Alana stated, each word chosen carefully.

"I am Naomi Mastairs," the woman at the head of the group of priests announced. "I have been named Lord

Balaam's successor. I wish the circumstances of my ascension to the position of High Priestess were different."

"I understand," Alana nodded. "Balaam gave his life in service to Lord Taelin by saving my life. In doing so, he also freed the souls of Thraal's victims in Tornith. I can not think of a more noble death for a High Priest of Taelin than that."

"Agreed," Naomi smiled. "You truly do possess the wisdom of Lord Taelin, Blademaster."

"Thank you, Lady Naomi," Alana bowed. She indicated the cairn carrying Balaam's body. "What is to be done with the body of my friend?" As she said the words, she realized that she meant them. At some point during the companions' travels, she and the High Priest of Taelin had become friends. She did not know how or why, but she was saddened to realize the fact when it was too late.

"In accordance with tradition, he is to be buried at sea," Naomi instructed. She gave each of them a paper boat with a candle in it. "Set the cairn adrift in the water. Then light those and set them adrift as well. You must watch the cairn drift away until you no longer see it. Only then may you leave."

"I understand." Alana nodded to the others. "It will be done as you have instructed."

"Lord Taelin chooses his Blademasters well," Naomi smiled. "See me at the Temple of the White after you have returned to Ravendale. I will no doubt have some work for you."

With that, Naomi, turned the group of priests around and headed off to Ravendale.

Alana nodded to Colwyn and William and the two men set the cairn adrift in the sea. After a few minutes, each of the four companions lit the candles in their paper boats and set them adrift after the cairn.

They watched the cairn float away, each lost in their own thoughts. Alana thought about life and death, and about how close she had come to losing her own life and the lives of her other friends.

Colwyn considered what life would have been like if Alana had died and then said a prayer of thanksgiving for Balaam's sacrifice.

Meryn thought that perhaps it was time to grow up a little and William contemplated love and what power it truly had.

And Cobalt thought about how close he'd come to losing a second Blademaster and wondered if it was time for Taelin to replace him with a younger dragon.

The sun drifted across the sky as they watched and waited. As the sun began to set, the cairn finally drifted out of sight.

Alana turned to Cobalt and stroked his neck. "Mighty dragon, go and rest. I do not think we will be in any danger from here to Ravendale. Should we need you, I can call you with the statue."

"As you wish my lady," the dragon rumbled. He backed away, turned and launched up into the air.

Alana faced Colwyn and heaved a heavy sigh. "My love, it has been a long, hard road. And I want to sleep in my own damn bed." She smiled weakly and then amended her statement. "Our own bed. Shall we go home?"

"I think that's the best idea I've heard in a long time," Colwyn replied. He took her in his arms and kissed her while William and Meryn shared a mischievous glance.

Hand in hand, Alana and Colwyn led the way back to Ravendale.

The Blademaster

Epilogue
Sunrise over Ravendale

FOUR FIGURES CRESTED THE HILL overlooking the city of Ravendale. They were leaning on each other, each visibly hurting from injuries sustained during their journey. They were split into two couples. One of the couples was a halfling with her left arm in a sling helping support a tall thin mage in white robes. The mage had a bad limp and was also supporting himself with his staff.

The other couple did not look as comical. Even with their injuries, they appeared to be serious and deadly. And they looked like they belonged together. The man was holding the woman up, his left arm around her shoulders, steadying her. The man had some links missing from his armor and a bandaged gash on his forehead that was still oozing a little. The woman's left thigh was bandaged tightly and she was wincing with every step.

The city of Ravendale, the home of these companions, was spread out before them. The taller woman looked up at the man beside her and smiled broadly.

"We made it, Alana," the man chuckled.

"It's good to finally be home, Colwyn," she agreed, leaning her head on his chest. What little energy she had left was fading.

"Yes, it is." Colwyn kissed the top of her head. "It will be nice sleeping in my own bed again."

"I've almost forgotten what its like to sleep in a bed," the halfling grumbled. "I bet I go right to sleep." It was a tribute to how tired the normally gregarious and talkative halfling was that that was all she said.

"Just so long as you don't keep me awake with your snoring, Little One," the mage chided. He turned to face the Blademaster. "What is next for us, Lady Alana?"

"Ask me again in a few days, William," Alana replied. "First things first, I want to sleep well for a change. I don't even want to think about what's next for a few days."

"I don't think it quite works that way for us anymore, my love," Colwyn said sadly. "Not since the Temple of the Blades. Nothing's the same for us anymore."

"I don't care," Alana snapped, a trace of her fiery spirit seeping through, despite her exhaustion. "We just saved the world. I think the world owes it to us to give us a little time to rest before we have to save it again."

"The High Priestess of Taelin has demanded that we make an appearance as soon as we arrive in Ravendale," Colwyn reminded her softly.

"She can wait," Alana grumbled. "I need at least a week to recover. Maybe two. We are all hurting and tired. I think that the world can wait until we are all healthy and rested for us to save it again."

Colwyn wrapped his arm tighter around Alana and nodded. "Then let's go home and hope the world sees it your way."

"At least you do, Col," she said.

The four friends slowly made their way into the township.

An old man was sitting on a rock not too far from where the four companions had crested the hill overlooking Ravendale. They had not noticed him because he had not wished for them to. But he watched as they limped down the hill towards their home, nodding to himself in satisfaction.

"I would say that the new Blademaster will do well," the old man said to the woman who had just appeared beside him. "Wouldn't you agree, Lady Solara?"

"She performed admirably in preventing Thraal from entering Calthea." Solara nodded. She crossed her arms as she looked down at the old man. "I have some concerns however, Lord Taelin."

"Concerns are to be expected, Lady Solara," Taelin said with a nod. He leaned back and watched a thrynda bird soar across the sky. "After all, the history of the Blademasters is not without concern and there hasn't been a new Blademaster in oh so long."

"It is not the past that concerns me, Lord Taelin," Solara sighed, "It is her companions that concern me."

"A true test of the Blademaster is the company she keeps." The god smiled at his companion. "You know that as well as I. Alana Steeldrake has chosen her companions well. I am especially impressed with the halfling."

"It is the halfling that concerns me the most. She is a thief and a liar." The woman scowled.

"You are just bitter because the halfling broke into your armory." Taelin laughed. When Solara did not respond in kind, he shook his head and sighed. "Yes, the halfling is a thief, however, those skills have already proven useful and will continue to do so. You did not know that I had placed Cobalt's summoning statue in the armory. Nor would you have given it to Alana had you known. Such a thing was irresistible to the halfling and, as a result, Alana now has her nathair an aeir a chosnaíonn."

"Cobalt is old and weak," Solara protested. "He should not be serving as nathair an aeir a chosnaíonn. He should still be in exile."

"We all have our opinions. You would rather have him die in shame?" Taelin raised an eyebrow. "He has a chance to redeem himself before it is his time to cross the veil. He has already saved the Blademaster once. He will do so again."

"I suppose," Solara sighed deeply. "What is next for the Blademaster?" The woman looked off towards the Temple of the White which was glowing blood red in the early morning light.

"You heard her," Taelin smiled broadly. He hopped off his rock and stepped over to the High Priestess of the Blades. "She has earned some time to rest up and heal. But soon enough, events will move again to where she will be needed. She will be ready then. I believe the situation that is brewing in Willowdale will prove to test her mettle."

"Bah." Solara scoffed. "Willowdale is nothing more than a den of murderers and cutthroats. It is hardly worth the attention of the Blademaster."

"I believe you will find that this Blademaster will keep her own counsel as to what she should bother with," Taelin laughed. "At any rate, there are things we should attend to, my dear."

"Of course, my Lord Taelin," the High Priestess of the Blades bowed slightly.

A slight wind rustled over where the god and the High Priestess had been standing moments earlier, spreading a few dry leaves over the rocks.

And the hill overlooking Ravendale was once more peaceful and quiet in the early morning light.

Appendix

Every effort has been made to keep things straight for the reader in the story, however, there are a lot of names and concepts. And so, I have provided this handy set of references for you. As the series grows, so too will this Appendix. I hope you all find this information handy.

The Appendix is divided into the following sections:

The Blademaster

Deities
(Alignment of the Deity is in Parentheses)
(G = Good Aligned, N = Neutral Aligned, E=Evil Aligned)

Ana (*AH-nah*) (N) Goddess of History

Aram (*AH-rum*) (N) God of Balance

Ceres (*SER-ees*) (N) Goddess of Love

Chemish (*KEM-ish*) (E) God of Magic (for evil aligned magic users)

Ferrin (*FER-un*) (G) God of Magic (for good aligned magic users)

Isis (*EYE-sis*) (N) Goddess of Life

Laeyra (*lay-EHR-uh*) (N) Goddess of Luck

Raeven (*RAY-vun*) (G) God of Nature

Ranthos (*RAHN-thos*) (E) God of the Moon

Serrin (*SER-un*) (G) God of the Sun

Taelin (*TAY-lin*) (G) God of Wisdom and Justice, also known as the Lightbringer, the Lord of the Light, and the Bringer of Light

Terra (*TER-uh*) (G) Goddess of Healing

Thraal (*THRAHL*) (E) God of Chaos, often referred to as the Dark God or the Bringer of Chaos

Torval (*TOR-vul*) (N) God of Magic (for neutral aligned magic users)

The Blademaster

Vash (*VAHSH*) (E) Goddess of the Seas

Veral (*ver-AHL*) (E) God of War

Xaria (*ZAHR-yuh*) (G) Goddess of Fertility

Zish (*ZISH*) (E) Goddess of Death

Places

The Southern Dales

The Southern Dales are the southernmost region located on the Continent of Calthea on the world of Calthea. Home to many races championed by the gods of good and neutrality, the Southern Dales are a region governed by a king who resides in a palace in Ravendale. Nobles known as the First Lords govern each of the ten territories reporting to the king. The rule fairly, the wisdom of Taelin guiding the leader's hands.

Arvendale – A medium sized city that is deep in the heart of the Southern Dales, on the other side of the Elven Woods from Ravendale and noble seat of the Arvendale territory. Dargan Starseeker, Colwyn's father, is the First Lord of Arvendale, and, although he does not necessarily recognize the fact, Colwyn is the heir to that title

Attendale – A city on the eastern coast of the Southern Dales and the noble seat of the Attendale territory

Barandale – A city on the western coast of the Southern Dales and the noble seat of the Barandale territory

Darcandale – A small city in the northwest of the Southern Dales and the noble seat of the Darcandale territory

Lovendale – A small port town on the southeast coast of the Southern Dales and the noble seat of the Lovendale territory.

Parciandale – A city in the north of the Southern Dales and the noble seat of the Parciandale territory.

Ravendale – The capitol city of the Southern Dales near the center of the Southern Dales and not too far from the Elven Woods. The noble seat of the Ravendale territory and home of the High Priest of Taelin.

Solvendale – A small town on the southwest of the Southern Dales and noble seat of the Solvendale territory

Talondale – A small merchant city in the southern part of the Southern Dales and noble seat of the Talondale region. Alana's hometown.

Valendale – A town a week's ride south of Ravendale and the noble seat of the Valendale territory. Home to the sage Isaiah.

Willowdale – A city in the far northeast of the Southern Dales. Also known as the Twice Dead City, Willowdale was once the noble seat of the former Willowdale territory, but that area of the Southern Dales has become somewhat vacant. Willowdale is known from time to time to be home to various outlaws and cutthroats

The Elven Woods – A dense forest to the southwest of Ravendale. Home to the Forestwalker clan of elves and the location of the Temple of the Blades

The Temple of the Blades – The ancestral home of the Blademaster. Here, Blademasters learn what they are to become. The Test of the Blades and all Blademaster weddings happen here. In addition, the Temple of the Blades is the location of the Legacy of the Blademasters.

The Wilds

The Wilds are the lands between the Southern Dales and Dracomyr. Each of the town in the Wilds is its own little kingdom, governing over itself. Unlike the Southern Dales or Dracomyr, there is no central council or government for the region.

Vikerin – A small villaige in the Wilds that is home to the largest temples for Taelin and Laeyra in the Wilds.

Dracomyr

Dracomyr is the northernmost part of the continent of Calthea. Dracomyr is home to the shadow creatures and the undead that Thraal loves. The capitol city is Tornith.

The Stonegate Mountains – A mountain range not too far from the Wilds that is home to several large clans of goblins.

Tornith – The capitol city of Dracomyr. The High Priest of Thraal serves in Tornith

Outworld

Outworld refers to places that do not exist as part of the world of Calthea per se.

Limbo – Limbo is a prison where Taelin trapped the essence of the Dark God for several hundred years. It is protected by a multiheaded dragon known as Mahumet

The Isle of Dragons – The Isle of Dragons is home to the dragons of Calthea. The Dragonic Council meets here to oversee law and order for the dragon nation. Although the Isle of Dragons does actually exist as an island on Calthea, it is considered to be part of Outworld as it is inaccessible to any but the gods and the dragons.

The Blademaster

People

Bothain, Albert – Proprietor of the Lucky Minotaur

Bunten, Hubert – A brute that occasionally can be found at the Lucky Minotaur

Dalphain, Caiaphas – High Priest of Taelin when the new Blademater, Alana Steeldrake, is born. Dies of old age

Darkholme, Adouon – High Priest of Thraal after the death of Drakkhous

Delwyn, Merinda – Priestess of Taelin sacrificed to Thraal and beloved of Balaam Otakis

Doilin, Altas – Legate of the Goblins in the Stonegate Mountains

Drakkhous – High Priest of Thraal. Killed by Alana Steeldrake

Kale, Richard – Protector of Raven Windrider

Kovalani, Mirian – Queen of the Forestwalker Elves and former lover of Colwyn Starseeker

Kovalani, Otan – Trainer of rangers for the Forestwalker Elves and brother of Mirian Kovalani

Marant, Lilliana – Priestess of Taelin that dies of the wasting sickness in the wilds and beloved of Darius Redwind

Mastairs, Naomi – High Priestess of Taelin after Balaam Otakis dies.

Otakis, Balaam – High Priest of Taelin after Caiaphas Dalphain dies. Killed by Drakkhous in Tornith while protecting Alana Steeldrake

Redwind, Darius – Priest of Taelin that becomes Drakkhous after he loses the woman he loves

Sapphire, Crystal – Last Blademaster named before the Great Purge

Starseeker, Colwyn – Protector to Alana Steeldrake and heir to the title of First Lord of the Valendale Territory

Starseeker, Dargan – First Lord of the Valendale Territory and Colwyn Starseeker's father.

Steeldrake, Alana – First Blademaster to be named in over 300 years.

Stonehands, William – Mage of the White that travels with Alana Steeldrake

Swiftfoot, Meryn – Halfling thief that travels with Alana Steeldrake

Talon, Isaiah – A sage

Tencis, Olianna – Priestess of Taelin in Tornith

Thames, Mariska – Priestess of Thraal and beloved of Adouon Darkholme

Vilas, Arthais – Senior Priest of Taelin in Tornith

White, Ash – Stable boy at the Lucky Minotaur. Brother of Gwendolyn White

White, Gwendolyn – Waitress at the Lucky Minotaur. Sister of Ash White

Windrider, Raven – The First Blademaster

Dragons

(Type is in parenthesis)
Good dragons are Gold, Silver, Bronze, Brass, and Copper
Neutral Dragons are Diamond, Ruby, Emerald, Sapphire, and Amethyst
Evil Dragons are, Red, Green, Blue, Black, and White

Alpharin (amethyst) Member of the Dragonic Council

Alpharis (bronze) Member of the Dragonic Council

Centrus (brass) Member of the Dragonic Council

Cobalthaxillius (gold) Nathair an aeir a chosnaíonn to Alana Steeldrake.

Cyrus (green) Member of the Dragonic Council

Eliazar (gold) Leader of the Dragonic Council

Esmertas (emerald) Member of the Dragonic Council

Firegem (ruby) Member of the Dragonic Council

Mahumet (multi headed good dragon) Guardian of Limbo

Mintakis (diamond) Member of the Dragonic Council

Onyx (black) Member of the Dragonic Council

Pyrus (copper) Member of the Dragonic Council

Sephiras (sapphire) Member of the Dragonic Council

Shakaaris (red) Member of the Dragonic Council

Snowfang (white) Member of the Dragonic Council

Talonwing (silver) Member of the Dragonic Council

The Blademaster

Trakkis (blue) Member of the Dragonic Council

The Elvish Language

(Author's Note: When I first decided that the Forestwalker Elves were going to have their own language and that it would be represented in the book, I thought I was going to make a language up. Then, I realized just how difficult that really is. I wasn't going to create a language for the Forestwalker Elves, but I still wanted to have a distinct language for them. Last year I hit on the perfect solution to my problem, and I put it into action.

The language for the Forestwalker Elves is the Irish language. I am currently learning the language. Those of you folks who speak Irish fluently (And I know there are, sadly, not that many of you) will most likely see that the translations are not very accurate. That's OK. They don't have to be. They just have to be good enough. And that's what I have.

Less than two million people worldwide speak the Irish language. I do not want the language to die as it is a truly beautiful language, which is why I'm learning it. My hope is that maybe some of my readers will see that this language is a beautiful language that needs to be saved. When I have children, I hope to pass the language down to them. But, for now, all I can do to save the Irish language is to use it. As the series goes on, I am sure this Elvish Language dictionary will grow. –Rick Bentsen)

An máistir na lanna – Blademaster

An té a chosnaíonn a – Protector

feithidí – A type of insect that releases silk that is woven into clothing by the Forestwalker Elves.

Múinteoir – A term of respect for a teacher of rangers in the Forestwalker Elves.

nathair an aeir a chosnaíonn – The dragon assigned to protect a Blademaster

Ní mór di a rachaidh isteach anseo chun aghaidh a thabhairt ar ndán di dul isteach le croí glan. Ní mór sí ag troid i gcomhréir leis an idéalacha Taelin agus Laeyra. Ní mór di cloí le Dlí na lanna má ghlacann sí ndán di. Teip ciallaíonn bás. – She who enters here to face her destiny must enter with a pure heart. She must fight according to the precepts of Taelin and Laeyra. She must abide by the Law of the Blades if she accepts her destiny. Failure brings death.

stát ndoimhneacht na tsíocháin inmheánach -- A technique used by elven rangers that allows them to be in a deep state of inner peace

Sí nach bhfuil grá nach bhfuil a fhios Taelin chun é Taelin ghrá. – She who does not love does not know Taelin for Taelin is love.

The Laws of the Blades

The First Law of the Blades:

You are commanded to love. Love your friends. Love your enemies. Love without reservation. Love without hesitation. Love without condition. Love without expectation of return. If you must fight, then fight with love in your heart. If you must kill, then kill with love in your heart. Never kill or fight with hate or anger in your heart. Hate leads to impotence, but love brings power. This is the law a Blademaster must live by more than any other or else she will be powerless to serve as she should. It is the First Law of the Blades because it is the most important. Live by it, or you will die.

The Blademaster

Blademasters and Protectors

Over the years of recorded history on Calthea, many women have held the title of Blademaster. Obviously, not all Blademasters have been mentioned in this series, but as Blademasters and their Protectors are mentioned, they will be listed here.

Blademasters of Old:

Raven Windrider and Richard Kale (The first Blademaster and her Protector)
Alyssa Nesbitt and Michael Westlund
Maria Davalos and Tarvan Draderis
Crystal Sapphire and Markus Sharde

Blademasters of Now

Alana Steeldrake and Colwyn Starseeker

The Blademaster

The adventures of Alana Steeldrake and her companions
will continue in

Willowdale

Coming April, 2014

The city of Valendale.

When they journeyed to Valendale to consult the sage
Isaiah Talon, the Blademaster and her companions found
the city vacant. Now, with Thraal's plans in Tornith
seemingly thwarted, the Blademaster and her companions
must now find out what happened to the people they knew
in that city.

New enemies and old friends will make this one journey
that Alana Steeldrake will never forget...

TURN THE PAGE
For a preview of Willowdale,
the second exciting book in
The Blademaster Chronicles

Prologue
The Nightstalker

The high Priest of Thraal scowled as he stormed through the ziggurat of Thraal in Tornith. It had been four days since the chosen warrior of that accursed god Taelin had killed his predecessor in the position of High Priest to Thraal. Adouon Darkholme was still angry about it. He had not particularly liked the lich. No one at the ziggurat of Thraal actually liked the lich. But the idea that someone could just waltz in and behead the High Priest was disturbing to him, especially since he held the position of High Priest now.

The fact that the Dark God had been freed from his prison did little to mitigate Adouon's anger. He wanted revenge on the Blademaster, and he intended to get it. One way or the other. He wanted to destroy her.

"I will have her head on my wall for a trophy," he vowed to himself. "She will pay for what she has done to you, Lord Drakkhous. I swear it will be so."

He swept down the stairs towards the High Priest's sanctuary. He had been the High Priest for four days, and had been named so by no less than the Dark God, Thraal. But he was having a hard time believing that the sanctuary was his to use. He was making very good use of it. Adouon was determined that no one would be able to do to him what Alana Steeldrake had done to Drakkhous. The lich had been very sloppy. He had underestimated the Blademaster and her companions. Adouon would not make the same mistake.

For the past three nights, Adouon had been working with his god about hoe best to dispose of the Blademaster. The Dark God had shown Adouon a plan of attack over the course of their work. This night, Adouon would learn the last of what he needed to know. It would be the beginning of the end for the Blademaster. Adouon reveled in that thought. It would be a glorious death. He could not wait for the execution of the Blademaster. It would be perfect. The Blademaster wouldd not survive the encounter. And she would suffer intensely for what she had done. As would her companions.

Even through Thraal had already given him most of the instructions for creating this new weapon, Adouon still did not know what to expect. It would be as much of a surprise for him as it would be for the Blademaster. He savored the unknown and knew that it would be good. Anything that Lord Thraal had imbued with power sufficient to kill a Blademaster in her prime had to be a good thing.

He entered the sanctuary alone. He had been instructed that no one was to hear the plans that Thraal had in mind for the Blademaster. It was not for anyone else to know what was to happen until the time was right. An evil grin spread across his face as he though of the Blademaster lying in a pool of her own blood. It was something that he could not wait to seel.

He knelt down before the small altar in the sanctuary and closed his eyes. The censer on the altar was full of burning incense, aromatic smoke wafting up to fill the room. He pulled the sleeves of his robes up to just past his elbows, and he pulled the dagger from his belt. There was one component left that needed to be added to the incense in order for Adouon's prayer of supplication to be heard. As he had the past three nights, he poked his arm lightly with the dagger, drawing off a single drop of his own blood on the tip of the dagger. He took the blood and added it to the burning incense. The smoke rising from the censer turned from a murky grey to a dusky red as the blood combined with the incense. This change in the smoke told him that all was ready for his supplication to be heard.

"Lord Thraal, hear my prayers," Adouon spoke softly, his voice low and deep in the silence of the sanctuary. "All has been prepared as you have directed. I await only the final instructions for this task. I ask that you come to me now and show me what I must do to rid Calthea of the Blademaster."

There was a silent whoosh in the air and all the candles in the sanctuary blew out all at once. The only light left was the soft glow emanating from the censer, bathing the room in an eerie red light. The soft red glow was barely enough to light the shadows around the altar. The first time that this had happened, it had caught Adouon off guard. It was the fourth night, and it had happened the same way each night, so he was used to it at this point. He also knew it meant that his Lord Thraal was about to appear in the sanctuary with him. It was exciting, alhough he had once found the prospect terrifying. But the fear had given way over the past four nights as he had realized just how much he was in Lord Thraal's favor. He knew that the previous three nights would have been possible without Lord Thraal's favor being upon him. He knew that successfuly ridding Calthea of the Blademaster would cause allow that favor to grow.

"You have done well, my High Priest," Thraal's deep, resonant voice sounded through the empty sanctuary. The Dark God made his presence felt to the High Priest. When Thraal lifted the darkness, Adouon could see the shapeless form on the other side of the altar, a tear of the very air floating in midair showing as blackness upon blackness. Although he had been freed from the prison that Taelin had kept him in four days before, Thraal still had not regained enough power to create a physical body for himself. It was something that would take some time. "I am well pleased with your work."

"Thank you, my lord," Adouon smiled and bowed to his god. "It is my pleasure to serve you."

"It is time for us to begin the final preparations for our revenge," Thraal continued. "I have gone over all of the incantations with you. You know what you need to do. Tonight will be your final instructions. Tonight you will learn about the person that you will need to use as a base for this weapon. The person must be selected very carefully or all will be for naught. There are very few of my followers currently in Tornith who exhibit the proper qualifications to become the instrument of our revenge. I will leave it to you to discover who among my faithful will be the one to become my chosen weapon. I believe that, when I give you the requirements, you will think of someone very quickly. I have someone in mind. I have no doubt that you will think of this person. I believe that she will be perfect for our purposes."

"What are the requirements, Lord Thraal?" the High Priest asked eagerly. Adouon pulled a roster of the followers of Thraal that were in Tornith. "What must I know to select the right person for this assignment?"

"To begin with, just as the accursed Blademasters are, my champion must be a woman," Thraal began. "Taelin and Laeyra, curse their eyes, are right in saying that women end up making better champions than men. I do not know the reasons why, only that it seems to be the truth. Maybe it is because women are not so easy to distract once they have their mind set on a goal. The reasons why matter not. It needs to be a woman who becomes my champion."

Adouon opened the roster of the followers of Thraal in Tornith and picked up a fresh quill and ink. He crossed off the name of every man on the list, leaving just the women, which cut the list of potential followers of Thraal by over half. It was still a large number though. He hoped that the rest of Thraal's requirements for this champion would narrow it down some more.

"What is the next requirement, my lord?" Adouon asked softly. HE looked over the names still on the list. "There are still too many for me to be certain I will have the right one."

"She must be human and she must be of the warrior class, not the priests or the mages," Thraal continued, his form writhing in excitement as he passed on the instructions. "This is very important. Only a human can effectively track and fight another human, snd as a warrior, she could use any kind of weapon. Doing otherwise would leave this instrument of our revenge at a distinct disadvantage. If we are to be successful, we must not give the Blademaster any sort of advantage."

"I understand," Adouon nodded as he crossed off more names the roster of Thraal's followers. "That certainly makes sense, my Lord. But that still leaves over a hundred of our followers. Surely there is another requirement? There are still far too many that fit the requirements for me to effectively choose one."

"She must be one of the elite warriors who were were made from the gentlest girls that were recruited. This will make her far more of a formidable weapon," Thraal continued with glee. "She must be absolutely ruthless and unswervingly dedicated to our purpose. She will have but one duty and she must be left to fulfill that duty as she sees fit. She must posess great focus and determination. Of paramount importance, though, she must have a great deal of hate in her heart. That hate will be the basis for her abilities. Only hate can counter love."

Adouon kept crossing names off his roster as he thought about what Thraal had said. First he eliminated all the women who were not elite warriors. That left about thirty women. He took those names and wrote them down in order of how ruthless they were. When he looked at the name at the top of the list, a sadistic smile slowly spread across his face. Without a doubt, she had to be the woman that Thraal had been thinking of. As he thought about it some more, he realized that she could have been the only choice for this assignment. Any of the other elite warriors would be good choices if she failed. He did not think that any of the others would be needed, though. He was supremely confident in the abilities of his top choice.

"Kera Rayden," Adouon announced quietly. He looked back at Thraal. "She is the only choice that I can see, my Lord Thraal. If she can not kill the Blademaster, I do not believe any of the other elite warriors could."

"It is agreed then," Thraal laughed. "Kera Rayden will become the first Nightstalker. You will perform the ceremony this very evening, Adouon. After the ceremony is complete, you will send her to the city of Willowdale. That is where she will attack and kill the Blademaster. See to it at once."

"It will be done just as you say, Lord Thraal,' Adouon bowed. "This night will see the beginning of our revenge upon the Blademaster."

"I know that it will be done," Thraal boomed out an evil piercing laugh. "We will speak again after she has been sent to Willowdale."

Thraal's form started to fade from view. Adouon stopped watching. He was already contemplating the ceremony. It was a ceremony that had to go just right or the Nightstarlker would not be created. Worse, Kera Rayden could die. That would be a waste of a good warrior. But the most important reason he could not fail was that it was a personal vendetta for him. What the Blademaster had done to Drakkhous had to be avenged. If not for the lich, then for Adouon himself. He still did not believe that someone had been able to simply remove the lich's head, and he was not about to sit and let that same thing happen to him. He believed that following Lord Thraal's directions for this ceremony, he would prevent that from happening to him. He wished that he could be there to witness the death of the Blademaster. It would make his revenge all the sweeter, but it was enough for him to know that, once the ceremony was complete and Kera Rayden was bound up in the power that Lord Thraal would gift upon her, the Blademaster's days would be numbered.

Adouon stood and stretched. It was time to find Kera Rayden to begin the ceremony. There was no time like the present. Adouon wanted to get started right away, because the ceremony did not have to be performed at any specific hour, according to Lord Thraal's instructions. Besides, the sooner they conducted the ceremony, the sooner the Nightstalker could start on her assignment to kill the Blademaster. He wanted to see the Blademaster quivering in fear and worry as soon as possible. He knew that Kera would see to that.

As soon as he left the sanctuary, he went looking for Mariska, the woman he had made his assistant. He had been impressed with the way Mariska had handled herself when the Blademaster and her companions had been at the ziggurat of Thraal. Well, he had really been impressed with her long before that. He had been keeping an eye on her since the day she had appeared at the doorstep of the ziggurat four years before demanding to become an acolyte to Thraal. The woman had been prone to flights of fancy, but she had also been a devoted acolyte and had served her Lord Thraal well. It had not been Meriska's fault that the Blademaster had escaped the binding spell that she had cast on her. The Blademaster's halfling companion had used the shadows as only a thief could and surprised Mariska by stabbing the woman in the back. It was just one more thing that the High Priest wanted revenge on the Bladeamster and her companions for. Adouon had been able to heal Mariska, but the near loss of her burned at him. The fire inside of him that longed for revenge against the Blademaster and her companions burned hot. He had come to realize that he loved Mariska. He had not let her know how he felt. After the healing, she had started to look at him in a different way. It was as if she knew his feelings for her without having been told. It was as if those feelings he had for her had been transferred to her during the link that was required for healing her. He thought about what he little he knew of how healing spells worked and realized that his feelings for her probably had been transferred through that link.

Adouon did not understand why he still felt that it was necessary for him to hide the fact that he loved Mariska. The lich had known, of course, but he had not given Adouon any trouble over it. Nor could he. Drakkhous had done all that he had as part of a deal with Thraal to return his true love back to the world of Calthea. Thraal did not seem to care if he loved Mariska, and Adouon knew that Thraal had to know his feelings about the priestess. It is difficult to hide one's true feelings from his god. Adouon knew that, so long as he did not allow his feelings for the priestess to interfere with his ability to do the Dark God's work, Thraal would not have a problem with his loving Meriska. So why did he feel it necessary to hide his feelings? One day, he would have the answer to that question. Until that day, he would keep his feelings for Mariska to himself.

He found her near the door leading to the stairwell up to the Great Fire and the sacrificial altar. Neither of them had been back near the Great Fire since the night the Blademaster was to be sacrificed. It wasn't for any specific reason that neither of them had gone up there in the four days since the attempted sacrifice. Adouon did not want to relive the memories from that night. He knew that going up there would bring all of those memories back. But the ceremony to create the Nightstalker had to take place up on the altar by the Great Fire. He was prepared to block out any unpleasant memories that were bound to come during the ceremony. He hoped that Mariska was prepared for that as well.

"Mariska," he said softly as he came up to her. "I need you to go find Kera Rayden as quickly as you can. I want you to bring her here to me. You will accompany us up to the Great Fire and assist me with a ceremony."

"I will be back with her presently, my Lord Adouon," Mariska smiled at him. She started to run off, but turned back to the High Priest. She ran her fingers through her hair. "What kind of ceremony is it?"

"Lord Thraal has given us the means to take our revenge on the Blademaster and her companions," Adouon grinned evilly. "Tonight we shall embark on our mission to kill the Blademaster. We will have bloody retribution for what she has done to us."

"I would be honored to help you with this worthy goal, my Lord Adouon," Mariska smiled. "The Blademaster must die for what she did to Lord Drakkhous. But know this. The halfling is mine to kill after what she did to me. I will bathe in her blood."

"I would not even dream of getting between you and the halfling, Mariska," Adouon laughed. He clapped her on the shoulder. "Now, go and find Kera Rayden. The sooner you bring her here to me, the sooner we can be on our way to avenging ourselves on the Blademaster and her companions."

The High Priest watched her go. There was a smile of satisfaction on the young priestess's face. He could understand why she felt so satisfied, as he felt much the same way. He knew that it would not be long before the new Nightstalker was created and sent on her way. It would be good to have the Blademaster sent to walk with Taelin and Laeyra. As far as Adouon was concerned, it could not happen fast enough. He knew that the Nightstalker would not fail. He longed to loose the Nightstalker on the world to do what she was going to do. He would love to be going with her, but he knew that she would prefer to work alone. That was just another reason she was the right choice to be the Nightstalker. She would not be distracted by any companions. Norwould be distracted by love interests, for she loved no one.

The one thing that he most piqued his curiousity about what was about to happen was how Kera Rayden would react to her new abilities and status in her god's eyes. He wasn't so much concerned about her reaction. He knew that she would accept it without question. It was not in her nature to do otherwise.

As he climbed the stairs to the Great Fire, Adouon thought about what he knew about Kera Rayden. She'd just turned thirteen when she was brought to the ziggurat of Thraal. She had been the gentlest of girls. Adouon remembered how she had feared everything when she first arrived. Her fear excited him, filling him with a sort of heady intoxication. He watched with pleasure as that fear was used to break her from of her foolish desire to follow Taelin. Her goal in life to that point was to become a priestess of Taelin. And she might well have been a good priestess for Taelin. Fate, however, had interfered with those plans. It had taken over four years for Adouon to turn her away from Taelin, but he had finally succeeded. She had been broken. Adouon believed that, because of how long it had taken to break her, Kera Rayden would have a special purpose in her service to Thraal..

Once she had been broken, Kera Rayden had served Thraal without question or hesitation. It amused Adouon to think about how, had she not been broken and made to serve Thraal, young Kera Rayden might have gone to fight alongside the Blademaster instead of now being sent to kill her. Fate was a funny thing sometimes. Adouon had no doubt that becoming the Nightstalker was Kera Rayden's destiny. He had once seen her take on four knights from the Southern Dales that had been sent to kill the lich Drakkhous. Not only did she kill all four of the knights, but in the brutality of her assault, she had continued hacking the four knights to pieces long after they had been killed. Adouon had admired her brutality he had vowed that he would keep an eye on her.

And he had. He had watched her blossom into an elite warrior, one beyond anything that the followers of Taelin could muster. She was a killer through and through, and a brutal one at that. She had been assigned the most difficult missions that the High Priest could find, and she had successfully completed them all. Her new abilities would make no difference in her service to Thraal. Adouon figured she would enjoy the extra power she was about the be granted by Thraal. He did not think he would need to worry about her. She would flourish in her duties as the Nightstalker.

He reached the top of the stairs and stepped out onto the top of the ziggurat. The heat from the Great Fire washed over him as he walked over to the sacrifical altar. He had not yet conducted a sacrifice for Thraal. He knew that one day he would sacrifice someone on this very altar, just as he had watched dozens of sacrifices conducted by Drakkhous. He did not think that he would enjoy the sacrifices the same way that Drakkhous had, but the lich had been depraved in ways that Adouon could never hope to be. He ran his fingers along the stone of the altar, feeling the warmth of the Great Fire. The Great Fire had never, in all the time that this ziggurat had stood in Tornith, been allowed to go out. It was imbued with a special magic that allowed it to burn without fuel. Adouon did not understand the magic involved that allowed such a thing to happen, but he did not need to. This was one of those times when understanding was not required, only obedience. He was determined that the Great Fire would not go out on his watch as High Priest of Thraal.

He'd left the door to the roof of the ziggurat open. He did not think that it would be long before Mariska would join him on the roof with Kera Rayden. He figured it would not take long for the priestess to find Kera. Mariska had ways of finding people quickly. Adouon had trusted on that ability when he tasked Mariska to find the woman who would become the first Nightstalker. He would wait patiently, although patience was not his strong suit. He just wanted this ceremony to be over so that the Blademaster would be on her way to the spirit world.

It was not long before his excellent hearing caught the sound of two sets of foot falls coming up the stairs. He did not turn, because he knew who it would be. No one else had any business coming up the stairs to the roof of the ziggurat. Unless a sacrifice had been called, none of the followers of Thraal came up to the Great Fire. He moved over to the other side of the altar. He made sure that all the preparations for the ceremony were in order. When he was satisfied that they were, he nodded to himself in silent satisfaction. Soon the foot falls stopped, and he looked up at the door to the ziggurat. When he saw Mariska and Kera in the doorway, he motioned them forward. They came and stood on the opposite side of the altar as he was.

"Priestess Mariska said that you desired to speak with me, my lord?" Kera asked softly. She was a very soft spoken woman, which had always rather surprised Adouon considering the ferocity with which the woman did everything else.

Adouon looked Kera Rayden over, nodding in satisfaction to himself. She was wearing her normal black leather armor. The armor shirt went all the way down to her wrists and came up all the way to her neck. Her hands were sheathed in black leather gloves, the back of the gloves armored heavily so that when she hit someone it would do as much damage as if she had hit them with a blunt weapon such as a club. The leather pants extended all the way down to her boots. Her boots came up almost to her knees and were heavily armored. The only part of her body not covered in armor was her head. She had long dark hair tied back in one long braid. Piercing blue eyes stared back at the High Priest as he looked her over. She stared back at him defiantly, as if daring him to attack her. He had no intention of doing so. She was as beautiful as she was dearly. She had no weapons on her at the moment, but the High Priest knew she did not need any weapons to kill.

"Yes, Kera, I do," Adouon smiled broadly. He motioned towards the altar. "You are here to help me with a small but important ceremony for Lord Thraal. I believe you will like the results of the ceremony as well."

"I have no desire for ceremony, Lord Adouon," Kera scoffed. "I am a woman of action."

"I know you are, Kera," Adouon nodded. "And I have action for you after the ceremony has been completed."

"Oh?" Kera raised one delicate eyebrow. "Who do you want me to kill?"

"The Blademaster," Adouon's smile grew wide and menacing. "When the ceremony is complete, you will be far more powerful than you are now. You will be the Blademaster's match. I expect that you will be able to kill her after Lord Thraal imbues you with the power he shall grant you this night."

"What do you want me to do, my lord?" Kera asked. Her voice betrayed how intrigued she was at the thought of having so much pwer.

"Lie on the altar," Adouon commanded. When she flinched, Adouon laughed. "No, you are not ot be sacrificed, Kera."

"I would hope not," Kera grunted as she lay down on the altar. "It would be hard for me to kill the Blademaster if

I were dead myself. Just get on with it, my lord, so I can be on my way to glorious battle with the bitch."

"Yes, it will be a glorious battle, indeed," Adouon murmured. He picked up the idol of Thraal that he had previously laid out on the altar. "You will once more do Lord Thraal proud."

Adouon closed his eyes and said a silent prayer to Thraal as he slowly circled the altar. He stopped on the opposite side of the altar than he had started on and looked down at Kera. She had closed her eyes, not sure she wanted to see what was about to happen to her.

"Lord Thraal, you have commanded this to woman to become your champion," Adouon began softly. "I demand, then, that you come and fill this woman with the power that you have promised to gift her. Take her hate and amplify it. Give her the power necessary to do what must be done. Allow her the power to rid the world of the hated Blademaster and her companions. I ask this as you have commanded me."

"It will be done,' Thraal's voice floated out from the Great Fire. "Kera Rayden, from now on, you shall be known as the first Nightstalker. You will stalk the Blademaster through the shadows of the world. The shadows shall be your weapons. You will do me honor by ridding Calthea of the Blademaster and her companions. So mote it be."

A shard of pure light burst off from the Great Fire and arced into Kera Rayden's body. The woman opened her eyes wide and light shot from her pupils off into the night. She screamed in pain and pleasure and arched her back. After a few minutes, the light faded, and Kera settled down onto the altar once more. She closed her eyes again and, slowly, her breathing returned to normal.

Finally she opened her eyes and settleed her gaze on Adouon. There was a power in that gaze. And a deep hatred he had never seen in her eyes before. He knew that the power transfer had been successful.

Kera Rayden was no more.

The Nightstalker had been born.

"I am ready, Lord Adouon," Kera said softly. "I am ready to kill the Blademaster for Lord Thraal."

"Then follow me to the portal. I will send you to Willowdale," Adouon nodded.

The Nightstalker stood from the altar and nodded. She swept down the stairs leading into the ziggurat to her quarters, where she picked up her weapons. When she met Adouon and Mariska down by the portal chamber, she was fully armed. With all of her weaponry, she looked to be an even more formidable woman than she had when she left the altar. She moved with an easy catlike grace, and every move was made with a definite purpose.

"The Dark God chooses his Nightstalkers well," Mariska said wryly. "The Blademaster will have a hard time with this one."

"That is the plan, Mariska," Adouon laughed. "Are you ready, my dear Kera?"

"I am ready, Lord Adouon," the Nightstalker nodded. "Send me though the portal."

Adouon led the way into the portal chamber. The portal was in the center of the room, a dark and swirling rip in space. Adouon stepped over to it and waved his hand in front of it.

"Willowdale," he said softly.

The darkness swirled faster in response to his soft command, and the image of a city floated in the swirling darkness. The image in the portal swirled in the darkness, eventually revealing itself to be a dark alley near the center of the city of Willowdale. Kera did not hesitate. She stepped through the portal and was gone in an instant.

"It is done," Adouon smiled. "The Blademaster will die by her hand very soon."

About the Author

Rick Bentsen released his first novel in 2001. It was a simple science fiction story that was somewhat well received. Although it never sold very well, the people that read his first novel enjoyed it immensely. From that first moment, Rick was hooked.

Rick has long loved science fiction and fantasy books and movies and that love has turned into a writing passion. He has recently added a mystery/thriller series to his normal science fiction and fantasy series as projects to complete.

Rick lives in southeastern Massachusetts which he believes is the most beautiful place in the world. Fall in New England, he finds to be the most inspirational time of the year with all the colors.

Rick can be reached through his facebook page (www.facebook.com/RickBentsenAuthor) or through his webpage at rickbentsen.com

www.ingramcontent.com/pod-product-compliance
Lightning Source LLC
Chambersburg PA
CBHW020831030726
47496CB00001B/190